Language, Discourse, Society

General Editors: **Stephen Heath, Colin MacCabe** and **Denise Riley**

Selected published titles:

Laura Mulvey
VISUAL AND OTHER PLEASURES

Michael O'Pray
FILM, FORM AND PHANTASY
Adrian Stokes and Film Aesthetics

Denise Riley
'AM I THAT NAME?'
Feminism and the Category of 'Women' in History

Moustapha Safouan
SPEECH OR DEATH?
Language as Social Order: a Psychoanalytic Study

Moustapha Safouan
JACQUES LACAN AND THE QUESTION OF PSYCHOANALYTIC TRAINING
(*Translated and introduced by Jacqueline Rose*)

Stanley Shostak
THE DEATH OF LIFE
The Legacy of Molecular Biology

Lyndsey Stonebridge
THE DESTRUCTIVE ELEMENT
British Psychoanalysis and Modernism

James A. Snead, edited by Kara Keeling, Colin MacCabe and Cornel West
RACIST TRACES AND OTHER WRITINGS
European Pedigrees/African Contagions

Raymond Tallis
NOT SAUSSURE
A Critique of Post-Saussurean Literary Theory

David Trotter
THE MAKING OF THE READER
Language and Subjectivity in Modern American, English and Irish Poetry

Geoffrey Ward
STATUTES OF LIBERTY
The New York School of Poets

Language, Discourse, Society
Series Standing Order ISBN 0–333–71482–2
(*outside North America only*)

You can receive future titles in this series as they are published by placing a standing order. Please contact your bookseller or, in case of difficulty, write to us at the address below with your name and address, the title of the series and the ISBN quoted above.

Customer Services Department, Macmillan Distribution Ltd, Houndmills, Basingstoke, Hampshire RG21 6XS, England

Before Modernism Was

Modern History and the Constituency of Writing

Geoff Gilbert
The American University of Paris

First published 2004 by
PALGRAVE MACMILLAN
Houndmills, Basingstoke, Hampshire RG21 6XS and
175 Fifth Avenue, New York, N.Y. 10010
Companies and representatives throughout the world

PALGRAVE MACMILLAN is the global academic imprint of the Palgrave Macmillan division of St. Martin's Press, LLC and of Palgrave Macmillan Ltd. Macmillan® is a registered trademark in the United States, United Kingdom and other countries. Palgrave is a registered trademark in the European Union and other countries.

ISBN 0–333–77051–X

This book is printed on paper suitable for recycling and made from fully managed and sustained forest sources.

A catalogue record for this book is available from the British Library.

Library of Congress Cataloging-in-Publication Data

Gilbert, Geoff, 1966–
    Before modernism was : modern history and the constituency of writing/Geoff Gilbert
        p.   cm. – (Language, discourse, society)
    Includes bibliographical references and index.
    ISBN 0–333–77051–X
    1. Modernism (Literature)   2. Literature – 20th century – History and criticism.   I. Title.   II. Series.

PN56.M54G55   2004
809'.9112 – dc22

                                                              2004046702

10   9   8   7   6   5   4   3   2   1
13   12   11   10   09   08   07   06   05   04

Printed and bound in Great Britain by
Antony Rowe Ltd, Chippenham and Eastbourne

This book is dedicated to the happiness of complex futures; to Jade and to Joe, and to all those other joes.

Contents

Preface: Things That Matter

> All that is 'advanced' moves backwards, now, towards that impossible goal, of the pre-war dawn.
>
> Wyndham Lewis.[1]

Modernism is most fully itself *before modernism was*: my book will be an elaboration on the terms of this sentence. The notion of the 'before' is a strange one in English, divided between indicating a spatial extension – what lies before us, a prospect; and a position in a temporal sequence – what came before, an antecedence. The meanings are distinct, but in practice they interfere with one another. When we stand before what lies before us, our spatial position is fringed with a temporal affect, an anticipation, anxiety, impatience, desire, dread. We find ourselves within an imagined sequence, temporally and affectively *before*. The sequence is only imagined: we can baulk at our prospects, turn away from them with regret or relief. But something will come: in that sense the presence of the spatial 'before' in our experience of time is an abstract one, which will fade in the face of the insistent concretion of temporal sequence. But the rising and fading of imagined prospects is part of the constituting texture of historical reality, and, more particularly, of the constituency – the urgent social thickness of desire and anticipation and frustration that lies beside historical narrative – of modernism.

This will not be an essay on temporality: when Sigmund Freud and Henri Bergson, two of the great modern theorists of memory and time, appear in the argument, they appear surprised by their excitement at war, and smoking cigars. The 'beforeness' of modernism will be explored in its affective immediacy, as it is given to us in a writing that is charged with project, and as it appears to us now, desirous and incomplete readers.[2] That is, the question of 'before' is a question of constituency: it depends upon the matter which makes up writing, and the arrangement of persons who are imagined to surround it. Mine is an historical book: the prospects that open up spatially before modernism, and the contexts which exist temporally before modernism, are historical prospects and historical contexts; they are surveyed and populated, in my account, by dogs and diseases and Poles and cigarettes and houses and ghosts and juvenile delinquents. These figures are located in space and in time: the spaces are organised, for the most part, around Britain; the time is the early decades of the twentieth century. Each of the figures has its fate, and those fates play out in historical sequences which are finished now; about which we can do nothing. What lay before them is now past. But the history which is appropriate to modernism, I will be arguing, cannot settle in this form: the urgencies we look for urgently in modernism demand a different shaping of history.

As Wyndham Lewis, the complex and troubling modernist writer and painter who will provide one recurring point of reference for my narrative,[3] put it, looking back in the 1930s at the practical failure of modernism:

> We are not only 'the last men of an epoch' (as Mr. Edmund Wilson and others have said): we are more than that, or we are that in a different way to what is most often asserted. *We are the first men of a future that has not materialized.* We belong to a 'great age' that has not 'come off'. [. . .] The rear guard presses forward, it is true. The doughty Hervert (he of 'Unit One') advances towards 1914, for all that is 'advanced' moves backwards, now, towards that impossible goal, of the pre-war dawn.[4]

Prospect is in the past, but it persists in the present as an affective if ineffectual project, driving history out of sequential shape. This history begins 'before' modernism, in the contexts to which experimental writing reacted and accommodated itself.

Modernism, my book will argue, is already there in the affective moment of its context. An example: in 1912, Leo George Chiozza Money, the liberal political economist, published a book called *Things That Matter.*[5] The subjects he discusses are recognisably important, both for historians in their attempts to understand the early twentieth century, and in their persistence as features of our contemporary world. Across analyses of education, franchise reform, unemployment, wages, and trade, he notes again and again how difficult it is to conceive of individual or collective agencies that could transform the world. The world he describes is heavy with mediation, composed of such a mass of confusing and contingent stuff that understanding and knowledge are both especially difficult to arrive at and, more importantly, irrelevant in directing us towards transformative actions.

For Chiozza Money, history has become heavy, and difficult to grasp or to transform; at the same time, the objects in which our relations to the world are concentrated have become flimsy and thin. In one chapter of the book, 'Our Chief Industry', he describes the dominance of 'rubbish' in a culture of over-production, in a world in which 'industry' has ceased to be a human attribute, and become a mediating institution.[6] Led by representations of what an ideal domestic life should look like, furnished fully with a growing number of necessary luxuries, much of our world has been cheaply and insubstantially made. The objects we produce, the intimate things that make up the fabric of our lives, extending us into the world and giving back to us a sense of being at home there, are increasingly – insultingly – unsatisfying:

> The poor man buys not a few good articles, but many pieces of rubbish. Instead of putting solid stuff into one comfortable room, he must pay respect to the 'drawing room' with which a thoughtful rubbish builder has provided him. The conventional rubbish house calls for conventional rubbish 'suites', for rubbish pictures in rubbish frames, and for rubbish ornaments. And what is a rubbish home without a rubbish piano?[7]

The hatred of badly made things is a recognisable period concern, and it echoes the terms of writers as disparate as Ezra Pound, Roger Fry, G. K. Chesterton, and H. G. Wells, whose various modernisms, medievalisms, and fabianisms focus on the need to materialise human belonging in the world in satisfying and well-made domestic objects. Chiozza Money's statement could also be read alongside the desire, expressed by Willa Cather and by Wyndham Lewis, to get rid of the clutter that is blocking potential formal creativities in fiction and in modern lives.[8] For Chiozza Money, this proliferating rubbish is shoddy physical evidence of a disastrous mediation of social relations by ungovernable economic and historical processes; the very signs of the lives we have, together, built for ourselves, warp and split, such that we cannot read or restore the conditions in which we exist.

Rather than focusing on modernism's attempts to build against this flow of rubbish, to rebuild the sign; and rather than reading modernism as part of an historical fabric which rips and tears towards a new aesthetic,[9] what I want to take from Chiozza Money's book is encoded in the animus of the writing. His is a book which does not lead easily towards the existing institutions of knowledge, for it accepts that knowing does not lead towards agency; that grasping and understanding the problem still leaves us helpless, unable to intervene formatively in the world. The rising stylistic energy of Chiozza Money's work registers the state of being blocked and irritated, of having nowhere plausible to turn. This is the energy and tone that my book will be tracing, in its attempt to register the presence of a modernism, before modernism was. This modernism is manifest not in the reparative drive towards an 'art' which will rebuild our world such that we can live there, nor as the exhilarating discovery of new formal possibilities within alienated fragments, but as another mode in which writing can do its work within modern history.

The figures of flimsiness are animated in *Things That Matter* by an appeal for constituency. It is this appeal, an urgent call out to a constituency of similarly blocked and damaged persons, that marks its historicity, or what I will be referring to simply, for modernism, as an engagement with modern history. As I have suggested, the book is recognisable to a reader today, for nothing but details have changed since it was written. The 'things that matter' to Chiozza Money are 'things that matter' equally to us now. In that sense, the book is negligible, for it made nothing happen: the weighty mediation it railed against proved properly impervious. But a reader of *Things That Matter* today will, I think, find herself experiencing an affect of longing, as well as a consolidated and potentially depressing recognition. For Chiozza Money's tone is filled with a frustrated hope that is foreign now for us: while he describes a world which resists critical knowledge and excludes transformative intervention, he fails to disguise his belief in alternative social relations. The book is subtitled 'Papers upon Subjects which are, or Ought to be, Under Discussion'. The heavy institutional passive voice of 'Subjects which are Under Discussion' reassures the reader, or alternatively dismisses him, with the claim that there is a committee of qualified individuals, a government or a royal society, which is dealing with these problems in his name. But that voice is doubled by a groundless parenthetical prescription – 'ought to be' – which is still searching for its constituency. To read this today is to be forced in retrospect to recognise that the constituency was not found, did not materialise; but at the same time it is to hear an appeal towards an open future. The energy in Chiozza Money's writing could not turn prescription into action, but it does persist in the affect of our reading, and that persistence gives history a different shape.

Robert Musil, in *The Man Without Qualities*, names this implausible persistence, a way of living and writing in relation to a prospect that does not obey the laws of the world, as 'the sense of possibility':

To pass freely through open doors, it is necessary to respect the fact that they have solid frames. This principle [. . .] is simply a requisite of the sense of reality. But if there is a sense of reality, and no one will doubt that it has its justification for existing, then there must also be something we can call a sense of possibility.[10]

This sense of possibility is tied to the counterfactual, to things which are fated not to happen.[11] But the relation between things which happen and those which do not, far from being a stable opposition, is complex enough to drive Musil's enormous novel. His elaboration of this relation, and his development of a narrative mode in which to express it, marked him, for Georg Lukács, as a modernist of the worst kind, as refusing to participate in the social project of constructing reality.[12] For Lukács, that shirking of engagement with the world, a privileging of 'abstract' over 'concrete' possibilities, is part of the 'ideology' of modernism, in which an absolute withdrawal from historical process and social relation is encoded. Musil, as if in response, stresses how fully embedded the sense of possibility can be in the social fabric of living:

the possible includes not only the fantasies of people with weak nerves but also the as yet unawakened intentions of God. A possible experience of truth is not the same as an actual experience of truth minus its 'reality value' but has – according to its partisans, at least – something quite divine about it, a fire, a soaring, a readiness to build and a conscious utopianism that does not shrink from reality but sees it as a project, something yet to be invented. After all, the earth is not that old, and was apparently never so ready as now to give birth to its full potential.[13]

There is heavy irony in this conjuring of a divine 'now', bursting unsatisfactory doorframes with its utopian futures. Musil's text will shuttle between an ironic instancing of the pathology of possibility, which leads to isolation and empty dreaming, and a writing which has faith in the capacity to invest the matter of our world with project. There are tunes to play on our rubbish pianos.

A modernism read within a history that we do not invest with this sense of possibility is worthless; to consolidate modernism as part of 'reality' is to betray it. This poses problems for a book such as my own, which aims, as many others have done, to place modernism within modern history. Chapters 1 and 2 will provide figures for modern history, in the forms, respectively, of the ghost in the empty house, and the juvenile delinquent. Here, as a first step in constructing a history which does not subordinate the sense of possibility to the sequences of reality, I want to reconsider the historicity of the term 'modernism'. The idea that modernism 'was', that in retrospect it can be placed stably in a narrative of the past, needs to be inflected by some of the resonance of prospect, of what lies before modernism as its condition in possibility. What lies before modernism spatially, the prospect of a possible world, is also part of modernism's temporal and social condition. Our assured employment, within the literary academy, of the word 'modernism', obscures this condition.

The problem with 'modernism' is that it does not mean very strongly. The term does not have the focus or the force definitively to include or to exclude any particular evidence, on either formal or historical grounds. This has led to critics multiplying and dividing modernism into modernisms, in an attempt to find something stable there.[14] But that search for a solid and material starting point is doomed to failure: the only history that 'modernism' has is an institutional history. This would not matter if the institutional history of 'modernism' in the Anglo-American academy had arrived at an internal coherence. But of course it has not: no single discourse explains why Getrude Stein and Wyndham Lewis and André Gide, for example, should ever have been comprehended within one single mental breath, certainly not one with enough force to blow away the substantial presence of, say, G. K. Chesterton. And this in turn might not matter if the loose and contingent arrangement of texts and historical moments with which the discourse on modernism operates were widely shared. But no bookstore outside a university would shelve the texts of modernism together; no reader innocent of university study of modernism would read Virginia Woolf and Ezra Pound for the same reasons.

Most of the other terms of literary study and literary periodisation are also heuristic and contingent, of course: 'the enlightenment', or 'romanticism', or 'realism', are all internally divided across a struggle to organise and to arrange materials which are to some extent recalcitrant. But the debates in each of these cases have at least some clear sense of purpose: we know that when we debate the terms of 'enlightenment', we engage arguments that have shaped, and continue to inform, the justification for uses of force in international politics, for example. When we consider the romantics, we might balance responsibilities to the wide usage of the term with an investigation of the ways in which modern subjectivity has been configured. Or when we talk about the values and limits of 'realism', we are defining and critiquing a shared and social project of representing the 'reality' of a world in which we work and belong. Each of these terms has three-fold solidity: they each signal an established and coherent discourse, an object that is shared beyond the academy, and a sense of purpose that is widely recognised.[15] 'Modernism' has none of this weight: it is flimsy, 'rubbish', because there has not been and can not be a plausible investment in its social fabric. When we use the term, we are in danger of appearing as dodgy salespersons, reassuring a sceptical customer.

It is easy to undermine the assurance of the Anglo-American institutions of modernism. There is a telling moment when Michel Foucault was asked where he places himself, in relation to 'modernism' and 'post-modernism'. He replied as follows:

> I must say, I find that difficult to answer. First, because I never really understood how modernism is defined in France. It's clear by Baudelaire, but after that it seems to lose meaning for me. I don't know in what sense Germans speak of modernism. I know that Americans are planning a kind of seminar with Habermas and me and Habermas proposed modernism as a topic. I'm at a loss; I don't know what that means or what the problematic is.[16]

Foucault's candour, however disingenuous it may be, produces, in me at least, a shudder or a frisson of embarrassed recognition. He feels in relation to 'modernism' an unsettlement, leaving him at a loss in the face of an unholy aggregation of Baudelaire, German philosophers, and the odd American celebrity event that he can only refer to as 'a kind of seminar'. It is hard to deny that this is more or less what has held 'modernism' together; and the contingencies within this arrangement can only be finessed away by a hardening of institutional assurance.

The isolation and incoherence and lack of project signalled by 'modernism' ought to be much more embarrassing than it currently is. Because 'modernism' does not have a formal unity or an historical drive, it has to be constituted afresh in the present, in the enunciation 'I am a modernist', uttered either by academics pledging a kind of allegiance to the institution (when responding to advertisements for university jobs, for example), or in secret dedication to dead writers' long-lost causes. That enunciation, while it shares something of the form of other rallying enunciations, such as 'I am a socialist', or 'I am a feminist', or perhaps even 'I am queer', is unlikely to provoke either coherent solidarity or coherent opposition. Outside its institutional function, it is a project that is empty enough, ethically and conceptually, to become a puzzling poetics or to signal pathology.

It is hardly surprising that the embarrassing constitution of modernism – a mixture of longing and melancholy and narcissism – should go hand in hand with an institutional retreat. The technicalities of practical criticism, new criticism, or textual post-structuralism, all of which are imbricated with moments of the enunciation 'I am a modernist', offer an intense if isolated structured labour, which helps to distract from the gap where modernism ought to be. The constitutional and the institutional energies that are gathered around modernism are radically opposed to one another; the invested subjunctive desire that modernism *be* is undermined by the assurance that it really *is* (in academic discourse) or that it really *was* (in historical sequence). Assurance works to contain embarrassment, hardening against it and denying its productivity, or at least its potential communication (there is nothing so contagious as embarrassment). That denial removes discourses of modernism from their relation to modern history, constituted as a history of possibility.

I have situated this embarrassment within contemporary academic discourses about modernism. But it is not entirely possible to separate the institutional from the constitutional moments of modernism, for the turn from embarrassed sense of project towards institutional consolidation exists as much within the object of modernist discourses, within the trajectories of most of the writers and groups that habitually are named 'modernist', as it does within academic discourses themselves. To take one central example, to which I will return in Chapter 3: when T. S. Eliot, who was, incidentally, very susceptible to blushing, formalises the project of his journal *The Criterion*, the two moments, of constitution and institution, are almost simultaneous. His 1923 obituary of Marie Lloyd describes a melancholy space where the music hall had been.[17] A vivid relation, a creative public interaction, between working people and the arts has been lost with her passing; culture is dying, for Eliot, as cultures die under colonisation. The image of a large working-class public, creative in their relation to their entertainments, noisy and vital, appears to signal an urgent project for the writers he will gather together in his journal. But what Eliot proposes is not the reconstruction or the reinforcement of threatened social relations: in his critical writings he does not imagine a world which is brought alive across a shared reading of *The Waste Land* or *Ulysses*. Rather, his response, later in the same year, in 'The Function of Criticism', is an institutional displacement of the whole problem. He promises, and places himself at the centre of, a policeable institution of criticism: 'a simple and orderly field of beneficent activity, from which impostors can be readily ejected'.[18] Eliot begins with a sense of loss, which he shares with a disenchanted public; he imagines for a second modernism as reparative social relation, and this brings great crowds of happier people briefly flashing into Eliot's thought. This is an embarrassing dream, and it is quickly replaced by the plausible prehistory of a discourse on modernism, impostors ejected, order established.

There is nothing necessarily progressive in returning to the productive embarrassment of the modernist constitution. The social arrangements which appear for a moment there, thickening the fabric of our desire for modernism, are not predestined to channel only the energies which would please this reader. In Eliot's discarded image of a popular cultural fusion, we can perhaps also sense hints of a nascent Fascism, and the Anglican Church, and even of *Cats*. When, in Chapter 4, I turn to the figure of the modernist dog, the social prospect which appears is a wild mixture of anarchic violence and national isolation. Or, in Chapter 5, while what is constituted around the practice of smoking may resist the deep determination of the human subject by historical sequence, at the same time it condemns the smoker to personal pathology, and leaves him vulnerable to control by Philip Morris, and the newer configurations of global economic power. The project of modernism is not an ethical project. There are good reasons to turn away from the embarrassments of constitution and towards the institution and its ordered discourses.[19]

The stable object which we can call 'modernism' is formed, in moments like Eliot's, as the object of a quasi-institutional discourse that has turned away from a vision of constituency. Modernism enters a history governed by distinctions and structures, by doorframes – however much we may sense that they are rubbish doorframes – and the sense of reality that accompanies them. But the point of modernism, modernism itself as a pattern of subjunctive desire, has been masked: there is only a trace within this discourse of the urgent groping towards a constituency of possibility that spreads out affectively before Eliot. That constituency of possibility is what we are in search of, I wager, when we read the works which we call, incoherently, modernism, and gather ourselves towards the risky enunciation: 'I am a modernist.' This book engages the search for that constituency, as it persists within modernism, before modernism was.

Acknowledgements

This is my first book: it has been a long time in the searching and the groping, and I have accumulated an embarrassingly large debt of gratitude in thinking towards it and in writing it. Financial support and collegial encouragement from St Catharine's College Cambridge and from the Faculty of English at the University of Cambridge made the early research work possible; the environment of the American University of Paris, and particularly the Department of Comparative Literature and English at AUP, has helped me to change much in the way I think about the subject of this book.

An earlier version of part of Chapter 1 was originally published as 'The Origins of Modernism in the Haunted Properties of Literature', in *The Victorian Supernatural*, ed. Nicola Bown, Carolyn Burdett, and Pamela Thurschwell (Cambridge: Cambridge University Press, 2004); an earlier version of Chapter 2 was originally published as 'The Manufacture of Inefficiency: Vorticists and Other Delinquents', in *Modernist Sexualities*, ed. Hugh Stevens and Caroline Howlett (Manchester: Manchester University Press, 2000). Grateful acknowledgement is made to the publishers and editors for permission to reprint that material.

I owe a lot to many people. I am happy to have this opportunity to thank (in the beginning): Isabel Ascencio, Barry Braybrooke, Lorna Macintosh, Alan Nickell, Donald Proctor, and Richard Spry. In Britain and America and in France, many friends and colleagues have helped me work on this project, directly and indirectly. I am very grateful to them all, and to those I have for the moment forgotten. Who knows how ideas come into being? – but it is clear to me that they fade and dwindle if they are not sustained by the right kind of social and intellectual environment. My ideas have been sustained by the example, the work, and the support of those around me (many of my ideas, in all probability, were stolen from those around me). Thanks to Tim Armstrong, Richard Beardsworth, John Bishop, Carolyn Burdett, Jonathan Burt, Alice Craven, Con Coroneos, Jason Edwards, Maud Ellmann, Jim Endersby, Andrew Fitzmaurice, Dennis Flannery, Caroline Gonda, Jeremy Green, Charlotte Grant, Helen Groth, Ellis Hanson, Nick Harrison, Paul Hartle, Andrew Hewitt, Alex Houen, Misha Kavka, Laura Marcus, Jodie Medd, Joe Mejia, Rod Mengham, Anna-Louise Milne, Chris Nealon, Alex Neel, Anna Neill, Ian Patterson, Richard Pevear, Rachel Potter, Jeremy Prynne,

Kristin Ross, Fiona Russell, Celeste Schenck, Adam Schnitzler, Morag Shiach, Lyndsey Stonebridge, Charlotte Sussman, Charles Talcott, Trudi Tate, David Thorpe, and Steven Turner. Librarians and archivists at the Cambridge University Library, the Library of the American University of Paris, The Bibliothèque nationale in Paris, Cornell University Library, and at the National Canine Defence League were unfailingly helpful. The editors who have worked on this book, particularly Paula Kennedy at Palgrave Macmillan, have shown exorbitant patience and confidence, for which I thank them warmly. David Haisley did much of the work of indexing. Thanks too to the students in Cambridge and at AUP, and to the audiences at seminars and conferences, who helped me to test and develop these arguments: I was particularly fortunate to find myself in the middle of the modernism conferences and seminars in London, Southampton, and Cambridge throughout the 1990s – there could not have been a better constituency with which to learn to think the thought of modernism. I have been very lucky in my families, and I thank them for all kinds of support and diversion and wisdom. Thanks to Isabel Ascenscio, Jade Ascenscio, Gail Gilbert, Jeremy Gilbert, John Gilbert, and Marjory Gilbert.

I would not have finished this book without the encouragement, the wisdom, the challenge, and the care, beyond the call of duty, beyond friendship, of Dan Gunn, Denise Riley and Pam Thurschwell.

Geoff Gilbert, Paris 2004

Introduction: Modern History and the Disavowal of Possibility

In the accidental ways of being a foreigner *away from home* [. . .] Wittgenstein sees the metaphor of *foreign* analytical procedures *inside* the very language that circumscribes them. 'When we do philosophy [that is, when we are working in the place which is the only "philosophical" one, the prose of the world] we are like savages, primitive peoples, who hear the expressions of primitive men, put a false interpretation on them, and then draw the queerest conclusions from it.' This is no longer the position of professionals, supposed to be civilized men among savages; it is rather the position which consists in being a foreigner *at home*, a 'savage' in the midst of ordinary culture, lost in the complexity of the common agreement and what goes without saying. And since one does not 'leave' this language, since one cannot find another place from which to interpret it, since there are therefore no separate groups of false interpretations and true interpretations, since in short there is no *way out*, the fact remains that we are *foreigners* on the inside – *but there is no outside.*

Michel de Certeau.[1]

It will then be the task of historico-philosophical interpretation to decide whether [. . .] the new has no herald but our hopes: those hopes which are signs of a world to come, still so weak that it can easily be crushed by the sterile power of the merely existent.

Georg Lukács.[2]

1

In my construction of 'queer conclusions', and of hopes which sign a weak new world, I will begin *inside* what is before modernism; will begin with a work by a writer who is not a 'modernist', however much we stretch and toy with definition. *The Adolescent* (1874) was the third in the sequence of major novels Dostoevsky wrote when he returned from exile, beginning with *Crime and Punishment* in 1866, and ending with *The Brothers Karamazov* in 1876. While it is almost impossible to summarise the plot, some of its materials can be assembled: the novel recounts the relations between Arkady, the nineteen-year-old adolescent of the title,[3] and those around him: his friends, his objects of desire, and his family. This family is complex. He does not bear the name of his father, Versilov, as his mother is married to Dolgoruky (both his mother and Dolgoruky had been serfs of Versilov). When Arkady comes to St Petersburg, he arrives with a burden of resentment against his father and against the world, which is compounded by the fact that his surname, Dolgoruky, is also that of a noble family, and so he has regularly to experience the difficulty of finding the right tone in which to deny that he is a Prince. The negotiation of these relations, the finding of an appropriate stance to take within what the novel calls a typically modern 'accidental family', is coordinated with the negotiation of entry into 'adult' life, an accommodation with a world which seems to be every bit as accidental as his family is.

The dynamic of the plot appears to be charged with an ethical dilemma. Arkady comes to St Petersburg from Moscow bearing a letter which may prove important – disastrously so – to the legal and emotional relations between many of the other characters, and he has to decide what to do with the power this evidence confers on him. But the relations are multiple and ambivalent and opaque, and the letter undergoes a series of accidents that mean its power is extremely uncertain. The relation between the uncertain ethical dilemma and the developments of the plot is at best tangential, and while the letter is often invoked, it is seldom clearly relevant; worse, it is not often in Arkady's control – it is at one point cut out of the lining of his coat while he sleeps, drunk – and the plot is moving so rapidly and randomly from one area of interest to another that it is difficult to grasp exactly what the moral problem is, that might be under scrutiny.[4]

The novel will not come into focus under these terms: in that sense, it is not like *Crime and Punishment*, or perhaps, it is even more extreme than that novel in decentring its central questions of moral choice. Indeed it does not really come into focus at all: the title that Dostoevsky initially considered for the novel was 'Disorder'. It ends with a gesture towards the future: Arkady gives the memoir which forms the body of the novel to a man who was once his guardian in Moscow, and who has played no part in the action of the novel. As with most of his actions, handing the manuscript over is heavily – convolutedly, apparently irrelevantly – qualified: 'Not that I needed anyone's advice so very much, but I simply and irrepressibly wanted to hear the opinion of this total outsider, even something of a cold egoist, but unquestionably an intelligent man.'[5] These qualifications bring the 'total outsider' back into the confusing ambit of the novel, which closes with a long extract from the letter he receives in response, ending in these paragraphs:

> 'I confess, I would not wish to be a novelist whose hero comes from an accidental family!
>
> 'Thankless work and lacking in beautiful forms. And these types in any case are still a current matter, and therefore cannot be artistically finished. Major mistakes are possible, exaggerations, oversights. In any case, one would have to do too much guessing. What, though, is the writer to do who has no wish to write only in the historical genre and is possessed by a yearning for what is current? To guess . . . and to be mistaken.
>
> 'But "Notes" such as yours could, it seems to me, serve as material for a future artistic work, for a future picture – of a disorderly but already bygone epoch. Oh, when the evil of the day is past and the future comes, then the future artist will find beautiful forms even for portraying the past disorder and chaos. It is then that "Notes" like yours will be needed and will provide material – as long as they are sincere, even despite all that is chaotic and accidental about them . . . They will preserve at least certain faithful features by which to guess what might have been hidden in the soul of some adolescent of that troubled time – a not-entirely-insignificant knowledge, for the generations are made up of adolescents . . .'.[6]

As a voice from outside, uninvolved with the novel's adolescent, this looks like a kind of tempered apology, suggesting that the novel is deformed by the personal and historical conditions of its production, and that such a deformation can have value only when picked up and worked on from some distant and matured position of transcendence, outside and in the future. The text itself, from this perspective, is adolescent material, a stage to be learnt from, rather than to be dwelt in or upon. The work and its historical context are chaotic, fortuitous, accidental, *raw*. These unambiguous and conventional negative value terms are imagined as the start of a simple, linear, temporal path that leads onwards to their redemption, to a time 'when the evil of the day is past and the future comes', when 'the future will find beautiful forms for portraying the past disorder and chaos'.

This relation between the negative and chancy present and a harmonious future is refused – or placed properly in transcendence – by the very design of the novel. In his notebooks for the novel, Dostoevsky first decides that this should be a first-person narrative, with Arkady as narrator. This is to be his first major first-person novel since *Notes from Underground*, although he had considered using the form for *Crime and Punishment*. Then he considers what lapse of time there should be between the events the adolescent describes and the present of his narration. How far towards the time when 'the future is in the past' should the narration advance? He considers a substantial period, five years, and then rejects the idea:

> *Can't make it* 5 years. The reader will be left with the crude, rather comical idea that 'There's that young adolescent now grown up, and perhaps holding a Master's degree, and a jurist, describing with great condescension (the devil only knows why) how foolish he used to be before,' etc. And thus the whole naïveté of the narrative is destroyed. And therefore, better let it be a year. In the tone of the narrative, the whole impact of a recent shock would still be apparent, and a good many things would still remain unclear, yet at the same time there would be this first line: 'A year, what a tremendous interval of time!'[7]

A year, rather than five years: the narrative structure lets us know that time has not brought the narrator of the novel to the transcendence of the 'future artist'. Five years would not have taken Arkady there either, except in condescending illusion, born of an interested or a resigned forgetting.

The imagined sentence – 'A year, what a tremendous interval of time' – is not, in the event, how the novel as published begins, but the irony imagined here is everywhere present in the novel, regulating its stylistic universe.[8] Reading is projected as happening in a future in which there will be knowledge, if not condescension. But at the moment of narration, and at the moment of actual reading, all that we have is a writing, delightful in its 'naïveté', which can give no account of itself. Arkady 'worries' at one stage that:

The reader will perhaps be horrified at the frankness of my confession and will ask himself simple-heartedly: how is it that the author doesn't blush? I reply that I'm not writing for publication; I'll probably have a reader only in some ten years, when everything is already so apparent, past and proven that there will no longer be any point in blushing. And therefore, if I sometimes address the reader in my notes, it's merely a device. My reader is a fantastic character.[9]

The particular productivities of the actual relation between narrator and his fantastic reader, under-determined, and articulated with a blush of embarrassment, will be subordinated to a future of maturity, clarity and proof. The adolescent narrator is constantly claiming and dismissing a project for the narration, attempting to impose a wise order on the events of his life, and equally constantly watching that order slide away from him. When he first describes one character, the informing intention of the description soon fades:

> By the way, everything I've been describing so far, with such apparently unnecessary detail, all leads to the future and will be needed there. It will all echo in its own place: I've been unable to avoid it; and if it's boring, I beg you not to read it.[10]

Needless to say, the description is not 'needed' in the future, and does not 'echo in its own place', for any temporal propriety, any sense that things 'lead to the future' is upset by contingency. He claims at another point that 'I notice that I'm setting a lot of riddles. Feelings can't be described without facts. Besides, more than enough will be said about all that in its place; that's why I've taken up the pen. And to write this way is like raving or a cloud.'[11] The 'why' of taking up the pen never quite finds its place: a purpose in writing everywhere does wonderfully devolve into clouds. On the first page, Arkady promises that 'there won't be anything more of its kind [an aside]. To business.'[12] But even sixty pages from the end of the book, events are moving faster than the narrative can control, generating fresh contingent delights and confusion and asides and clouds of words: 'But again, anticipating the course of events, I find it necessary to explain at least something to the reader beforehand, for here so many chance things mingled with the logical sequence of this story that it is impossible to make it out without explaining them beforehand.'[13]

We will never know 'the logical sequence', because it cannot be imagined anywhere apart from 'chance things', and thus it can never be imagined to have stopped being formed. Against the thwarted desire for ordered time, in which the narrator could mature, and raw and accidental events could be turned into form, Arkady takes pleasure, and the narrative builds its elaborate energies, from contingency, from chance things. The thematics of the accidental family are reflected in a prose of accidental joys. The movement of prose and the confusion of the family combine, when Arkady tries to understand how his mother and father first became lovers:

> I only want to say that I never could find out or make a satisfactory surmise as to precisely how it started between him and my mother. I'm fully prepared to believe, as he assured me himself last year, with a blush on his face, even though he told me about it with a most unconstrained and 'witty' air, that there was not the least romance, and that it all happened *just so*. I believe it was just so, and that little phrase *just so* is charming, but still I always wanted to find out precisely how it came about with them.[14]

What Arkady has inherited, what he discovers in his father, is less a place in the world or an idea of his origin, than a blush, and a pleasure in contingency. In terms to which the argument will return in Chapter 2, the temporality of the Freudian 'family romance' is displaced by an attachment to the present. Things are constantly happening 'suddenly' or 'immediately', and even the most highly charged plot elements are undercut with stray contingent stuff, which, as Richard Pevear notes, is all regarded by the narrator as 'stupid': that perfectly adolescent word.[15] Of course, to an extent this is given as characteristic of Arkady the adolescent; but it is also the source of the particular pleasures and insights, the particular textual productivity, of the novel.

This novel, I would argue, can productively be read as modifying, without displacing, Bakhtin's account of Dostoevsky as a dialogic novelist. Bakhtin suggests that, for Dostoevsky, ideas and social visions are materialised in conflicting voices and positions, which no single perspective can mediate: 'Dostoevsky found and was capable of perceiving multi-leveledness and contradictoriness not in the spirit, but in the objective social world. In this social world, planes were not stages but *opposing camps*, and the contradictory relationships between them were not the rising or descending course of an individual personality, but the *condition of society*.'[16] In *The Adolescent*, all positions are concentrated in un-developing Arkady, and in an aesthetic of 'chance things' which happen 'just so'. All wisdoms that claim to have ironic control over, or to be a progressive development from, his youthful naïveté are drawn back into his adolescent temporality. The work of writing shadows him closely in its way of knowing the world. Positions and perspectives retain their irreducible autonomy – there is still, as in Bakhtin's account, no ideal mediation of differences in voices, and thus no ideal mediation of differences in social position, no transcendent state – but the positions cohabit *within* the figure of the narrating adolescent.

The following is one example in which contingent detail resists narrative ordering, becoming itself an order, which competes with the construction of the plot:

> That same day I had to see Efim Zverev, one of my former high-school comrades, who had dropped out of school and enrolled in some specialized higher institute in Petersburg. He himself is not worth describing, and in fact I wasn't friends with him; but I had looked him up in Petersburg; he could (owing to various circumstances that are also not worth talking about) tell me the address of a certain Kraft, a man I needed very much, once he came back from Vilno. Zverev expected him precisely that day or the next, and had informed me of it two days before. I had to walk to the Petersburg side, but I wasn't tired at all.
>
> I found Zverev (who was also about nineteen years old) in the courtyard of his aunt's house, where he was living temporarily. He had just had dinner and was walking around the courtyard on stilts.[17]

Things happen and there is no point in explaining how. The stilts, needless to say, do not serve any function in the plot; nor are they *only* characteristic of a young energy, to be located in the characters' adolescences. They provide the strangest kind of pause, a vantage point or a slightly ridiculous elevation, from which to view the onrush of event, and the attempt to construct form.

I begin my book with this aspect of Dostoevsky for two reasons. First, almost the whole range of writers who are called modernist read his work intensely, with various mixtures of fascination and repulsion; I want to argue that consciousness of a modernist constitution becomes visible in these troubled readings. With Dostoevsky, something within the project of literature becomes difficult and urgent. And second, this knowledge and this project are difficult to integrate or incorporate.

The consciousness which appears in the reading of Dostoevsky is embarrassing: it is very difficult to sustain (it is 'stilted', we might say); the modernists turn away from it or place it at a safe distance or step down from it, in order to save the plausible institutional formation of 'modernism'. This consciousness and its mode of knowing are encoded within Dostoevsky's novel as a kind of sudden proximity – 'better let it be a year' – which is transferred both to the unsettling sense of proximity that British writers felt to Dostoevsky and to the problem of the kind of distance at which modernism itself most happily appears. As Dostoevsky is to the 'modernists', I shall suggest, so are they to us.

Indestructible furniture and fitful imagining

What turns some away from Dostoevsky, what causes others to hesitate before a dangerously slippery slope, is not only laziness: I believe that it is fear. . . . His truth is too urgent, too indiscreet, too extreme, not to appal those who pass their lives in trying to cleanse themselves of the guilt of the human condition, or to evade it. They hope to re-assure themselves by smiling away his barbarian excesses! If the fear of recognising themselves, for good or for ill, did not grab them viscerally [*ne les tenait aux entrailles*], would they display such a furious energy in building up, between themselves and that monster, the barrier of borders, the defence of climate and civilisation? 'Dostoevsky', they say, 'is only valuable as an artist of his race. We don't have to make him our business [*Nous n'avons rien à démêler avec lui*]. His particular genius consists in this: that he is the most Russian of the Russians.'

Jacques Copeau.[18]

I want now to coordinate this version of Dostoevsky with a series of modernist encounters with his work.[19] While some British writers were already aware of his writing, either in the original or through French translations, the Russian writer became properly a fixture in Britain through Constance Garnett's translations, published between 1910 and 1920. Virginia Woolf, writing in 1917, notes that 'his books are now to be found on the shelves of the humblest English libraries; they have become an indestructible part of the furniture of our rooms, as they belong for good to the furniture of our minds'.[20] Katherine Mansfield, in 1919, writes of a 'cult' of Dostoevsky, seeing in 'Dostoevsky's influence upon the English intellectuals of to-day the bones of a marvellously typical Dostoevsky novel'.[21]

Dostoevsky is at once indestructible furniture and cult: the first result of this is that his name becomes easy shorthand for a compound mental, physical, and economic state: feverish, convulsive, impoverished, and idealistic – modern. Katherine Mansfield enjoyed regular weeping drunken evenings, which friends called her 'Dostoevsky nights'.[22] André Gide, in France, refers to Dostoevsky in the same way in his second mention of the writer in his journal. Describing a Phalange banquet in 1908, he notes:

> At the moment of the toasts a young fool who is not given the floor when he wants to recite some of Royère's poems goes off in the wings and breaks the mirror in a private dining room. 'Very Dostoevsky,' says Copeau, with whom I walk home.[23]

The references to Dostoevsky are easy and light: they encode a pressured and impulsive way of living. These references can be multiplied usefully, to thicken our sense of what was widely and immediately seen in his writing, and of how that vision is transferred to a way of living. Bronislaw Malinowski, the Polish anthropologist to whom my argument will turn in Chapter 3, has been considered, by Mark Manganaro and more recently by Michael North, as providing an important and revealing parallel for literary modernism.[24] While working in the field in the Trobriand islands, he repeatedly struggles to banish his 'Dostoevskian reactions': an affective complex including nostalgia for Poland, a general *ennui*, an ambivalence about novels, and his attachment to the more literary and bohemian culture he associates with his friend and ex-lover Stanislaus Ignacy Witkiewicz. These reactions have to be tamed in the name of professional ambition and epistemological clarity. T. S. Eliot, to give just one more example of this widespread use of Dostoevsky's name as shorthand, retrospectively described his married life with his first wife Vivien as 'like a Dostoevskean novel written by Middleton Murry'.[25]

These are entirely casual expressions: they are part of the ordinary un-thought language of early twentieth-century modernist culture. They do not pretend to read Dostoevsky carefully, and they are not considered acts of self-description. The Russian writer seems to provide an immediate and handy name for a contemporary way of being. The semantic reach of this use of his name is loose, but relatively circumscribed: it indicates a slightly abject loss of control, a shameful but broadly private failure, a claustrophobic energy derived from the difficulty of living. These meanings appear to have their origins in an amalgam of Russian politics, the particular foibles of Dostoevsky's characters, and aspects of the writer's biography: his economic difficulties, the relation between his politics and his religious thought, and his epileptic body.[26]

These tropes continue in more considered readings of Dostoevsky. For Woolf, the writing of all the Russians, in English translation, is like men 'deprived by an earthquake or a railway accident not only of all of their clothes, but also of something subtler and more important'. This is a very strange passage. Woolf first appears to be talking about something lost in translation, something at once blatantly, nakedly, and disastrously in your face, *and* impossibly 'subtle', as it *can't* be read in Dostoevsky and the other Russian novelists, because of a cultural and linguistic distance. But this sense of an unreadable absence, the sense of something that is pointedly lost in the texts, soon becomes the kind of essential presence – that presence which is repeatedly referred to as the 'Russian Soul' – that cultures and languages only serve to obscure. 'They have lost their clothes, we say, in some terrible catastrophe, for some such figure as that describes the simplicity, the humanity, startled out of all efforts to hide and disguise its instincts, which Russian literature, whether it is due to translation or to some more profound cause, makes upon us.'[27]

We find sketched here, then, an extreme case of the structure that, T. J. Clark has suggested, is definitive of modernism in painting (although I think that the argument can be cautiously applied to literary modernism too). In *Farewell to an Idea*, Clark, poignantly, attempts to break with modernism, to recognise both that it is over and also that it only ever had the kind of presence that a dream has. Clark's book is built in wonderful and careful critical exegesis of the historical forces of hope and of change that are concentrated in the modernist artwork; but the investment he makes in this reading is signalled as a melancholy attachment.[28] Melancholy, in which the ambivalent attachment to an uncertainly defined lost object kills the subject, slowly, from within, blocking her capacity for life, must be turned into an act of mourning. Modernism must become an historical object, in order to allow us openly to live towards the future. For Clark:

> Modernism had two great wishes. It wanted its audience to be led toward a recognition of the social reality of the sign (away from the comforts of narrative and illusionism, was the claim); but equally it dreamed of turning the sign back to a bedrock of World/Nature/Sensation/Subjectivity which the to and fro of capitalism had all but

destroyed. I would be the last to deny that modernism is ultimately to be judged by the passion with which, at certain moments, it imagined what this new signing would be like. Cézanne and Cubism are my touchstones, and Pollock in his drip paintings. But at the same time I want to say that what they do *is* only imagining, and fitful imagining at that – a desperate, marvellous shuttling between a fantasy of cold artifice and an answering one of immediacy and being-in-the-world.[29]

Modernism has only the power of fitful imagination: it is neither constant nor material in its making of the world. We can see a recognition of both parts of Clark's definition of modernism in Woolf's description of the Russians, and of Dostoevsky. The social reality of the sign could not have a clearer figuration than in the vision of something which is lost in translation, something which is affective because it cannot be transparently read. And at the same time, this absence, re-coded by Woolf as a simplicity and a defenceless nakedness, becomes the ground on which humanity is reconfigured, 'Nature/Sensation/Subjectivity' in Clark's terms; the 'bedrock' of 'simplicity and humanity' in Woolf's. It is hard, though, to build anything on this intrinsically unstable bedrock: for Clark it is made unsteadily up of convulsions, 'fitful imagining'; for Woolf it appears only as part of a 'terrible catastrophe', and as such is weak: naked and vulnerable.

Clark suggests that this impossibility of solid construction is further definitive of modernism, and this is the reason why his book wishes, finally, to say 'farewell' to the idea of modernism:

> Modernism lacked the basis, social and epistemological, on which its two wishes might be reconciled. The counterfeit nature of its dream of freedom is written into the dream's realization.[30]

Nothing is known or lived here; modernism was *only* dreamed. The very material objects of modernism bear the traces of this history of something faked, as they are produced in wishful evasion of knowledge of the social relations that subtend their production. Clark here approaches Georg Lukács's terms for thinking about literary modernism as an 'ideology', in which formal experiment, the forging of dreams of freedom, is grounded in a pointed ignorance of social and historical condition.

This – to transfer Clark's argument to modernist writers – is to envision the modes of experience of the modernists, their Dostoevskean reactions, Dostoevskean nights, Dostoevskean marriages, as only reflections of their ungrounded aesthetic dreams. It would reduce those moments, as Lukács does, to a kind of pathology, without social reality. But Lukács's argument, in 'The Ideology of Modernism' (1957), is arrived at after long wrestling with Dostoevsky. In *The Theory of the Novel*, which he wrote in 1914–15, and published in 1916, Lukács had tentatively appealed to Dostoevsky as offering a future for fiction beyond the novel, and with that future for fiction, a new world:

> It is in the words of Dostoevsky that this new world, removed from any struggle against what actually exists, is drawn for the first time as a seen reality. That is why he, and the form he created, lie outside the scope of this book. Dostoevsky did not write novels, and the creative vision revealed in his work has nothing to do, either as affirmation or as rejection, with European nineteenth-century Romanticism or with the many, likewise Romantic, reactions against it. He belongs to the new world. Only formal analysis of his works can show whether he is already the Homer or the Dante of that world or whether he merely supplies the songs which, together with the songs of other forerunners, later artists will one day weave into a great unity: whether he is merely a beginning or already a completion. It will then be the task of historico-philosophical interpretation to decide whether we are really about to leave the age of absolute sinfulness or whether the new has no herald but our hopes: those hopes which are signs of a world to come, still so weak that it can easily be crushed by the sterile power of the merely existent.[31]

When he writes the 1962 Preface to *The Theory of the Novel*, Lukács is embarrassed about these fervent passages, from which he distances himself historically: 'We have every right to smile at such primitive utopianism, but it expresses nonetheless an intellectual tendency which was part of the reality of that time.'[32] They are his adolescent excesses: like Arkady's manuscript, they are raw, young historical material, perhaps an internalising of the historical disorder of wartime Europe, and as such they require a mature – possibly a condescending – framework. He notes that the book and its dreams were an historical error: 'it was written in a mood of permanent despair over the state of the world. It was not until 1917 that I found an answer to the problems which, until then, had seemed to me insoluble.'[33] The error, which will be corrected by his Marxism, is the fake dream of a modernist, dreamed weakly, in despairing identification with Dostoevsky.

In his later terms, what Lukács finds in Dostoevsky is merely an 'abstract potential' which is improperly severed from the lived social fabric of the world. The 'signs of a world to come', which stand against the 'sterile power of the merely existent', can only, in this argument, signal ideological evasion of a 'concrete' social project. They burgeon forth as a 'subjectivity' which is morbid and 'psychopathological'; and 'the protest expressed by this flight into psychopathology is an abstract gesture; its rejection of reality is wholesale and summary, containing no concrete criticism. It is a gesture, moreover, that is destined to lead nowhere; it is an escape into nothingness'.[34] Nothingness and abstraction are correlated:

> The possibilities in a man's mind, the particular pattern, intensity, and suggestiveness they assume, will of course be characteristic of that individual. In practice, the number will border on the infinite, even with the most unimaginative individual. It is thus a hopeless undertaking to define the contours of personality, let alone come to grips with a man's actual fate, by means of potentiality. The *abstract* character of potentiality is clear from the fact that it cannot determine development – subjective mental states, however permanent or profound, cannot be here decisive.[35]

Possibility, the dream of a new world, modernist fiction, are all only abstract. They have no real presence in the world because they cannot define the contours of personality, or determine development, and as such they remain wholly subjective, and that subjectivity can only be seen to be pathological. Development and character, the agencies through which humans enter into dialectical relations with history, depend on the concrete realisation of potentiality through action.[36] This is why he has no time for André Gide (the Gide of *Les Faux-Monnayeurs*), or for Musil, in whom the 'sense of possibility' is raised to a method; and why, in general, he sees modernism as an 'error'.

Lukács makes this argument in the name of the social being of man, his existence within a network of meaningful and material human relationships. Literature can only have its life within this set of relations. Modernism, by this token, cannot contribute to the work of history because it begins by positing an a-social individual, and an a-social origin for literary creation; because it begins by situating the individual and the work of writing outside the lifeworld. As a result: 'We see that modernism leads not only to the destruction of traditional literary forms; it leads to the destruction of literature as such.'[37] While

I want to resist Lukács's conclusions, that modernism is not part of the work of history because it is an ideology and a pathology, I also want to recognise something in this insight. Lukács is useful in noting that there is a kind of writing which has a problem with its relation to the lifeworld and the public sphere, and that this problem issued at once in a vision of the impossibility of 'literature as such', and in a difficulty of living. These are the terms that arise from the encounter with Dostoevsky.[38] The question – for Lukács, for Clark, and for the rest of this introduction – is whether this embarrassing moment describes also a social arrangement and a productivity in the world, and thus whether we lose a resource for social imagination, in writing modernism off.

Sudden brothers

Like Woolf, Katherine Mansfield finds a disturbing nakedness gathering around Dostoevsky, but for her the mechanisms of disrobing are less enigmatic. She argues that there is good reason to be defensively casual around Dostoevsky, to take him superficially, as a way of parrying his shock:

> For if we do not take him superficially, there is nothing to do but to take him terribly seriously, but to consider whether it is possible for us to go on writing our novels as if he had never been. This is not only a bitterly uncomfortable prospect; it is positively dangerous; it may well end in the majority of our young writers finding themselves naked and shivering, without a book to clothe themselves in.[39]

The illusory protection of literature is at stake here, as a medium and a practice which can defend young writers from the world by allowing them to feel at home there. Dostoevsky – if he is taken seriously – threatens to remove that protection, and the result is an embarrassing and uncomfortable absence of books.

John Middleton Murry is willing to take Dostoevsky very seriously indeed; he seems even eager to risk nakedness and cold. His enthusiastic hailing of the Russian writer, as 'a phenomenon which has lately burst upon our astonished minds, [. . .] towards which an attitude must be determined quickly, almost at the peril of our souls,'[40] implies a welcoming of the impossibility of a comfortable relationship between literature and living. Dostoevsky, he argues, as Mansfield does, and as Lukács, in my construction, does, destroys the position of literature in

the world: 'the novels of this great novelist have in them explosive force
enough to shatter the very definition of the novel'.[41] It does this first
by destroying temporality; with that destruction a viable relation
between fiction and life is undone:

> A novel [. . .] *represents* life. Life is a process, whose infinite variety
> cannot be staled; it is a movement in time. Therefore a representa-
> tion of life must, like its exemplar, be permeated with this sense of
> process and movement; in the pregnant phrase of a French novelist,
> it must be, as it were, *baigné dans la durée*, bathed in a sense of time.
> It must be enveloped in that air in which our physical bodies are
> born and are nourished, come to maturity and pass on to death.
> Lacking this atmosphere, the men and women which the novelist
> created must inevitably languish and die. [. . .] But the human con-
> sciousness depends on the being of the physical body, and the being
> of the physical body can be represented only as a process in time.
> This is the essential condition upon which life may be represented.
> Where the sense of time is, the sense of growth and progress, there
> is life. Probability and truth in the novelist's art depends primarily
> on this.
>   Whether by deliberate process or by unconscious instinct, Dosto-
> evsky set himself in his works to annihilate this sense of time.[42]

This is a particularly debilitating version of literary self-consciousness.
Here a consciousness of self separates out from an asphyxiated body, a
body whose continuity in time has been annihilated. A relation forged
in the novel between consciousness and life, by which the novel can
make claims to probability and truth, is interrupted. And, again as for
Mansfield and as for Lukács, there is an articulation of these questions,
about how writing places itself in relation to probability and possibility, with a strange unmasking of literature and materialisation of the
book. For Murry, if Dostoevsky is a novelist, then the novel is 'only a
convenient name for a number of pages sold at a price agreed by the
bookseller'.[43]

Taking Dostoevsky seriously, then, for these writers, reveals something
– economics, suffering, the materiality of the book – beneath or behind
the protections of literature. This something appears to be both around
the literary text, in its social scene, and within it. According to Jacques
Copeau, quoted above, fear is produced here as a result of recognition:
something constitutional, a grabbing in the guts which responds to the
urgent appeal of Dostoevsky. This is why, for Copeau, writers turn away

appalled from their troubling fascination with his work, and replace him at a safer distance. Lawrence was perhaps, characteristically, the most vehement of all the British writers in his rejection of Dostoevsky's work.[44] He violently abjects the Russian writer, and with him his friend Murry.[45] Writing about the 1916 selection from *A Writer's Diary*, and Murry's introduction to it, he states: 'I call it offal, putrid stuff. Dostoevsky's big and putrid, here, Murry is a small stinker, emitting the same kind of stink. [. . .] I can't do with this creed based on self-love, even when the self-love is extended to the whole of humanity.'[46] The image of a rancid self-love which so appals him, appears to concretise Lawrence's deep erotic ambivalence about relations between men: one of his more extraordinary images of Dostoevsky is of him burying his head in the earth 'between the feet of Christ' and thus ending in a posture where his buttocks are shamelessly exposed and vulnerable.[47]

Like Lawrence, Joseph Conrad demonstrably adumbrates Dostoevsky's writing extremely closely, especially in *Under Western Eyes*.[48] And like Lawrence, the sense that Dostoevsky has got inside him disturbs him intensely. André Gide describes a meeting with Conrad, in which they understand one another on all subjects except for that of Dostoevsky:

> As he never gave his opinion about anything without solid knowledge, his judgments were very strong; but as they accorded with my own, the conversation went on smoothly. On only one point were we unable to establish an accord. The mere mention of Dostoevsky's name made him shudder [*frémir*]. I think that a few journalists, by clumsily comparing them [*par des rapprochements maladroits*] had exacerbated his Polish exasperation against the great Russian, with whom, nevertheless, he has secret but obvious similarities [*avec qui nonobstant il ne laissait pas de présenter des secrètes ressemblances*], but whom he cordially detested, such that one could not speak of him in front of Conrad without stirring afresh his vehement indignation.[49]

The name and the idea of Dostoevsky set Conrad's body vibrating. Clumsily placed too close to Dostoevsky, he shudders and becomes vehement, the very secrecy of the similarities between the writers appearing – for Gide – as a physical reaction.

This is a particularly interesting meeting, as Gide, and the *Nouvelle Revue Française*, in which this acount of Conrad was published, remained close to Dostoevsky. If British modernism, in my account, enters its institutional history by turning away from Dostoevsky, a very different relation between literature and the social is imagined in the *NRF*, in identification with the Russian writer. Gide's own study of Dostoevsky is openly narcissistic: 'like the bees of which Montaigne writes, I have preferred to search in his work for that which is suitable for my honey [*ce qui convient à mon miel*].'[50] He finds a sensual openness in Dostoevsky into which he can extend his own sense of project, and that of the *NRF*.[51] This openness is entirely inward, a honeyed distillation; at the same time, it is a social relation. Henri Massis, in his virulent attack on Gide as revealed by this book, disapprovingly notes both of these aspects of the relation between the writers. On one hand, *Dostoïevski* is perfect evidence of what is wrong with Gide: while he has sought for a writer who is different from himself, who 'trembles with energy', such that one is led to hope that finally he will be able to 'make contact with an object' rather than only with further versions of himself, we are left once again within Gide's narcissism. At the same time, through the mediation of Dostoevsky, the already dangerous influence of Gide is extended yet farther: 'he is looking to seize [Dostoevsky] in order further to extend his influence, to make his concerted tone heard across the disconcerting voices of the powerful novelist'.[52] The combination of narcissism and influence, for Massis, produces a public pathology in which Gide need not feel the force of a disciplinary guilt. 'What he wants is to recover a harmony which does not exclude his own dissonance, a law which does not demand that he feel otherwise than he does.'[53]

It is clear I think that Massis's disgust at Gide is socio-sexual.[54] His imagination of a social narcissism, extending sensually out into a world of selves, which are conceived as similar to Gide rather than marking a difference from him, calls up the full force of Massis's vehemence, and the full weight of his Catholic orthodoxy. Something must be disciplined here. Gide's friends occasionally thought the same. Roger Martin du Gard worried that publication of *Si le grain ne meurt* and *Corydon*, and the scandal which he believed would be the response to their relatively sensual and relatively open depictions of homosexuality, would be 'harmful to the full and final expansion of your gifts'.[55] The mode of social relation that Gide's writing implies will impede development towards a 'full and final' writing position, will leave him in a formless present tense. And du Gard correlates Gide's desire to be arrested in this position with his reading of Dostoesvky, noting that '[f]or months he has been living in daily intimacy with Dostoevsky [. . .]. The idea of public confession is infectious.'[56]

When T. S. Eliot writes his 1923 letter from England in the *NRF*, he distances himself actively from this contagious strain of precipitous narcissistic social imagining. He counsels the choice of Henry James rather than Dostoevsky as a model:

James did not bring us 'ideas', but rather a new world of thought and sentiment. Some have looked to Dostoevsky for this new world, others to James; I tend to think that the mind of James, so much less violent, so much more sensible and more resigned [*à tel point moins violent, à tel point plus raisonnable et plus résigné*] than that of the Russian, is no less profound, and that it is more useful, more applicable to our future.[57]

James offers a pragmatic resignation to the future, as counterweight to the violent attractions of Dostoevsky.

The mixture in Dostoevsky, and around him, of a narcissistic intimacy and a violent precipitation, imaged in *The Adolescent* in the delightful proximity of narrator to his younger self and to a fantasised reader and to the contingencies of the world, and developed in the sensual expansions of the *NRF*, are the reasons why 'modernism' hardens against him. Woolf remained troubled and fascinated by Dostoevsky from the moment of her first recorded contact with his work. This was on her honeymoon in Venice, from which, writing to Lytton Strachey, she notes that 'It is directly obvious that he is the greatest writer ever born: and if he chooses to become horrible what will happen to us? Honeymoon completely dashed. If he says it – human hope – had better end, what will be left but suicide in the Grand Canal.'[58] It is a wonderfully complicated marriage scene – she writes to the ambiguously sexual Strachey, who had of course proposed marriage to her in 1909, and perhaps invokes the late honeymoon of George Eliot, whose husband Johnny Cross leapt into the Grand Canal in 1880.[59] Her capacity to remain within this scene – to persist in socio-sexual complexity, to make a life rather than an institution of marriage – depends upon Dostoevsky's writing.

Two elements in his work which fascinate her prove exactly the reasons why she must reject him: the elements of speed or suddenness,[60] and of a crowded intimacy of bodies without structuring differences. Dostoevsky goes wrong when he goes too fast. She notes:

[H]ow often in guessing the psychology of souls flying at full speed even his intuition is at fault, and how in increasing the swiftness of his thought, as he always tends to do, his passion rises into violence, his scenes verge upon melodrama, and his characters are seized with the inevitable madness and epilepsy.[61]

There is a strange folding together of the author and the text here, as if, in Bakhtin's terms, speed collapses the dialogic registering of objective social conditions into an unsustainable monologue, which internalises social contradictions as an intermittent body.[62] The text, like Conrad, shudders.

The convulsive body appears with a rapid crowd. The destruction of the 'time sense', which Murry had announced, is at least partly a result of there being too many unhierarchised disorderly presences on the scene. Woolf is explicit about this in the same review. 'Sometimes [. . .] it seems as if from exhaustion he could not concentrate his mind sufficiently to exclude the waifs and strays of the imagination – people in the streets, porters, cabmen – who wander in and begin to talk and reveal their souls, not that they are wanted, but because Dostoevsky knows all about them and is too tired to keep them to himself.'[63] This is a fairly precise echo of the terms of Eliot's institutional displacement of problems of constitution, which I cited in the Preface, where the problem of a melancholy culture, a culture lacking a vital relation to its arts, gave rise to the image of a noisy crowd, which then required the calming order of a structured institution of criticism, with the power and vigilance to eject unwelcome intruders. Some crowded constituency – 'waifs and strays of the imagination' who give life to the dead phrase 'fellow sufferers' – has got too close for modernism's comfort.

Before Modernism Was

There are five chapters to my book. Each is a kind of case study, in which a figure for the modernist constitution is introduced and its constituency explored. In order of appearance, these figures are: the ghost which crowds out empty houses and disturbs their market value; the adolescent boy, anxiously scrutinised by psychology and sociology; the 'Pole', awkward Central-European cousin to attempts to make Europe central to the world; the dog which is part of the family but may well harbour rabies; and the smoker who clings to a habit that she does not wish to understand. The cast of figures is by no means exhaustive: any number, almost, of other presences could be conjured up in their places. Such necessity as they have resides in an exemplary intensity. They are contingently intense for me, to begin with, in my own version of the embarrassing enunciation 'I am a modernist', which gathers into it a range of contents – I am a nervously home-owning self-exiled smoker who fears dogs and still dreams of his adolescence. They are intense too to some extent for the world in which modernism emerged, and for the world in which it unstably persists.

These are *figures* of the modernist constitution – that which appears before modernism – in two senses. First: they appear, materially, as solid bounded objects, which are part of a historically particular experience. Second: they are to be understood as rhetorical figures within systems of representation, or discourses. In rhetoric, a figure is defined as a deviation from a representational norm. The combination of these two figures of the figure – a bounded material body, and an abnormality within representation – provides the kind of historicity which I will argue that modernism has, in its emergence, and in its intense appeal to us for recognition.

Chapter 1 finds modernism in empty, haunted houses. The materiality of this figure is shaky, aligned as it is with ghosts which evade positivist recording; but at the same time, that spectral presence has very material effects. The ghost in the empty house affects the market value of the property. Discourses which attempt to place property at the centre of our identities, which attempt to sustain the idea of a *home* which can be both shelter and an extension of ourselves, within a world traversed by inhuman movements of capital, are shown to be troubled by these revenants. The figurations – the exorbitant processes of literature – which mark modernist writing, shadow closely the figure of the ghost. In this chapter I read a range of writers who are considered modernist, as they attempt to create the properties of modernism in relation to questions of money and value: works by Virginia Woolf, Henry James, and Wyndham Lewis are analysed in relation to discourses of literary and domestic property, and in relation to the burgeoning market for popular fiction, including the literary commodity, the 'ghost story'.

In Chapter 2, the ghost gives way to more excessively *raw* material. The adolescent boy, in his delinquency and his difficulty of employment, is the closest thing to a hero, in my book. Like Dostoevsky's Arkady, the youths who appear in this chapter are filled with a contradictory contingency which has its roots deep in the embodied sense that, to repeat Chiozza Money's terms from the Preface, the world is 'rubbish'. This knowledge does not dismay the adolescent, but it cannot be absorbed by the discourses that attempt to contain him – the chapter looks at the valiant attempts, within juvenile justice, debates on unemployment, and psychology, to register and demarcate the presence of the sulky teen. The adolescent cannot be absorbed by discourses because he is not a species of the 'subject': in general, my book has no use for that term, as it finds everywhere that 'interpellation' of the subject is only partial, and is everywhere stymied by the energies of the figures it attempts to control. The writers who sustain the adolescent figure of the modernist constitution in this chapter include the contributors to the 1914 Vorticist journal *Blast*; but I also find modernist textual practices emerging within non-literary works: psychologist Stanley Hall's extraordinary prose, and Judge Lyndsey's hysterically imperative legal writing, are both part of the urgent fabric of the modernism that I construct.

The combination of an approach to the material figures on which modernism depends with a reading of the rhetorical figures through which it appears, takes my book close both to deconstruction and to cultural studies. I have learned a great deal from work in these modes, and I would be pleased to claim an affiliation with both tendencies in writing about literature in history.[64] But I hope also that the assurance which has marked the institutional legitimacy of both of these approaches will be troubled a little in my book; and that something of the urgency with which both of these approaches appeared can be registered here. Deconstruction was never just a mode of registering the incompletion of the subject; it was always also a path to the openness of the human future. Cultural studies was not just a way of bringing new subjects into universities; it also hoped to reform the social relations within which academic thought happened.

In Chapter 3, the scene of modernism becomes increasingly international. The limits of the British focus of the earlier chapters had already been challenged, by, for example, the trans-national movements of capital which undermine the material fabric of the home. Here, the figure for modernism, the 'Pole', is a radical migrant, found travelling between Poland, Brittany, Paris, London, and the Trobriand Islands. In order to create stable discourses, such as the discourse of 'modernism' or that of anthropology, a geographical stability is imagined: a Centre is given to the world. But the imagination of that centre is constantly overlaid with more material figurations, including the intractable political problems encountered in defining or governing 'central Europe'. The chapter discusses at some length the work of Polish anthropologist Bronislaw Malinowski, as he faces a choice of terminus for his anthropological writing: either he can take it back to Poland, where it would become part of a conflicted modernist culture; or he can – as he in the end does – place it in the academic centre of the world, in London.

These two geographical trajectories, one of which is governed by 'a sense of reality', the other existing only as part of the 'abstract' possibility which is materialised in Poland, compete with one another, and in that competition, a place for the emergence of modernism is defined.

Modernism in Chapter 3 reflects something which cannot be separated from geography. It is forced to keep on moving, as there is no stable ground on which it can rest, no agreed borders to contain it. In Chapter 4, I consider a drive within modernism – the drive to abstraction – which hopes to hold things still. The name I give to this drive is 'quarantine', and my chapter investigates a series of possible relations between the creation of abstract artworks and the attempts to seal Britain off from international flows of money and disease. I read this drive through the figure of the dog, looking at a rich complex of legal and medical discourses that emerge around dog-breeding and rabies scares; I read works written by dogs and about them alongside early twentieth-century feminism and modernist writing on aesthetics. The dog is an overlooked proximate presence within the set of relations which make up human social identities;[65] our attempts to give form to the dog channel all kinds of historical anxieties about modern life.

The book ends up in smoke. Chapter 5 begins with Sigmund Freud's surprising assertion that his smoking habit, like his Jewishness, is a 'private affair', and has nothing to do with psychoanalysis. As the discourses and institutions of psychoanalysis take their form within a history that connects the First World War to the Second, I argue in that chapter that the place of the private, outside psychoanalysis, becomes an increasingly important one. The disastrous private addict, as he appears just outside the discourse of psychoanalysis and as he is attacked within a range of British popular fictions, is my final uncomfortable figure for the constitution of modernism. Smoking displays the damage of historical relations, while allowing the individual to 'cope' with history; and in that display it refuses the full subjection of the individual to her history, maintaining an under-determined kernel – a place where a cigar is just a cigar – within historical and cultural explanation. Smoking also produces smoke, an inchoate signal of something burning in our past, to which must attend; something urgent before modernism was.

1
Property: The Preoccupation of Modernism

[Spirit] dwells in heaven and dwells in us; we poor things are just its 'dwelling', and if Feuerbach goes on to destroy its heavenly dwelling and force it to move to us bag and baggage, then we, its earthly apartments, will be badly overcrowded.

Max Stirner, *The Ego and Its Own*[1]

Jetzt wär es Zeit, daß Götter träten aus bewohnten Dingen . . .
Und daß sie jede Wand in meinem Haus
umschlügen. Neue Seite. Nur der Wind,
den solches Blatt im Wenden würfe, reichte hin,
die Luft, wie eine Scholle, umzuschaufeln:
ein neues Atemfelde.

Rainer Maria Rilke[2]

The introduction has suggested that the modernism which my book will be tracking is an oddly substanced figure, a material irruption that rises affectively up within regularities of discourse and institution, glimpsed sweatily but unsurely by the reader. This first chapter will look to the most literal rendering of that notion of the revenant – the figure of the ghost. I am interested here in a long-standing relation between ghosts and properties: in the case of houses, ghosts may make property more interesting and singular, attaching forgotten histories to the functional structure of the building; but they also disturb its market value. Houses with ghosts are empty because they cannot be sold or rented. In the case of literature, the development of the ghost story is part of the regularisation of a market for popular fiction, an attempt to get rid of the unpredictable mysteries of the relation between literary value and the career of authorship, the attempt to make a living from fiction. The crossing of these two figures of the ghost indicates a place for modernism to emerge. It has been long understood that one of the things that modernism in literature and the arts may be is a different kind of property, something valued socially and culturally in a different way than the properties within a general economy. This understanding invites sociological, economic, or historical reduction. This chapter will both accept and finally be forced to relinquish this invitation, for what that property is devolves into questions of valuing that can neither escape from nor settle in sociology, economics or 'history'. Literary property will be the focus, but the chapter will start with the details of the housing-property market in Britain at the turn of the century, and the ghosts that obstruct its ideally inhuman functioning.

One of the first things the Society for Psychical Research did after its foundation in 1882 was to set up a committee to investigate haunted houses. This committee ran into problems almost immediately. Not only, as they later discovered, were ghosts notoriously shy of their investigative machineries; but the properties – the houses themselves – behaved strangely when approached by psychic investigators.

The Society was one of a proliferation of late-Victorian institutions. It included many notable figures among its members – Henry Sidgwick, professor of moral philosophy at Cambridge University, was one of the founders; Henri Bergson and William James were both honorary presidents. The Society aimed to resituate the supernatural: to take it away from shadier spaces and replace it within relatively positivistic scientific discourses. There is nothing inherently disastrous to such a project in a failure to record supernatural phenomena: ghosts have a right – almost a duty – to be tricky, and that kind of difficulty can be understood as merely a spur to further creativity in experimental design. What is more difficult for an experimental science to absorb is the reflection on the material conditions – the houses as properties – which aren't easy to separate from the phenomena – the ghosts – themselves.

The first report of the committee acknowledges the problem:

> The owners of houses reputed to be haunted are reluctant to make the general public, or even a select portion of it, partakers in the privileges which they themselves enjoy. The man who admits the possibility of any house being haunted runs the risk of being regarded as

a visionary; but the hint of such a possibility in the case of a man's own house is, none the less, commonly regarded by him as impairing the value of his property.[3]

This worry is confirmed by another member, writing ten years later about the reluctance of one informant to say too much about his house and its ghost: he 'was for a time unwilling to give further accounts, lest the house, which belonged to a friend of his, should again become depreciated in value; as it appears from Miss Morton's record that it has previously been [it was rented for £60, less than half its market value, in 1879–80]'.[4] Somewhere, before the problem of recording unstably material phenomena, another materiality insists. A ghost in the house affects its value; a privilege recognised by risky visionaries is undervalued by the common regard. This problem can't be seen as merely the irruption of extraneous and singular anomaly, because there is no more articulate ground for property values than that of the common regard. That is, within a free market, price is the point of operation of the invisible hand; exchange value is the immanent expression of a harmonious social totality.[5] And the search for ghosts stumbles on incoherencies within this consensus.

The committee responds with a reactive overvaluation:

> We would earnestly entreat our members and friends who are so fortunate as to inhabit haunted houses, to afford us an opportunity of visiting them. [. . .] we are willing to incur much trouble and expense for the chance.[6]

Several years later, the committee has investigated much inflated rumour, but still no measured ghosts. Their labours are not entirely without product. They have arrived at some sort of understanding, for they have 'gained some experience in a rather difficult art, the negotiation of leases for "haunted houses" '.[7] The project of tracking apparitions has taken a detour into the heart of market operations.

The present chapter will follow this detour: first in a reading of a short story which I argue is placed at one programmatic origin of British modernism, Henry James's 'The Jolly Corner', which appeared first in Ford Madox Hueffer's (later Ford) *The English Review*, in 1908; then in a reading of a 1911 story by Wyndham Lewis. This latter story is also somewhere at the bottom of modernism, but contingently so, and with a different sense of propriety. My reading of these two texts concentrates on one central figuration: where a ghost arises from the emptiness of a house, and the house's emptiness – or perhaps better its simultaneous emptiness and excessive inhabitation, vacancy and overcrowding – signal something already present in the materiality of the property market. This will be an essay in reduction, then, pushing stolidly on through ghostly apparitions towards the historical and material ground they so flimsily obscure. But, as the experience of the Society for Psychical Research suggests, the material *as* property is no stable base from which to determine superstructural or symptomatic effects such as ghosts.

I want to take this pattern, where the ghost keeps re-appearing within the material explanations which would aim to exorcise or to regularise it, as a model for what to do with another kind of reductive ambition. In modernism's claim for origination, modernism disavows its relationship to the literary marketplace; imagines itself as free and autonomous in relation to its economic conditions. That freedom is conceived as alternately serene or critical, as disinterested or determinedly negating. Much recent work has heartily and usefully debunked this conception, in the name of social history. Lawrence Rainey, for example, argues that 'modernism, among other things, is a strategy whereby the work of art invites and solicits its commodification, but does so in such a way that it becomes a commodity of a special sort, one that is temporarily exempted from the exigencies of immediate consumption prevalent within the larger cultural economy, and instead is integrated into a different economic circuit of patronage, collecting, speculation, and investment'.[8] In concentrating on the integration of modernism within a socio-economic story, this body of work has been in danger of misreading disavowal – the blind break for freedom – as simply disingenuousness, and thus of losing the charged ambitions of this odd moment of writing.[9] That charge has a historical resonance that will not be contained by literary history, and I suggest that the history of modernism's urge to autonomy may be best approached through the strangenesses of properties, and the ghosts that they breed.

As clear as the figure on a cheque

Virginia Woolf, in 'Mr Bennett and Mrs Brown', her by turns retrospective and prospective account of the origination of modernism, an origin she sees as both datable to a vague-precise moment in or around 1910 and as still wilfully straining for consolidation at the date of the essay's publication and republication in 1923 and 1924, sees a properly autonomous modern fiction as requiring the wholesale destruction of houses. The problem with the fiction which has gone before – specifically that of Bennett, Wells, and Galsworthy – is that it has depended upon a dodgy synecdoche: they 'have laid an enormous stress upon the fabric of things. They have given us a house in the hope that we may be able to deduce the human beings who live there.'[10] For Woolf, this does not work. Character has been obscured by the details of property and the rattle of narration: in Bennett's *Hilda Lessways*, for example, 'we cannot hear her mother's voice, or Hilda's voice; we can only hear Mr Bennett's voice telling us facts about rents and freeholds and copyholds and fines'.[11] There is a failure of integrity which betrays a lack of 'interest[] in character in itself; or in the book in itself. [. . .] Their books, then, were incomplete as books, and required that the reader should finish them, actively and practically, for himself'. We are led back outside into the world, where to complete the activity of reading we may have 'to join a society, or, more desperately, to write a cheque'.[12]

Modernism – for Woolf, 'Modern Fiction' – has as its purpose to save in one swoop the autonomy of the artwork, its 'completeness', and the autonomy of the person from the world of societies and cheques. So the buildings have to go. 'At whatever cost to life, limb, and damage to valuable property Mrs Brown must be rescued, expressed, and set in her high relations to the world [. . .]. And so the smashing and the crashing began. Thus it is that we hear all round us, in poems and novels and biographies, even in newspaper articles and essays, the sound of breaking and falling, crashing and destruction.'[13] This noisy clearing of the ground may be something she hears as problematic and strained in other modernists, but it is a scene of which Woolf is fond; indeed I'd want to argue that the active erosion of physical structures is one of the competing strains in Woolf's aesthetic. When 'Time Passes' (vaguely-precisely the ten years from 1908 to 1918) in *To the Lighthouse*, darkness floods in to the Hebridean holiday home of the Ramsays:

> Nothing, it seems, could survive the flood, the profusion of darkness which, creeping in at keyholes and crevices, stole round window blinds, came into bedrooms, swallowed up here a jug and basin, there the sharp edges and firm bulk of a chest of drawers. Not only was furniture confounded; there was scarcely anything left of body and mind by which one could say 'This is he' or 'This is she'.[14]

The confounding of furniture and the approach to an effacement of personhood look set to take the whole house with it, to the point where 'some trespasser, losing his way, could have told only by a red-hot poker among the nettles, or a scrap in the hemlock, that here once some one had lived; there had been a house'.[15] This uncertainly motivated wanderer, at once actively trespassing and passively lost, light himself of property, reads personhood – against the Mr Bennetts – elegaically from the effacement of property. 'And so the smashing and crashing began'.

Of course, the house does not go this way: through the sniffily valued efforts of Mrs McNab and Mrs Bast, described as 'a force working; something not highly conscious; something that leered, something that lurched',[16] the house is restored to its holiday distinction. But the movement which would have levelled it to the undifferentiating ground is continued. The redemptive aesthetic enclosure and the corresponding rescuing and expressing of Mrs Ramsay are heavily and pointedly dramatised, in the simultaneous solution to the formal problems of Lily Briscoe's painting and completion of the long-postponed trip to the Lighthouse. But that resounding closure is far from satisfying; or perhaps far *too* satisfying.[17] There persists an alignment of the vision of the novel with those 'destructive elements' which would have houses and forms collapse.[18] Lily herself articulates it:

> One wanted fifty pairs of eyes to see with, she reflected. Fifty pairs of eyes were not enough to get round that woman with, she thought. Among them must be one that was stone blind to her beauty. One wanted most some secret sense, fine as air, with which to steal through keyholes and surround her where she sat knitting, talking, sitting silent in the window alone; which took to itself and treasured up like the air which held the smoke of the steamer, her thoughts, her imaginations, her desires.[19]

This secret sense, ghostly in its vacancy and profusion, follows closely the path of the flood of darkness which had earlier effaced body and furniture together. The idea that getting rid of the house will give us 'the person' and the 'complete' artwork disavows this alignment, where the aesthetic sense necessary to give us the person is the same destructive dark force that will cause the house to crumble. The movement of disavowal is complete when it imagines writing as founded on the generalised inheritance of a 'room of one's own', protected from all propertied interferences, or when it forgets about the cheque presented at the moment of purchasing the novel in its eagerness to imagine that the autonomous artwork has nothing to do with the writing of cheques. In this movement Woolf tends towards the easily won 'form' which is celebrated by Roger Fry and especially by Clive Bell as an unanxious coordination of significance with emotional disinterest within the work of art.

What is I think most powerful about Woolf, what distinguishes her from the main currents of Bloomsbury, is the way in which the *movement* of disavowal on which the autonomy of the individual or the artwork depends is given noisy and destructive agency. The escape from the Edwardian novel of property places its own 'enormous stress upon the fabric of things'. What Woolf imagines as being programmatically and metaphorically done to properties from outside – the crashing, the stress on the fabric, the breaking of windows – is already ramifying within individual houses, in the physical, civic and economic structures of dwelling. One estate agent's journal notes that 'Twelve small houses in Stepney have been unoccupied for some time past, and on a recent visit to the neighbourhood the owner was unable to find the houses. In fact five of them had entirely disappeared [. . .].'[20] Low interest rates in the 1890s led, in London, to a building boom of unstoppable momentum, which met a fall in real wages, and a substantial rise in interest rates, from the beginning of the new century.[21] The result was a very visible juxtaposition of unoccupied and overcrowded properties. This pressure on central-London property lent further momentum to the expansion of urbanisation outwards into cheaper land. Part of the effect of this was to produce a very substantial random and unstable 'unearned dividend' for those who happened to own these areas. And none of these processes was easily either predicted or controlled. Banks would not lend to landowners on the promise of urban expansion, and so the development of suburbs proceeded irregularly, according to speculative investments: 'There is not a town in England where you may not find secluded plots of building land, which the tide of building has passed by on either side, from no apparent cause, and left in abandoned sterility.'[22] The rent gradient, which indicated property becoming cheaper with distance from urban centres, did not reduce pressure on the centres, because, public transport still being relatively expensive, the very or even the moderately poor were unable to afford to commute.

These stresses on the fabric of property should be understood in the context of changes in the structure of wealth in Britain through the long *fin-de-siècle*. The value of British agricultural land plummeted: in 1878, according to José Harris, land constituted one quarter of the national wealth; by 1914, less than one twelfth.[23] Land had been the ground, both material and symbolic, of social hierarchy in Britain: wealth, power, and land ownership had circumscribed relatively congruent constituencies. So we might expect the collapse in land values to have led to a dramatic confounding of economic and social distinction; towards at least a potential inchoacy of power. But access to property in Britain at the end of this period was probably more unequal than at any time in national history (and, incidentally, than in any comparable European country). The de-materialisation of capital did not have democratising effects.

The Liberal government of the latter part of the Edwardian period tried repeatedly to rationalise this situation. This is the preoccupation of the Edwardians that worries Woolf, with 'rents and freeholds and copyholds and fines'; although it is also a preoccupation shared by Paul and Minta in *To the Lighthouse*, whose relationship looks like the clearest version in the novel of the 'change in human character' for which Woolf's essay demands representation. They no longer love one another, but their relationship has somehow been 'righted' by a social sense that can absorb his affair with another woman who shares his position on 'the taxation of land values'.[24] That tax was proposed to normalise the unearned dividend from urban expansion and to level out the rent gradient, and, along with new rating policies, to pay for the amelioration of human conditions from the rise in urban property prices, to humanise the movements of exchange value. But the phenomena themselves were perhaps too odd, local, and rapidly changing to be covered by any rationalising plan at the level of the State. The limits here of humanist, reformist, and politically consensual policy (the limits, I would say, of liberalism), are marked by their baffled confrontation with the details of a spectralised economy of property. J. A. Hobson, an influential left-liberal thinker, realised that 'nothing less [than the beginnings of an unceasing and an enlarging attack on the system of private property and private industrial enterprise] can fulfil the demand, which Mr. Churchill has expressed, that "property be associated in the minds of the mass of the people with ideas of reason and justice"'.[25]

Was the whole house crowded from floor to ceiling?

Algernon Blackwood, in his first published story, 'The Empty House', fictionalises the situation of the Society for Psychical Research. The story concerns the investigation of a building which, although it 'seemed precisely similar to its fifty ugly neighbours, was as a matter of fact entirely different – horribly different'.[26] The building's difference results in, and realises within the fiction, its collapsed market value, expressed in the haunted emptiness of a house which cannot be rented or sold.

Two psychic researchers, Geoffrey Shorthouse and his aged but intrepid aunt, investigate the house and attempt to get rid of the ghost, in order to make the house inhabitable, and thus to normalise its value. The ghosts in the empty house embody a glitch in the operations of the market. Their apparition is clearly class-marked. They arise from downstairs in the kitchen and scullery, and descend from upstairs 'somewhere among those horrid gloomy servants' rooms with their bits of broken furniture, low ceilings, and cramped windows'.[27] Within the representation of an abnormal house, they are excessively present manifestations of the properly invisible servants who maintain propriety, a registration of the different kinds of inhabiting that maintain an idea of 'home'. They might also remind us of one of the examples Woolf gives of the 'change in human character': 'In life one can see the change, if I may use a homely illustration, in the character of one's cook. The Victorian cook lived like a leviathan in the lower depths, formidable, silent, obscure, inscrutable; the Georgian cook is a creature of sunshine and fresh air; in and out of the drawing room, now to borrow the *Daily Herald*, now to ask advice about a hat.'[28]

But the details of Blackwood's scene are very slightly skewed from a simple expression of the repressed materiality of the domestic. What these ghosts object to – which objection is what makes them manifest *as* ghosts – *is* the fact of representation or rationalisation. They don't want to be measured or evoked, but to be left alone: 'The whole dark interior of the old building seemed to become a malignant Presence that rose up, warning them to desist and mind their own business.'[29]

This subtilisation of the problem of class occurs through a full identification of the ghosts with the property, with the 'whole dark interior of the old building'. This is not just an evasion: as Churchill and Hobson suggest, a crisis of legitimation appears in the form of a malignant, irrational something undermining the conditions through which the material can be represented as property. This articulation of the particular demands of *literary* property with the relations between houses and their ghosts is taken up in Blackwood's third book, *John Silence: Physician Extraordinary* (1908).[30]

John Silence, Blackwood's 'physician extraordinary', is called in to solve the case of Felix Pender, an increasingly successful humorous writer, living in a 'rising' district of London (one, that is, where property is becoming increasingly expensive). Under the effects of 'psychical invasion', by a previous, long dead, proletarian, and possibly Irish,[31] occupant of the house, Pender has lost his marketable facility. After a battle of psychic and moral wills, Silence exorcises the ghost, and Pender's talent is restored.

Pender's problem is not one of productivity: in fact, 'he works like a fury'. What is wrong with the writing, what makes it 'nothing', unthinkable, is that it is not saleable. 'He can no longer write in the old way that was bringing him success.' ' "[He] produces nothing" – [Pender's wife] hesitated a moment – "nothing that he can use or sell" '. The fear is economic. 'Unless something competent is done, he will simply starve to death'; starve to death, and lose his hold on the house.[32]

The story investigates a problem of value, then, but not a simple one. It covertly admires this new production, considering it 'most damnably clever in the consummate way the vile suggestions are insinuated under cover of high drollery'. These 'vile, debased tragedies, the tragedies of broken souls', products of 'the kind of bad imagination that so far has been foreign, indeed impossible, to [Pender's] normal nature', and productive of laughter that is 'bizarre, horrible, disturbing',[33] in their effectiveness, their ability to evince a different sort of response from the reader, are rather a challenge to than an evacuation of Pender's sense of literary value. Pender is becoming a proto-modernist.[34] The right of Pender to occupy this house and to participate in its capital growth depends upon his relation to a literary marketplace. This happy situation is fraught with instabilities. The ghost, and the writing practice it incites in Pender, express something of the logic of this instability. Through its agency – already a vacancy and a superfluity of agency – the house threatens to become empty or overcrowded. While the aetiology of only one ghost is given in the story, that ghost appears as multiplied excessively: 'Was, then, even the staircase occupied? Did *They* stand also in the hall? Was the whole house crowded from floor to ceiling?'[35] And within this scene, an unnameable and unsaleable creativity – the production of nothing – is imagined.

John Silence solves the case in two stages. First, and indeed silently, he takes over Pender's rental payments.[36] Then, he exorcises the ghost, and with it the spectre of modernism. In the relay between property value and literary values, both within the fiction and around it in the relation between Blackwood and his readers, the ghost and the writing it dictates are a pressing anomaly. Without them, a consensus about value can be produced and maintained.

Writing about the production of these early stories, Blackwood suggested that 'Something in me, doubtless, sought a natural outlet'. This 'something', he claims, is the 'accumulated horror of his years in New York'.[37] As he describes it, the horror was of life among the lumpenproletariat, living as a casual labourer, sometimes sick, among criminals and bohemians. At the same time, this horror is of ambition, of the speed of American capitalism. 'I realised how little I desired this [speed, display, advertisement] and glittering brilliance, this frantic rush to be at all costs sharper, quicker, smarter than one's neighbour [. . .] I missed tradition, background, depth.'[38] He is looking for a practice which will evade these two horrors, the two faces of homeless capital, and he finds it in writing. The books he writes stave off this horror at the same time as they express it. They sold well enough to support Blackwood's subsequent retreat into the compensatory fantasy of a rural sublime: 'With my typewriter and kit-bag, [I took] my precious new liberty out to the Jura Mountains where, at frs. 4.50 a day, I lived in reasonable comfort and wrote more books.'[39] But his writing needs its implication in the economies that it helps him to escape. *John Silence: Physician Extraordinary* was itself part of a speculative literary market: it was, for instance, the first book in Britain to be advertised on roadside billboards.[40]

In one of the many new manuals for authors which are both symptoms of the new literary business and attempts to control its implications, Walter Besant, president of the Society of Authors, estimated, wildly, that since the middle of the nineteenth century, due to the Education Act of 1870 and the opening up of colonial markets, the potential readership for a novel in English had risen from around fifty thousand to more than 120 million.[41] With this massively inflated speculation about the reach of fiction, there were considerable shifts in the economies of authorship. The royalty system opened authorship to freedom of labour (or latent pauperism).[42] The census of 1881 included 3400 self-identified authors; by 1891 the number had risen to 6000; by 1901 to 11,000.[43] These new speculators are offered the kinds of status which went with landed properties. Besant argues that while the nineteenth-century novelist had little chance even of a peerage, 'it is now well known that a respectable man of letters may command an income and a position quite equal to those of the average lawyer or doctor. It is also well known that one who rises to the very top may enjoy as much social consideration as a Bishop and as good an income.'[44] But the conditions which make this status possible – all of those new and marginal readers; all of one's cooks flitting up the stairs in search of the *Daily Herald* – are also those which produce the ghost of the mob, the negation of the consensus which secures the stabilities on which the social consideration of a Bishop depends.[45] 'Writing fiction [. . .] becomes a wild gamble instead of a moderately remunerative occupation.'[46]

Modernism is an effect of and a response to this. David Trotter, for one, has pointed to the way that a mass market opens up the possibility for specialised market fractions to be defined against it.[47] But the sense of something gone wild, the anxious or exhilarated sense of the anarchic threat of market expansion and literary speculation, is lost in his immensely productive account of the relation between the textual development of modernism and the structure of the reading public. He loses the sense of the *why* of modernism, the sense clearly there in Woolf's demand for the rescuing of Mrs Brown from buildings and Mr Bennett. He loses the dialectical relations between a consolidated mass market and its implausible fractions, a hope for wholeness both signalled and mourned in the withdrawal of modernism to an immaterially stable room of its own while the buildings crash down around it. Trotter saves a liberal accommodation of individuals to the texts which please them, against the haunting sense that liberalism – for better or for worse – is not in control of the forces building and destroying its world. This is to deny – or to relegate to a space *within* representation – the excesses and vacancies of agency that crowd and abandon the liberal individual; to get rid too quickly of the ghost.

Not the ghost of a reason

Ford Madox Hueffer (later Ford) set up *The English Review* in 1908. Its aim was to inaugurate a new standard and frame for literary value, as well as to consolidate a function for the valued literature. Its professionalism is defined against the marketplace, through disavowal. The first issue quotes with pride from a letter from Shaw, which it glosses as 'at once [. . .] a benediction and [. . .] a prophecy of [financial] disaster'.[48] Douglas Goldring, Hueffer's assistant, describing the care with which Hueffer and Joseph Conrad worked and reworked the statement of the journal's mission – which Violet Hunt called 'that sweet and fatuous circular' – complained that 'with my experience of "commercial journalism" gained in the well-run office of *Country Life*, it all seemed rather babyish'.[49] In one of the constructions of affiliation through which the idea of 'modernism' is immanently produced, Ezra Pound described *The Little Review* as continuing in exactly this anti-market tradition: '*The Little Review* is now the first effort to do comparatively what *The English Review* did in its first year and a half: that is, to maintain the rights and position of literature, I do not say in contempt of the public, but in spite of the curious system of trade and traders which has grown up with the purpose or result of interposing itself between literature and the public.'[50]

But the exemption from market rationalities, where rights and positions are maintained 'in spite of' the market, and where the autonomous is posited against the curious system of the mediated, is not conceived only for art's sake. *The English Review* had a substantial political section, analysing for instance the structure of British unemployment, the intractable problems of the Balkan crisis, the possibility of a National Insurance scheme. To these problems, the journal offered 'The Critical Attitude': an attitude fostered by the literature which it aimed to print. The icons throughout were Flaubert and Henry James; and their work was ascribed considerable political potential: not through moral or ideological compulsion – the last thing one would associate with the reading of either author is a strongly unifying or an uplifting idea – but through the spectacle of disinterested literary value itself, and through the notion of 'really reading'. 'Flaubert said that had the French really read his "Education Sentimentale" France would have avoided the horrors of the *Débâcle*. Mr James might say as much for his own country and for the country he has so much benefited by making his own'.[51]

Aside from the unexamined 'quality' exemplified by James and Flaubert, the journal had some difficulty in defining the new literature it sought. It comes closest by contrast, defining new creation through obituary. First Swinburne dies. The magazine wants to recognise both the overwhelming 'epic volume' with which Swinburne is still felt and the distance between Swinburne and the sort of contemporary writing which *The English Review* exists to publish. 'There are to-day so many things to see, so many to "take stock of," that we none of us dare to generalise. We realise very fully that if to-day we generalise in one direction, tomorrow fresh facts will come to upset our theories.'[52] The hygienic scare-quoting of the accountant's phrasing is clearly in the manner of Henry James; and at the same time it is a measure of the difficulty of saying *what* literature – or the critical attitude – does with 'things'. Meredith, in the next issue, 'follows Mr. Swinburne into the shadows; and now, indeed, the whole Round Table is dissolved'.[53] The problem is to find a presence to replace this legendary dissolution. That is *The English Review*'s conscious literary purpose: to find and encourage a new literary voice. But when that new voice appears, it is difficult to characterise. When Edward Thomas reviews Pound's *Personae* the review is appreciative, even excited, but he finds it possible only:

[t]o say what [Pound] has not. [. . .] He has no obvious grace, no sweetness, hardly any of the superficial good qualities of modern versification; not the smooth regularity of the Tennysonian tradition, nor the wavering, uncertain languor of the new, though there is more in his rhythms than is apparent at first through his carelessness of ordinary effects. He has not the current melancholy or resignation or unwillingness to live; nor the kind of feeling for nature that runs to minute description and decorative metaphor.[54]

Pound's modernism fits the bill, but only in so far as it is a negative presence, adumbrating the appropriate shade of the missing Swinburne and Meredith.

When it comes to embodying this ghostly negative, the journal publishes literature about property. The first issue started the serialisation of Wells's *Tono Bungay*. The novel begins with the collapse of the world organised around the great estate; the disintegration of a spatial organisation of distinction. This is the property plot I outlined earlier: a vision of property consolidated by its relation to land and signalling social organisation gives way catastrophically on to an era of speculation. The novel plots the movements of a fortune based on a drug, 'Tono Bungay', described as 'nothing coated in advertisements' which is the – absent – centre of an advertising and financial industry.[55] Riches proliferate through this wild gamble, but they will not consolidate. Specifically, the house the newly paper-wealthy protagonist attempts to build sprawls and hesitates and will not take form. '[Financiers] all seem to bring their luck to the test of realization, try to make their fluid opulence coagulate out as bricks and mortar. [. . .] Then the whole fabric of confidence and imagination totters, and down they come.'[56] This is much closer to Woolf's vision than the schematics of 'Mr Bennett and Mrs Brown' will admit: a new-liberal stress on the fabric of things is entirely consonant with the modernist 'sound of breaking and falling'.

Pride of place in the first issue was given to Henry James's story 'The Jolly Corner'.[57] As Michael Anesko demonstrates, James had already shown himself sensitive to the details of the literary marketplace; and in at least one late story he displays intimacy with the kinds of property terms that dismayed Woolf. The two female cousins in Henry James's story, 'The Third Person' (1900), have unexpectedly inherited a house that is haunted.[58] The ghost – a hanged smuggler ancestor, 'third person' to their strange couple – both enables and troubles their intimacy; certainly it adds a kind of frisson and interest and history to their ownership. They describe this interest as an 'unspeakable unearned increment':[59] referring again to the 'unearned dividend' which provoked attempts at liberal tax reform. Like Pender in the Blackwood ghost story, they find this anomaly increasingly difficult to live with: they strive to exorcise the ghost. And there is something telling, if schematic, jokey, and bizarre, about the logic through which they do finally normalise and quiet their house:[60] one of the cousins replays the ancestral crime, smuggling a Tauschnitz paperback across from Paris. This strange, if lightly handled, transfer between the details of the literary marketplace and those of the terms of anarchic property values is crucial; and it is much more profoundly at the heart of 'The Jolly Corner'.

'The Jolly Corner' tells the story of Spencer Brydon, returned to his native New York after 33 redemptive years of refinement in Europe. He is shocked; and shocked by the manner in which he is shocked.

> Proportions and values were upside-down; the ugly things he had expected, the ugly things of his far-away youth, when he had too promptly waked up to a sense of the ugly – these uncanny phenomena placed him rather, as it happened, under the charm; whereas the 'swagger' things, the modern, the monstrous, the famous things, those he had more particularly, like thousands of ingenuous inquirers every year, come over to see, were exactly his sources of dismay. [. . .] It was interesting, doubtless, the whole show, but it would have been too disconcerting hadn't a certain finer truth saved the situation. He had distinctly not, in this steadier light, come over *all* for the monstrosities; he had come, not only in the last analysis but quite on the face of the act, under an impulse with which they had nothing to do. He had come – putting the thing pompously – to look at his 'property', which he had thus for a third of a century not been within four thousand miles of; or, expressing it less sordidly, he had yielded to the humour of seeing again his house on the jolly corner [. . .].[61]

The 'house on the jolly corner', as the story is already intimating, will be the site of a process of refinement. It signs the less sordid, the less pompous than 'property'. It signals, both as object and title, the ideal of a motivation which can face up to this inversion of values and proportions, an impulse (both in the last analysis and on the face of things) with which the monstrous speculative architecture has 'nothing to do'. And it is the finer truth which will, with the mysterious agency craved by the *English Review*, 'save' the undefined situation; which will defeat the horrors that Blackwood also associated with New York.

But the separation of kinds of value is unstable. Brydon's refinement – exactly that which recoiled from all that 'swagger' – is and always has been built upon his happily disavowed implication in the crazy financial logic which drives New York up. And he is about to become considerably richer as a result of a market in which a house that has fallen down is worth more than one standing:

> He could live in 'Europe,' as he had been in the habit of living, on the product of these flourishing New York leases, and all the better since, that of the second structure, the mere number in its long row, having within a twelve-month fallen in, renovation at a high advance had proved beautifully possible. [. . .] The house within the street [. . .] was already in course of reconstruction as a tall mass of flats [. . .][62]

Like Blackwood's 'Empty House', this 'structure' is un-marked; it is a 'mere number in its long row'. Only its collapse allows the singularities and anomalies which reside within the empty space of the commodity, and within the space of the social consensus upon which exchange values depend, to be expressed. It is harder for Brydon to separate his impulses from *this* monstrosity.

No longer hygienically distanced from the tainted sources of his dividend, Brydon turns to Alice Staverton in order to learn a new and adequate way of relating to his property; and particularly of possessing and valuing the empty house on the jolly corner. She is

> the delicately frugal possessor and tenant of the small house in Irving Place to which she had subtly managed to cling through her almost unbroken New York career. If he knew the way to it now better than to any other address among the dreadful numberings which seemed to him to reduce the whole place to some vast ledger-page, overgrown, fantastic, of ruled and criss-crossed lines and figures – if he had formed, for his consolation, that habit, it was really not a little because of the charm of his having encountered and recognized, in the vast wilderness of the wholesale, breaking through the mere gross generalization of wealth and force and success, a small still scene where items and shades, all delicate things, kept the sharpness of the notes of a high voice perfectly trained, and where economy hung about like the scent of a garden.[63]

She has managed a resistance to the economy which is unaccountable; which escapes absolutely any mapping in money. This is the voice of Mrs Brown, perhaps, heard across and despite the noises of Mr Bennett. Perhaps it is not surprising that her relation to the property is pointedly vague: she is 'possessor and tenant', subtly clinging to it, rather than either exclusively owning or renting it. This 'small still scene' of cultured aestheticism demands and drives a work of adequation.

Brydon's first move is to keep *his* property – the house on the Jolly Corner – empty and unsold; and indeed to display its emptiness to Alice. 'He only let her see for the present, while they walked through the great blank rooms, that absolute vacancy reigned'.[64] He refuses to capitalise on, or to instrumentalise at all, the house as property. The refusal and the emptiness interrupt market value through the production of a significant nothing.

> the beauty of it – I mean of my perversity, of my refusal to agree to do a 'deal' – is just in the total absence of a reason. Don't you see that if I had a reason about the matter at all it would *have* to be the other way, and would then be inevitably a reason of dollars? There are no reasons here *but* of dollars. Let us therefore have none whatever – not the ghost of one.[65]

Brydon disavows absolutely, denying *interest* all the way through to the ghost. When he attempts to insist, the narration checks him, freeindirect discourse providing the juice in which he is to stew: 'He had found the place, just as it stood and beyond what he could express, an interest and a joy. There were values other than the beastly rent values, and in short, in short – !'. Alice Staverton follows up: her interjection is brutal, and absolutely to the point:

> it was thus Miss Staverton took him up. 'In short you're to make so good a thing of your sky-scraper that, living in luxury on *those* ill-gotten gains, you can afford to be sentimental here!' [...] He explained that even if never a dollar were to come to him from the other house he would nevertheless cherish this one; and he dwelt, further, while they lingered and wandered, on the fact of the stupefaction he was already creating, the positive mystification he felt himself create.
> He spoke of the value of all he read into it [...].[66]

This explanation is indeed a 'positive mystification', frankly white-washing the failure to respond to Alice's audit of his sentimental construction of value. And it is significant that the move towards blatant mystification and stupefaction is imagined and experienced as creative; is valued as an exorbitant act of reading. Any reader who enjoys late James must share this baffling sense of value.

Alice suggests further, having seen Brydon surprisingly competently 'stand up' to the representative of the firm which is turning the 'other' property into a skyscraper, that if he had stayed in New York he would have 'discovered his genius in time really to start some new variety of awful architectural hare and run it till it burrowed into a goldmine'.[67] This is the trigger for the rest of the plot, which fairly romps onwards from this point. Brydon haunts his own empty house, attempting to find out what he would have been like had he stayed, and finally meets the ghostly figure of his counterfactual possibility. The frisson is in a confusion of pronouns, in the possibility of their identity, or in the interrogation of the mode of his identity with this other self.[68]

But I think that there is a sense in which this line of analysis is just so much more generic stupefaction. Alice Staverton's brutal question is not about identity but about relation; not about whether he could have *been* a New York property speculating billionaire, but about the fact that his refined difference is already implicated in the monstrosities of the world of property. I am suggesting that the story is at least partially reflexive: that it is interested in the relation between an achieved textual refinement and the sordid implication of the story as literary property in the wild spaces of domestic property, and that it figures this refinement as positive mystification; as a valuable and creative disavowal. In his autobiography, James speaks about the mutually exclusive physicalities of writing and money; here he describes his first payment:

> I see before me, in the rich, the many-hued light of my room . . . the very greenbacks, to the total value of twelve dollars, into which I had changed the cheque representing my first earned wage. I had earned it, I couldn't but feel, with fabulous felicity: a circumstance so strangely mixed with the fact that literary composition of a high order had, at that table where the greenbacks were spread out, quite viciously declined, and with the air of its being also once for all, to 'come' on any save its own essential terms, which it seemed to distinguish in the most invidious manner conceivable from mine.[69]

The claim here is of absolute spatial exclusion: money, with its 'queer [. . .] rather greasy complexion',[70] can not be on the desk at the same time as writing. And the agency of the writing subject is baffled before both: money arrives with fabulous felicity; literary composition has its own vicious and inscrutable terms. But this was also the scene in which James discovered his vocation. Michael Anesko, discussing this moment, has suggested that:

> We should recognize that money alone is not the primary vehicle for reconciling James's attitudes toward art and the marketplace. What renders 'literary composition of a high order' compatible with 'sordid gain' is precisely the 'positive consecration to letters' James experienced [. . .] his signal commitment to the literary vocation.[71]

'Positive consecration' fulfils here the same function as the 'positive mystification' that Brydon dwells on, that he feels himself create. It is a sort of disavowal: imagining literature happening in a place which has 'nothing to do' with the desk that in turns the money and the writing paper occupy. Within 'The Jolly Corner' we can trace the movement of that disavowal: a leaving behind of, rather than a response to or a refinement of, Alice's brutal acknowledgement of a structural dependence between the two realms. As in Woolf, literature requires a moving away from property; but, again as in Woolf, the story aims less at an achieved stillness at the end of the process – an achieved autonomy of person and of artwork – than at a representation of the very movement of disavowal.

This movement is inscribed in the particular mode of textual refinement, the convolutions of figurality, that marks James's high distinction. This is the economically implausible writing of a risky visionary, too expensive of readerly attention to sell simply, to become the happy commodity 'ghost story'. But its condition of possibility – its exploitation of the new market fractions thrown up in reactive response to a speculatively consolidated world of the literary commodity – is as tied to the logic of the commodity as the value of the house on the jolly corner is tied to the monstrously coining 'other structure'.

The 'real' ghost, that is to say, is the wrong kind of figure. It is given, generically, in advance, as that which the plot will produce. Brydon knows all along 'what he meant and what he wanted: it was as clear as the figure on a cheque presented in demand for cash'.[72] The distinctly Jamesian haunting stands at a refined distance from this blatancy.

It had begun to be present to him after the first fortnight, it had broken out with the oddest abruptness, this particular wanton wonderment: it met him there – and this was the image under which he himself judged the matter, or at least, not a little, thrilled and flushed with it – very much as he might have been met by some strange figure, some unexpected occupant, at a turn of one of the dim passages of an empty house. The quaint analogy quite hauntingly remained with him, when he didn't indeed rather improve it by a still intenser form: that of his opening a door behind which he would have made sure of finding nothing, a door into a room shuttered and void, and yet so coming, with a great suppressed start, on some quite erect confounding presence, something planted in the middle of the place and facing him through the dusk.[73]

The persistent haunting is by the literary figure, by the 'quaint analogy'. The ghostliness which the story realises settles at one remove from the fictional world, within the world of figures. In her deconstructive reading, Deborah Esch suggests that Brydon 'cannot read the word "figure", though he uses it repeatedly, because he cannot tell (or admit) the difference between its literal and figurative senses'. Esch establishes this difference as one between 'the figure on a check, a number that represents a fixed amount of money and can be exchanged on demand for that sum, and the "strange figure" of his earlier analogy – the prosopopoeia – to which he is attempting to assign as stable a significance by literalising'.[74] Esch's perception of the problem of figuration is acute, but for me it signals a radical difficulty in establishing the 'literal' in the space of the economy, where the material depends for its capacity to be maintained on a speculative field of property. And so when Esch concludes that 'The "ordeal of consciousness," in this exemplary Jamesian narrative, is a function of the processes of figuration that it thematizes – of the ordeal, that is, of reading and writing',[75] I would agree entirely. But I would suggest that the strain in actually ('really') reading and writing is materially continuous with the field of property that Brydon, in attempting to elevate his conscousness above it, marks as 'disavowed' by figuration. Haunting is performed by the value of prose, inflated by a strangely creative force of positive mystification; the ghost figures whatever it is that seeks an absolute distinction between that value and its massy sustenance. However hard the severance is wished, what is figured is also propertied, and is none the more literal, non the less spectral, for that.

I have suggested that this story is placed at one of the programmatic origins of modernism, charged there with instancing a mode of 'really reading' which is adequate to modernism's conditions in liberal crisis. The charge itself, the demand that writing extricate itself from the conditions that grossly generalise without at the same time disappearing into thin air, is what appears as a ghost. This ghost is troubling to Blackwood's ambitions of producing a writing on which one can live; it competes as a darkly erosive force with Woolf's luminous enclosing of the autonomous person and her artwork; it survives as a movement inhabiting, but in no sense at home in, the very fabric of literary and domestic property.

When modernism lays claim to autonomy, it has to extricate itself from the field of property. The values for which it is to stand, either actually or potentially, are opposed to the instrumental creations of markets and money. When it comes to figuring the positive values, the positive place or presence of modernist writing in the world, a range of terms are evoked which appear to exist apart from the world of property: ghosts, singularity, destruction; but as I have been arguing, this opposition between the material and the immaterial, between property and that which evades it, is already functioning within property itself. The movement of disavowal which would inaugurate the specific form of the art work is already at work within the stable properties the work of art disavows. For this reason, the distinction which founds modernism must be reimagined. Modernism is not distinct from other forms of literature, such as Blackwood's popular ghost stories; and modernism's value is not distinct from other forms of value, such as market value. Rather, modernism, in the form of the ghost in the empty house, signals the historicity and thus the fragility of the particular operative distinctions on which genres and markets and properties depend, as they reach out towards unconvinced and unsatisfied constituencies for support.

The wearying solicitation of emptiness

When *The English Review* finally realised Shaw's 'prophecy of disaster' and ran out of money after twelve months of Hueffer's editorship, his assistant, Douglas Goldring, set up a journal of his own: *The Tramp: An Open Air Magazine*. It answers to a fantasy, like Blackwood's fantasy of a life spent frugally writing in the Jura mountains, of transcendence of the strenuous problems of modernity and the neuroses of the urban crowd through the creation of the individual without properties. It is a magazine of outdoor life, fêting, and advertising, the life of the vagabond, without the inertia of property, travelling with only what he can carry on his back. The fantasy is of escape from the crowded and unconsensual civic space into a realm constrained only by the imagination. According to Harry Roberts, writing on 'The Art of Vagabondage', '[i]t is only the tramp who is able to realise the meaning of Maeterlinck's statement that we all live in the sublime'.[76] This shattering escape is associated with the transcendental freedom of 'genuine' literature. Goldring 'argued endlessly with [Wyndham] Lewis and Ezra [Pound]' that '[e]very genuine artist [. . .] is born free', and that '[o]nly if he allows himself to become enslaved by commercialism or by conventions does he require to break his self-imposed shackles'.[77]

But this fantasy of freedom from property (and from the regulative exchanges of commerce and convention) is commodified in the magazine. The advertisements encode the subtext. There, life in the sublime meets more realistic goals. 'Readers of THE TRAMP [Ozonair Ltd announces] who are, or should be, lovers of fresh air, will learn with particular interest and delight how the office and sitting-room can be ozonised, and pure "sea" air introduced at a moment's notice into the otherwise unhealthy atmosphere of rooms in crowded cities.'[78] Nomadic relation to modernity is a refreshing fantasy of escape, constantly protected from its realisation in identification with less savoury images of the propertyless, urban nomads and street arabs, the lumpenproletariat and the bad *bohème*. ' "Homeless, Ragged and Tanned" ', one advert reasoned, 'sounds very well in a song, but the filthy vagabond squatting in the road-side grass does not add to the delight of a country walk. THE CHURCH ARMY asks for the support of all who love the country for its LABOUR HOMES throughout the land for reclamation of vagrants, loafers and beggars.'[79]

After publishing three stories in *The English Review* (each of which has something to say about property and the literary market),[80] Wyndham Lewis was having difficulties establishing a market for his writing. He had approached the celebrated literary agent J. B. Pinker to place his work. Pinker failed, perhaps because of having too rational or strategic an attitude to the literary market. Lewis retrieved his stories from Pinker, noting that 'I can probably place all of them, if I have them at once, and as they are unmarketable, in a different way [from his failed popular novel *Mrs Dukes' Millions*], this chance may not recur'.[81] The singular home for these differently unmarketable writings was *The Tramp*, where he published four stories, including 'Unlucky for Pringle'.[82] Like 'The Jolly Corner', Lewis's tale is a kind of ghost story, in which ghostliness is correlated with the intricacies of property. Here, rather than dealing with the spectacular and chancy landscape of New York real estate, the concentration is on the exploitation of 'fag-end leases': the purchase and letting of houses which have come close to the end of their lease-hold term. And again, as for Woolf, the mode of narration is strung out between an attempt to give us 'the person', and the fascinations of property.

Lewis is a very different kind of writer from Henry James: at the beginning of his career rather than nearing its end; consciously avant-garde rather than spinning out extravagantly the possibilities within traditional forms; in stylistic temperament blunt rather than refined. To attempt to read them together across the linked spaces of *The English Review* and *The Tramp* is to face the full difficulty of thinking about 'modernism' as defined by a set of common properties. What they may share is a ghost and its accommodation; a sense which ramifies within stylistic self-awareness – within the figuralities that mark their texts off in different ways as struggling with stylistic and generic norms – of their own conditions of production. That is, they stage their own relationship – as wrought or overwrought pieces of writing, writing that risks 'producing nothing', noisy and incomplete movements of disavowal – to the interrelated questions of property and literary property which this chapter has been articulating. This may be, as I have suggested, a particularly reductive account of what modernism is; but that reduction indicates a ground in property which is not stable, and thus calls up the positive mystification of the ghost.

The plot of Lewis's story is in some ways parallel to that of James's. James Pringle has returned to London from Paris and is looking for somewhere to live. He lodges with a French family, and during the course of his residence, the husband, a prematurely retired chef, develops a mysterious illness which is related vaguely to Pringle's pleasure in his intimacy with their lives and their apartment. Similar to James, then, is the way in which a relation to a home appears mysteriously to clarify something about the central character, something which inheres in a way with the domestic space too odd to explain in fully rational terms. Dwelling calls up writing. Lodging is, according to the narrator, one of Pringle's preferred habits.

'Apartments to let.' That sign never lost its magic for James Pringle. For others a purely business announcement, for him it appeared a soft and almost sensual invitation. It was the pleasant and mysterious voice of innumerable houses. A street with many of these signs almost agitated him. [. . .] Perhaps the ideal vocation for Pringle would have been that of a broker or sheriff's officer – an affable, rather melancholy one. As it was, he was a landscape painter, whose circumstances confined his occupation of houses to rooms at ten or fourteen shillings a week, with north lights.[83]

As contrasted with James, there is a distinct lack of tension in the telling here. Three aspects are loosely related: a 'seduction narrative', where Pringle is called 'sensually' rather than contractually by vacant properties; a whimsical sense that he ought to have been more fully ensconced in the world of property, as a broker or a sheriff's officer rather than a painter; and a circumstantial explanation. That looseness seems to be the result on one hand of a distance between the narrator and the character, and of a relative lack of interest in his subjective motivations ('perhaps the ideal vocation . . . '); and on the other hand of an uncomplicated direct access to the character's psyche ('A street with many of these signs almost agitated him'). The source of complication in the James story is not present here: there is no space for the rising investigation of the ontology of character that I associated there with a movement of disavowal. Pringle is just what the narration says he is.

Lewis's reduction of Pringle is confirmed by the rapid dismissal of his status as 'artist', as someone who might compete with the designing authority of this story, and its replacement by the description of his 'circumstances': what 'landscape painter' signals is a particular property bracket ('rooms at ten or fourteen shillings a week, with north lights'). He is known as Bennett knows Hilda Lessways.

In the case of a man of genius the mediocrity of his daily life – his lodging, however mean, with the rest – takes a warmth and vitality from him. No doubt Goethe felt somewhat the same glamour in living in his own house in Frankfurt-on-Main as any educated man would feel if he suddenly became the tenant of Goethe's house. An exhilaration, almost excitement, is reflected back to the artist from anything. Pringle, not possessed of exceptional gifts, had been strangely endowed with this gusto for the common circumstances of his life; or, rather than definitely 'endowed with', I should suppose it to have developed in the following way. Originally seeking merely for suitable conditions for his work, etc., but conceiving of these conditions too fastidiously and morbidly, gradually this got the upper hand, as it were, so that it seemed almost – as I have described my friend – that his sole preoccupation consisted in sampling these conditions.[84]

Reduction is insisted upon: the work of 'art', Goethe's revivifying of the world through its artistic inhabiting, here collapses into an identity of work and context. Like the ghost-hunting of the Society for Psychical Research, the initial impetus towards 'work' is diverted towards a 'preoccupation' with its conditions in property. The reduction of art to context undoes the disavowal upon which modernism is ostensibly founded.

Again, there is a mimetic accommodation of the prose to its unresisting subject. Where James's narrator expresses, in straining accord with Brydon, the difficulty of conceiving what exactly comprises his character, admitting at one point that an 'acute [. . .] certainty' experienced by the character is 'determined by an influence beyond my [the narrator's, as implied author] notation!',[85] Lewis's narrator is exceedingly relaxed. The markers of potential indeterminacy, the supposing and seeming and 'as I have described', do not open up any kind of doubt. Hypothesis simply stands; the specificities of narration have all the flagrant redundancy of the 'etc.'.

There is a self-consciousness about narration, then, but one in which consciousness does not trouble its object. 'The foregoing narrative is, no doubt, in every essential detail exact, as it is compiled from facts and impressions then directly noted and received, and from my exhaustive intuitive knowledge of Pringle.' This 'intuition' seems to signal the kind of interest Woolf takes in Mrs Brown: the narrator suggests that 'it would be simpler for me to describe [. . .] even his most secret reflections, than what passed between us in the bar of the public-house'. But these secret reflections are secret even to Pringle. The story is about Pringle's 'eccentricity', but it notes that 'the existence of any eccentricity in Pringle was not so much as hinted at between us, or, for that matter, often realized by him'. Pringle, were he to tell his own tale, would fall back it seems on 'commonplace psychical formulas. For example, his delight in the landlord or landlady would appear as a gleeful or humorous "interest in character"'; while the narrator, 'having the key to my friend's strangeness, had no difficulty in casting this back into its original and veritable idiom'.[86]

That idiom is the idiom of property. Pringle's search for lodgings is difficult, and he finds himself reluctantly drawn towards a building in which he has lived before. Marchant, the owner, is a slum landlord: from the narrative's description, we can surmise that he is one of those speculators who bought up 'fag-end' leases, the very cheap property that was nearing the end of its leasehold period. 'His business in life was to exploit poor old ramshackle houses that could be obtained cheap. He would install himself in them, let every available cranny, and live there until they fell to pieces. One felt that this one might at any moment take a terrible revenge.'[87]

> Every time that he was at a loss where to turn, and had rejected one idea after another, Marchant's house – in which he had sworn never to live again – presented itself in its inviting probable emptiness, low rents, and accommodating landlord. He seemed fated to go there, and unable to escape it. Had there been nothing else against it, the fact of its facility and the wearying solicitation of its emptiness was enough to repel him.
>
> He felt that going there was a stale compromise, and that it had something insufferably ready-made, lax, and roomy about it. But now at one o'clock he gave way, but somewhat in exasperation, determined, as he said to himself, to 'get it over'.[88]

The figurative language is striking here. A landlord is 'accommodating'. The compromising easiness of the rooms is expressed as 'roomy'; vacant spaces are 'empty'; and it is from this that their uncanny compulsion derives. This is 'ready-made', even 'lax' writing, finding within the thing represented the means of representation itself. The building does indeed present itself 'in its inviting probable emptiness', rather than having to be represented. There is no purchase for figuration at all here, no space or too much vacancy altogether for any work of writing to happen. As for Pringle, so for the prose, the relation between the work of writing and its condition collapses into an identity as literal as the figure on a cheque. Modernism seems here to disappear: the distinction between this story and the tepid travel tales that fill the journal is unaccountable.

Pringle lodges with the French family. At first, things go well. 'In a week Pringle was savouring the delights of "lodging" as he had never done before, having lost less by actual inhabiting than usual.'[89] But this convergence between the idea and the experience of lodging is not stable. Pringle's interest in his new home, in the space and in the family, begins to produce illness and discomfort, until he has to leave. The logic is not easy to follow, at a psychological, economic, or even syntactical level. Pringle has become a ghost, but again, the distinction between the literal and the figurative which would be necessary to keep the ghost and the material distinct is not easy to maintain:

> He had passed like a ghost, in one sense, through a hundred unruffled households. Scores of peaceful landladies, like beautiful women caressed in their sleep by a spirit, had been enjoyed by him. Their drab apartments had served better than any boudoir. But at last one of the objects of his passion had turned in its sleep, as it were, its sleep being the restless slumber of the sick – had done more than that, had cried out and chased Pringle away. His late landlord no doubt gave the sleepwalker or spirit in Pringle a considerable shock. I found him very much shaken.[90]

Naming the ghost opens a confusion of figures. What *is* the object of Pringle's passion? The antecedent is the generic landlady, but the relation imagined with landladies is itself only figural: they are enjoyed 'like beautiful women' enjoyed by spirits. And the context confuses further. It is M. Chalaran who is in 'the restless slumber of the sick' in the fiction, but the restless turning he does is only a figure – 'as it were' – for what the 'object' does. Pringle becomes a ghost here, or rather his ghost, the 'spirit in Pringle', habitually unruffling, has ruffled and been shaken, as though by a ghost. And all of this is shadowed first in the revenge of the property, where it is drably related to questions of poverty, and leasehold, and landlords.

Unlike Brydon and Blackwood, Pringle is not allowed to settle. The story does not exorcise the spirits which keep writing destructively apart from property. But the mobility of Pringle and of Lewis is not separate from property. We should remember the implausible conditions of the story's appearance: this is the right site, for a moment, for 'differently unmarketable' writing, and a reader could be forgiven for not noticing that it is a modernist work within a market-driven magazine. The story does not implicitly claim by a tension of narration or a striving for distinction to disavow its relation to economic interest, and to property. Unlike the work of James or Woolf, it does not strain to imagine a value which would have nothing to do with houses; the space of writing here does not attempt to reform the indeterminacies of property, with the effect of falling buildings, crashing and destruction. Nor does it imagine writing in the commodified form of an ideal vagrancy, as lived by

Blackwood and as sold as a fantasy in *The Tramp*. The ghostly centre of the writing, its original idiom, rather, is identical with its properties, with their terrible revenges and their ghosts. It leaves those properties, shakily standing.

2
Boys: Manufacturing Inefficiency

He was so young
That explains so much
No book ever explained what to be young is
But they look so important for that.

Mina Loy[1]

On connait moins bien l'adolescent que l'enfant.

Françoise Dolto[2]

The destructive character has no interest in being understood.
Attempts in this direction he regards as superficial. Being mis-
understood cannot harm him. On the contrary he provokes
it, just as oracles, those destructive institutions of the state,
provoked it.

Walter Benjamin[3]

There may be no more predictable anguish than that which obtains
between the adult and the adolescent, which issues in eternal and
undeniable reproaches of injustice and incomprehension: it isn't fair;
you just don't understand. In each of the epigraphs to this chapter
there is a conflict between young people (Benjamin's 'destructive character'
is 'young and cheerful'[4]) and knowledge. The importance of books,
the impersonal assurance of Dolto's psychoanalytic 'on', the state – all
are embarrassed in the face of the figure of youth. There is even a
suggestion that ignorance of the adolescent is the ground on which
knowledge is built and shared. My argument in this chapter will develop
this insight. Adolescence is modern not because it is new (although a
new set of discourses do gather around the figure of the adolescent at

the beginning of the century), but because it signals what has to be ignored if a vision of historical continuity is to be constructed. This ignorance takes the form of a definitional exclusion of the figure of the adolescent (he is represented as a 'stage' which is passed through and over); and this diachronic process is shadowed by a way of imaging the idea of knowledge itself. Ways of talking about what we know, about the relations between knowing and acting, are troubled by the figure of the adolescent, such that every scene of adult knowledge is undermined by someone somewhere sulking in their room or slamming angrily out of the house. This problem cannot be contained, either, exactly as a mystery (although that is what psycho-analysis ends up counselling), for the adolescent cannot simply be sit-uated as an object. We have all been adolescents, and however difficult it may be to recognise the self in those embarrassing photographs (which tend to be rarer in the family album than those of our other ages), it is not easy, either, to say that that graceless avatar has been entirely left behind.

This chapter will, then, consider the figure of modernism as youth, and more specifically as adolescence. The materials I draw on include debates around juvenile justice and juvenile labour at the beginning of the century. The point of this investigation is to get at something within the promise of modernism which is encoded as a refusal of knowing: like Dostoevsky and his adolescent, the agency discovered here is reg-istered affectively but can not be folded easily into the institutions of knowledge. The adolescent and the modernist, I shall conclude, are less minor species of the subject, to be conjugated as so many reflections of discursive and historical process, than a different way of accounting for the placing of the person in relation to an historical account of meaning. This is still a question of historiography: my aim is still to define how to think about 'modern history' as a context for the pro-jects of modernism, rather than to find history dissolving into an endless textual movement, uninformed by persons and their agencies. But, as my introduction argued, the history has to be written from a position still baffled by many of the problems that it surveys: as Charles Altieri argues, to 'be historical' involves taking the work of dialectics seriously; but the modernism and the modern history I am interested in registering will neither allow any shadow of the developmental to encroach upon the dialectical nor enter into easy converse with the assured historian.[5] A history which is too assured, too adult, is in danger of falling into Loy's trap, and giving fresh space and angry impetus to the sulky contempt in its object.

In a 1915 letter to Augustus John which ends with a threat of physical violence ('being active and fairly strong, I will try and injure your head'), Wyndham Lewis, a few years on from the beginnings touched on in the previous chapter, now almost established as a Vorticist painter and recently the editor of the briefly sensational *Blast*, asserts a significant but unstable difference between John's way of being an artist and his own.[6] The letter and the threat continue the theme of an article in *Blast* in which Lewis, while acknowledging that John is, 'in the matter of his good gifts, and much of his accomplishment, a great artist', and that he was part of an 'eruption of new life', inaugurating 'an era of imaginative art in England', suggests that his vitality has now leaked away: 'he had not very great control of his moyens, and his genius seemed to prematurely exhaust him'.[7] What is wrong, and what is signalled in the distinction between *Blast* and John, is partly a question of affiliation, a repulsion common in formalist modernism against a *fin-de-siècle* aestheticism in which Lewis yokes John's 'boring Borrovian cult of the Gitane'[8] to Sickert, Nicholson, and even to Oscar Wilde. But Lewis is also, in the terms of the article in *Blast*, making a point about the history of aesthetic value. As the imagined eruptive energies have been exhausted, John has become publicly and stably – inertly – successful. 'The gypsy hordes become more and more languid and John is an institution like Madame Tussaud's, never, I hope, to be pulled down. He quite deserves this classic eminence and habitual security.'[9] This generational revolt is a recognisable avant-garde strategy: art must continually rejuvenate itself by maintaining a critically aggressive relation to the stability of stable values. But it is also a very fragile one: it predicts that *Blast*'s novelty and shock are the inauguration and the repetition of a fatal process, in which the creative 'eruption of new life' is recontained by the history it sought to interrupt.

   In a different register, without the background of violent threat, Ford Madox Hueffer explains why he has been supportive of *Blast*, a journal in which his writing looks distinctly out of place:

> I support these young men simply because I hope that in fifteen years time Sir Wyndham Lewis, Bart, F.R.A., may support my claim to a pension on the Civil List, and that in twenty years time the weighty voice of Baron Lewis of Burlington House, Poet Laureate and Historiographer Royal, may advocate my burial in Westminster Abbey.[10]

Hueffer, with much of the same ambivalence with which Lewis congratulates John on his 'classic eminence', suggests that *Blast*'s aggressive attacks on the sites of the establishment (including the Royal Academy, located in Burlington House, and the monarchy) are the parricidal preface to an identification with those institutions. Instanced here is what Pierre Bourdieu has argued to be the narrative of the modern aesthetic economy. The heterodox symbolic capital annexed through occupying the position of advanced and oppositional artist anticipates a legitimated pay-off. And it is a version of this story that Freud has taught us to recognise as the inevitable condition of gendered human subjectivity and historical process. The son's desire to destroy the father is an expression of his sorry fate: the father occupies exactly the position destined for him. Rebellion motors reproduction. '[T]he whole progress of society', as Freud puts it in 'Family Romances', 'rests upon the opposition between successive generations.'[11]

So is this what Lewis means when, in the letter to John, having backhandedly reassured him that '[y]ou will enter the history books, you know, of course!', he adds: 'Blast is a history book too'? For it strikes initially as the strangest of statements. *Blast* calls strenuously for an art which 'plunges to the heart of the present', evading the determination of historical process by willing its abolition. 'Our vortex is not afraid of the past: it has forgotten it's [*sic*] existence.'[12] This art of a present that is outside historical time corresponds with the historical exemption of the Vorticist artist. 'The moment a man feels or realises himself as an artist, he ceases to belong to any milieu or time. Blast is created for this timeless, fundamental Artist that exists in everybody.'[13] By calling *Blast* a 'history book too', is Lewis conceding that the claim to stand outside and both calmly and violently against the movements of history is either ill-fated – subject to an inevitable containment by the history it has forgotten – or in bad faith? Is blasting the British Academy just the most efficient way of getting into it? Is the angsty outsider simply waiting for the moment when he can write dominant history himself, as the Historiographer Royal of Hueffer's cynic scenario?

This would leave Lewis knowing what, according to Paul de Man, Nietzsche knows. Attempting to oppose 'history' with a modernity which 'exists in the form of a desire to wipe out whatever came earlier, a point of origin that marks a new departure', Nietzsche understands that modernity is 'a generational power that not only engenders history, but is part of a generational scheme that extends far back into the past'.[14] Rebellion not only necessarily fails but also gives substance and duration to exactly the flattened history it aims to reject. Becoming conscious of this, Nietzsche is forced to fall back on a metaphysical idea of 'youth' as an extra-historical source of creative generation, and then fall further back into the concession that youth must become conscious in its turn, and thus subject to the same inevitable absorption in a fatal historical process. Literature somewhat frantically traces the movement between the attempt to attain the immediate horizon of modernity and youth, and the reabsorption of that attempt into an inexorable history. It is obvious that this explication of what a history book is will not suffice as self-description for *Blast*, however strongly it may explain what is really happening in its moment. Something young is lived here which calls for its register. There has to be another sense in which *Blast* is a history book too. When it posits an art outside historical process, it does so from a very specific site, placed both geographically and temporally: 'The Great London Vortex' (the geography of this story will reappear in Chapter 4). This position in its particularity offers access to the *texture* of contemporary British history, which *Blast* conceives as a peculiar tranquil continuous revolution. Here I think *Blast* doubles de Man's call for a new mode of literary history, which abandons 'the pre-assumed concept of history as a generative process [. . .]; of history as a temporal hierarchy that resembles a parental structure in which the past is like an ancestor begetting, in a moment of unmediated presence, a future capable of repeating in its turn the same generative process'.[15] But it doubles this historiography substantially, in a state of being, rather than critically. As opposed to 'Latin' cultures, thrilled by the experience of modernity into what Lewis diagnoses as a 'romantic and sentimental' revolutionary aesthetic, 'In England [. . .] there is no vulgarity in revolt./ Or, rather, there is no revolt, it is the normal state.' This is why 'consciousness towards the new possibilities of expression in present life [. . .] will be more the legitimate property of Englishmen than of any other people in Europe'. This consciousness is shot through with the paradoxical structure of 'modern history' or 'normal revolt'; it is 'Chaos invading Concept and bursting it like nitrogen' (the impossible chemistry is very probably a mistake – Lewis in *Tarr* had shown himself happily incompetent in these matters – but it is also finely apposite: nitrogen is a very stable gas); or it is 'insidious and volcanic chaos', while at the same time 'bare[ ] and hard[ ]'. And it has a single determinant, the willed industrial production of 'the modern world', whose machinery 'sweeps away the doctrines of a narrow and pedantic Realism at one stroke'.[16]

When, in 'The New Egos', Lewis defines again the modern individual and its appropriate aesthetic, he isolates a figure disappearing into the conditions that stand against it. As opposed to the 'civilised savage, in a desert city, surrounded by very simple objects and restricted number of beings', whose ego is adequately defined by or confined to the contours of the body, 'the modern town-dweller of our civilisation'

> sees everywhere fraternal moulds for his spirit, and interstices of a human world.
> He also sees multitude, and infinite variety of means of life, a world and elements he controls.
> Impersonality becomes a disease with him
> [. . .]
> Dehumanisation is the chief diagnostic of the Modern World.
> One feels the immanence of some REALITY more than any former human beings can have felt it.
> The superseding of specific passions and easily determinable emotions by such uniform, more animal instinctively logical Passion of Life, of different temperatures, but similar in kind, is, then, the phenomenon to which we would relate the most fundamental tendencies in present art, and by which we would gage it's [sic] temper.[17]

The art of dehistoricised 'individuals' is at the same time an art of individuals who are penetrated by their historical environment. These 'new egos' can barely be conceived of as subjectivities at all, so completely is their interiority (and the adequate formal presentation of it) invaded by the 'Reality' of the object world. But at the same time, this indeterminate product of the modern environment is unanxiously in 'control' of these conditions, producing from their prosthetic multiplicity forms that express the altered ego of the modern artist as agent rather than object of this history. By something like a mimetic submission to historical conditions, which are gently vital with normal revolt rather than inertial or confining, *Blast* claims to incorporate and thus to identify with modern historical process itself.

This identification, a mode of becoming conscious of insubordinate identity, is named 'adolescent':

> 1. Beyond Action and Reaction we would establish ourselves.
> 2. We start from opposite statements of a chosen world. Set up violent structure of adolescent clearness between the two extremes.
> 3. We discharge ourselves on both sides.
> [. . .]
> 8. We set Humour at Humour's throat. Stir up Civil War among peaceful apes.[18]

This adolescent is distant from the ideal youth of de Man's Nietzsche. The oppositional escape from historical temporality here signs an expressive participatory articulation of historical contradiction. This articulation expands upon the earlier stated intention, 'to destroy politeness, standardized and academic, that is civilized, vision': to bring about, that is, something like a state of nature.[19] The state of nature, what remains when the 'doctrines of a narrow and pedantic Realism' are swept away, is irreducibly historical.[20] Sounding through Freud's plot, where 'the opposition between successive generations' is over-whelmingly expressed into 'the whole progress of society', we can perhaps hear the muffled and distorted echo of Marx and Engels: 'the history of all hitherto existing society is the history of class struggles'.[21] The German phrases are not related to each other;[22] I am not claiming that Freud *refers* to Marx here. However, because they share significant historical conditions, we might expect that the two totalising explanations of social history, that of Freud and that of Marx, should overlap. 'Family Romances' plots the successful 'liberation' of the individual from the 'authority' of his parents as a daydream of social mobility:

> At about the period I have mentioned, then [the antecedent of this 'period' is vague, stretching between 'the period before puberty' and its persistence 'far beyond puberty'], the child's imagination becomes engaged in the task of getting free from the parents of whom he now has a low opinion and of replacing them by others, who, as a rule, are of higher standing.[23]

The plot in which adolescent rebellion appears as a stage which is necessarily overcome depends upon a dematerialising internalisation of class as fantasy. The family 'Romance' dramatises an evasion of the contradictions between development and structure that are concen-trated in the adolescent predicament. The brief emergency of the ado-lescent and the avant-garde, momentary respite from historical inevitability, lodges contradiction solidly within the style of the devel-oping body.

Of course, 'civil war' was already in the air. The years before 1914 saw a series of relatively autonomous threats to the reproduction of social and political structures: militant suffragist activity, a wave of increas-ingly politicised strikes, debates about Home Rule in Ireland; a loose for-mation that is often referred to as a 'crisis of liberalism'. The classically apocalyptical account is Dangerfield's (1936), depicting a society which would have become ungovernable had it not been for the irruption of the First World War.[24] Most recent historians, refusing the temptation to grasp together and complete the separated struggles on the fronts of labour, gender, class, and nation, have disagreed about what this crisis was: not so much about the scale and extent of the disturbances as about how to read the meaning of their *tone*; how to read the aggressions and anxieties involved in the participation of representations in this moment. This historiography is rightly suspicious of attempts to ascribe consciousness to historical process.[25] But what it may evade is the dialectical challenge involved in reading fractured attempts – like *Blast*'s, like the adolescent's, like modernism's – to grasp and embody this moment.

Modernist fiction, as Patricia Meyer Spacks argues, is fixated on the figure of the awkwardly positioned youth.[26] The altered *Bildungsroman* of Forster, Woolf, Richardson, or May Sinclair attaches its point of view to a position within generational struggle that refuses its issue. We might suggest tentatively that this is a working out of a generational question within the novel form. Classic realism could be understood to define itself in the moment of George Eliot's review of *Wilhelm Meister* (and Lewes's 1855 biography of Goethe); in this moment adolescence is safely stationed outside the processes of realism. Modernist fiction makes its claims to separation from the realist tradition by undoing this exclusion. The heroine of Sinclair's *Mary Olivier* (1919), for example, arrives at an identity, that of 'poet', which is an alternative to marriage or motherhood, and which is strongly associated with the continuation, even the permanent installation, of an ineffectual rebellion against her (now dead) mother. Or Lily Briscoe, in *To the Lighthouse* (1927), is expressed in an aesthetic vision which holds her in relation to the broadly parental figures of Mr and Mrs Ramsay, without allowing her to progress to an identification with either of them. In Forster's *Maurice* (written in 1914, first published in 1971), a sustainable homosexuality is imagined as a loyalty to adolescent passions and ideals in the face of 'maturing' pressures; and the formal adolescence of the novel sponsors its uplifting ending in the face of the doom dictated by a responsibility to realism.[27]

In these books, an aesthetic and an ethical position which underwrites the design of the novel is understood as a more or less rebellious persistence in the position of adolescence. Formal modernism, which requires a conscious refusal of something in the novel form, imagines adolescent authorships. *Tarr* (1918), Wyndham Lewis's own *Bildungsro-*

man, presents what looks like a movement past the awkward age: the novel follows Tarr into marriage and a productive working life. But the significance of the forms of marriage and work has been emptied out. Tarr's distinction as an artist, an asserted ironic distance from the subjected, 'bourgeois', behaviours of his body and its culture, is presented, and uncomfortably valued, as masturbatory and infant rebellion. His modernist interiority is represented as an aesthetic production which is at the same time a constituting disorder which holds him back from fulfilling the forms of everyday life.[28]

Blast, uneasily enacting an aesthetic rather than figuring it as the novels do, has an eccentric relation to the moment of liberal crisis. It certainly does not imagine itself as part of a broad alliance to overthrow the liberal state, but it does seem to recognise that this political turmoil is its condition and its opportunity. From a similar historical vantage point to that of Dangerfield, Lewis remembers that 'we were not the only people to be proud about at that time. Europe was full of titanic stirrings and snortings – a new art coming to flower to celebrate or to announce a "new age"'.[29] Where *Blast* becomes an important historical document, and where modernism becomes a significant index, is in its expressive exemplification of the problem of how to recover or otherwise respond to the complexities of agency and inefficiency in this moment. To read *Blast* demands the negotiation of a distance between statement and meaning that accommodates both an aggressive and a proleptically disenchanted awareness of powerlessness. When it imagines its own cheery putsch – 'A VORTICIST KING! WHY NOT?' – or when it claims as its purpose the escalation of a conflict – 'Civil War among peaceful apes' – it does it, and undermines it, with a clarity it names 'adolescent'. I want to take this seriously in all its histrionic comedy, for in the history and culture of the adolescent body, which is as modern as Vorticism and as much of a 'comic earthquake',[30] we can begin to locate the 'new ego' that *Blast* imagines for modernism. And this seems to me a step towards responding appropriately to the demands encoded in 'liberal crisis'; a way of resisting the position of historiographer royal; a means of sketching a way of knowing that is adequate to the problematic raised by the epigraphs to the present chapter.

J. C. Squire, in *The New Statesman*, describes the Vorticists as 'a heterogeneous mob suffering from juvenile decay'.[31] This external ascription is mirrored internally, though with its value terms of course inverted. When the manifesto 'blesses' France, it finds itself in the

BALLADS of its PREHISTORIC APACHE
Superb hardness and hardiesse of its
Voyou type, rebellious adolescent.
[. . .]
GREAT FLOOD OF LIFE pouring out
of wound of 1797.
Also bitterer stream from 1870.[32]

This passage collects a wide range of references. The 'rebellious adolescent' is glossed as the 'voyou type', the word 'voyou' covering a range of attitudes, from the relatively comfortable 'scamp' or 'rogue', through to the full-blown 'delinquent' or 'hooligan'. This latter end of the spectrum is indicated by the 'Apache', violent knife-carrying gangs of street youth.[33] There were regular scares that this kind of 'foreign' street violence was infecting British gangs.[34] To suggest that the 'apache' is 'prehistoric' is implicitly to challenge a contemporary sense that this violence is new, an interruption of a traditional lawfulness. But the passage goes on to align that prehistoric condition with a fairly specific historical narrative: the 'voyou type' crystallises the 'normal state of revolt' that is the bitter afterlife of the post-revolutionary débâcle and of the excessive internal violence France experienced after the Franco-Prussian war.[35] Any sense, that is, that the history of France is the history of an enlightening bourgeois republic carries with it a bitter and an energising undercurrent, which the 'voyou type' embodies as politics, as a 'violent structure of adolescent clearness'.[36] The troublesome adolescent, on the threshold of socialisation but aggressively unwilling to proceed, evading history in order the better to reveal it, asserting and apparently experiencing a *difference* which science, law, and politics want to read as just a stage to be overcome in the normal developmental narrative, is a powerful figure both for the 'history book' which *Blast* embodies and for the uneasy suspicion that it will all come to nothing.

A machine in the tentative

The American psychologist Stanley Hall's massive 1904 study, *Adolescence* is usually credited with bringing the term into popular usage and stabilising it as an object of investigation. It is exhaustive and definitive in its conceptualisation of the adolescent, but at the same time riven with the problems of concept and definition which seem always to adumbrate these juvenile data. The book is driven, Hall says, by love for its object:

As for years, an almost passionate lover of childhood and teacher of youth, the adolescent stage of life has long seemed to me one of the most fascinating of all themes, more worthy, perhaps, than anything else in the world of reverence, most inviting study, and in most crying need of a service we do not yet understand how to render aright.[37]

Calling for 'a service we do not yet understand how to render aright', Hall's 'almost passionate' love marks a point of uncertainty which attracts the abundant fascination of Hall's science. Culture must learn from adolescence, even become adolescent, in order to serve the adolescent adequately. This is vital for Hall because adolescence 'and not maturity as now defined, is the only point of departure for the super-anthropoid that man is to become. This can only be by an ever higher adolescence lifting him to a plane related to his present maturity as that is to the well-adjusted stage of boyhood where our puberty now begins its regenerating metamorphosis.'[38] The logic here is odd. The new Adolescence, forged with love from recognition and doubt, is to be a surpassing of maturity in the same way that maturity realises the potential of childhood; at the same time the development to the higher adolescence stands apart from the normal process ('the whole progress of society') of well-balanced children moving towards the 'habitual security' of adulthood. The whole tendency to think in terms of developmental sequence asks to be folded into a different shape of knowing. Maturity must hold itself back within the crisis of adolescence in order to evolve.

There are eight chapters in Hall's first volume:

    I: Growth in Height and Weight
    II: Growth of Parts and Organs During Adolescence
   III: Growth of Motor Power and Function
   IV: Diseases of Body and Mind
    V: Juvenile Faults, Immoralities, and Crimes
   VI: Sexual development: Its Dangers and Hygiene in Boys
  VII: Periodicity
 VIII: Adolescence in Literature, Biography, and History

The first chapters describe a movement inwards, which promises also a gauging and an integration. As we move from the measurements of the outside of the adolescent body to the organs, the muscle, and the mind, we are offered a trajectory from description to explanation; from 'height and weight' towards 'function'. And the tendency towards explanation is shadowed by a drive toward evaluation, from 'diseases' towards 'faults' and 'crimes'. 'Function', given briefly here, is the key turning point in the text, as it attempts to hold together the ways that adolescent bodies move and their position and purpose within culture. 'Culture' operates within the same problematic space for Hall. Generally used with the sense of 'the development of the body', it continually reaches also towards the place of that body within larger socially signifying networks.[39]

The adolescent body is at an awkward age; 'this is an age of wasteful ways':

> At puberty [. . .] when muscle habits are so plastic, [. . .] kinetic remnants strongly tend to shoot together into wrong aggregates if right ones are not formed. Good manners and correct motor forms generally, as well as skill, are the most economic way of doing things, but this is an age of wasteful ways, awkwardness, mannerisms, tensions that are a constant leakage of vital energy, perhaps semi-imperative acts, contortions, quaint movements, more elaborated than in childhood and often highly unaesthetic and disagreeable, motor coordinations that will need laborious decomposition later.[40]

The difficulty of Hall's argument, the difficulty of the idea of function and culture generally as they try to bridge bodily development, intrinsic purpose, and intersubjective meaning, is that the referent of 'this age' is significantly double. Here, the etiology of wasteful inelegance (the self-difference in adolescent agency) is within the adolescent body: the muscles, having grown at different rates, are disharmoniously arranged, producing what Hall, with fabulously disarming disrespect for other discourses, calls a 'psychosis in the muscle habits'. I assume that these are psychotic, oddly, because liveable: they produce an ambiguity of being rather than a neurosis which would rise towards consciousness. And this purely mechanical disarrangement is understood both as an effect and as a determinant of consciousness; as 'partly the same instincts of revolt against uniformity imposed from without, which rob life of variety and extinguish the spirit of adventure and untrammelled freedom, and make the savage hard to break to the hardness of civilisation'.[41] Again Hall's prose is of the most splendid mimeticism. When Hall describes the adolescent as 'hard to break to hardness', he represents a bodily disarrangement which functions as an instinct which knows the distinction between self and other, and which thus is positioned to produce an historically operative, a representational, hardness. Hall's phrase is also conscious of an affiliation between the adolescent body and resistant colonised cultures. Thus for Hall the inefficient effect of uneven growth, the clumsy and gangling adolescent, expresses a jerky resistance to the demand for graceful and efficient subjection.[42] And this resistance is oddly creative as well as critical: 'Youth tends to do everything physically possible with its body considered as a machine in the tentative.'[43] For Hall, this randomising of gesture is a good thing, a 'spurty diathesis' producing a reservoir of potential, an 'alphabet' out of which unforseeable new capacities, 'complex and finer motor skills',[44] will be built.[45]

'This age', then, expresses outwards from the adolescent body. But it is also always an historical reference for Hall. 'Changes in modern motor life have been so vast and sudden as to present some of the most comprehensive and all-conditioning dangers that threaten civilised races.'[46] Juvenile imbalance and juvenile potential are over-determined by the processes of industrial and urban culture, processes which themselves destabilise, randomise, and energise the body and its meanings. The inefficiency which is the adolescent body's critique of, and alternative to, the shapes and functions of its culture is produced in that culture. Cyril Burt, psychologist to the Education Department of London City Council, to whose influential writing on juvenile delinquency my argument will return, describes how life in the modern city interrupts concentration and continuity of behaviour:

[T]he street not only offers direct enticements to theft and wilful mischief, but also makes the worst sort of training ground for the sober citizen of the future. Sustained and systematic activity is there impossible. If the small boy starts a round of marbles, the rain or the traffic will presently interrupt it. If, with a lamp-post for a wicket and a bit of board for a bat, he tries a turn at cricket, the constable will presently move his little team along. But far more enthralling than any organised game of strenuous sport is the crowded succession of inconsequent episodes which a day in a London thoroughfare unfailingly affords – a man knocked over, a woman in a fit, a horse bolting off with the cart on the pavement, a drunkard dragged along to the police-station by a couple of constables, a warehouse or a timber-yard blazing in the midst of twenty fire-engines. Life for the street arab is full of such random excitations; and becomes an affair of wit and windfalls, not an opportunity for steady, well-planned exercise.[47]

This wild exterior to the disciplinary machineries of the household, the family, the workplace, and the school is a familiar ground for theories of the modern and the modernist.[48] The 'random excitations' and 'inconsequent episodes', in which the police are every bit as involved as more obviously convulsive types, penetrate the adolescent proto-modernist and block any accession to 'sober' citizenship. The distance between subject and object on which representation and plausible identity depend is represented as constantly collapsing: the 'subjectivity' of the 'street arab' is so completely full of the world of the street as to seem to identify with it, without remainder.

What writing about the adolescent reveals is that this place, the environment in which the 'new Ego' of *Blast* is to be formed, far from being a marginal spasm, irruptive into a stable centre, is an exemplary modern site. Rather than the demonic and dangerous exterior to the stability of the family, the workplace, the culture, it is significantly continuous with what I want to risk calling the *materiality* of these institutions; a materiality which the adolescent helps both to create and to reveal. For the stage of confusion in the family, where the adolescent proves resistant to the structures of power which the idea of a family is supposed to embody, may be more a model for the family as institution than a moment of exception to it (a more docile and projective vision of the same story will be told through the figure of the dog in Chapter 4). The economic power which the adolescent wields, with his wage often necessary to sustain the family but seldom sufficient to form a new nucleus, distorts clean structures of authority. Unable, for the most part, to earn enough to set up a separate household where economic activity would feed back into reproduction of the congruence of family and society, the adolescent dislocates ideas ('Family Romances' as well as 'the doctrines of a narrow and pedantic Realism') from practices of power.[49] The family's role as a vehicle for the idea of history is troubled here. The historically distended interface of generational struggle, swollen with the contents of 'this age', may mark the contradictions within the form of the family, at once model and instrument of social reproduction and a site for the irruption of modern history, of materiality as 'normal revolt'.

Hence we could say that the adolescent is the result of too complete a relation to the social and historical environment, rather than a momentary liberation from it. It is significant that a young delinquent sounds a troubling note at the end of Foucault's *Discipline and Punish*. He signs less a resistance to disciplinary control than a radical *difference* from the disciplinary schema which Foucault's study charts. For Foucault this is a moment of wildness, a singularity outside the networks of power and discourse: it gives rise to an anarchist critique of the modern subject, aiming to 're-establish or constitute the political unity of popular illegalities'.[50] Following Michel de Certeau in his critique of Foucault's genealogies of power, we could suggest that it marks the persistence of the possibilities of practices – 'tactics' – which do not give rise to discourses; the possibility of a materiality which is prior to and other than disciplinary formation, rather than the promise of a singularity which escapes it.[51]

In the workplace, too, debates which gathered around the juvenile labour question complicate the attempt to distinguish between the disruptive spaces of the street and the disciplinary institutions of labour. The prolongation of industrial adolescence is producing unemployable adults, and thus no adults at all:

> it has been universally agreed that the problem is largely caused by young people leaving school at the age of 14 with a limited amount of education and taking up 'blind alley' occupations, which offer them a relatively high commencing wage but a minimum of industrial training, and leave them at 17 or 18 a 'drug in the market' incapable and impossible to absorb, except perhaps at times of unusual trade prosperity.[52]

Responsibility is first confidently assigned and then tends towards tautology: the problem is caused by . . . the problem, which is experienced or described by the boy. As Reginald Bray argues in *Boy Labour and Apprenticeship*, by failing to capitalise himself, the boy is heading towards a 'blind alley'[53] which concretely mirrors his lack of mature vision. Unemployable at the age of eighteen (his place will be taken by a younger and cheaper worker), his development into a 'sober citizen' and his unfolding into the position of legitimate householder and parent will be truncated. The solution is to return to a structure of apprenticeship, where the boy is installed within a protective and disciplinary developmental process at the same time as he develops the skills to compete in the labour market.

Arnold Freeman argues against Bray's sense that there is a solution, exposing the faulty logic of his position. Unemployment, he argues, is

> a phenomenon [. . .] largely independent of the character and training of the worker, but inherent in industrial conditions. [. . .] [T]he direct value of the industrial training of youth [here he quotes Beveridge] 'as a remedy for unemployment is somewhat limited; it

cannot touch the causes of industrial fluctuation or in practice prevent casual employment'. Thus, while the training of youth is questioned on the highest authority as a remedy for Unemployment, the treatment of the Boy Problem in this connection has served to hide aspects of it which would seem to be far more important than that of the so-called 'blind-alley'.[54]

No amount of training, no work done on the adolescent, can resolve the problems inherent in the structure of the labour market. The problem, for Freeman, is that industry is incompletely modern, and relying on casual and unskilled labour to supplement its inefficiency. The adolescent is merely a reflection of a more fundamental problem of function and culture, his 'character' never formed because he exists in an unsteady and an inconsequent relation to his activity, subject to what Freeman capitalises as the 'Change of Jobs'.

This is what Freeman refers to as the 'manufacture of inefficiency in the majority of boys between school and manhood':

> We must think of the boy of 14 as standing at the centre of a circle, from which shoot radii towards the circumference, representing the adult environment. All of these radii are in the right direction, and if they were prolonged by continued education they would finally bury themselves in the circumference. As it is, they fall short; the boy is subjected to social and industrial conditions that speedily destroy the standards of value which the school has created; the radii atrophy, and adequate relations between the boy and his environment are not established.[55]

In these environments, then, the natural – the educated – impulses of the boy are diverted such that he will age on an orbit which never connects with adulthood; adolescence lost in space, discovered as an effect of this 'culture', as contradiction between structure and development, may be prolonged indefinitely.[56] Freeman understandably backs away from the implications of this, suggesting that the question of 'whether [existing social and industrial conditions] are satisfactory in themselves is [. . .] beyond the purview of this investigation'. Public action has become necessary, he urges, but 'such action cannot take the course of altering in their general features either the social or the industrial structures upon which this society is at present based: it can only concern itself with such modifications as will ensure to the nation's youth preparations for the functions of adult life'.[57] This is a characteristic response, and it should be understood as driven by the need to save an idealised notion of 'history' and 'subjectivity', such that the youth must be prepared for 'the functions of adult life' even where those functions do not correspond with existing practices. This is an uncomfortably brazen ideological move. A consciousness is registered here before being rejected.

The adolescent is formed in the unthinkable interruption of an ideal history by material conditions, at the place of a cancelled expression of structural contradiction. But what does the boy know about it? Where is his agency located relative to this crisis, or to this fearful revolutionary horizon? Freeman argues that the boys he studies have 'no politics'; that they 'know nothing' about politics. One typical boy

neither knew nor cared about politics; nor about any of the parties or principal current measures (excepting, as always, Votes for Women and the Insurance Àct!). He apparently did not even know of the existence of Mr. Asquith, nor of either the present or the late leader of the Opposition. But he knew of Mr. Lloyd George's existence [. . .] ([. . .] Mr. Joseph Chamberlain, he knew, in common with practically every other boy.)[58]

The exceptions here are by no means random. They describe the political positions which contribute to the 'crisis of liberalism' which I suggested is modernism's condition, the field of conflict opened up by *Blast*'s 'adolescent clarity'. And Freeman's response is to argue that such a symptomatic political ignorance must be roped off:

[In three or four years] the youth will be entitled to vote;[59] as we have seen, he is, at present, hopelessly ignorant of political and social questions. It might not, perhaps, be ill-advised for us as a nation to admit to the franchise only such men and women as can pass a reasonable test in matters which every voter ought to know.[60]

After the war, Freeman produced a pamphlet entitled *How to Avoid a Revolution*.[61]

How does this pointed ignorance relate to the innocence that Lewis claims retrospectively for Vorticism, an innocence which he links to the autonomy of art? He describes a meeting with Asquith, the liberal Prime Minister unknown to adolescents, who 'unquestionably displayed a marked curiosity regarding the "Great London Vortex", in which he seemed to think there was more than met the eye. He smelled politics beneath this revolutionary technique.' Lewis states that 'I, of course, was quite at a loss to understand what he was driving at.'

> for my part I was an artist, first and last. . . . But the Prime Minister of England [*sic*] in 1914 could not be expected to accept this simple explanation. For the destruction of a capital city is a highly political operation. And these blasting operations, so clamorously advocated, suggested dissatisfaction with the regime as well as with the architecture. And 'Kill John Bull With Art!' the title of one of my most notorious articles – there was a jolly piece of sansculotism. What could that mean, if it did not point to tumbril and tocsin.[62]

What, indeed, could that mean? The politics of *Blast*, strung out between its innocence and the Prime Minister, and anticipated in the truncated aggression of its prose, cannot be reduced to a question of intention. It appears rather as a demand for a political imagination that will not subordinate the moment of adolescent refusal and threat to the history, 'the whole Progress of Society', in which it is subsumed. History, Lewis suggests, in a resumption of Hall's fascination, arrests at this moment of failure, turning back on its adolescence as the proper way forwards.

> We are not only 'the last men of an epoch' (as Mr. Edmund Wilson and others have said): we are more than that, or we are that in a different way to what is most often asserted. *We are the first men of a future that has not materialized.* We belong to a 'great age' that has not 'come off'. [. . .] The rear guard presses forward, it is true. The doughty Hervert (he of 'Unit One') advances towards 1914, for all that is 'advanced' moves backwards, now, towards that impossible goal, of the pre-war dawn.[63]

This demand, as debates around juvenile justice in this period demonstrate, is the proper content of the adolescent interior, of the 'boy's own story'.

The boy's own story

In the period between the Children's Act (1908) and the Children and Young Persons Act (1933) there were a number of shifts in the theory and practice of juvenile justice in England, in response to a perceived rise in the incidence of crimes committed by young people. There was a move to separate out juvenile justice, and juvenile crime, ever more completely from the adult justice system: to run separate courts, with a differently trained and briefed judiciary, and to shift gradually from punishment towards reform.[64]

Cyril Burt was perhaps the most comprehensive and influential writer on the problem of juvenile delinquency. Writing in 1925 in *The Young Delinquent*, he states the principle on which the distinction between modes of criminality on the basis of age is justified.

> It is a maxim of criminal law that no person is to be considered guilty unless his act was the outcome of a guilty mind. [. . .] Legal guilt itself thus depends upon a guilty condition; and this in turn, it is held, depends partly upon age. With adults, the unlawful act in itself may be sufficient proof of a guilty state of mind – of criminal malice, negligence, or knowledge. But [. . .] the law presumes that [the juvenile offender] acted as he did without criminal intent; and the burden of proving a guilty state of mind, either from the child's previous declarations or from his subsequent concealment of his deed, is cast upon the prosecution.[65]

While the normal adult's interiority is fully expressed in his action, the juvenile is imagined to be opaque. Burt's categories of 'juvenile offence' are classed under emotional properties (anger, acquisitiveness, grief, and secretiveness), where we would tend to range adult offence under kinds of action or types of object. While we can read the adult's guilty mind directly from his criminal behaviour, the guilt or criminality of the delinquent is radically interior, and must be expressed, not in the coded form of behaviour, but in a consciousness that the delinquent avows, in declarations and concealments.

We need to know different kinds of things about the juvenile offender in order to pronounce him guilty. A 'case history' is necessary, Burt argues. This is not by any means a new suggestion, and it draws on the experiments in juvenile courts in the USA.[66] William Healey of the Juvenile Psychopathic Institute in Chicago had pioneered the systematic use of what he called the 'Boys [*sic*] own story', asking young people who had been arrested to tell their personal history in such a way as to understand how they had become criminals. 'The most striking thing that I found was youngsters saying, after they had dug it out of their unconscious, "Now I know." Kid after kid, either in those words or other words similar to them, told me that now for the first time he knew why he stole or ran away or something.'[67] And, like Freud's 'talking cure', this revelation of previously submerged determinants is part of the process of reform. Once the juvenile offender has narrated himself, has placed himself in a story of causes and effects, Healy argues, he finds that he can function within society: the clash between the bodily culture of the adolescent and the culture in which it functions will just disappear.

Of course a talking cure in which the entry to analysis is through the courtroom is not dealing with the same structuring of symptoms as psychoanalysis. Freud comments on the *impossibility* of the proper analysis of delinquents in his foreword to *Wayward Youth* by August Aichhorn, at the same time as he recognises a unity of purpose between Aichhorn's disciplinary education and his own psychoanalysis:

> One should not be misled by the statement – incidentally a perfectly true one – that the psycho-analysis of the adult neurotic is equivalent to a re-education. [. . .] The possibility of analytic influence rests upon quite definite preconditions which can be summed up under the term 'analytic situation'; it requires the development of certain psychic structures and a particular attitude to the analyst. Where these are lacking – as in the case of children, of juvenile delinquents, and, as a rule, of impulsive criminals – something other than analysis must be employed, though something which will be at one with analysis in its *purpose*.[68]

The adolescent cannot engage with the process of analysis, for Freud (this is striking, given how many of his patients were young women; and how important the position of adolescence appears to be to, for example, the 'Dora' case). Anna Freud later repeated that the analysis of adolescents was impossible. She notes that:

> When, in our capacity as analysts, we investigate mental states, we rely, basically, on two methods: either on the analysis of individuals in whom that particular state of mind is in action at the moment, or on the reconstruction of that state in analytic treatment undertaken at a later date. The results of these two procedures, used either singly or in combination with each other, have taught us all that we, as analysts, know about the developmental stages of the human mind.
>
> It happens that these two procedures, which have served us well for other periods of life, prove less satisfactory and less productive of results when applied to adolescents.

'Mental states' cannot be made present to analysis nor constructed in analysis. The transference cannot be successfully produced and managed, and thus the 'analytic situation' cannot be brought into being, it seems, because the adolescent is detached from the libidinal structure of the family, and engaged instead (it is a strange but telling opposition) with the moment of living. 'Whatever the libidinal solution at a given moment may be, it will always be a preoccupation with the present time and, as described above, with little or no libido left available for investment either in the past or the analyst.'[69] Anna Freud counsels simply waiting until the stage is passed.

The relation between the recording of the 'boy's own story' and analysis is both invoked and denied. Certainly, the results, in the practice of Healy, are not those of psychoanalysis. What seems to be a process of plumbing and re-ordering psychic material, of internal surveillance, opens up on to wider territories. Judge Ben Lyndsey, who used similar methods to those of Healy, in a more impassioned and much less systematic way, reads deeply into the evidence of juvenile crime and finds an imperative rather than data:

> I began to deepen and broaden that work, to peer from effect to cause. And across my range of vision rolled cotton mill and beet fields with their pitiable child slaves and the dance halls and vice dens of the underworld.
>
> And I found that these influences that were undermining childhood were in league with the capitalistic powers of Special Privilege, the real political masters of our city and state.
>
> In short, I faced a whole system and the System's State.[70]

The message Lyndsey receives from the adolescent interior is a message of clarity, urgency, paranoia, and obligation. He went on to agitate for women's suffrage, strikers' rights, a minimum wage for women and children, child labour laws, companionate marriage, and birth control.

For Hall, adolescent culture is a combination of the delinquent physiology of pubertal disharmony and the structural disgrace of modern industrial inefficiency. This vision of culture demands a separated space of juvenile justice. In Lyndsey, the vision has taken a new form: the lack of correspondence between the interiority of the boy and the meaning of his actions leads on to the need to hear the boys' own story, which expresses, in the imperative mood, injustice and contradiction.

The problem is also the solution: the juvenile delinquent. Youths are convicted not for committing particular crimes but for *being* juvenile delinquents.[71] That is, the court exists simply to categorise and to exclude the troublesome evidence of the adolescent, and the incoherent culture on to which the adolescence gives access. The court offers a way of enclosing the cognitive threat posed by the adolescent. Burt quotes a London magistrate: 'with vigilance sufficiently increased, the number of charges [in Juvenile Courts] could be doubled, trebled, or quadrupled', and goes on to argue that 'by pressing the definitions for such offences as the infringement of police regulations or for such delinquencies as those connected with sex, and by isolating petty thefts at home, one could expand the percentage [of delinquents] to almost any degree'.[72] This image of a whole phase of life taken out of the social and into the space of criminal justice is a strange fantasy. Yet, according to one historian who has worked through the police records for one English town, which reported a 300 per cent rise in juvenile crime figures between 1880 and 1910, this is how the court functioned. There was almost no rise in traditional crime, rather a new attention to 'offences' such as 'malicious mischief, loitering, and dangerous play [sliding on bridges, street football, the discharge of fireworks]'.[73] Here the law approaches Stanley Hall's suggestion, paraphrasing Lombroso, that all adolescents by nature are criminal:

normal children often pass through stages of passionate cruelty, laziness, lying, and thievery. He reminds us that their vanity, slang, obscenity, contagious imitativeness, their absence of moral sense, disregard of property, and violence to each other, constitute them criminals in all essential respects, lacking only the strength and insight to make their crime dangerous to the communities in which they live.[74]

A new mode of criminality is described which concentrates historical process safely within what will not quite reduce to a stage in bodily development. 'A stage of life, adolescence, had replaced station in life, class, as the perceived cause of [juvenile] misbehaviour.'[75] It is exactly the mobile idea of the stage – what Habermas refers to as the 'echo of the developmental catastrophe',[76] the resounding of the destructive critique of the adolescent against the givenness of moral judgement – that proliferates and crystallises as an appeal to respond to what *Blast* calls the 'reality of the present'.

My chapter began by claiming that the adolescent interferes with knowledge. Social categories and psychological models and historical narratives appear unable to contain the figure of the adolescent, except in the form of a moment which will pass, or an illegality to be excluded from the institutions of knowledge, but not to be offered the substance of the outlaw. This may be a necessary structuring: it is not that the adolescent, or modernism, provides an alternative way of knowing the world, which could somehow be chosen over those which emerge from the lifeworld, which time and history have given us; but neither can the adolescent ever quite be excluded from the scene of the constitution of knowledge in modern history, not until we have become fully at home in this world. The maladjustment of individuals to 'history', or their penetration by all that is not ideal in modern history, that which is material or that which demands change, gives rise to the constituency of writing and the body of adolescent critique. The adolescent and the avant-garde, echo of the developmental catastrophe, persist as the pressing knowledge that from the beginning things did not need to be the way that they are.

3

Poles: The Centre of Europe

> Mr Conrad is a Pole, which sets him apart, and makes him, however admirable, not very helpful.
>
> Virginia Woolf.[1]

> Remember how we considered Conrad a traitor.
>
> Stanislaw Ignacy Witkiewitz.[2]

Conrad is not helpful to Woolf, as she thinks about how modern fiction might respond to modern life, because he is Polish. This is an odd argument for many reasons, but in this chapter I want rather to follow its logic: there is something in being 'Polish' which has to be excluded from consideration when 'modernism' is being built as a narrative of change and development, a narrative which can be attributed to a form like an institution. Conrad has a particularly complex relation to the marketplace and to the language, and a particularly complex set of affiliations, which will not allow him to help Woolf build her story. For Witkiewicz, Conrad is not enough of a Pole; has betrayed something in his movement to the 'centres' of European culture. He issues this reminder in a letter to Malinowski, the anthropologist, as he considers making his career and his life in Britain, at the London School of Economics, rather than in Poland. While this betrayal is of course at least partly about simple national solidarities, there is a wider problem encoded in the idea of the persistence in Polishness. When Alfred Jarry introduced *Ubu Roi* with these directions: 'The action, which is about to start, takes place in Poland, which is to say, nowhere',[3] the reduction of 'Poland' to 'nowhere' might be seen to characterise the ideal of some pointed metaphysical absurdity. Conversely, the substitution of 'Poland' for 'nowhere' gives useful historical reference to the irresponsible aspects of modernist literature. If modernism is not fully responsive to the 'world' in its material instance, the resources on which it draws in refusing the world are not necessarily themselves other-worldly. Perhaps this can be made clearer by returning to Lukács's critique of the 'ideology' of modernism, discussed in my introduction. Unlike the realist novel, for Lukács, modernism refuses to engage with the given fabric of identity and action. Whereas the novel considers 'possibility' in a concrete way, as that which is realised in particular actions 'in the world'; modernism sits impossibly alone, thinking 'possibility' and 'the world' in merely abstract terms. I do not think there is a space in Lukács's argument for something such as 'Poland', that nostalgic project which emerges out of the clashes of geopolitics; to admit the unhelpful reality of Poland would muddy the ground on which his distinction between abstract and concrete possibility is constructed. In an attempt to chart this difficult territory, this chapter will look to the languages shared between literature and ethnography as they try to come to terms with the sort of world in which Poland is central.

One of the aims of this analysis will be to provide a contextual framework within which to read 'The "Pole"', Wyndham Lewis's first published fiction, which appeared in Ford Madox Hueffer's journal *The English Review* (which I discussed in Chapter 1) in May 1909. That issue of the journal defines the awkward place into which modernism was emerging, and my first chapter thought about that place in terms of property. The emergence of modernism is also articulated with political geography, and this will be the point of focus here. In my earlier discussion, the pressing absence of Swinburne's 'epic volume' was manifest as a ghostly figure within the relays of domestic and literary property. His absence, and the need to find a literary voice which can both replace him and mark the fact that writing like his is no longer the right sound to give the world, is also a matter of geopolitics.

The English Review did not publish literature exclusively. Each issue ended with a substantial section, generally around fifty of the two hundred pages, called 'The Month', dealing with current affairs. These pages, in this first year of the journal, were particularly obsessed with the politics of Central Europe. The clumsy and temporary settlement of the Balkan crisis is the subject of an editorial in the issue in which Lewis first published. It icily welcomes the settlement.

The joy felt over the settlement of the Balkan question had about it something sinister, something oppressive. The stock markets rose, an ideal fell [. . .]. And yet, no doubt, the settlement is in many ways a most useful piece of work. It is useful because it relieved many apprehensions. [. . .] It shows us, in fact, that as between nation and nation we stand exactly where we did, exactly where we have always stood. It shows us that now, as always, treaties are things to be tranquilly broken, as soon as you have behind you a sufficiency of armed strength. And it is very well that this fact should have been reasserted.[4]

Condemnation of Prussian expansionism slides into an awkward recognition that 'Prussia is perfectly within her rights. She stands very much where we did not so very long ago. She wants what we wanted then, what today we have got.'[5] This recognition, according to the editorial, is what is so important, so useful, about the settlement:

It has proved that small States can expect no mercy. It should prove to us that if we sink to the level of a small State we need expect no better a fate than is that of Poland to-day [. . .]. Poland, with its ancient glories, its romance, its chivalry, Poland, because it was once so formidable, is divided up, is held down, by three mighty Powers.[6]

This cynical recognition of the anarchic claims of power over 'civilisation' is, I think, one kind of reason why Swinburne's 'epic volume' is no longer possible. Swinburne is 'epic' in his full-throated participation in the processes of late-romantic nationalism; the problem of Poland suggests that this mode will not serve; a new literary voice is necessary. The relationship between the two aspects of the journal, its literary project, and its political criticism, is an Arnoldian one. Great Literature fosters a 'Critical Attitude' which is seen, somehow, to stand as both a transcendence and a solution of the involved problems of politics and history. But, in the face of the problems of central Europe, this critical attitude has little instrumental force. Henry W. Nevinson, writing in the first issue, analyses and tabulates the claims of the various parties: their conflicting demands, and their conflicting historical claims. 'At the moment of writing', he concludes, 'there lies the Balkan problem, plain for anyone to read, though not to solve.'[7] The absence of a new voice, the unseizable ghostly presence that Pound's poetry presented to *The English Review*, matches the difficulty of taking a position on the questions of central Europe; the embarrassment of a Great Nation's relation to Little States.

By the 1920s, the moment of high modernism had solved this problem; or at least T. S. Eliot thought that it had. In his 1923 review of *Ulysses*, he accepts that the certainties of the age of the novel have passed, that the novel 'will no longer serve'.[8] But *Ulysses* – and he is clearly talking about his own contribution, *The Waste Land*, too – represents, not the puzzling problem of modernism in *The English Review*, but a new method, the 'mythical method'; 'It has the importance of a scientific discovery.'[9] Famously, this method has politically and historically transformative powers. It is 'a step toward making the modern world possible for art'; it outlines the possibility of 'ordering, of giving a shape and a significance to the immense panorama of futility and anarchy which is contemporary history'.[10] It is very likely that Eliot is thinking, in this image, about the new forms which the problems of central Europe have taken after the war; the new conflicts arising from the Russian Revolution and the Versailles treaty.[11] The guarded triumphalism of this article, and of 'The Function of Criticism' of the previous month, figures modernism in a very different way from the complicated and nervous cynicism of the 'Critical Attitude' of *The English Review*.

At the same moment, claims similar to Eliot's were being made in a different discipline. In 1922, Bronislaw Malinowski, the Polish anthropologist, published *Argonauts of the Western Pacific*, an analysis of the Kula: a ritualised system of exchange which holds together the communities of the Trobriand Islands, north of the East tip of Papua New Guinea.[12] Malinowski's account replaces images of the 'savage' as irrational and anarchic with a 'functionalist' explanation. 'Ethnology has introduced law and order into what seemed chaotic and freakish. It has transformed for us the sensational, wild and unaccountable world of "savages" into a number of well ordered communities, governed by law, behaving and thinking according to consistent principles.'[13] This scientific comprehension will, he hopes, ground a centralised 'Wisdom' with the power to control the crisis of a central Europe itself grown all too savage, 'when prejudice, ill will and vindictiveness are dividing each European nation from another, when all the ideals, cherished and proclaimed as the highest achievements of civilisation, science and religion, have been thrown to the winds'.[14]

Malinowski's monograph, the model until recently for British social anthropology, was based on fieldwork carried out during the First World War. His fieldwork diary, published in 1967, makes available a counter-ethnography, a competing account of cultural contact which embodies a knowledge which was passed over in the finished monograph.[15] It is an extraordinary document, detailing obsessively and repetitively Malinowski's violent mood swings; his lusts, drug intake, his shifting attitude to Poland, and his overriding professional ambitions. One reviewer argued that 'fieldworkers' diaries are meaningless to anyone except themselves, the product of a sort of suspended state between two cultures'.[16] This chapter will claim that the viewpoint from that 'suspended state' is meaningless in a significant way. Referring to Michael Levenson's claim that 1922 was the most important year for modernism not because of the publication of *The Waste Land* and *Ulysses*, but because of the institutional success of Eliot's editorship of *The Criterion*,[17] Mark Manganaro has argued that the simultaneous 'accession to cultural legitimacy' of modernism and functionalist anthropology is 'not sheer coincidence'.[18] I want to elaborate on that, and to advance a further claim: that the 'meaningless' counter-ethnography of the *Diary* and the primitivist 'false start' of Lewis's first short stories share conditions of possibility; that a reading of the experiences that threatened to disrupt Malinowski's institutional success will illuminate a modernist dead-end, and elucidate modernism's investment in 'The "Pole"'.[19]

The Diary also helps to explain a different tone which underlies the authority Eliot and Malinowski claim in the early 1920s. The opening of *The Argonauts of the Western Pacific* is elegaic.

> Ethnology is in the sadly ludicrous, not to say tragic, position, that at the very moment when it begins to put its workshop in order, to forge its proper tools, to start ready for work on its appointed task, the material of its study melts away with hopeless rapidity. Just now, when the methods and aims of scientific field ethnology have taken shape, when men fully trained for the work have begun to travel into savage countries and study their inhabitants – these die away under our very eyes.[20]

This fatalism, an innocent or bewildered restatement of *The English Review*'s assessment of the relation between Little States and Great Nations, is a result of the ambition that issues in *The Argonauts of the Western Pacific* and a professional career at the London School of Economics, rather than in the *Diary* and a modernist career. It displaces a whole series of losses on to a fatal resignation: loss of his relation to Poland, loss of adolescent attachments, loss of the uncomfortable and violent emotional responses of the *Diary*.

The tone, and the specific reference, appear in Eliot's writing too, in 'In Memoriam, Marie Lloyd', published in the second issue of *The Criterion*. The 'encroachment of the cheap and rapid-breeding cinema' has led to the 'decay of the music-hall';[21] and with it, Eliot suggests, will disappear the possibility of dignity and interest in the lives of working people:

> In an interesting essay in the volume of *Essays on the Depopulation of Melanesia*, the psychologist W.H.R. Rivers adduced evidence which has led him to believe that the natives of that unfortunate archipelago are dying out principally for the reason that the 'Civilisation' forced upon them has deprived them of all interest in life.[22]

The processes of modernisation will have a similar result: 'it will not be surprising if the population of the entire civilized world rapidly follows the fate of the Melanesians'.[23] This is the ground on which the order called for in 'The Function of Criticism' must obtain.

> I was dealing then [in 'Tradition and the Individual Talent' (1919)] with the artist, and the sense of tradition which, it seemed to me, the artist should have; but it was generally a problem of order; and the function of criticism seems to be essentially a problem of order too. I thought of literature then, as I think of it know, of the literature of the world, of the literature of Europe, of the literature of a single country, not as a collection of the writings of individuals, but as 'organic wholes', as systems in relation to which, and only in relation to which, individual works of art, and the works of individual artists, have their significance.[24]

These 'organic wholes', concentrically involving the nation, Europe, and the World, are not based in a project of re-instituting excitement in life – not in the revivification of Melanesia – but in a critical displacement. The editorial principle of *The Criterion* was to discuss, not politically topical issues, but political theory.[25] What is called for is not a world re-enchanted by the reading of *Ulysses*, but personal control of 'the emotions and feelings of the writer',[26] an ordered field of criticism, a properly managed profession: 'a simple and orderly field of beneficent activity, from which impostors can be readily ejected'.[27]

The function of criticism, then, for Eliot, might well be to provide a surrogate order within which the problems of personality, of relation to the material and political world, can be proleptically resolved.

To mangle Freud's famous formulation: Where literature in history was, there professional criticism shall be. Freud's phrase – 'Where Id was, there shall Ego be' – itself enacts a displaced resolution of the problems of contested territory in Central Europe.[28] What he calls the 'work of culture', performed by an ideal psychoanalysis, appears in its context, in his lecture on 'The Dissection of the Psychical Personality', in the *New Introductory Lectures on Psychoanalysis*, as a hasty resolution, in terms which have strong advertising appeal for the profession of psychoanalysis, of problems of topography raised in the lecture. Freud has noted that the psychic divisions between the superego, id, and the ego are not clear cut, using an analogy to explain. 'I am imagining a country with a landscape of varying configurations – hill-country, plains, and chains of lakes –, and with a mixed population: it is inhabited by Germans, Magyars and Slovaks, who carry on different activities. Now things might be partitioned in such a way that the Germans, who breed cattle, live in the hill-country, the Magyars, who grow cereals and wine, live in the plains, and the Slovaks, who catch fish and plait reeds, live by the lakes. If the partitioning could be neat and clear-cut like this, a Woodrow Wilson would be delighted by it [. . .]. The probability is, however, that you will find less orderliness and more mixing.'[29] The impossibility of a clear dissection of the psyche mirrors the impossibility of a stable apportioning of the territories of central Europe.[30] This difficulty – the difficulty of thinking the relationship between psyche and culture – is displaced, rather than solved, in Freud's lapidary formula.

Eliot's ambitions are similar, and similarly evasive, to Freud's. In place of the messy relations between artists, the 'unconscious community' which is buried under a disordered history, a conscious critical effort must be made. 'As the instincts of tidiness imperatively command us not to leave to the haphazard of unconsciousness what we can attempt to do consciously, we are forced to conclude that what happens unconsciously we could bring about, and form into a purpose, if we made a conscious effort.'[31] The disenchanted population of 'In Memoriam Marie Lloyd' – Melanesians, Poles, Proles and underdisciplined writing – returns as the mob to be excluded from this cleansed consciousness and this ordered professional field.

Polish action

When Malinowski left for New Guinea, anthropology was not yet a profession. Its research work was done by anybody: by missionaries, adventurers, colonial officials. And its written results, at least in England, were not clearly separated from studies of the classics, travel writing, or literature. The comparative ethnology of Frazer and the Cambridge Classicists may have brought some sort of relativism to bear on Western cultural and political traditions, but it did so from a standpoint that was 'literary' in the most intractable and culturally implicated way. Frazer's *The Golden Bough* grew out of the notes to a translation of Pausanias.[32] Andrew Lang translated Homer, wrote anthropology, which Freud refers to in *Totem and Taboo*, and wrote a novel in collaboration with Rider Haggard,[33] all feeding his compendious work on children's fairy tales. Rider Haggard's author narrator, Alan Quatermain, offers his services to anthropology,[34] and had he been just slightly more real he could have joined the adventurers, traders, missionaries and colonial officials who provided the information upon which Frazer performed his comparative syntheses, and who sent photographs to the *Strand* for printing as 'curiosities'. Literature was imagined by Walter Besant and others as spreading inexorably and profitably over the empire, and was clearly being fed by the return of travellers' accounts; and anthropology was selling like popular fiction.[35] Peter Keating reports 'a close connection between the views of popular anthropologists like E. B. Tyler, Max Müller and Andrew Lang, and the even more popular novel of Empire, that was to hold until discredited by the development of sophisticated field-work techniques. Much of this literature was as conjectural as science fiction.'[36]

Early in *Argonauts of the Western Pacific*, Malinowski distances himself from this culture on empiricist grounds.[37] The ability of casual field-workers to observe without prejudice, he argues, is compromised by their having their 'own business' to perform in the object community:

> None of them lives right in a native village, except for very short periods, and everyone has his own business, which takes up a considerable part of his time. Moreover, if, like a trader or a missionary or an official he enters into active relations with the native, if he has to transform or influence or make use of him, this makes a real, unbiased, impartial observation impossible, and precludes all-round sincerity, at least in the case of the missionaries and officials.[38]

The ethnographer's tent, proudly displayed as the first illustration in *Argonauts of the Western Pacific* (Fig. 1, facing 16),[39] stands for a way of living that is entirely different: a professionalism that 'labour[s] on a field so far only prospected by the curiosity of amateurs'.[40] This professionalism, membership of a 'disinterested' scientific community, depends on an alienation from his own culture that allows him to become part of the culture being observed. The 'goal is, briefly, to grasp the native's point of view, his relation to life, to realise *his* vision of *his* world'.[41] As he put it in 1915, in the period of his first enthusiasm for fieldwork, 'My experience is that direct questioning of the native about a custom or belief never discloses their attitude as thoroughly as the discussion of facts connected with the direct observation of a custom or with a concrete occurrence, in which both parties are materially concerned.'[42] Malinowski's 'participant observation' strives towards an immediate apprehension, the state when 'their behaviour, their manner of being, in all sorts of tribal transactions, became more transparent and easily understandable than it had been before'.[43] This immediacy, a knowledge that dispenses with the distance between subject and object to incorporate the social totality to be known in the practices of adaption to that totality, is the state of 'being there', the representation of which, Clifford Geertz argues, guarantees the effect of authenticity.[44]

This paradox, whereby being professional is achieved by a passage through alienation from the cultures of 'civilisation', is resolved by the introduction of the idea of modernism.[45] Malinowski's academic and social background was in the advanced 'Young Poland' movement: candid and enthusiastic about sex, a culture of positivism and romanticism, Mach and Avenarius as well as Nietzsche and Bergson.[46] His unpublished essay on Nietzsche, for instance, puts his methodological ideas into philosophical contexts.[47] Paul Carter makes the same connection: 'The meaning [Malinowski] discovered in native life was the meaning he would give his own life; and, what is more, it would license his going back, his return to the centre of European culture. The anti-intellectualism of his determination to submit himself, suspending judgement, to the supple and subtle river of phenomena as they passed before his eyes, to whatever came into his mind, was itself a signature of his European culture and the historical and aesthetic crises associated with Modernism.'[48]

Malinowski suggests that this modernist epistemology can be achieved simply by being Polish, when he speculates: 'I am not certain if this joining in is equally easy for everyone – perhaps the Slavonic nature is more plastic and more naturally savage than that of Western Europeans.'[49] Thus Polishness and modernism become a first step in a movement towards the 'centre'; they mark a temporary alienation of identity in the service of supervening professional ends.[50]

But this gravitation of 'Polishness' and 'modernism' towards the centre, the elision in Carter's argument of Malinowski's Central-European culture with the 'centre of European culture', is not inevitable. Something crucial has been hidden in the process: the whole problem of Great States and Little Nations that provided focus for *The English Review*. It obscures a significant *choice* of destination for Malinowski, and for modernism. He vacillates in the *Diary* continually over whether he should return to Poland or to England; sites, at the time of Malinowski's fieldwork, with very different statuses, and very different histories.

Poland had not existed as a state since the 1770s; had been divided and redivided according to the fluctuating ambitions and fortunes of the three empires, Russian, Prussian, and Austro-Hungarian, which had colonised its territories.[51] To be 'Polish' was, as one historian puts it, 'to belong to a community which has acquired its modern sense of nationality in active opposition to the policies of the states in which they lived'.[52] Polish Action – the action which is about to start takes place in Poland, which is to say, nowhere – is lived against or despite the structures in which it takes place. This community is 'functional' in a sense which disturbs Malinowski's descriptive categories. The functionalist method has no place for Polish Action: 'Ethnology has introduced law and order into what seemed chaotic and freakish. It has transformed for us the sensational, wild and unaccountable world of "savages" into a number of well ordered communities, governed by law, behaving and thinking according to consistent principles.'[53] This Central European problem, the 'Polish Question' that accompanies the emergence of modernism, which seems to be resolved in *Argonauts of the Western Pacific*, appears as a series of methodological difficulties, and the associations that cluster around them, in the *Diary*.

Disenchantment

As *The Diary* reveals, participant observation, the suspension of cultural identity as the first step towards the professional centre, was not altogether comfortable for Malinowski. Rather than smoothly *being there*, within the objectified totality of Trobriand culture where '[the ethnographer's], life soon adopts quite a natural course very much in harmony with his surroundings',[54] Malinowski experiences life as part of a frustrating processing of relation to it: an erotic cycle of repulsion, boredom, and fascination, sometimes performed in bad faith, sometimes violently charged. Sometimes he dreams of complete assimilation, at other times is repulsed. 'The natives still irritate me, particularly

Ginger, whom I could willingly beat to death. I understand all the German and Belgian colonial atrocities. I am also dismayed by Mrs Bill's relations with a handsome nigger from Tukwa'ukwa.'[55] At one point in his diary, he muses, quoting Conrad in English:[56] 'On the whole my feelings towards the natives are decidedly tending to *"Exterminate the Brutes"* '.[57]

At such moments, Malinowski takes refuge in literature. Reduced to one 'humanising' moment in *Argonauts of the Western Pacific*, where he admits that the initial difficulty of fieldwork led to 'periods of despondency, when I buried myself in the reading of novels, as a man might take to drink in a fit of tropical depression and boredom',[58] his struggle with the novel fills the *Diary*. This entry, from October 1914, is typical, and repeated daily at times. 'I promised myself I would read no novels. For a few days I kept my promise. Then I relapsed.'[59] There are other lapses that seem more methodologically significant: his craving for European company, his periods of idleness, the way he slips into an attitude of distrust towards the Trobriand Islanders; but it is his inability to stop consuming narrative, losing himself in books (particularly the romance fiction of Haggard, Stevenson, and Kipling), which really disgusts him. '[T]he time I made the mistake of reading a Rider Haggard novel' represents the nadir.[60]

Literature keeps taking him out of the present into 'the company of Thackeray's London snobs'.[61] The literary is seen to stand between the ethnographer and his object, its way of representing the primitive adulterating the ideal empiricism which is Malinowski's aim. 'Wasted all day Saturday 17 and Sunday 18 [. . .] reading *Vanity Fair* and in my desperation – complete obfuscation, I simply forgot where I was.' Sometimes this mediation is seen simply to block the view. 'We sailed past a little uninhabited island [. . .] I felt too rotten to look and was bogged down in the trashy novel.' At other moments there is a romantic atmosphere, allowing intuitive knowledge of the savage, that cuts through appearances and short-circuits the proper processes of research. 'For the first time I heard the protracted, piercing sound of a shell being blown – *kibi* – and with it a monstrous squealing of pigs and roar of men. In the silence of the night it gave the impression of some mysterious atrocity being perpetrated and threw a sudden light – a somber light – on forgotten cannibal ceremonies.'[62] This bleeds into a fear that Malinowski might *write* a popular novel, rather than a scientific ethnography.[63] A non-empiricist comparativism threatens to return with this literary epistemology; a simple evolutionist characterisation replacing the difficult articulation of an alien culture in functionalist terms.

Most revisionist readings of Malinowski's work have suggested that the revelations contained in the *Diary* are simply falsifying: they negate the claims made in *Argonauts of the Western Pacific* about the value of 'participant observation' as a methodology, and suggest that this way of becoming intimate with the Other – which Malinowski in one place calls 'ethnographer's magic' – is either an act of pure projection, or merely a rhetorical effect. But the *Diary* embodies a sort of knowledge too, which the model of two cultures – the West and its Other; the 'centre of European Culture' and its peripheries – is too blunt properly to conceive. Pierre Bourdieu articulates the possibility of this other kind of knowledge in his ethnographic work in Algeria during the Algerian revolution. This work, perhaps most powerfully expressed in 'The Disenchantment of the World' (1963), tries to understand the modes and meanings of action within the colonised community.[64] The ambitions of the Algerians, their sense of identity, the relevance of their traditional patterns of behaviour, have been eroded by the impact of rationalising French land laws, and by structures of government within which their concepts of authority and identity have no place. Like 'Poles' in Central Europe, Algerians under French rule do not find themselves reflected (as Algerians) in the objective structures within which they have to work and survive. In this context, Bourdieu argues, the traditional actions of the Algerian community are subtended by disenchantment: actions and identities are performed in the anticipation of their failure or futility. But as a result of this estrangement, traditional actions take on new meanings: wearing the chechia or the veil becomes an act of resistance, the manifestation of a constituency of dissidence. Such actions no longer have meaning only as a function in a unified culture, but express also a relation to the colonising power.[65]

Malinowski comes close, at one point in *Argonauts of the Western Pacific*, to recognising the horizon of disenchantment, at the only moment in that book where he recognises the effect of the presence of colonial government. He had theorised the function of magic and myths within the context of the Kula, the circuit of trading voyages. They work to consolidate a unified worldview, where the objective world and subjective experience reflect one another nicely:

I spoke above [. . .] of the enlivening influence of myth upon landscape. Here it must be noted also that the mythically charged features of the landscape bear testimony in the native's mind to the truth of the myth. The mythical world receives its substance in rock and hill, in the changes in land and sea. The pierced sea-passages, the cleft boulder, the petrified human beings, all these bring the mythological world close to the natives, make it tangible and permanent. On the other hand, the story thus powerfully illustrated, reacts on the landscape, fills it with dramatic happenings, which, fixed there for ever, give it a definite meaning.[66]

This epic enchantment of experience and objectivity can no longer be maintained for the Trobriand Islanders, which provides one motivation for its construction in anthropology. Their economy is 'distorted' by their relations with pearl traders; their social structures by the superimposition of colonial government. In Malinowski's account, this measure of alienation can lead only to the destruction of their culture. 'The undermining of old-established authority, of tribal morals and customs, tends on the one hand completely to demoralise the natives and to make them unamenable to any law or rule, while on the other hand [. . .] it deprives them of many of their [. . .] ways of enjoying life [. . .]'.[67] This loss of *joie de vivre*, mingled oddly with the difficulty of government, he is convinced, is what leads to the disappearance of individuals and cultures that he mourns in the opening passage of *Argonauts*, quoted above. This, remember, was also Eliot's diagnosis in the essay on Marie Lloyd. Stanley Hall noted a hard amalgam of the ungovernable and the culturally destabilising in the figure of the adolescent. But Malinowski does not recognise that the loss of obvious function for many traditions may turn them into a resistant practice, what Bourdieu calls 'colonial traditionalism',[68] the index of a resistant maintenance of community against the evidence of its insignificance; nor does he imagine that the resistance of 'natives' to law (both scientific and jurisprudential) might be anything other than a mark of degeneration.

The Diary, again, tells a different story. Ethnographic sympathy – 'becoming a savage' – might be possible for Malinowski, not because his 'Slavic Nature' is plastic, but because of an homology of positions. Poland and the Trobriand Islands are in no sense identical: in terms of Malinowski's material position relative to their community, he can be easily considered to function in a position like that of the colonial government. But his relation, as a Pole, to the structures of State power in Europe is paralleled by the estranged identities of Trobriand Islanders within a colonial organisation. And this homology is not recognised as knowledge, but appears in his *Diary* as a failure, or an interruption of knowledge: a disenchantment. He accuses his informers of lying when they don't match their objectifying function;[69] he is irritated when they laugh or make a game out of the business of supplying him with information;[70] he gets annoyed when one of them asks him about the war in Europe. Johannes Fabian notes that 'At least twenty times [Malinowski] reports on situations when the present with its demands became too much to bear. [. . .] All this, I believe, is not only evidence of Malinowski's psychological problems with fieldwork, it documents his struggle with an epistemological problem – coevalness'.[71] The ethnography of the uncomfortable and unequal co-existence of cultures is written in the disruption of ambition and knowledge, the irrational desires and actions of the 'suspended state' excluded from *The Argonauts of the Western Pacific*. 'At night, a little tired, but not exhausted, I sang, to a Wagner melody, the words "Kiss my ass" to chase away *mulukwausi* [flying witches].'[72]

Malinowski recognises obliquely that his *own* disenchantment might be a sort of knowledge, might have some sort of tradition or function, when he refers to his frequent lapses into depression as his 'Dostoevskean reactions';[73] or, invoking his friend and sometime lover,[74] the Polish avant-garde artist and writer Stanislaw Ignacy Witkiewicz (Stas), refers to 'doubts à la S.I.W'.[75] These depressions, the failure of scientific confidence and ambition, are linked throughout to a mode of perception associated with modernism, and – ambivalently – with repudiated sexual desires and his sense of duty to Poland. They produce a state of 'continuous ethical conflict. My failure to think seriously about Mother, Stas, Poland – about their sufferings there and about Poland's ordeal – is disgusting!'[76]

All of these problems converge at several moments in the *Diary*. Here is one particularly impacted example:

Talk with Tiabubu and Sixpence – momentary excitement. Then I was again overcome by sluggishness – hardly had the strength of will to finish the Conrad stories. Needless to say a terrible melancholy, gray like the sky all around, swirling around the edges of my inner horizon. I tore my eyes from the book and I could hardly believe that here I was among neolithic savages, and that I was sitting here peacefully while terrible things were going on *back there*. At moments I had an impulse to pray for mother. Passivity and the feeling that somewhere, far beyond the reach of any possibility of doing something, horrible things are taking place, unbearable. Monstrous, terrible, inexorable necessity takes on the form of something personal. Incurable human optimism gives it kind, gentle aspects. Subjective fluctuations – with the leitmotiv of eternally victorious hope – are objectivised as a kind, just divinity, exceptionally sensitive to the moral aspect of the subject's behaviour. Conscience – the specific function that ascribes to ourselves all the evil that has occurred – becomes the voice of God. Truly, there is a great deal to my theory of faith.[77]

Malinowksi collapses from the 'momentary excitement' of fieldwork into literature and lassitude. The external world is replaced ('needless to say') with an atmosphere deriving from Conrad. This substitution, a failure of will, is marked by a theoretical regression: Tiabubu and Sixpence, members of the culture to which he is attempting to be present, are figured, in terms of the evolutionist language he repudiates, as 'neolithic savages'. He has relaxed out of the present into the distant and literary past. The present returns as the problem of Poland, *'back there'*, ravaged by fighting on the Eastern front, where Poles are fighting in the armies of both Russia and the Central powers. The strain involved in being present to the 'excitement' of cultural contact, and to the demands of Polish identity, is opposed to theoretical regression, figured through literature. The rest of the paragraph charts Malinowski's recovery. It accelerates through an abstraction of the problem to its theoretical resolution in his 'theory of faith', on which he congratulates himself. But this resolution is purely theoretical: the real problem, the problem of the coeval, is displaced; it finds only surrogate solution in the field of professional ambition.

That professional ambition is accompanied by a domestic ambition: 'At present, if I am strong enough, I must devote myself to my work, to being faithful to my fiancée, and to the goal of adding depth to my life as well as my work.' On the second and longer fieldwork expedition, Malinowski gradually convinced himself that he was engaged to Elsie Masson (E.R.M. in the diaries), and that she must be the only object of his sexual interest. She represents 'the Promised Land' of an 'atmosphere naturally harmonizing with mine'; the harmony he is able only fitfully to realise in his ethnographic role. He is able to daydream about 'the possibility of a professorship [. . .] and plan[ ] lectures, receptions, etc., with E.R.M. as my wife'. This is a resolution of his 'suspended state'. It conflicts with his Polish identity: 'If I married E.R.M., I would be estranged from Polishness'; and it is understood as a subjugation of his modernist epistemology: 'Nor can I bear the Dostoevskean reactions I used to have – some sort of hidden aversion or hostility, mixed with a strong attachment and interest.'[78] Witkiewicz, writing to Malinowski in 1921, when Malinowski was about to decide to turn down the chance to return to a professorship in Cracow in favour of his job in London, reminds him of these other attachments, calling up Malinowski's responsibility to a whole set of adolescent allegiances.[79] 'I'd so like you to become Polish again. It's a pity to lose one's nationality that way. Remember how we considered Conrad a traitor.'[80]

Excluding these haunting obstacles, Malinowski is left alone:[81] 'I analysed the nature of my ambition. An ambition stemming from my love of work, intoxication with my own work, my belief in the importance of science and art [. . .] ambition stemming from constantly seeing oneself – *romance of one's own life*; eyes turned to one's own form. [. . .] External ambition. When I think of work, or works, or the revolution I want to effect in social anthropology – this is a truly creative ambition.' He dreams of 'homo-sex., with my own double as a partner. Strangely autoerotic feelings; the impression that I'd like to have a mouth just like mine to kiss, a neck that curves just like mine, a forehead just like mine (seen from the side).'[82]

These exclusions are tightly linked with the dehistoricisation of the ethnographic object. The first premise of functionalism is that the culture in question is to be considered as a totality; and that in this particular case, the Kula (a system of give and take, manifesting and producing value, and expressive of the structure of relations that makes up the community) is understood to be the foundation of that enchanted unity. The debts incurred in exchange are not experienced merely as individual burdens, but revivify the experience of relationships within a social whole. And those relationships, rather than being conceived of statically, are constantly remade through acts of exchange. Malinowski lists the seven classes of exchange that correspond to all possible modes of relation between two individuals in this culture.[83]

In rejecting the experience of relation to the material culture around him, in controlling his 'lusts and aversions' and concentrating on his ambitions in the British academy, Malinowski radically straitens the kind of productivity which can be described here, and limits what the object of anthropology can be: he is unable to imagine how his labour could operate within the culture of the Kula, or what relationship is expressed in his interaction with the Trobriand Islanders. What this totality does not include is Malinowski. It is not that it would be theoretically impossible to think about the exchange of knowledge as relationship-creating or expressive. He describes instances of ideas or information functioning both as commodities, when the Trobriand Islanders sell the rights to particular dances to other tribes, and as inalienable gifts, when fathers pass on the knowledge of certain sorts of magic to their sons.[84] He could have theorised the information they pass on to him as a commodity exchanged for the tobacco he brings with him; or as a tribute, expressing the status he is accorded. In a letter to Elsie Masson, he notes the experiences on the basis of which both these possibilities could have been articulated:

> This village is [. . .] a good ethnographic hunting ground – scarcity of tobacco [. . .].
> By the way, I was known before as *Matuna Omarakana*, 'the man from Omarakana'. Now I hear myself announced by the term TOLILIBOGWO or TOLIBOGWO ('the man of the old talk' or to put it nicely the 'Master of Myth'); – there is of course no reverence associated with this designation.[85]

Nor does the totality include the relations with pearl traders or with local government, although these are also based in exchange. This production of totality through exclusion is a denial of his experience, and of the historical conditions within which his contact with the Trobriand Islanders takes place. It is the institution of a *distance* between the professional ethnographer as the author of *Argonauts of the Western Pacific*, and the messy field of cultural contact:

> In Ethnography, the distance is often enormous between the brute material of information – as it is presented to the student in his own observations, in native statement, in the kaleidoscope of tribal life – and the final authoritative presentation of the results. The Ethnographer has to traverse this distance in the laborious years between the moment when he sets foot upon a native beach, and makes his first attempt to get in touch with the natives, and the time when he writes down the final version of his results.[86]

The 'traversal of this distance' marks, I think, a return to the culture of the novel. Formally, Malinowski's actual experience of the Trobriand Islands is transformed through the generalised viewpoint of a fictional narrator. He invites the reader to 'Imagine yourself suddenly set down surrounded by all your gear, alone on a tropical beach close to a native village, while the launch or dinghy which has brought you sails away out of sight': 'launch or dinghy' being a particularly weird insertion of indeterminacy into a remembered scene.[87] The standard form he uses throughout the text hereafter is: 'Returning to our imaginary first visit ashore'.[88] In a letter to Frazer, he remarks that his work should be 'accepted, not because of its scientific value (whatever that may be) but because it ought to be a book that *sells*'.[89] This imagination of market success is mirrored in the shaky gesture of the terms of the subtitle, 'enterprise' and 'adventure'. They mark features of the islanders' lives, but slide all too easily into becoming a generic marker of the sorts of imperial romance against which his project had been initiated; and against which his Polishness and his desires had struggled.

The orientation of the book towards a literary market thoroughly implicated in centralising and hierarchical structures is expressed as (and expresses) a movement, a shift of emphasis, from solidarity to profit:

> Perhaps as we read the account of these remote customs there may emerge a feeling of solidarity with the endeavours and ambitions of the natives. Perhaps man's mentality will be revealed to us, and brought near, along some lines which we have never followed before. Perhaps through realising human nature in a shape very distant and foreign to us, we shall have some light shed on our own. In this, and in this case only, we shall be justified in feeling that it has been worth our while to understand these natives, these institutions and customs, and that we have gathered some profit from the Kula.[90]

The call for solidarity happens at the same time as the turn back from the object economy towards the culture within which *Argonauts of the Western Pacific* is to be circulated, as that solidarity is to be realised as 'profit'. Rather than conceiving ethnography as a practice in relation to the communities expressed and maintained by the Kula exchange, it is seen as an object to be traded within the European, particularly the British, cultural marketplace. This profit is consolidated in Malinowski's successful career at the London School of Economics, an institution whose history anticipates that of Malinowski's text. Founded by money left for Sidney Webb to use in the interests of the Fabian movement, it was the centre of that movement's shift from the support of direct action towards a distanced theoretical interest. Beatrice Webb noted in her diary that 'Last night we [the Webbs] sat by the fire and jotted down a whole list of subjects which want elucidating – issues of fact which need clearing up. Above all, we want the ordinary citizen to feel that reforming society is no light matter and must be undertaken by experts specially trained for the purpose.'[91] To this end, Harold Laski was prevented from publishing on political topics in the popular press.[92]

The dividend to be obtained from this institutional organisation, as I noted at the outset of my chapter, was to be a transportable and un-situated 'final synthesis'; a universal 'Wisdom' which might regulate a European culture grown all too savage itself, 'when prejudice, ill will and vindictiveness are dividing each European nation from another, when all the ideals, cherished and proclaimed as the highest achieve-ments of civilisation, science and religion, have been thrown to the winds'. But, for Malinowski at least, it is achieved only at a heavy cost. This wishful appeal to a theoretical world order that replaces and resolves the resistance of 'Polish Action' should be read against the elegaic tone of the opening of *Argonauts of the Western Pacific*, and the last entry in the *Diary*. 'I shall experience joy and happiness and success and satisfaction in my work – but all this has become meaningless. The world has lost colour.'[93]

Taken for a 'Pole'

Malinowski finds that his will to live in the world in its full complex-ity, with its Great States and Little Nations, with Poland and homo-sexuality and affect as constitutive aspects of the world, is opposed to the professional urge to order it and clarify it. A particularly modern productivity is more or less abandoned here; the mode of writing sketched in the diary which registers something of the disenchanted power of Polish Action, something of the rich difficulty of living in the world, is given over in favour of an institutional reproduction. The remainder of this chapter will attempt to describe some of the struc-tures through which that ambivalent productivity might persist at least as a colouring of knowledge.

Paul Carter describes how emerging from the Mont Cenis tunnel into the light of Italy was a revelation for Adrian Stokes, the English painter and writer on aesthetics and psychoanalysis: 'the new vitality he experienced in the south was inseparable from its novelty: The pecu-liar zest he attributed to certain architectural milieux sprang from the sense they gave him of astonishment, surprise, of being in a state of per-manent apparition.' He finds this state confirmed by the experience of William Walton. When the train 'came out on the Italian side they found the most marvellous sun. He never recovered from this moment of revelation, the shock of seeing such brilliant light.' Carter wants to suggest that the 'clarity of light (and life) [in a new southern environ-ment] may throw the muddiness of one's former existence into clear and critical relief', but also that life in a new country may be difficult.

The new country exists as an aesthetic whole, over against the person who comes into it, already complete before the existence of the observer. '[T]he very completeness of this new world, its self-containedness, threatens to re-enclose the migrant psyche, to reduce it once more to passivity'.[94]

I have suggested that Malinowski's reaction to such a revelation, and to the threat which it brings with it, was to initiate a long process of self-control, and social, political, sexual, and psychic re-orientation. Ambition, a realistic attitude to his future based upon a return to England and the liberal academy, was his way of controlling both the excitement of revelation and the fear of dissolution. Malinowski's reaction can be surrounded by a variety of other possibilities, suggested or enacted by more or less analogous cases. Stanislaw Ignacy Witkiewicz accompanied Malinowski to Australia, on the way to the fieldwork sites. It is difficult to reconstruct this moment: little material exists, and less has been translated, but it is clear that he was to be the official photographer and draughtsman on the expedition.[95] His fiancée had recently committed suicide, and this was to be the beginning of a new life for him. He is shocked, here in Ceylon, by the light:

> I'm unable to describe the wonders I'm seeing here. These things are absolutely monstrous in their beauty. Meadows flooded with water in the midst of forests. Strange olive-green calami. In little ponds, purple-violet water lilies. The vegetation madder and madder, and the people more and more gaudily, but wonderfully dressed (violet, yellow, and purple, sometimes emerald green), which along with the chocolate and bronze bodies, and the strange plants in the background, creates a devilish effect. [. . .] The lakes are covered with flowers going from scarlet and orange vermillion to violet and lake. [. . .] All this causes me the most frightful suffering and unbearable pain, since she's not alive with me. Only the worst despair and the senselessness of seeing the beauty. She won't see this – and I'm not an artist. . . . Everything is poison and brings close thoughts of death. When, when will this inhuman suffering end?[96]

Foreign light externalises the sorts of expressionism which interested Witkiewicz, who experimented with writing and painting under the influence of various drugs. The impossibility of making sense or living comfortably (he planned carefully one of a series of suicide attempts while in Australia) is the condition of his self-presentation as an artist, and the guarantee of his neo-romantic modernism. He sees this in the new world. From a very different perspective, this account of life in the South Seas as the externalisation of an economically irrational modernist sensibility is confirmed by Ellis Silas, a watercolourist and illustrator who visited the Trobriand Islands a few years after Malinowski.[97]

Silas finds it impossible to paint there. The light obliterates the picturesque, dissolving mass and producing a grotesque effect, suggesting both modernist use of colour and formal abstraction. 'When fine weather set in, the colouring became so intense as hitherto it had been dull; some of the effects were startlingly crude and frequently theatrical which treated as purely decorative schemes presented unlimited possibilities, but generally the powerful sunlight destroyed the large masses, the effects being kaleidoscopic.'[98] A modernist aesthetic, as economically ruinous as the ghost which possesses the humorous writer discussed in Chapter 1 above, presents itself here before being rejected; it takes all of Silas's considerable phlegm to recover himself and paint as if he had never had the experience. Writing in *The New Age*, Huntley Carter entitles an article about the series of exhibitions in the Grafton Galleries which introduced Post-Impressionism to the British Gallery circuit, 'The Post-Savages', finding in such work a call to empiricism as the basis of a new self-discovery. 'From all the works that count at the Grafton Galleries just now, comes this insistent, exhilarating cry. We must, will be ourselves. We will see with our own eyes, do with our own hands, think and talk in our own language.'[99] He is answered, in the letters pages, by the sort of spluttering response that is as much the intended product of modernism as the work itself. The letter completes the relation between modernism, savagery, and light that has marked the effect of a 'new country'. 'From the time of the great colourists there had gradually developed a subtle seeing into the play of colour and light and shade in flesh; Manet revolted against that, and painted flesh as the common man sees it in a searchlight of day, crudely and strongly [. . .] and he infused everything with an intense vulgarity.'[100]

The relationship between primitivism and modernism is, then, already established,[101] both discursively and as a problem of *value*. In this context, it is not surprising that Wyndham Lewis, going South into 'primitive' Brittany (as Witkiewicz had done, in preparation for his first visit to Malinowski in London in 1911, when he went to study with the Polish artist Slewinski, a pupil of Gauguin, in Pont-Aven), should find himself becoming modern. He describes, in retrospect, how the sunlight and the clarity, the 'wild and simple country', of Brittany made possible the objectification of the Breton communities into 'little monuments of logic'.[102] The functional communities of 'Inferior Religions', the religious fascinations that structure his stories, are also the presentation of 'sun-drunk insects'. Martine Segalen notes that:

> We must beware of judging the people of Bigouden [South West Brittany] as the travellers of the late eighteenth century and early nineteenth century were so ready to do. [They] related the same old diagnoses and the same old vision of the stick-in-the mud peasant, incapable of any kind of innovation and more interested in dancing and drinking than in working. The theme of the peasant as blinkered, whether by idleness [. . .] or by ignorance and poverty [. . .] is one that recurs over and over again.
>
> But surely what we are dealing with here is a different kind of economic logic, one wholly alien to observers who were imprisoned in pre-capitalist, capitalist, productivist, or modernist, straitjackets?[103]

Clearly Lewis is performing exactly this projection: he imagines participants in the object culture as blinkered; as identical with their sociological objectification. 'Moran, Bestre, and Brobdingnag *are* essays in a new human mathematics. But they *are* each simple shapes, little monuments of logic' (emphases mine).[104] The names of characters and the names of his stories are conflated; both become 'essays', both formulations and experimental monuments. But Lewis too is held in this environmental determination, where culture and nature and representation become one. 'Mine was now a drowsy sun-baked ferment.'[105] The light of Brittany, according to Lewis, led to a shock of cultural estrangement that initiated a break with the academic artistic practices he had learned at the Slade and the pastiche Shakespearean sonnets he had written, and originated his first real writings. 'It was the sun, a Breton instead of a British, that brought forth my first short story – *The Ankou* I believe it was: the Death-god of Plouilliou'.[106]

The story does produce the stereotyping that Segalen warns of: it is a perfect example of modernist primitivism. But from the act of stereotyping, which produces a logic within which the modernist is also represented, Lewis produces an account of the economy of art which owes a great deal to the economic complexies that Segalen suggest 'primitivism' ignores. The set of cultural and geographical relations concentrated within the scene of modernist primitivism, and the range of powerful desires that follow the articulations of these relations, become the basis for a reflection on the economics of modernist cultural production. This writing is set to fulfill the blocked promise of Malinowski's *Diary*.

The story describes the powerfully disturbing effects which reading Breton folk tales has on the integrity of the narrator's person. The Ankou, the blind death god, about whom the narrator has been reading in a guide book, appears.

> Where he had come was compact with an emotional medium emitted by me. In reality it was a private scene, so that this overweening intruder might have been marching through my mind with his taut convulsive step, club in hand, rather than merely traversing the eating room of a hotel, after a privileged visit to the kitchen. Certainly at that moment my mind was lying open so much, or was so much exteriorized, that almost literally, as far as I was concerned, it was inside, not out, that this image forced its way. Hence, perhaps, the strange effect.

But such dislocation is unable to take the narrator fully into the superstitious field of the myth. He attempts to be affected: 'I said to myself that, as it was noon, that should give me twelve months more to live. I brushed aside the suggestion that day was not night, that I was not a Breton peasant, and that the beggar was probably not Death. I tried to shudder.' But it is not possible. 'I had not shuddered. His attendant, a sad-faced child, rattled a lead mug under my nose. I put two sous in it. I had no doubt averted the omen, I reflected, with the bribe.'[107]

Superstition, and the powerful congruence of a story with its culture, give way to distance, and fiction, with the compensatory exchange of a couple of coins. Ludo is not the death god, but everywhere people still feel obliged to propitiate him. They have to hurry to pay him, or he moves on. They protest: 'The people around here spoil him, according to my idea. He's only a beggar. It's true he's blind. [. . .] He's not the only blind beggar in the world.' But when Ludo approaches, the speaker 'pulled out a few sous from his pocket, and said: "Faut bien! Needs must!" and laughed a little sheepishly'.[108] He is the centre of a pattern of behaviour – an 'Inferior Religion' in Lewis's terms – which is not the one the narrator imagines, but which operates with the same reluctant and 'sheepish' necessity on the Breton community, structuring it not by conscious belief, but at the level of incorporated practice.

The narrator explores this structure, and meets Ludo again. 'Although I was now familiar with Ludo, when I looked at his staring mask I still experienced a faint reflection of my first impression, when he was the death-god. That impression had been a strong one, and it was associated with superstition. So he was still a feeble death-god.' But this recognition comes just as the structuring centre of the story shifts. Asking, carelessly, whether 'Perhaps you've met the Ankou', he watches as Ludo begins to experience pains. 'I had the impression, as I glanced towards him to enquire, that his face expressed fear.'[109]

'Perhaps', the narrator wonders, 'I had put myself in the position of the Ankou, even – unseen as I was, a foreigner and, so, ultimately dangerous – by mentioning the Ankou, with which he was evidently familiar. He may even have retreated into his cave, because he was afraid of me'. He is implicated in the story now, held in a tradition of a culture which is not his. Properly, this authorises the tale, makes the narrator the fictional *creator* through his ability to produce the analytical, abstracted social dynamic which the plot both represents and serves. The author becomes, all unawares and foreign, the operator of the cultural necessity which structures that community. Rationalisation will not work. 'Later that summer the fisherman I had been with at the Pardon told me that Ludo was dead.'[110]

Keith Spence has argued that the myth of the Ankou is the sort of story a community tells itself to explain or enact the arbitrary nature of death, including cultural death, or disenchantment. Spence retells one story which 'concerns the blacksmith at Ploumilliau, who mended the Ankou's scythe when he should have been at Midnight Mass, and died the next morning for his pains. Indeed you are as likely to die if you do the Ankou a good turn as you are if you cross him in some way.'[111] These legends, like most stories of prophecy, express a structural relation to the inevitability of death, and how that structure supervenes over the contingent or the plausible world of practical judgments. This is one of the features of contemporary art, a feature as driven by superstition as is any inferior religion, as Lewis expresses it in *Blast*. 'In a painting certain forms MUST be SO; in the same meticulous, profound manner that your pen or a book must lie on the table at a certain angle, your clothes at night be arranged in a set personal symetry [*sic*], certain birds be avoided, a set of railings tapped with your hand as you pass, without missing one.'[112]

The dying Breton tradition, within which the narrator finds himself as he becomes Lewis, the modernist author of another story of the Ankou, is a resistant one. The first of the books about the 'last' Bretons was published in the first half of the nineteenth century.[113] 'Brittany' had not appeared on the French maps since the revolution. France's centralised education system, acting particularly against the Breton language, was as direct and pervasive as the forces of market expressed in the spread of empires. La Braz's collections of folk-tales express the anarchic and necessary fates which attempt to subject Brittany, but which render it instead resistant, alienated, aesthetic in the powerful way that the Kula hinted at when it became an objectified novelty working against Malinowski's ambitious trajectory. Spence quotes one of the tales of the lost city of Ys, which marks a fatalism (all stories of the lost city fail to lead to its recovery) which is still resistant:

> Two young men from Buguélès used to go every night to cut seaweed at Gueltraz, which is against the law, as everyone knows. They were busy about their task when an old woman, bent under a load of firewood, approached them. 'My lads,' she said, appealing to them, 'please could you carry this load to my house? It's not far, and you'd be doing a great favour to a poor old woman.' 'Too bad,' said one of them, 'we've better things to do.' 'And,' said the other young man, 'you might report us to the customs men.' 'Curse you!' the old woman shouted. 'If you had answered yes, you would have saved the city of Ys.' And with these words she disappeared.[114]

This story is part of a 'colonial traditionalism', to return to Bourdieu's terms.[115] While it describes the inevitable overwhelming of Breton culture, in the act of description it performs and maintains that doomed culture; the lost city of Ys is another powerful instance of the 'nowhere' of Jarry's Poland. Lewis's emerging modern authorship is lodged within this logic.

Now, it is clear that to speak of Lewis as a Breton separatist is not quite right. However, he is, briefly, mistaken for a Pole. 'On first arriving, I was taken for a "Pole," and the landlady received my first payment with a smile that I did not at the time understand. I think she was preparing to make a great favourite of me.'[116] This definition is 'functional': the term refers to anyone, usually Russian or Polish, who has left home to come to Brittany. Lewis, who enjoys this sort of strange generalisation, gives us further information; indeed the whole essay purports to describe the mode of being of this group, to convince us that they do form a viable grouping, however unlikely they may sound.

> A young Polish or Russian student, come to the end of his resources, knows two or three alternatives. One is to hang himself – a course generally adopted. But those who have no ties [. . .] take a ticket to Brest. They do this dreamily enough, and of late years almost instinctively. Once arrived there, they make the best of their way to some one of the many *pensions* that are to be found on the Breton coast.

The address had been given to them perhaps by some 'Pole' who had strayed back to his own country prior to his own decease or to hasten somebody else's.

They pay two or three months' board and lodging, until the ten pounds is finished, and then, with a simple dignity all their own, stop paying. The hosts take this quite as a matter of course. They henceforth become the regular, unobtrusive, respected inhabitants of the house.[117]

The migration is often political, the 'auriole of a political crime' legitimating the Pole's status,[118] and this formal 'political' character is associated with the status of the Pole as 'artist', whether or not he should actually create. 'A good many "Poles" are painters – at least until the ten pounds is spent, and they can no longer get colours.' The definition, it is claimed, is not Lewis's, but is performed by the Breton peasant community. '"Polonais" or "Pole," means to a Breton peasant the member of no particular nation, but merely the kind of being leading the life that I am here introducing cursorily to the reader.'[119] And so the logic by which Lewis can become a 'Pole' involves his finding himself positioned within a process at once superstitious, political, and economic; that process is both created and inhabited by his authorship, is at once material and fictional.

Gauguin, for Lewis, is the prototypical Pole. The discovery of Gauguin is 'no small matter in the establishing of the "Pole." Gauguin might almost have claimed to be the founder of this charming and whimsical order.'[120] The position of 'Pole' becomes possible because of the example of Gauguin, at the intersection of two cultures and economies, that of 'primitive' Brittany within modern France, and that of the contemporary art market.[121] Robert Goldwater notes that each of Gauguin's moves, from Paris to Rouen, from Pont-Aven to Le Pouldu, from Panama to Martinique, from Tahiti to Dominique in the Marquesas, is a voyage deeper into 'the primitive'. But it is also a move 'always from a place where it costs little to live, to another where it costs even less'. Gauguin's optimistic belief is always that 'to live like the natives costs nothing'.[122]

Gauguin's is a myth of primitivist abundance, just the sort of generalisation that Malinowski was at pains to correct. Lewis's cultural account of Gauguin, however, is not about an arcadian plenitude. It does imagine how the artist can live in society on nothing, but it explains this in terms of a strangely figured debt; a debt that inheres not in the 'pure value' of art, for which society necessarily owes the artist something, but in a complex of historical misunderstandings.[123] 'The "Pole's" own explanation of the astonishing position in which he finds himself, if by chance he realises the abnormality of it, is that they are afraid to let him go for fear of losing their money'.[124] This debt is seen, in Lewis's strange account, to be based in a Breton myth constructed to account for their contact with the modern-art market, when men from Paris came to offer mysteriously enormous sums of money for Gauguin's pictures.

> A good many 'Poles' are painters – at least until the ten pounds is spent, and they can no longer get colours. The Bretons have never yet quite got over the shock Monsieur Vollard and others gave them in coming down from Paris *en coup de vent* and offering them a thousand francs – without a word of warning or a preliminary low offer to *ménager* their nerves – for Gauguin's sketches that these hosts of his had confiscated in lieu of rent. The sight of a constant stream of breathless gentlemen, with the air of private detectives, but with the restless and disquieting eyes of the fanatic, often hustling and tripping each other up, and scrambling and bidding hoarsely for these neglected pictures, moved deeply their imaginations. These enthusiasts indeed defeated their own ends. For months they could induce no one to part with the veriest scrap of paper. The more they offered, the more consternated and suspicious the peasants became. After the visit of one of these gentlemen the peasant would go into the church and pray. After that, feeling stronger, he would call a family council, get drunk, and wake up more bewildered and terrified than ever. I think that many Gauguins must have been destroyed by them, in the belief that there was something uncanny, devilish and idolatrous about them, – they determining that the anxious connoisseurs suing for these strange images were worshippers of some inform divinity.
>
> However, many of them did at last part with these pictures, receiving very considerable sums. The money once in their pockets they forgot all about Gauguin. This new *fact* engrossed them profoundly and exclusively for a time – they pondering over it, and turning it about in their minds in every direction. At last, with their saving fatalism, they accepted it all. These matters have been no small factor in the establishing of the 'Pole.' Gauguin might almost have claimed to be the founder of their charming and whimsical order.[125]

The 'Pole' is able to live in Brittany not because of any 'natural' condition, but through a confusion of values arising from the intersection of cultures. The value of concentrating on Lewis is discovered in this account. What Lewis hopes for is not the profit that Malinowski envisions, nor a simple market success in Britain. Rather, he hopes for a career within the clash of values, the futilities and anarchies squeezed out of the modernist public sphere in Eliot's restitution of the 'world' as an organic totality.

Anthropology and modernist primitivism set out in search of an enchanted world in which we could have been at home, in which art and culture and life would have been the same thing. Malinowski and Eliot attempt to construct the worlds of knowing, the institutions of anthropology and modernism, as monuments to this lost possibility, pure and whole and entirely beyond history. That history, modern history, as my previous chapter argued, is peopled with adolescents rather than with noble savages; to live in modern history is to be constantly unsettled by an adolescent within. Modern history, we can now add, happens in Poland; or rather, there is no modern history which does not recognise that Poland, or the Trobriand Islands, or Algeria, or Brittany, are central to the world, along with the economic, political, and historical forces which are felt most clearly in our relations to these places. The modernism which Lewis feels coming into existence in Brittany involves finding himself negotiating the complex network of exchanges and misunderstandings through which Brittany and Poland persist. This modernism is entangled with the desire for a transcendence of history, with a desire to be at home in the world. But the aim of modernism, as this chapter has conceived of it, is not to reach that home, and to establish and save culture, but rather to *persist* in relation to the stubborn complexities of the world.

4
Dogs: Small Domestic Forms

Who is the third, who always walks beside you?
T. S. Eliot, *The Waste Land*

I am Caesar. The King is My Master.
Where's Master, by Caesar, the King's Dog

The previous chapter found a missed prospect in the space of 'Polish Action', an awkward articulation of market possibilities with the incoherent stories of geo-politics. This prospect is of a particularly difficult way to live; there is a whiff of pathology in the disenchanted refusal of ambition and heuristic clarity sketched there, without even the bright blind energies of the figure of the adolescent to spark it with some kind of young hope. There is not very much *will* involved in the modernism discovered stubborn and persistent here. The present chapter will describe a contrasting tendency in modernism and in its relation to territories. It will register the will to form that works against the dissolving energies negotiated by the modernism of my previous chapter. If modernism as just described negotiates the realities of the world, it is also ranged against those realities. The present chapter will look at the movement of separation from the world, for which the abstract artwork is the emblem. The abstract artwork is *quarantined* against the world; my argument will explore the literal scope and the metaphorical resonances of this figure of quarantine. The desire to protect the will and the artwork from the world, a desire that is fundamental to modernist abstraction, is hedged by anxieties. I intend here to construct a social history of this quarantined will to form, and of its attendant anxieties. I will begin with Edwardian dog-breeders. The proximity of their language to that of British modernists on the subject of abstraction establishes the dog for this chapter as something between an analogy for, and an instance of, the abstracting will. I will continue with a wider account of the insularity which is a condition of both British dog-breeding and British modernism. The island is imagined as a space protected against flows of capital and of undifferentiation; but here I will suggest that its insularity is as much an effect of as a ground for the abstracting will. Turning to an apparently underdetermined alliance between the women's suffrage movement and organizations for the defence of dogs, I will consider the reflection of this international vision of quarantine in the domestic British setting. The menace of rabies, against which quarantine is a defence, is easily compounded with other menaces, including that of female sexuality. The disproportionate anxieties that gather around rabies and venereal disease offer one conduit through which the forces operative in the women's movement can enter the space of the abstract artwork. But the nature of the relays between the domains which the modernist abstract artwork draws on also makes the political potential that appears here hard to sustain. The forces of feminism, anti-capitalism, and the promise of autonomous abstract art all appear to coalesce here, but only if the abstracting will accepts to conceive of itself as a rabid dog.

The tendency to wry faces

Some British dog-breeders were anxious at the beginning of this century, and their anxiety is registered as a twinge over the form of the bulldog. It is still a popular breed, perhaps more popular than ever. It is, after all, 'so essentially *the* national breed.'[1] But the Kennel Club, the British organisation for dog lovers and dog breeders, is gently worried. The contemporary bulldog is tending 'to go high on the leg, with deficiency of brisket, and an inclination to coarseness'. Some problems seem to have been held in check: the 'great outcry against button ears' has died down, 'for nowadays one sees comparatively few dogs with bad ear carriage'. But then there is the terrible – terrible because potentially so easily corrected – 'tendency to wry faces'.[2]

The national breed is inclining to expressive forms which trouble this observer. This is part of the problem of selective breeding very generally. The willed creation of form, separate from the idealised but implacable regulations of nature, is an anxious mode. *The Kennel* accepts that the typologies of form and breed have been freed from nature's syntax:

Nature is concerned with the survival of the fittest; and her fittest is not necessarily the best from man's point of view, but is rather that possessing to the greatest degree the ability to thrive and increase under natural conditions. The qualities demanded by the struggle for existence in wild life were totally different from those now sought by breeders. It was of vastly more importance, for instance, that the undomesticated dam should be able to protect her young and hunt food for them and herself, than that she should have heavy bone or abundant wrinkle.[3]

Dogs are perceived to have shifted from qualities 'demanded' to qualities 'sought'; from the embedded instrumentality of 'fitness' towards the categorical appeal of the 'best'. Expressing the freed will-to-form of the dog-breeder, the idea of type has been severed from all mundane relations. We can hear the language of description prised apart from function, and even from mimesis. 'Wrinkle' no longer indicates in the first instance a general or recognisable 'wrinkliness', but rather the type-defining corrugation of the ideal specimen. 'Heavy bone' is less a quantifiable measurement, than the nominal incantation of the initiate. This free-floating technicity rebounds easily into a nervous or a sneering irony.

Some whole breeds, it is feared – not yet the British bulldog, but who knows for how long? – have attained so finely to their type as to become, in the catch-all phrase of the period, 'degenerate'.[4] In her article 'Is the Dandie Degenerate?', Kate Spencer bemoans the effects of a recent 'craze for soundness' in the breed. Again, the problem lies in the drift of 'soundness' away from a referent in nature:

They determined to have soundness at any cost: and they got it, but at what a sacrifice! Dogs were bred from solely for the good points they possessed, and type went by the board. The foreface has increased in length, with the decline of the full hazel eye, till it seems we are going to emulate fox- and Irish terriers with their lengthening jaws and diminished skulls.[5]

The pursuit of type here has attacked the very capacity for recognition, the intimacy of relation between humans and their pets. The products of abstraction, of the will to form, look back with a new gaze. The degenerate Dandie 'has a sour and crafty look which repels one'.[6] This is what is feared for the national symbol, for the bulldog. Through a process of willed development, the form through which the nation mediates some of its ideals – of courage, tenacity, of heroic stupidity – may ossify and repel.

The process of abstraction which has the dog autonomous, form mediated only by its doggy matter, is itself partly responsible for this state of affairs. But it is compounded, and the anxiety to which it gives rise is intensified, by a circumstance very particular to Britain. Quarantine restrictions, designed to combat a possible spread of rabies into Britain from the continent, had made the breeding of dogs across British borders prohibitively expensive of time and money (quarantine fees at the turn of the century were between five and ten shillings a week).[7] Hence British types, isolated from genetic involvement with their continental cousins, had diverged widely from them, becoming intensely British. Degenerate canine abstraction is an anxious insular effect.

One contributor to *The Kennel* places anxiety about dog types within this context, marking the overdetermination of the shift from 'fittest' to 'best' with a national isolation. Here the object is the Daschund:

> *Panto rei* – everything moves. As in ancient Greece, so in modern times. That is life, the 'eternal circulation of things' is its expression, not only in the individual, but in the life of nations. Exchange what you have to give of your best intellectual possessions, your finest products of art. Exchange the professors of your universities, as America has done with the Continent before now. 'Canine sport is employed [*sic*] art' is the phrase of one of the leading German authorities connected with the dog world. Therefore to this branch of sport applies what I have said before. Exchange its products. Let the dog have his share in improving life, for he is the being standing nearest to man.[8]

The logic may not be impeccable here, but the animus is clear. The insularity of the British dog world, and British insularity more generally, are leading to relative regression, expressed in the shape of the dog and its relations with humans. 'The quarantine regulations [. . .] will always prevent Englishmen getting the standard of foreign breeds in absolute conformity with that prevailing in their native lands'; whereas, 'If you study the pedigree of an Airedale bred in Germany you will find that nearly always it contains a large proportion of imported blood, with the consequence that the standard of excellence nearly approximates to that of the English.'[9] This tendency, afflicting the supple coupling of man and his most proximate ally, may reinforce a national regression.

And the mechanism of regression is quarantine: the enforcement of the insular form of the nation.

Quarantine and the island of abstraction

The second half of this chapter will return to the specifics of British dogs; to their abstractions and their repulsions. But for the moment I want to leave them in what is for now an indeterminate relation to a discussion of painterly abstraction in Britain before the First World War. Their approach to an anxious transcendence of instrumentality and mimesis, and the concentration within their forms of both an historical genesis of their nervy autonomy (the relation between structures of quarantine and the nature of the dog) and a reflection of political anxieties about Britain's place in Europe, I want to argue, models strongly the historicity of abstraction.

Abstraction is a particularly impacted site for the work of historicisation. To recognise sufficiently the claims and ideals specific to aesthetic forms and intentions without losing sight of their physical and discursive location is still a challenge for modernist criticism. This challenge is particularly pressured around a movement like modernism, for which the autonomy of the arts is so definitionally central. For Andrew Benjamin, developing Clement Greenberg, abstraction is central to, and definitive of, the specificity of art. Abstraction performs 'the recognition and the affirmation within art's own work of there being something integral to specific artistic activities'.[10] This recognition and affirmation allows us to imagine the purified history of a specific agency. The abstract artwork, mediated only by its relation to its own medium, concentrates its separated intention. Its relation to representation need not even be imagined as one of negation, as a critical alternative to the world, for the source of its signifying power is in its own work. Because its logic is held to its proper place, the agency concentrated in abstraction can break absolutely from the syntactical inertias of the representational imagination, can breathe forth the instated possibility of independent creation.

This ideal is too valuable to sacrifice cheaply to the demands of an historicist reduction which would align the agency of the artwork with the determinations of external forces, short-circuiting its specificities and the freedoms which they cause to be imagined; or to a post-structuralist dispersal of that agency within an endless discursive indeterminacy. For Charles Altieri, the definitional break which abstraction mimes, bodying forth idealisable universals of form while resisting adamantly all received ethical forms for those universals, has methodological as well as ethical consequences. If a modernism which is arranged around the claims of abstraction is 'not a better way to read nature and history, but a better way to read against nature and history',[11] a reading of this act of reading, of this agency, had better, it seems, begin and most probably end with the will concentrated, recognised, and affirmed within the artwork.

What happens then to history? Altieri's answer to this is subtle and valuable. History, rather than being imagined as the determining condition of the aesthetic object, appears as a question of method, in the details of the dialectical relation between the situation of the historian and the predicament and challenge of the artwork. The modernist act of abstraction works within circumstances that it cannot fully grasp. It thus calls to those who come after it to complete the task which it has only begun. At the same time, the historian also operates within conditions that are not of her own making, and thus appeals to the resources of past imagination to guide and support her negotiation of the world.[12] To envision this theatre of agency as operating through the forms of abstraction is to maintain a maximum of imaginative possibility. But, as my introduction argued, there is a danger that this imaginative possibility will be straitened by the same terms – art, 'modernism', abstraction – which allow it to be engendered. The term may confirm the institutional processes that separate the engaged receiver of the gift of art from the difficulties of living.

This problematic will be focused here through a more local one: how can I speak of an abstract art happening in Britain?[13] To address this question is to challenge two different kinds of account, which have become entangled: those which place British modernism within a larger European art history (by which abstraction arrives in Britain from elsewhere); and those which situate aesthetic agency within the space of 'art'. A cartoon version of my answer is already growling away in the anxious form of the bulldog, grown autotelic and deficient of brisket; and become that way through an articulation, both historical and historiographical, of context: through the system of quarantine which isolates Britain as an island within a sea of canine exchange.

A more material version will begin, again, with Wyndham Lewis, the writer and Vorticist painter, apostrophising his situation. *Blast*, the 1914 journal of the Vorticists, stands as a manifesto for a particularly English (the Vorticists' term) version of modernist art. It defines Vorticism against Cubism and Italian Futurism, claiming a distinction on two grounds. In the first place, unlike Cubism, the Vorticists address the terms of modernity. While there is much to learn from Cubist painterly flatness, from their heavy intensification of impressionist experiment, 'However MUSICAL OR VEGETARIAN A MAN MAY BE, HIS LIFE IS NOT SPENT EXCLUSIVELY AMONGST APPLES AND MANDOLINES.'[14] The static realisation of form's independence is too easily, and too inconsequentially, won.

In contrast to Futurist work, the Vorticist relation to the forms or experiences of modernity is both active and specifically painterly. Futurism is attacked for its excessive excitement about the things of modernity: speed, modern conflict, technology. 'Cannot Marinetti, sensible and energetic man that he is, be induced to throw over this sentimental rubbish about Automobiles and Aeroplanes, and follow his friend Balla into a purer region of art? Unless he wants to become a rapidly fossilizing monument of puerility, cheap reaction and sensationalism, he had better do so.'[15] Futurism, in *Blast*'s account, loses itself to the energies with which it has become identified, and becomes a laughable parody of the world: 'The futurist statue will move: then it will live a little: but any idiot can do better than that with his good wife, round the corner. / Nature's definitely ahead of us in contrivances of that sort.'[16] The stance and distinction of Vorticism are imagined as the expression of a location, a gathering of a specifically English genius. The appeal of Vorticism is to be more stable and painterly than Futurism, and more modern than Cubism, and these twin advances are secured by their relation to their location.

Part of the mode of this self-positioning consists in 'Blasting' and 'Blessing' aspects of the contemporary world. England, having been blasted for its climate, is blessed in different terms. It is congratulated 'for its ships', for its ports ('restless machines'), for its seafarers: 'THEY exchange not one LAND for another, but one ELEMENT for ANOTHER. The MORE against the LESS ABSTRACT.' This blessed England exists as part of a composition, gaining definition through insularity: 'THIS ISLAND MUST BE CONTRASTED WITH THE BLEAK WAVES'; with 'the vast planetary abstraction of the OCEAN'. 'England', as an 'island', is itself an abstraction: an 'Industrial Island machine, pyramidal workshop, its apex at Shetland, discharging itself on the sea.'[17]

In order to become the location whose genius an abstract art will express, this England must undergo its own prior abstraction. This modernism will be powerful in so far as it is local, then, for 'Just as we believe that an art must be organic with its Time / So we insist that what is actual and vital in the South, is ineffective and unactual in the North.'[18] And, while this context has its value on the grounds of some representable characteristics, such as a tradition of seafaring and an industrial history, it is also an abstracted object. England becomes an island, usefully ignoring the problem Ireland poses to any political concentration of national identity, and happily pinching the specificities of Scotland into the diminishing tip of the pyramid, a form which appropriates the prestige, particularly high at this moment, of Egyptian forms, which are being imagined by some as the origins of all art; and by others placed in an iconic position within discussions of abstraction.[19]

This is not, then, any simple insertion of abstract art into a material context which exists prior to it. The context is organised through the abstracting vision of Vorticism: turned into a geometric, non-mimetic, machine-like productive form.[20] And this contextual abstraction in turn informs and guarantees an image of subjective agency: the 'ego' of Vorticism, and the peculiar edgy aggressive stylistics which I discussed in the context of adolescence in Chapter 2. *Blast* also identifies this stylistics, under the name of 'humour', as 'English':

> BLESS ENGLISH HUMOUR
> . . .
> BLESS this hysterical WALL built round the EGO.
> BLESS the separating, ungregarious, BRITISH GRIN[21]

The autonomy of this art movement is enclosed by a wall of style which itself derives from and expresses a national character; and that national character is secured by an insularity which is partly abstracted and partly representational. The boundary which, composed of coasts, ports, and oceans, secures the productive vision of an Industrial Island machine, also marks and encloses the abstracting will.

A similar process is at the centre of Lewis's novel of this period, *Tarr*. The central character, the British abstract painter Tarr, has some difficulty working in his new studio in Paris. The room is full of the inertial force of other inhabitings; it concentrates the forceful syntax of practical entanglement from which abstraction has to break.

> This large studio-room was worse than any desert. It had been built for something else, and would never be right.=A large square white-washed box was what he wanted to pack himself into. This was an elaborate carved chest of a former age. He would no doubt pack it eventually with consoling memories of work. He started work at once, in fact. This was his sovereign cure for new rooms.[22]

Work here, breaking 'at once' with the informing powers of environment, transforms that environment, 'cures' it, into a responsive abstraction. The dwelling becomes a machine. Contextual determinations are mastered doubly. This rebounds inwards too, as Tarr's interiority confirms the nested series of artworks, an unbroken chain in which environment, artist, and artwork are yoked to the abstracting will.

> A woman had in the middle of her a kernel, a sort of very substantial astral baby. This baby was apt to swell. She then became *all* baby. The husk he held was a painted mummy case. He was a mummy case, too. Only he contained nothing but innumerable other painted cases inside, smaller and smaller ones. The smallest was not a substantial astral baby, however, or live core, but a painting like the rest.=His kernel was a painting. That was as it should be.[23]

The lazy and brittle reliance on an idealised gender difference should sound sufficient warning here: there is something unsatisfactory about this model, stamped through from kernel to studio with the signature of achieved will. The satisfied mastery of environment and interiority by an organising aesthetic shuttles between a rebarbative and an inconsequent distinction. The studio and its abstract inhabitant are in danger of being either ignored or roped off absolutely from any active relations with the world. What is especially interesting in this context is the way in which *Tarr* dramatises these anxieties about the status of an achieved abstraction.

Writing in retrospect about the moment of *Blast*, Lewis suggests that the correspondence between artwork and environment, the Vorticist abstraction of context, was a poorly conceived intention. Here he is discussing specifically the architectural environment, but that stands, for Lewis as for many other modernists, as synecdochical for context very generally, particularly the political context:

> the pictures produced by myself, and other painters of similar aims, [. . .] were rather pictorial *spells*, as it were, cast by us, designed to attract the architectural shell that was wanting, than anything else. And, in the early stages of this movement, we undoubtedly did sacrifice ourselves as painters to this necessity to reform *de fond en comble* the world in which a picture must exist – for its existence is obviously contingent on, and conditioned by what the architect produces. In the heat of this pioneer action we were even inclined to forget *the picture* altogether in favour of the frame, if you understand

me. We were so busy thinking about the sort of linear and spatial world in which the picture would have its being and thinking about it in such a concrete way, that we sometimes took the picture a little for granted. It became merely a picture X – a positional abstraction, as it were.[24]

This is a most graphic statement of the dangers that Altieri suggests attend a reductive historicism, experienced this time from within the moment of production. The aesthetic dimension has been collapsed into wider determinations; the aesthetic object is impoverished; and with it are lost the kinds of specific contribution that painting might have made to the repertoire of ideals available to social and political imagination.

Yet this piece of journalism, written in a moment of disenchantment, is not quite right about the situation of *Blast* and its abstract island; a situation which is more than merely positional. I noted earlier that the coast operated as the locus of a distribution between abstract and representational energies: it is striking how much British abstract art from this period concentrates on coasts, ports, shipping. On one hand, the coast is the defining idea of the abstracting movement, turning the British Isles into 'England', separating the unexcited formalism of Vorticism from an insignificantly modern Cubism and an excessively historically identified Futurism, embodying willed vortextual form. On the other hand, it locates the material objects and forces which mirror both the form of Vorticist art *and* its relation to context, its modernity. When Lewis argues that 'consciousness towards the new possibilities of expression' will be 'more the legitimate property of Englishmen than of any other people in Europe', he does so on the grounds of an industrial pre-eminence; a familiarity with the forms of the industrial world. 'England' has invented this industrial modernity, and with it has abolished realist or mimetic dependence.

Machinery is the greatest Earth-medium: incidentally it sweeps away the doctrines of a narrow and pedantic Realism at one stroke.[25]

The modern activity of machinery is incidental because it merely adumbrates and locates the true creative force of abstraction; realism is 'narrow and pedantic' when it imagines a static, non-dialectical relation between representation and its objects. This same familiarity with the abstracting force of machinery has driven a geographical movement at once expansive and compacting: 'By mechanical inventiveness, too, just as Englishmen have spread themselves all over the Earth, they have brought all the hemispheres about them in their original island.' And that variety and plenitude, to complete the movements of abstraction, does not come back in the form of material objects, or even as their representation – not as 'the complication of the Jungle, dramatic tropic growths, the vastness of American trees'. Rather, the world returns as a modernity through which these objects are partially abstracted. The contents of the world stand concentrated in the coastal and industrial machineries that define the genius which has driven the expansive movements of trade: '[I]n the *forms* of machinery, factories, bridges, and harbours, we have all that, naturally, around us'.[26]

This original island, unlike Tarr's studio or the fantasised and disappointed architecture which Vorticism projected, is not reducible either to the ideal emanation of the artwork, corresponding to it and confirming it as the result of another *spell*; nor to the registering of a material or discursive context which determines Vorticist painting and thought. Rather, the island here signals an abstraction which is rhetorical, but whose rhetorical force inheres in its autonomy. For me to give this formulation substance and energy will require my moving now in two directions. First, I want to thicken my description of what abstraction is for Lewis; then, to investigate the historical conditions within which the vision of a wilfully insular industrial Britain functions.

Willhelm Worringer, the German art theorist who writes at the beginning of the century, offers the most compelling contemporary theorisation of what abstraction is for Lewis. Lewis knew his work thanks to the explanatory zeal of T. E. Hulme, and was happy to recognise a tight match between Hulme's theoretical writing, which draws heavily on Worringer, and his own practice as an artist. He suggests, slightly improbably, that:

> All the best things Hulme said about the theory of art were said about my art. [. . .] We happened, that is all, to be made for one another, as critic and 'creator'. What he said should be done, I did. Or it would be more exact to say that I did it, and he said it.[27]

Worringer describes two distinct aesthetic tendencies: the urge to empathy, which produces an art of organic forms; and the urge to abstraction, which is focused in geometric patternings. These divergent tendencies correspond to two states of the relation between cultures and their environment. In periods where this relation is experienced as one of comfort in, and mastery over, environmental forces, art feels free to roam abroad, enjoying itself in, extending itself into, the forms of the external world. For this, the urge to empathy, 'Aesthetic enjoyment is objectified self-enjoyment.'[28] The urge to abstraction, by contrast, begins in fear and 'space shyness'. It 'is the outcome of a great inner unrest inspired in man by the phenomena of the outside world'. It results in an art which *saves* objects from the space of contingency, history, and indeterminacy through a process of abstraction. This fear-filled art is characteristic of primitive peoples:

> The happiness they sought from art did not consist in the possibility of projecting themselves into the things of the outside world, of enjoying themselves in them, but in the possibility of taking the individual thing of the external world out of its arbitrariness, of eternalising it by approximation to abstract forms and, in this manner, of finding a point of tranquility and a refuge from appearances.[29]

This accords to some extent with Andrew Benjamin's argument about abstraction. It stresses the reduction of forms to flatness; it coordinates that reduction with a relation to a necessity which is wholly internal to the medium, which does not answer to the demands of the outside world. But, unlike Benjamin and the tradition on which he draws, it also offers an aetiology of autonomy. It locates the 'break' between the space of will worked out in the artwork and the conditions of existence within a story of blocked mastery over the environment.

Worringer's argument is immediately important for someone in Lewis's position. It breaks with an art history that sees a single developmental direction: the evolution of technical mastery of the materials of painting in the service of representation. This mode of thinking had characterised the valorisation of 'English' art through the nineteenth century.[30] That historical account had defined itself against, for example, Celtic art (in, for example, discussions of the Book of Kells), which it dismissed on the grounds of its geometrising abstractions (such that abstraction became a key term in the Irish Renaissance). Worringer thus provides a ground for a distinction from a *genealogical* account of Englishness; unlike the thought of Bell and Fry, his account has a combative direction, calling up the possibility of, even the pressing need for, a new art practice. Further, this direction loads abstraction with distinct and contemporary prestige. It asserts a greater spiritual depth to abstract art: its inturning agoraphobics trump everywhere the trivial arts of empathetic enjoyment. That depth is sponsored by the alignment of geometric abstraction with the increasing prestige of primitive, Byzantine, and Egyptian art.

When T. E. Hulme summarizes, applies, and transmits Worringer's work, both in his general theoretical writings on art and in his writing about the work of Lewis and his contemporaries, he stresses the profundity of artistic volition in geometrical abstract art.[31] Abstract art is profound because it instances the laws and forms of necessity, regulating and disciplining the limitations of purely human values (Lewis refers fondly to him as 'Hulme of Original Sin'). It shadows too a political critique of the democratic social organisations that foster the rule of human values.

Worringer gives Hulme the terms with which to imagine and to herald a radical change in sensibility, and a political change to consolidate that. Hulme also meditates on the mechanisms of that change, and here his work displays an unusual arrangement of interests. The urge to abstraction will appear both as the object of political and emotional clarification and as implicated in the rhetorical processes through which that clarification is to be encouraged. For Hulme, human self-consciousness is inertial and muffled by social media. The developing sensibility, which corresponds to Worringer's urge to abstraction and shyness of space, will not recognise itself, or manifest itself, in identities and agencies. Rather, this striking change in cultural processes appears embedded in the adjectives and epithets used about art, which arrive without clear motivation. 'At the present time you get this change shown in the value given to certain adjectives. Instead of epithets like graceful, beautiful, etc., you get terms like austere, mechanical, clear cut, and bare, used to express admiration.'[32] The new age is discernible through a linguistic epidemiology, rather than heralded with an eureka:

> Most of us cannot state our position, and we use adjectives which in themselves do not explain what we mean, but which, for a group for a certain time, by a kind of tacit convention become the 'porters' or 'bearers' of the complex new attitude. [. . .] which we cannot describe or analyse.[33]

Hulme's work has as its function and political mechanism to spread and energise a new vocabulary. It is remarkable primarily for the animus it invests against the terms of the organic, the fluxive, and the democratic. It has rhetorical designs, acting through the prestige and circulation of epithets to clarify and consolidate a shift in political and aesthetic sensibility.

To enter into politics and to engage with history, for Hulme, is to intervene in a struggle between the linguistic diseases which aim to infiltrate and to possess the passive human agent. But this struggle is radically asymmetrical. The new age of abstraction, an isolate agency born of space-shyness and retiring from democratic flows, where the psyche retreats to the abstract enclave of inhuman necessity, requires a quarantine of the sensibility. Anti-mimetic politics and aesthetics are imagined as bringing an end to rhetorical tangle. The agent, separated from the syntax and semantics of environment, approaches to inhuman necessity, to a condition of abstract insularity. Hulme himself provides a set of associations which may help to thicken the sets of relations between these fields – between abstraction and quarantine – in an essay on 'The Art of Political Conversion'. The essay argues for a need to innoculate against deeply-held prejudices which turn out merely to be effects of prestigious vocabulary. Hulme does this through observing

> my own change of mind on the subject of Tariff reform. I was, I suppose, the typical wobbler, for while politically inclined to be a Protectionist, yet [. . .] theory pulled me in the opposite direction. Now amid the whirlwind of that campaign, I noticed that two apparently disconnected and irrelevant things stuck in my head had a direct influence on my judgement, whilst the 'drums and tramplings' of a thousand statistics passed over me without leaving a trace. The one was a cartoon in *Punch* [. . .] The other was an argument [used] by Sir Edward Grey. 'To attempt', he said, 'to bind the Empire together by tariffs would be a dangerously artificial thing: it would violently disturb its "natural growth". It was in opposition to the constant method which has made us a successful power.' This had a powerful effect on me [. . .] for this reason: that whereas we all of us had a great many emotions and nerve-paths grouped round the idea of Empire, they were by this argument bound up with Free Trade. It seemed to bring Protection in conflict with a deeply seated and organised set of prejudices grouped around the words 'free' and 'natural'.[34]

The historical coordinates here are clear: Hulme refers to the debates between Joseph Chamberlain and liberal advocates of free trade over British economic policy between 1903 and the general election in 1906. And Hulme's relation to this debate is again significantly double. On the one hand, what this story of political conversion through the estrangement of lazy appeal to the 'free' and the 'natural' is meant to do is to argue for the necessity of a competing rhetoric, aligned here with Tariff Reform, looking for a concentration of intention through the performance of insularity. (Hulme looks enviously for that concentration towards the will distilled in the necessary unfolding of 'German unity', itself confirmed by heavy trade protection.) On the other hand, that model – the state argued for – of a willed national politics, separated from the extensive appeal of nature and freedom encoded historically in the patterns of free trade, will herald an end to rhetorical drift. Politics will subsume economics; abstraction will dominate the mimetic.

Blast's insistence that the coast be the boundary of 'England' as an abstract island may not be a trivial one, then, in relation to my question about what it means to speak about abstraction happening in Britain. Britain itself is abstracted, rhetorically, as a means of imagining the inauguration of a concentrated political will; and that abstraction itself is imagined, in its autonomy, as the end to historicisms that depend upon an undeterminable discursive movement. Abstraction loads the distribution between environmental economics and state politics; between history and agency.

It has become something of a cliché to speak of this period, the long *fin-de-siècle*, between the Boer War and the First World War, as a time of national anxiety; as a time when anxiety is focused on the form of the nation. The rise of competing industrial powers, particularly Germany and the USA (both tariff-protected against imports from Britain), the collapse of agricultural production, and the decline in manufacturing output, all signal an increasingly problematic balance of trade. Throughout this period, the balance of payments was supported by invisible exports, and by the revenue from British shipping which serviced foreign trade. Both looked likely, in the long term, to exacerbate the balance-of-trade problems. None of the projected outcomes was attractive: contemporaries envisaged enforced deflation to reduce foreign imports, with consequent unemployment in Britain, or a general migration of labour and industrial capital, leaving, in Beatrice Webb's vision, the City of London as 'an island of capital in a sea of foreign investment – the land given over to sport.'[35]

J. A. Hobson, the liberal theorist, sees this condition as implying 'the most important change in modern history.' For him, trade protection is the wrong way to manage

the growing severance between the political and economic limits of national life. Protection represents an effort to prevent industrial interests from wandering outside the political limits of the nation, to keep capital and labour employed within the political area, confining extra-national relations to commerce within the narrower limits of the term [. . .]. It represents the struggle of a deformed and belated nationalism against the growing spirit which everywhere is breaking against the old national limits.[36]

For Hobson, protection is a 'fearful' doctrine; shrinking back from the 'coming internationalism'; deformed and belated, proposing 'a process of narrow intellectual in-breeding.' This is 'space-shyness', a process of political quarantine that threatens to result in a deficiency of brisket, and wry faces on the national form.

Here the idealised agencies of abstraction and tariff reform meet: not in the burgeoning forth of a leading idea, but in the insistence on a truncated and insular autonomy. The determining forces that surround this separated agency do not exactly infect or inflect it, but they are never left behind. They register as the anxiety which attaches to autonomy, the vibrating movement of its rhetorical status; or as the set of affects into which that anxiety is transformed, including the hysterical walled-in Ego of *Blast*'s stylistics, and the single-minded bluster with which, for example, Chamberlain counters Asquith's statistics with the driven reduction of politics to abstracted will: 'I am interested in the Facts, not the Figures.' What this affect signals, in relation to the history of aesthetic autonomy, of abstraction, is less the performed separation of the abstract object from the syntaxes of politics and practical life, than a recognition of the forces that surround and motivate the struggling for ideal and for form. These forces operate within a distribution between aesthetic and environmental codes; a distribution between abstraction and representation, politics and economics, modernism and late capitalism.

The dog hates it, of course

> Our Vortex rushes out like an angry dog at your Impressionistic fuss.
>
> Wyndham Lewis[37]

Responding to the fear of flows of disease and capital, attempting to establish a will which is insulated against the uncertainties of modern international history, quarantine generates a form which cannot shake off the anxieties against which it is established. The dog and the modernist art work will not be still. In the following section of my chapter I will turn to the energies internal to British domestic history, as they become affixed in their turn to the form of the dog and the diseases and threats it is imagined to harbour. The concentration will be on the extended struggle between the National Canine Defence League and the State over the domestic dog. New Dog Regulation Legislation in the 1880s allowed the police to empound or to muzzle any dog found without its owner in an area where rabies was suspected. These extraordinary powers express in a displaced manner attitudes towards other sorts of social control. In 1900, the National Canine Defence League (NCDL) reported the case of a woman who was 'annoyed by frequent domiciliary visits from the police, who have forced themselves into the lady's bedroom at night, to see if the dog was muzzled'. The overreaction of the police (to very limited outbreaks of rabies) enacts a classic dirty joke. It is worth remembering in this connection that Freud says of the smutty joke that, 'If a man in a company of men enjoys telling or listening to smut, the original situation, which owing to social inhibitions cannot be realized, is at the same time imagined. A person who laughs at smut that he hears is laughing as though he were the spectator of an act of sexual aggression.'[38] There is a series of anti-suffrage postcards showing the silencing, control, and muzzling of woman as dog. One postcard from 1909, marked 'BEWARE OF SUFFRAGISTS', shows a woman, with a leash round her neck, having her tongue cut out with scissors.[39] In the same year, the National Canine Defence League reported 'a truly fiendish outrage upon a pet dog belonging to Mrs Johnson, of Caterham. The dog was out of the house for half an hour, returning with its tongue cut out at the roots, and had to be destroyed.'[40] The joke about woman, and the violent act against the dog, are linked casually but deeply in the social history of this period.

The second annual report of the Manchester Society for Women's Suffrage describes a case testing the definition of the word 'man', and the implications for women's representation, in the 1867 Franchise Reform Act, which gave a limited number of working-class men the vote. The register of electors accidentally included some women's names. It was questioned whether the courts had the right legally to remove these names from the register. 'One of the judges suggested that he would have the right to remove the name of a dog [. . .] from the register, and therefore, by implication, identified the political status of women with that of domestic animals.'[41] The distinction between object and person is of course muddied by the animal. Here the grounds of that distinction in terms of their different mediations by the State are called into question.

The relation between men, women, and rabies is faintly present in the iconic poem of modernism, T. S. Eliot's *The Waste Land*, a poem that keeps the dog far hence that's friend to men (suggesting that the threat comes from the domestic and familiar rather than from the distant and conventionally ferocious, from the friendly dog rather than from Webster's original 'wolf that's foe'), but fails to eradicate the dog from a poem that fears death by water – hydrophobia. That poem is haunted, throughout, by the trace of presence, a guarantee of reference, banished from the poem, but always felt there.

Who is the third, who always walks beside you?[42]

We know how this is supposed to be read, because the footnotes tell us that in this section of the poem one of the 'themes' is 'the journey to Emmaus', in which the sensation of the presence of Christ kept overtaking the disciples. And this idea is, again according to the footnotes, mixed up with ideas 'stimulated by the account of one of the Antarctic expeditions (I forget which, but I think one of Shackleton's): it was related that the party of explorers, at the extremity of their strength, had the constant delusion that there was *one more member* than could actually be counted'.[43] The notes casually encourage a mixture of the transcendental and the heroic; and this has been the dominant direction of readings of the poem from I. A. Richards onwards. This is the direction that indicates 'modernism' as a victory over the modern world, elevating the modernist object in a kind of negative transcendence.

It is hard, however, for even this poem to shake off the materials of the world. In 1919, when beginning to write *The Waste Land*, Eliot's household – himself, Vivien, and their dog – was caught up briefly in a rabies scare. Eliot writes to his mother: the letter begins with his own worries that he may catch Vivien's influenza, and then basks in the attentions he has been offered by the editor of *The Athenaeum*. Then it passes to subjects more serious:

> I have been trying the last two afternoons to buy a muzzle for our dog. We have a dog – a very small Yorkshire terrier with hair over its eyes, a waif which followed me in the street. We have had it some time. It is of very good breeding, and was beautifully trained by someone and a good companion for Vivien when she is alone during

the day. Lately there was a dog accused of rabies near London, and so all dogs must be muzzled. The shops have been besieged by frantic people wanting muzzles, all bringing their dogs. I waited in a queue for half an hour yesterday and the woman just ahead of me bought *three* – and there were no more of the size. I managed to get one today, and then had to buy a file and a pair of pincers to alter it to fit. The dog hates it, of course.[44]

The transference between the frantic muzzle-buying crowds of women and Eliot's own discomfort, picking up on the scene of a potential contagion from his sickly wife,[45] is the kind of material that Michael Levenson has put at the centre of his unusually modest and careful reading of *The Waste Land*'s politics. Levenson begins with the sense that Eliot's work is 'a poetic improvisation within a social convulsion', and develops a carefully dialectical reading of the personal politics of Eliot's poem from a sense of how, for Eliot, 'it is terrible to be alone with another person'.[46] The modernist object becomes in part a way of assuaging that terror, of creating something by which we can be less alone, and which is neither another person (particularly, for Eliot, not a woman) nor the rubbish which litters the given world. Douglas Mao has explored very beautifully the range of affects which this conception of the object arouses for modernism;[47] here I want to continue to imagine this abstracted object as a dog.

There were two major aspects in the dog movement in this period: the debates around the rabies scare of the 1890s, and the general move to liberate dogs from bondage. The 'rabies question', which debated the right of the government to muzzle or destroy dogs suspected of having rabies, lingered on throughout the Edwardian period (although rabies had been eradicated from Britain by 1902). Traces of it are there in Eliot's 1919 letter. Part of the power of the rabies question derives from its repetition of the arguments for extension and repeal of the Contagious Diseases Acts which went on throughout the 1870s and early 1880s. The medical profession, Parliament, and the movements to resist them, repeat the attitudes and language developed through the debates about the regulation of venereal diseases in their consideration of how to control rabies.

The campaign for general emancipation of dogs runs alongside the Edwardian campaigns for Women's suffrage. It acknowledges common ground with, for instance, the Women's Social and Political Union, and adopts parallel methods in prosecuting its cause. Charlotte Despard (leader of The Women's Freedom League, a breakaway group from the

WSPU), speaking to the National Canine Defence League in 1910, argued: 'I want to say to those that are here, both men and women, that [the representation of the dumb and the helpless] is the desire that is at the back of our great women's movement (cheers)'[48] Answering her, the chairman, Mr. H. Baillie Weaver, rather cryptically declared: 'the sooner you get Women's Suffrage, the sooner will you succeed in emancipating dogs from cruelty (loud and prolonged cheers).'[49] The Kennel Club was clearly distancing itself from the League as well as from the suffragette movement when it argued that 'No Government could say that we have unduly worried them with petitions, or accuse us of imitating the methods of the suffragettes.'[50] Like the suffrage movement, the League realised that the opposition position was strongest when unarticulated: it demanded public debate.

Concern for dogs, however, acts as a 'safe' cause for the displacement of anxieties about women's demands for political power. In the imagined absence of the little woman, man may have to concentrate his affections in his relationship with the little dog. The dog-liberation movement first appeared as an extension and a change of emphasis in the broader animal-liberation movement. The RSPCA (Royal Society for the Prevention of Cruelty to Animals) was set up in 1820, and concerned itself mostly with the welfare of working animals and the abolition of certain sorts of blood-sport, such as bull-baiting. Along with the temperance movement, this marks an attempt to adjust to the new domestic ideals of an industrial age. 'Blood sports clashed not only with the specific demands of factory work but, more generally, with the whole emerging domestic way of life.'[51] Dogs were almost entirely neglected by the RSPCA until the latter half of the nineteenth century, the period when the domestic pet became a widespread adjunct to the middle-class family. The League's concentration on the dog marks a shift in focus from the construction to the reproduction of a middle-class domestic ideal.

This imbrication of an imagination of the space of the family with discourses about dogs is one route for the transfer of an animated concern about gender on to the figure of the dog. The other, as I have suggested, is in the way that the rabies legislation repeats certain elements of earlier legislation, directed at women. The Contagious Diseases Acts of 1864, 1866, and 1869 were initially understood as entirely local and pragmatic pieces of legislation; or, at least, they had their rationale as acts of limited scope to deal with particular problems in particular places. The Military had become worried about the levels of venereal disease among member of the forces in southern naval towns.

In response to this concern, the acts gave the police the power to subject women suspected of being prostitutes to vaginal examination for signs of VD. The acts were widely supported in Parliament, as well as by the medical establishment and the Anglican clergy. It was only when there developed a movement calling for the extension of this legislation and regulation throughout the nation, on the model of the French Bureau des Moeurs, when a pragmatic grounding in its 'exceptional status as national defence legislation'[52] was transposed into claims of a general moral nature, that organised opposition developed. The repeal campaign, led by Josephine Butler, caused bills for the rescinding of the Acts to be introduced into Parliament every year throughout the 1870s, until a motion was passed against the compulsory examination of women in 1883, and full repeal was achieved in 1886.[53]

Part of the problem with the acts, and the probable reason for the eventual success of the repeal campaign in exposing its ideological incoherence, was that there was little attempt made to define the prostitute. William Acton, the author of *Prostitution*, and prominent in the extensionist campaign, came to believe that the category was so obvious as not to need statutory definition. The Assistant Commissioner of the Metropolitan Police proposed 'that any woman who goes to places of public resort, and is known to go with different men, although not a common prostitute, should be served with a notice to register'.[54] This position, unable to conceptualise itself, is loaded with a knowingness that attests to the hidden agenda of the acts: to control the 'unowned' sexuality of the 'common' woman and thus to enforce a structure of sexual power and an ideal of domestication which is not explicit, but which the debates raised by the Contagious Diseases Acts repeal movements bring to the surface.

The extensionist argument aimed to enforce the difference in kind between state-regulated and privately owned female sexuality. The enforcement of the distinction between prostitute and domestic woman was an attempt to disavow the relation of sympathy developing between them, since, as some feminists argued, the act of inspection *produced* the distinction, by institutionalising the prostitute. In the face of the notion that marriage, like prostitution, resembled a contract 'in which women exchanged themselves – their legal rights, their property, their bodies, and the fruits of their labour – for a wage paid in the form of material subsistence',[55] the extensionist movement felt the need to define woman as *naturally* complementary to man. Given that this 'natural pair' implicitly but knowingly conceals a particular economic relation, enforced in the interests of a particular political structure, that structure requires, for its 'natural' reproduction, the passive compliance of women.

To question these structures of sexual and domestic power required a different conception of where disease, and its opposite, health and order, were to be located. That is, the notion that prostitutes were an original reservoir of venereal disease, and that the disease passed as if directly from prostitute to pure woman, had to be replaced with a theory that dealt with the role of the male in the spread of contagious disease. The successful publicity around the use of the speculum in the painful and intrusive examination of women – the practice that Josephine Butler characterised as 'instrumental rape' – had two effects. It invoked the agency of men, in the figure of a demonised medical profession, and thus made possible a different image of the source and mechanisms of disease. Butler was able to argue that venereal diseases were 'really' spread from man to man, with woman the innocent victim of vicious male practices. It also allowed middle-class women to sympathise with prostitutes, as they imagined that, within the terms of the acts, they could be taken, violently, for prostitutes themselves. Thus the gap between 'pure' and 'fallen' woman could be bridged by an act of sympathy. This dual process, the invocation of the male's role in the transmission of disease, and then the revoking of male mediation in an act of sympathy or identification of the middle-class woman with the prostitute, was one of the founding moves of one aspect of the women's movements. It operated to short-circuit the structures of homosociality that later were defined by Eve Sedgwick, drawing on the work of Gayle Rubin.[56] It cast firmly in gender terms what is also a class issue: the acts have also been understood in relation to 'a tradition of repressive social legislation that tried to enforce a social discipline on the unrespectable poor.'[57] It produced a framework within which altered sexual practices such as psychic love, lesbianism and chastity (issues discussed in modernist feminist circles, and regularly in the columns of *The New Freewoman* or *The Egoist*) could be seen as necessarily related to a campaign for women's emancipation.[58]

At the same time, it made the relationships *between* men available for inspection. It was an easy move from recognising the agency of men in the transmission of disease to the removal of women entirely from this economy.[59] Josephine Butler recounts a case where:

> 70 men were found affected by recent venereal sores of a bad kind, not one of them having seen the face of a woman for more than a year. To such dissolute soldiers the cowardly official says, 'Inform,

inform us of the *woman* who has infected you.' The men ashamed to confess that they had infected each other point to any woman who comes first.[60]

In this phase of the women's movement, the key sites are the coastal towns of Southern England, anticipating the sites of interest in the rabies legislation, and doubling the geography of protectionists and Vorticists as they try to will their original autonomy into existence. The disease that threatens to enter there, and which is figured as animal female sexuality, is discovered, in the critique offered by the women's movement, to be already present within the institutions that are to be protected.

In the parallel debates about dogs and 'their' diseases, pointing to the first safe target, the dog who comes first, *The Lancet*, the journal of the British Medical establishment, argued that 'Wandering dogs are the chief agents in the propagation of rabies, for the reason that they are more exposed to contamination than those which are properly cared for, and also because rabid dogs, even when carefully guarded, seek to wander from home.'[61] Or, again, the *Lancet* urges, 'the whole problem [of rabies] is not a medical but a sociological one. The remedy [. . .] is that every dog without an owner, every stray dog, and every unmuzzled dog, regardless of ownership, must be taken and painlessly killed.'[62] The danger of rabies comes from unowned dogs; and rabid dogs *become* unowned. For David Syme, in *Rabies* (1903), a dog which does not respect its master is clearly suffering from rabies, and thus demented, perverse: 'every one of the [. . .] senses is grossly exaggerated and more or less perverted. [. . .] It must, for example, be a spectral delusion of simply the weirdest character which will drive a rabid dog [. . .] to spring at its master or mistress as at a fiend.'[63] The National Canine Defence League introduced several aid programmes to support a relation between master and dog which was not based in economics, an idea of ownership which was naturalised to look more like 'marriage'. When dog-registration taxes were introduced, or when the Government charged extortionate quarantine fees for the dogs of soldiers returning from the Boer war, the League stepped in to ensure that the relationship between dog and man should not be dependent on ability to pay. 'Many appeals were made to the committee [. . .] for their assistance to defray the cost of the taxes upon dogs kept by people in poor circumstances. In every case strict enquiries were made as to the circumstances and worthiness of the applicants, and when found to be deserving the tax was paid; in fact, no deserving case was refused.'[64] This policing of the concept of ownership allowed the League to shift the terminology of the wandering dog from the 'stray' to the 'turned-out dog'.

Against the National Canine Defence League's position, that every 'turned-out' dog was potentially an 'owned' dog, the government, along with the medical profession, equated the wandering dog with the rabid dog. Dog Regulation Bills allowed local authorities in areas where rabies was suspected to exist to impound any stray dog or any dog without a muzzle. In 1887, in the South of England, according to the League, 'not only was the muzzle imposed upon the slightest pretext and over an altogether absurd radius of miles, but, together with the muzzle, came wholesale and unnecessary slaughter of healthy dogs, a slaughter which last month reached its culminating point at the Brighton Dogs Home, when the ruthless massacre of 121 healthy dogs was carried out on the advice of the Board of Agriculture.'[65] The medical profession reckoned that the muzzle was a perfectly painless addition to the dog, which *realised* its nature: the dog could do everything but bite, which is not part of its function or nature as a domestic animal.[66] A dog, that is, should have no nose, and no teeth, it should have a muzzle. And if it does not display this public lack, it should *be* muzzled. This general imperative is a move, within the Dog Regulation movement, akin to the shift from pragmatic to moral justification of the Contagious Diseases Acts. It involves the enforcement of a distinction between owned and unowned dogs, and the subordination of both, to the owner and to the state. This shift interfered with the development of the sympathy or identification with the dog that informed the National Canine Defence League agitation. The *Kennel*, again in opposition to the League, argued that 'Sympathy, carried to the verge of madness, is altogether impracticable in the struggle for existence and in the face of many seen and unseen enemies.'[67] In fact this 'misguided sentiment', like the misguided sympathy with the prostitute, 'affords an example of our very national existence being threatened if our soldiers and sailors who guard our fortresses and man our fleets are stricken with disease'.[68]

Like the campaigns for the repeal of the Contagious Diseases Acts, the National Canine Defence League campaign for reform of dog regulation acts opened up the potential for altering the structures within which dogs (and some of the issues they take with them) were imagined, by offering an alternative model of the social pathology of rabies. There are two different accounts of rabies offered in competition with that of the medical profession and the State.

The first is the denial of the existence of rabies, which was not irrational, given that rabies was eradicated in 1902, long before the rabies scares ended, and given that there was no consensus about the mechanism of rabies, which led to many misdiagnoses (Tetanus and Delirium Tremens were both regularly reported as rabies cases). Further, the graphic publicity about the disease led to some cases of hysterical rabies. 'The long and variable incubation period [it has been claimed that it can take up to two years to appear] is a desperately worrying time. [Anyone bitten by a dog suspected of having rabies] feels as though a death sentence were hanging over them. No wonder that, amongst less resilient personalities, extreme anxiety may lead to symptoms of hysterical pseudo-rabies.'[69] The League was able to claim, in 1887, that 'in every instance [when the league investigated] the alleged rabies turned out to be no rabies at all'.[70]

The second argument, that rabies was to some extent spontaneously caused by the actions of restraint designed to keep it in check, was the most widespread, and most influential, because most successfully schematic. Again, the *Lancet* describes and rejects the argument. 'A number of the [medical] profession have been strongly protesting against muzzling dogs, as in their opinion it is calculated to produce rabies and to develop in rabid dogs a tendency to bite, and also [. . .] a muzzle may also cause madness, and so rabies may develop *de novo* without contact with another diseased animal.'[71] The National Canine Defence league made this case in a letter to Lord Salisbury in 1899:

> If the possible existence of rabies in the country were admitted, your memorialists submit that the muzzle, being a distinctly insanitary method, would have the tendency to increase the disease rather than to diminish it. Its cruelty stands attested not only by the common-sense of every dog owner, but also by the common consensus of medical opinion, leading veterinary surgeons and canine experts to generally affirm that it is cruel directly by restricting a dog's power of breathing, injuring its eyesight, and inflicting many serious wounds; and indirectly by compelling many dog owners, for fear of fines for non-muzzling, to keep the poor animals chained, confined, or shut up in back yards.[72]

This pathology implies that the rabid dog is produced by the very methods that it is claimed prevent rabies, against a government arguing that it is not in the nature of the wandering dog to be affected by the muzzle.[73]

To understand the intent and force of these arguments, it is necessary to understand more about the disease.[74] Because, like syphilis, the disease affects the nervous system and the brain, it produces itself as a demented sensation narrative, already so close to a horror story that it is impossible for the patient *not* to make the connection. Death is generally caused by bodily failure as a result of prolonged terror and suspense rather than by an organic mechanism within the disease; and this again brings 'real' and 'hysterical' rabies closer together: people die of hysterical rabies in exactly the same way as they die of real rabies.

The first stage, an indefinite period of time (between a few days and many months) after the bite, produces troubling reactions. The patient feels 'restlessness, depression, a feeling of tension, nightmare or inability to sleep, and a sense of foreboding'.[75] The dog with rabies, at the corresponding stage, becomes either unsociable or manic: 'the first sign to be noticed in dogs is a change in temperament. Dogs that are normally friendly tend to seek solitude and creep under furniture or beds. [...] Sudden bursts of excessive affection are commonly seen at this stage.'[76]

The second phase is more disturbing still. Tears flow without stopping. The voice changes: 'cries of alarm may be distorted by paralysing or swelling of the vocal cords which alter the voice so that shouts sound more like barks'.[77] As the human becomes a nervy, tearful, and feminised dog, so the dog's voice changes. What has been more accurately described since as a 'throaty howl',[78] tended to be read, at the height of the rabies scares, as 'expressive of the animal's excitement and agitation. The bark has not the normal, full, sonorous ring, but is rather an hysterical *falsetto* screech of excitement.'[79] The rabies victim has his private modernist phantasmagoria:

Hearing, sight, taste, and even smell itself, are intensely acute, being exaggerated to the point of pain, and but broken and falsifying media to the mind. The sudden opening or shutting of a door, a brusque tone of talk, a sip of water or beef-tea, a sudden flash of light as from the opening of a hunter's watch or from the light of a mirror, the merest sniff of ammonia; any of these trifling irritants of sensibility never fails to bring on convulsions. [...] Amidst this chaotic disturbance of sensibility there is, however, no evidence of the higher mental faculties being impaired. There is evidence only of the deranged framework of sensation. [...] one of the memorable symptoms [...] which presented itself [to one victim] was the persistent fancy that some poplars, adjoining his bed-room window, were gigantic men peering in on him! Had there been no poplars there would have been something else to have served as the same falsifying basis of horror; – a solitary boulder or two, perhaps, in a field, like a weird head and shoulders cropping up through the soil.[80]

This nervous degenerate modernist excitement, taken along with the vicious feebleness of the dog, is explicitly a feminisation, both of the dog and of the rabid victim: 'rabid animals very rarely kill people outright. This may be explained by a lack of persistence and sense of purpose in the frantic attacks by these sick animals.'[81] In fact, the disease is seen to confirm, as well as to produce, this feminisation: the rabies 'of a resolute, strong-nerved man is a very different disease from that of the timorous, effeminate, "neurotic"; for the entire nervous system of the former is a very different structure with respect to the rabies-germ from that of the latter'.[82]

And, of course, the most publicly spectacular symptom is 'hydrophobia'. Originally used as a synonym for rabies, it now describes one symptom of the disease in humans. It has been called, in a medical text that becomes infected with the literary qualities of the disease, 'the most terrible and mysterious symptom in the whole of medicine'.[83] Along with other forms of morbid sensitivity, and driven by a huge thirst, 'the patient picks up a cup to drink, but, even before the liquid has touched his lips, his arm shakes, and his body is contorted by violent jerky spasms of the diaphragm and other inspiratory muscles. The head is jerked back, the arms are thrown upwards and the spasm may affect other muscles until the whole body is arched back into an involuntary "back-bend" At the same moment the patient experiences great terror.'[84] While the destruction of some of the control mechanisms of the brain does mean that there is a material danger of liquid entering the lungs, this symptom has been remarked before this material connection with pain and danger has developed. 'Hydrophobia may be produced by the sight, sound, or mention of water, or even by the arrival of someone whom the patient suspects may be bringing water.'[85]

However, there is a problem with the objectification of the rabid agent, human or canine, as an hysterical dog-woman, the problem posed by another 'mysterious fact' about rabies. 'For reasons which are unknown rabies is up to seven times commoner in men than in women',[86] and, on closer inspection, its symptoms seem to speak, not of feminisation but of a hypostatization of aggressive masculine sexuality. 'In [some] patients there are bizarre abnormalities of function of the hypothalamus and amygdaloid nuclei producing increased libido (satyriasis, nymphomania), which drove one patient to attempt sexual intercourse thirty times in one day. Patients may also experience severe pain in the penis, unprovoked penile erections (priapism), and spontaneous ejaculation of semen, and may commit acts of indecent exposure and attempted rape.'[87] The dog, too, becomes hyper-sexed. Friendliness develops into sexual arousal. The transposition of this blatant and uncontrolled male sexuality into metaphors of hysteria and possession, which result from contact with woman as dog, seems to perform a denial of masculine sexuality as well as to protect the innocence of the relation of devotion which exists between the man and the dog as the model of the domestic. Of course, the gender of the bitten man and the biting dog may be a mystery to medicine because it has a repressed social cause: men 'wander' more than women. But perhaps also the dog that bites the man rather than the woman, in his rabid and hyper-sensitive condition, 'knows' something.

Dog knowledge, what is known about dogs and what dogs appear to know, is also knowledge about the material structures of gender. The dog, man's best friend, promises both the idealisation of, and a material compensation for the loss of, the sense that these structures are natural. The dog is the symbol of trust and of human trustworthiness, and a warm object which provides comfort to betrayed humans. In its rabid state the dog is represented as caught up in the wild relay of ideas between fields; across representations of the dog the politics of international trade are connected to those of gender. The dog is a vector of liberal crisis. The rabid dog is cousin to the adolescent delinquent described in Chapter 2, who gave occasion for an affective knowledge of the structures of history, which knowledge could not be incorporated within institutions of knowing. We might remember from that chapter that the suffrage movement and Joseph Chamberlain's protectionism were two of the areas of politics which the adolescent knows about; and that this knowledge, for Arnold Freeman, was enough to prove that the adolescent 'knows nothing' about politics, and should be excluded from the polis. In the case of the adolescent, the problem was solved by an act of definitive exclusion, through the invention of the 'juvenile delinquent'. 'Modernism', as an institutional category, I argued, performed a similar function, enclosing and defusing the cognitive threat posed by modernism's constitutional energies. The fate of dog knowledge, and of the knowledge anxiously surrounding modernist formal abstraction, will be a similar one.

Unshackled

The National Canine Defence League campaigns were not only, or even primarily, about rabies. The various other campaigns tended, however, to borrow the heat and focus of the rabies issue. The League argued that the rabies scares of the 1890s had been dreamt up by the medical profession in order to collect dogs for vivisection, just as it had been argued that the venereal disease scares had been in some measure a front for the recruitment of prostitutes. And the State action, in muzzling dogs and causing them to be chained up, as well as *producing* the rabid dog, was seen as a special case of individual cruelty. The annual report of the National Canine Defence League for 1898/9 is 'a record of unceasing heavy and important work which has grown to be, more or less, a fight and a protest, not only against official callousness to the sufferings of dogs, but also against active and aggressive cruelty to them by those who should be the official protectors of our dumb friends...'.[88] Given that cruelty to animals was seen as proof of animality, the movement is also that of an enlightenment process,[89] the liberation of oppressors from their own prejudices through the liberation of dogs from their chains (in the National Canine Defence League literature, dogs are always 'chained' up, never 'roped', 'tied', or 'leashed').

In 1906, in the regular 'Dogs in Bondage' column, part of a long campaign to 'bring [both magisterial and lay opinion] to recognise that perpetual bondage is as harmful to dogs as to human beings',[90] Ouida, the popular Victorian melodramatic novelist, realised her vocation and published 'A protest against chains', which was later issued as a National Canine Defence League leaflet.

> Throughout the country there may be heard the almost incessant wailing and moaning of chained dogs; dogs left in solitude to pine away their lives; ill-fed, unpitied, often unvisited for days altogether, left to lose their intelligence, their beauty, their health and strength, in a torture undeserved and wholly inexcusable. Is it not possible to awaken some consciousness in the owners of these martyrs that every kind of disease is created and propagated by the inaction and neglect in which these poor helpless good creatures are kept? [...] His barking and howling are so incessant that his owner never attends to it night or day.[91]

This image of a suffering hidden within, and obscured by, the practices of domesticity is powerful. As another contributor put it in 1914 '[Bondage] is an evil which does not thrust itself into the public eye, because so many of our poor dogs are hidden away in private yards, but it is undoubtedly one of the most prevalent injustices of which dogs are the victims.'[92]

When Christabel Pankhurst argued, in a text called *Unshackled*, that 'Women had greater justification for militant methods than the unemployed, because, unlike men, they were without any constitutional means of gaining their end',[93] she was arguing from within a similar shift of focus in the franchise movements, made possible by the Contagious Diseases Acts repeal campaigns. The exact identification of State power with patriarchy was a strategic claim, of course, as the conflation of a whole range of regulative mechanisms with 'cruelty' in the arguments of the National Canine Defence League was strategic.

However, this parallel can be taken only so far. The knowledge that came out of the Contagious Diseases Acts repeal campaigns became a source of power for the women's movement, while the knowledge that rabies produced was never really about dogs or disease at all. The recognition that dogs were in chains was at least partly a discursive displacement, a bad joke born of the inability to contemplate the demands of women and the shifting structures of domestic history. Leaflet 379 in the National Canine Defence League series worries: 'Those who are nearest and dearest to us, those who we trust with our happiness and our good name, may become traitors to his faith./ His DOG always remains faithful.'[94] When the League conjures up the image of cruelty: 'a man might [kick] his dog half to death because his wife hadn't got the tea ready',[95] it looks like a displacement of the more likely scenario, in which he attacks the woman. The domestic dog becomes the repository for an ideal that is under threat; which 'woman' may no longer be destined to embody. When the Government proposed destroying half of Britain's dogs during the First World War to avert possible food shortages, the League's successful campaign focused on the need of Britain's soldiers to have 'someone faithful' at home to imagine and write to – woman, presumably, no longer fulfilling that role. Richard Aldington, imagist poet and modernist entrepreneur, celebrates this moment, the dog again appearing within a circuit of phobically disavowed homosexuality: 'Friendships between soldiers during the war were a real and beautiful and unique relationship which has now entirely vanished, at least from Western Europe. Let me at once disabuse the eager-eyed Sodomites among my readers by stating emphatically once and for all that there was nothing sodomitical in these friendships.' The 'nothing sodomitical' follows the model of the love of dogs: 'Probably a man must have something to love – quite apart from the "love" of sexual desire. (Prisoners are supposed to love rats and spiders.) Soldiers, especially soldiers overseas in the last war, entirely cut off from women and friends, had perforce to love another soldier, there being no dogs available. Very few of these friendships survived the peace.'[96]

In the campaign for emancipation, then, the dog loses its ability to produce the threat of rabies, and becomes instead a guarantee of the increasingly fraught language of common humanity. The extraordinary knowledge brought forth from the alliance of the common prostitute and the un-muzzled dog gives way to unreconstructed common sense. The National Canine Defence League sees its future as institutional, imagining 'that the Society shall be, not merely a present power in the land, but an Institution for the protection of dogs so long as England remains a nation – an Institution as firmly established as Parliament itself, or the Courts of Justice'.[97] By 1914, they were comfortable enough about their relation to State power to applaud the training of the first police dogs.

By this stage, those who do not like dogs are simply and unfathomably *perverse*, rather than understood to be ideologically determined. 'The small group of interested people who are engineering the campaign had a definite purpose in view, and they combined forces with those who, *for some reasons or another*, are unhappily prevented from appreciating the true value of a dog's love and companionship.'[98] It seems as if the emancipation of dogs is a kind of rehearsal of an 'idealised' suffrage, where change in social practice leads to no change in social structures at all. The public is constantly reassured that if a dog is turned loose, nothing at all will happen. 'Give dogs their freedom. Do not make them chained prisoners. Make them your free and happy companions and friends. They will repay you with devotion and fidelity.'[99] This sort of story is repeated interminably: 'When the [unapproachably vicious] dog was loosed from its bondage it was discovered, to the apparent astonishment of his staff, that he was not in the slightest degree fierce.'[100] Scores of reports of dogs rescued from cruel masters to become the valued pets of middle-class families are presented in the League's literature.[101] The dog has become a compensation to the man for the lack of the lack he had projected into the woman. In 1913, at the high point of suffragist militancy, the League published a leaflet quoting from Maeterlinck's 'On the Death of a Little Dog':

> He loves us and reveres us as though we had drawn him out of nothing [. . .] he is our intimate and impassioned slave, whom nothing discourages, whom nothing repels, whose ardent trust and love nothing can impair. [. . .] He has loyally, religiously, irrevocably recognised man's superiority and has surrendered himself to him

body and soul, without after thought, without any intention to go back, reserving of his independence, his instinct and his character only the small part indispensable to the continuation of the life prescribed by nature.[102]

This completely negative conception of the dog guarantees male self-love. This function of the love of a man for his dog is perfectly captured in *Captain Loxley's Little Dog*, a popular Edwardian dog novel. 'The light of the signal flare fell on Bruce's face as Big Master looked straight into his eyes. There he saw wonderful things; saw devotion, saw his King, his Country, saw all a sailor lives – and will die – for.'[103] Big Master does not, of course, see in the eyes of the dog, or in his relationship to Little Bruce, any evidence of the less wonderful things that sailors die *of*.

Round to the centre himself

In her diary for September 1933, Virginia Woolf records a long and happy conversation with T. S. Eliot. They talk partly about their anxieties: Woolf's nervousness about what will happen with *Flush*, her portrait of Elizabeth Barret Browning through the eyes of her dog; Eliot's difficulties with the last stages of his disentanglement from Vivien, which involves rephrasing her insanity as hysteria (he will not, Woolf reports 'admit the excuse of insanity for her – thinks she puts it on; tries to take herself in'). Woolf is pleased with the long conversation, and with the peace of its having ended and become available both for reminiscent savouring and for the analytical work of her journal: 'I shall walk on the downs and think of Tom & my parched lips with some degree of pleasure.' She can save the pleasure through the analysis, I think, which focuses on the enlarging defensive egotism of Eliot, which had left little room for herself: 'Yes I like talking to Tom. But his wing sweeps curved & scimitar like round to the centre himself. He's settling in with some severity to being a great man.'

Eliot – 'round to the centre himself' – has been pompous about his critics:

> He said that he no longer <thought> felt quite so sure of a science of criticism. He also said that people exaggerate the intellectuality & erudition of his poetry. 'For example Ross Williamson in his book on me . . .' He said that very seriously. I couldn't quote Holtby with the same candour. Ross apparently attributed the dog, in Tom's quotation from Webster, to profound associations with the dog star. Not a

bit of it says Tom: I was having a joke about Webster. I connect all this with his bubbling up of life.[104]

It is hard not to feel a certain kind of despair here at the abounding dullnesses. This is where modernism has ended up in 1933. Literary criticism is a field in which the writer is on first-name terms with the critics, whom he tolerates. Critics dully chase symbols, 'decoding' profound meanings behind textual slightness. The poet retreats coyly from those readers who treat him too seriously: he was only having a joke, that is not what he meant at all. At the same time, the poet takes public pleasure in having earnest readers, in having a 'book on me'. All of the stress of the dog, exactly the stress with which the space of modernist will is brought into being, has gone out of modernism. When Eliot claims that 'the dog that's friend to men' is only a joke within the space of literature, something private between himself and Webster, modernism has either been realised as part of literary history, or it is over.

5
Smoke: Craving History

the effect of the war on literature seems to me mainly to have been a winnowing away of those interests which have never been very firmly rooted in our habits.

Edmund Gosse[1]

the craving for something to hold by which is outside [the self], and which cannot have grown out of the inner persuasions of men

Guy Thorne[2]

In 1926, Ernest Jones was worried about Freud's 'conversion' to faith in thought transference. He was nervous about what public knowledge of such an enthusiasm might do to the image of psychoanalysis in Britain. Freud counsels calm, giving Jones lessons in how to close the subject:

> When anyone adduces my fall into sin, just answer him calmly that my adherence to telepathy is my private affair like my Jewishness, my passion for smoking, and other things.[3]

Here Freud seems to have internalised a set of politic public limits; to have pragmatically regulated his own responsibility for the discipline of psychoanalysis. While all of psychoanalytical knowledge must authorise itself by a detour through Freud, rooting itself in Freud and his self-analysis, not everything Freud does or thinks nourishes his discipline. His sins are his alone; they are his 'private affair'.

This chapter will avoid the main topic of Freud's exchange with Jones – telepathy or thought transference – to concentrate instead on the other proprietary private affairs:[4] 'my Jewishness, my passion for smoking'. It will treat them exactly *as* Freud's private affairs: that is, as having their meaning within a place which is neither 'public' and 'historical', nor 'personal' and 'psychical' in the senses defined by psychoanalysis. Eli Zaretsky has suggestively argued that one kind of history of psychoanalysis would articulate its discourse with the discursive construction of 'personal life' under capitalism. Psychoanalysis reflects, and offers the potential to reform, a structured relation between the three terms through which capitalism reproduces: the economic, the familial, and the personal.[5] Freud's pragmatics here outline a further and distinct region of experience that will be systematically excluded from psychoanalysis in the very process of its public construction between the author and his discipline. And, in relation to Zaretsky's argument, we might at least hope that attention to the dynamics of psychic underdetermination can offer some critical leverage on the narratives which psychoanalysis and the twentieth century share.

Smoking, which led eventually to the cancer that killed him, was one of Freud's enduring passions. We might even suggest that he was more faithful to the habit than he was to any of the particular concepts or methods of psychoanalysis itself. He was never comfortable, and could rarely work, without cigars. But this passion, and the remarkable psychic efficacy of smoking, remained determinedly un-analysed, even when these worked against the discipline's demands: he suggested that 'his passion for smoking hindered him in the working out of certain psychological problems'.[6] Freud may never actually have said that 'sometimes a cigar is only a cigar', but the remark is certainly not an arbitrary one: it does not imply that other objects could replace the cigar in the sentence. There is something in the transaction with the world through smoke that needs to be protected; that is insistently removed from the grasp of psychoanalytic explanation.

After a heart attack in 1930, Freud was forced to curtail his smoking drastically. '[S]ince then' he wrote to his wife, 'I really feel like a changed person. Except that that changed person also has a great longing for the missing cigars.'[7] His condition deteriorated. From a sanatorium, he wrote dismally to Sandor Ferenczi:

> The recuperation began with the painful recognition that a cigar smoked on 25/4 would have to be the last for a long time. On 4 May I was able to travel to Berlin almost fully recovered. I am feeling fairly healthy here, but it was an act of autotomy, as the fox performs in

a snare when it bites off its own leg. I am not very happy, but feeling rather noticeably depersonalized.[8]

This metaphor of autotomy is striking: it calls for analysis without being an analytical metaphor. A process of recovery or coping is described in which something is left behind, neither restored nor reintegrated nor mourned. The remaking of the self is sadly and markedly partial. Freud is 'fairly healthy', but 'noticeably depersonalised'. There is something melancholic in the tone of this, but the object which has been lost is so clearly indicated that melancholy seems to be the wrong term. The severed limb is not an object, either, of ambivalence; it is more stolid and external than that: sometimes a cigar is only a cigar. Freud smoked again a month later.

The metaphor reappears, in a very different context, eight years later. Through 1938, Freud began to realise that his situation, as a Jew in Nazi-controlled Vienna, was becoming untenable. He attempted to reassure himself by imagining that the Catholic Church would not allow violence against the Jewish population, and that Austrians would not be as 'excessive' as Germans in their anti-Semitism. Yet gradually he had to yield before the evidence. Staying was impossible. In May, he wrote to his sister-in-law:

> They say that when the fox gets its leg caught in a trap, it bites the leg off and limps off on three legs. We shall follow its example.[9]

Again, no analytic restitution or modulation of loss is imagined. Freud will just have to manage on three legs, unbalanced, limping. We are taken to the heart of the Oedipal story here, and Freud of all people has no answer to the riddle, not when it is posed in this context, at this moment. The organic and historical forces ranged against Freud, those of cancer and central-European anti-Semitism, did not appear without warning; Freud was aware of the threatening development of both for most of his life. Why, then, should he find himself so entirely without psychoanalytic resource? What might it mean that he responds to the withdrawal of nicotine or the forced uprooting from Austria with the image of drastic and irreparable self-mutilation?

Cathy Caruth's account of the way that trauma connects the thought of psychoanalysis to its history also draws attention to the moment of Freud's leaving Austria under the pressures of gathering anti-Semitism. This moment is inscribed as an aporia – the interference between two avowedly contradictory prefaces – within the texture of *Moses and Monotheism*, the work that Freud began in Austria, discontinued when he realised that its publication would draw Nazi attention to the institutions of psychoanalysis, and then completed in Britain. 'Freud's writing', for Caruth, 'preserves history precisely within this gap in his text; and within the words of his leaving, words that [. . .] convey the impact of a history precisely as what *cannot be grasped* about leaving.'[10] What this history signals is the disruption of the single story of the subject – the story of monotheism, of the relation to the primal father, of the disciplinary completion of psychoanalysis, perhaps also the story of Freud's own 'father complex' – by a knowledge that is difficult to articulate within psychoanalysis, of the 'inscription of the Jews in a history always bound to the history of the Christians'.[11] This knowledge, this historicity, is then re-inscribed as the historicity of psychoanalysis, the way in which the future truth of the institution is written into 'the endless survival of what has not been fully understood. If psychoanalysis is to be continued in this tradition, it is paradoxically in what has not yet been fully grasped in its survival that its truest relation to its insight must be found.'[12] History is figured as the trauma-ridden history of an institution, and read deep in the gaps of discourse. The place of history is in what Caruth calls the 'ethics of memory'; in the activity of relation between the contemporary thinker and her tradition.

My chapter will shadow Caruth's work quite closely. But my interest is less in the – broadly deconstructive – historical making and unmaking of knowledge and its institutions than in the gestures and practices that bear and express historical knowledge differently. Knowledge is expressed in limping, becoming 'noticeably depersonalised', being addicted, and 'coping' with history. To begin to re-read the relations between psychoanalysis and history from within these gestures, yoking together Jewishness and smoking in a private and under-protected place, is not to suggest that either psychoanalysis or Freud is revealed as having failed, leaving Freud and his legacy open to attack from an outside of which psychoanalysis can give no account. But neither can all of this knowledge be fed back into the 'survival' of psychoanalysis as discourse and institution. Rather, an account of the way in which privacy is positioned and given a home, both contingently and historically, outside the institutionalising of psychoanalytic knowledge, may allow us to read the relations not only between psychoanalysis and its history, but also between the subject and its histories and destinies. The resolute underdetermination of the private suggests that while violent physiological and political forces may rise up against human pleasure and our identity, there are places in human life that do not need to be informed. This vision of the human is not an ethical one; it may open on to difficult territories: damage, instability, incoherence even. The difficulty, and for my argument the interest, is to read this story of damage without setting it in stone. Those objects we rely on, to help us get through history, may turn out time after time themselves to be as deadly as smoking. But this is an historical truth: even where it most unstoppably informs the shape of the psyche and our understanding of what it is to be human, it is neither human nature nor the necessary logic of the psyche. Even if there is no subject innocent of it, trauma is only historical; it is not history.

To tolerate life

'All my libido', Freud complained, beside himself with an emotion which it is hard to name, in 1914, 'is given to Austro Hungary'. There is a proper awkwardness in this phrase, in the incommensurability of its terms: a technicist word that roots emotion somewhere in reformulated biology and an artificial composite state, one given to the other. It reeks of historical contingency, and the excited Freud is positioned as the ideological subject within the scene, obscuring that contingency by investing his nature in both terms, lending them mutual life. The evident local historicity of this emotion should rub off, I think, on the more plausible formations that Freud uses in his writings around this time. When in 1915, for example, he calls nations 'the collective individuals of mankind',[13] we should hear the same contingencies sounding through the post-romantic truism. The individuals are as historical as the nations and as local and temporal as the forces that hold them together. And the nations are at war.

This is at least part of the reason why it may have become inevitable that smoking and Jewishness be left outside psychoanalysis, when psychoanalysis prides itself on, and indeed is almost defined by, its radical inclusiveness. The First World War provided a field on which psychoanalysis could prove itself as a therapeutic method; at the same time it placed psychoanalysis within a scene in which the relation between the individual and history was intensely pressured. Psychoanalysis, that is, becomes publicly powerful as a mode of comprehending, healing, and reforming the relations between personal life and historical structures at a time when those relations are unusually straitened. The (relative) public success of the institution is grounded here; at the same time, in response to historical pressures, a space outside psychoanalytical knowledge, the space of the 'private affair', is quietly defined.

This story begins with the First World War. As Freud puts it, with startling banality: 'This episode [. . .] has not been without importance for the spread of the knowledge of psychoanalysis.'[14] The experience of a huge number of cases of shell-shock made two points clear. First, it became evident that the root of the problem could not be traced to any positivistically imagined origin; that the cause of shell-shock was not neurological damage. Patients displayed the same kinds of symptoms whether or not they had been exposed to physical trauma. Second, there was no easy relation to be drawn between the inciting cause and the amplitude or type of the symptoms; the same experience would affect different individuals in radically different ways. In these conditions, many doctors were successful in relieving symptoms with some more or less Freudian techniques, from the recall and analysis of dreams, through simple conversation aimed at the recollection of lost memories both from the experience of war and from earlier periods in the patient's life, to methods discarded by clinical practice but with some relation to psychoanalysis, such as hypnotic suggestion and cathartic abreaction.[15]

These broadly psychoanalytical techniques, it should be noted, were used within a military framework, as alternatives and adjuncts to, for example, the threat of court martial and electric shock therapy.[16] They shared the same ends as these other techniques, and it was fairly widely agreed that, in many cases, therapeutic methods were more successful than other techniques in making sick people back into soldiers.[17] The other alliances which we might imagine analysis as entering into have no place in this frame: alliances with conscientious objectors, or with the deserters who, as Freud briefly and retrospectively acknowledges in *Group Psychology and the Analysis of the Ego*, react to a situation of probable death by rationally refusing the demands of discipline 'in a justifiable manner'.[18] Psychoanalysis's relative success coincides with a straitening of its field of action, and the occupation of some potentially uncomfortable positions. The institution becomes identified with the new wartime nationalisms.

The 1918 International Psychoanalytic Congress, held in Budapest just before the end of the war, was the first to attract representatives of the national governments of the Central Powers. There was talk of government support for psychoanalytical centres for the treatment of war neuroses; and the psychoanalysts responded by speaking appropriately about shell-shock. Papers from this congress were published as the inaugural volume in the institution's new series of publications.[19] Karl

Abraham, in one of the presentations, distinguished between the neurotic, who in the face of probable death produces symptoms which inhibit him from exposing himself to danger, and the healthy soldier. His example is of a soldier wounded three times by shrapnel, increasingly severely, then blown up and left unconscious for two days, but who does not become neurotic. He argued that 'the healthy person is able to accomplish a complete suppression of his narcissism: he loves according to the transference type, and so is capable of sacrificing his ego for the whole'.[20] The healthy person, that is to say, is the happily and unquestioningly potentially-dead person; and psychoanalysis, the conference claimed, is able to make more people healthy than other methods. The argument that leads to this claim aligns the rhetoric of ego analysis, for the moment at least, with the gruesome propaganda of, for example, Maurice Barrès, as well as with the military writing of Generals Foch and Joffre.

The prospect of the instrumentalisation and partial legitimation of the institution motivates, structurally at least, a lack of questioning about the interests of the patient. A kind of 'reality principle' is at work here, which overcomes the doubts and cavils about the relation of the individual to historical and social structure which are encoded within neurosis. The operation of that principle – where some of the possibilities, desires, and scruples of psychoanalysis are sacrificed to a historically plausible narrative which might ensure the survival of the institution – can be seen within certain of Freud's wartime writings.

The sacrifice is painful, as though there were some kind of transferability between the lives of soldiers and the institution. 'Thoughts for the Time on War and Death' charts the work of mourning which psychoanalysis performs in order to adjust itself to this newly imagined instrumentality. The essay opens with an acknowledgement of losses and disillusionment:

> We cannot but feel that no event has ever destroyed so much that is precious in the common possessions of humanity, confused so many of the clearest intelligences, or so thoroughly debased what is highest. Science herself has lost her passionless impartiality; her deeply embittered servants seek for weapons from her with which to contribute towards the struggle with the enemy.[21]

With this collapse of standards, and the debasement of values, other ideals are lost: the possibility of international communities, non-national citizens, scientific impartiality, faith in the state, free thinkers.

The result of these losses is disillusionment. But under the pressure of the reality principle, cathexis must be withdrawn from the lost ideals.

> There is something to be said, however, in criticism of this disappointment. Strictly speaking it is not justified, for it consists in the destruction of an illusion. We welcome illusions because they spare us unpleasurable feelings, and enable us to enjoy satisfactions instead. We must not complain, then, if now and again they come into collision with some portion of reality, and are shattered against it.[22]

Psychoanalysis accedes to the call of 'reality', which is here evidenced in the behaviour of nation-states during wartime. And that accession happens under the sign of something which looks very much like trauma: the shattering collision with an unmanageable and shocking external reality. Psychoanalysis appears here as the war-neurotic patient, to be put back together as a functioning agent, a kind of stoic soldier, within a totalitarian vision of the nation-state. It 'should not complain', but should give up illusions about the possibility of civilised behaviour in the name of this reality, and specifically civilised international behaviour. 'Thoughts for the Time' ends by extending the injunction against complaint towards a speculative imperative: 'Is it not we who should give in, who should adapt ourselves to war? [. . .] To tolerate life remains, after all, the first duty of all living beings.'[23] And life has become identified with the supervening, incontestable, and avowedly cruel and deceitful wartime national interest. Something like this process is encoded within the easy equation of individuals and nations.

This kind of resigned 'toleration', by which individual interests are subordinated to a powerful rather than an ideal national collective, was embraced by other thinkers important to our sense of the shape of modernism. Henri Bergson, whose works were widely read by British modernist writers and have since been seen as usefully explanatory of modernist goals and techniques, contributed to the discursive ground on which the shape of the war was determined. The suppression of the fact of individual death through the imagination of a hypostatised collective will finds analogies in Bergson's pre-war thought. The following passage is from *Creative Evolution* (1907), Bergson's most widely popular work:

> All the living hold together, and all yield to the same tremendous push. The animal takes its stand on the plant, man bestrides ani-

mality, and the whole of humanity, in space and in time, is one immense army galloping beside and before and behind each of us in an overwhelming charge able to bend down every resistance and clear the most formidable obstacles, perhaps even death.[24]

This analogical connection between life and the army is given concrete form in Bergson's propaganda writings, of the same moment as Freud's 'Thoughts for the Times', some of which are collected as *La Signification de la Guerre*.[25] In this pamphlet, his conversion of his own theories into propaganda is exemplary of what Freud describes: 'Science herself has lost her passionless impartiality; her deeply embittered servants seek for weapons from her with which to contribute towards the struggle with the enemy.'[26]

Bergson is aware, painfully so, of the power of his institutional position and of the emotional charge of his arguments relative to that: he is President de l'Académie des Sciences Morales et Politiques. As he puts it, ringingly: 'I did not imagine that I would come, to the most formal meeting of the year, driven by a force greater than my will, to throw down, from this position of elevation, a roar of horror and of indignation.'[27] Much of Bergson's emotion is registered in conventional propaganda, in the usual lists of German crimes: '*incendie, pillage, destruction des monuments, massacre de femmes et d'enfants, violation de toutes les lois de la guerre*'.[28] At this level, the force greater than his will is simply the force of duty to patriotism. This is also, however, a search for the *meaning* of the war; an attempt to construct in advance 'how a philosopher can speak about it'.[29] Luckily for Bergson, the responsibilities to patriotism and philosophy are not incompatible:

> It has been said that the last word in philosophy was 'understand, and don't get annoyed'. I don't know, but if I had to choose, I would far rather, in the face of crime, get annoyed, and not understand. Luckily, the choice does not have to be made. There are angers which draw strength, on the contrary, from going deeper into their object; the strength to maintain themselves or to make themselves new. Ours is that sort. We should clear up the meaning of this war: it will make us feel all the more horror for those who wage it against us. Nothing, anyway, is easier. A little history, a bit of philosophy will be enough.[30]

The pamphlet goes on to turn the terms of *Creative Evolution*, the distinction between the torporous slide into mechanism and the flexible development along the right evolutionary path, in tune with the *élan vital* – between, in the terms he uses in the pamphlet, 'la force qui s'use et celle qui ne s'use pas' – into the distinction between Germany and France. Bergson nationalises the *élan vital*, and conflates it with the force of patriotism which causes him to speak. He had seen Life, which term he hypostatises and capitalises in *Creative Evolution*, as characterised by a 'gentle slope'.[31] This slope begins to seem very much less gentle in its new role, in the force of ideological conformity which General Foch brings to bear in the collective will of the disciplined army: 'Only thus [through the notion of group psychology] can we explain why in certain solemn moments on the field of battle a whole army, without knowing why, feels itself carried forward as if it were gliding down an inclined plane.'[32]

The life which Bergson defines and which becomes an ideological force in the war is the life that Freud's essay has suggested it is the 'first duty of all living beings' to tolerate. We can imagine other possibilities, other effects of the breakdown of the illusion of a world that harmoniously responds to the subject's desires.[33] If there is an unease about 'Thoughts for the Time on War and Death', though, it is possibly less in its accommodation to this bleak and historically specific vision of extraordinary conditions, than in the way that they become normalised and generalised. Or, rather than strong argument being given for the psychic normality of the wartime nation, alternative constitutions, alternative political and geographical configurations are stylistically discredited, turned into fantasy. Anything else, including the vision of what the world used to be like before wartime, is represented as a dream landscape. I cannot find another example in Freud of the odd lyricism with which he de-realises the world before war:

> Anyone who was not by stress of circumstance confined to one spot could create for himself out of all the advantages and attractions of these civilised countries a new and wider fatherland, in which he could move about without hindrance or suspicion. In this way he enjoyed the blue sea and the grey; the beauty of snow-covered mountains and of green meadow lands; the magic of northern forests and the splendour of southern vegetation; the mood evoked by landscapes that recall great historical events, and the silence of untouched nature. This new fatherland was a museum for him, too, filled with all the treasures which the artists of civilised humanity had in the successive centuries created and left behind. As he wandered from one gallery to another in this museum, he could recognize with

impartial appreciation what varied types of perfection a mixture of blood, the course of history, and the special quality of their mother-earth had produced among his compatriots in this wider sense. Here he would find cool inflexible energy developed to the highest point; there, the graceful art of beautifying existence; elsewhere, the feeling for orderliness and law, or others among the qualities which have made mankind the lords of the earth.[34]

All political or psychic articulation of the pre-war world is compressed into the oddly absolute image of paralysed individuals, of those 'by stress of circumstance confined to one spot'. For others, there is no possibility that these varieties of mastery over and accommodation with the world could come into conflict with one another; no sense that claims ideological and material are encoded in the 'varied types of perfection' of this pre-Oedipal mother-earth and fatherland. This frictionless, harmonious, disarticulate place is created to be punctured by the weapons of instrumentality; it is utopian to the extent that it drives the argument towards the necessity of wartime subjection as a firming-up of the terms it so excessively dissipates.

The move towards reality, to taking death seriously, to wartime subjection, is aligned with a range of ideas, as 'the tendency to exclude death from our calculations in life brings in its train many other renunciations and exclusions'. Casually, death is seen as underpinning the seriousness of living: 'Life is impoverished, it loses in interest, when the highest stakes in the game of living, life itself, may not be risked. It becomes as shallow and empty as, let us say, an American flirtation, in which it is understood from the first that nothing is to happen, as contrasted with a Continental love-affair in which both partners must constantly bear its serious consequences in mind.'[35] The role of America in Freud's psycho-political topography at this moment is important. His veritable hatred for Woodrow Wilson as the president of a nation which in his view can participate in war and in European politics without risk, surfaces continually in his writings about and around the war. The only good thing to come out of America – 'the only excuse [. . .] for Columbus's misdeed' – is tobacco.[36]

The rejection of internationalism and the rejection of American flirtations are accompanied by a rejection of fiction.

It is an inevitable result of all this ['all this' is rather vaguely indicated – it includes the need to consider death as part of the richness of life and an unwillingness to countenance death as a part of the individual life] that we should seek in the world of fiction, in literature and in the theatre compensation for what has been lost in life. There we still find people who know how to die – who, indeed, even manage to kill someone else. There alone too the condition can be fulfilled which makes it possible to reconcile ourselves with death: namely, that behind all the vicissitudes of life we should still be able to preserve a life intact. [. . .] In the realm of fiction we find the plurality of lives which we need. We die with the hero with whom we have identified ourselves, yet we survive him, and are ready to die again just as safely with another hero.[37]

As in the utopian space of frictionless pre-war internationalism, fiction allows its audience to have its cake and eat it, to experience the richness of a life of risk without having to subject the organism to that risk. Once it is accepted that war can stand for reality, fiction will also have to be dismissed: 'It is evident that war is bound to sweep away this conventional treatment of death. Death will no longer be denied; we are forced to believe in it. People really die; and no longer one by one, but many, often tens of thousands, in a single day. And death is no longer a chance event. [. . .] Life has, indeed, become interesting again; it has recovered its full content.'[38]

Contemporary with the modern composition

Literature, at least in its realist mode, as a supplemental representation of life, becomes unnecessary, impossible, obscene, in relation to the newly 'interesting' life of the national subject in wartime. The stress this development causes is evident in literary production of the period across Europe,[39] evident both as a refusal of fiction and as a disciplinary regeneration. Here, for example, is Henry James, improbable propagandist, writing in the same year as Freud, about France:

It takes our great Ally, and her only, to be as vivid for concentration, for reflection, for intelligent, inspired contraction of life toward an end all but smothered in sacrifice, as she has ever been for the most splendidly wasteful diffusion and communication; and to give us a view of her nature and her mind in which, laying down almost every advantage, every art and every appeal that we have generally known her by, she takes on energies, forms of collective sincerity, silent eloquence and selected example that are fresh revelations – and so, bleeding at every pore, while at no time in all her history so completely erect, makes us feel her perhaps as never before our incalculable, immortal France.[40]

From being the site of the 'splendidly wasteful diffusion' of literary experiment, France is becoming a place of contraction and intention; is becoming eloquent in its call to national identification or myth. Identity with the nation is almost irresistible, and demands renunciation of divergent fictional aspirations. The reward is in the phallic bleeding of a communion in national sacrifice. This new sense of nationalism, sometimes known in France as the *union sacrée*, is built on a totalising of the social base, where criticism or political differences are either deferred or subordinated to the larger mystical unity of nation – what Freud and Bergson both call 'life'.[41] Politics, imagined as a debate between different interests over the future of the community, and as a debate about what the constituencies of community are, becomes unthinkable.[42] This community without difference is then consecrated as a supervening agency. To be part of this France, then, is to sacrifice the situated interests of the individual to its larger agency. As Maurice Barrès, one of the most vehement of patriotic authors during the war, put it: 'the men are admirable, that is to say, they are ready to sacrifice themselves'.[43] This vision of the admirable individual, one which repeats that of Abrahams, is finally consonant with Freud's notion of the first duty of the living being, and it is a vision incompatible with fiction.

It is not clear whether the end of fiction imagined here is the end or the apotheosis of modernism. The war did see a return to realist modes, and renewed interest in traditional forms.[44] For Edmund Gosse, writing in 1916, the advent of war produces a concentration of behaviour that leaves no space for literary experiment: 'the effect of the war on literature seems to me mainly to have been a winnowing away of those interests which have never been very firmly rooted in our habits'. With some glee he predicts that 'We may probably hear very little more about "vorticists"'.[45] But while it is true that *Blast*, the journal of the Vorticists, folded after its second, 'war' issue, that may be because there was a troubling *identity* between war and Vorticism, rather than an incompatibility. Perhaps the most pointedly situated modernist representation of the war is Margaret Anderson's 'The War', in her avant-garde journal *The Little Review*: a single blank page, footed by the parenthetical phrase '[We will probably be suppressed for this.]'[46] This might suggest that modernism has nothing to say to or about the war, that it is struck dumb. But that silence is recuperated as agency by its generic situation: it will call down social and political censorship. The journal had made a splendidly ambivalent speciality of blankness, including an almost entirely empty issue, 'published' in September 1916, in which the absence of writing was intended as a negation of the writings – not worth the paper they were printed on – which other journals published; and an absent issue, censored by the US Post Office for obscenity, in October 1917, which again became a signal instance of the value of the journal. To this variety of blanknesses might be added the October 1916 issue, which did not appear at all, presumably for financial reasons.

Gertrude Stein, the very icon of 'splendidly wasteful diffusion and communication', also argues that modernism and the war are contingently interchangeable, in a piece written eight years after the end of the war. 'Composition as Explanation' gives an account of the genesis of her own changing styles which is also an account of the conditions of possibility for experimental writing in general. She suggests that writing be defined in the double sense of 'composition'. On one hand composition is 'the thing seen by every one living in the living that they are doing, they are the composing of the composition that at the time they are living is the composition of the time in which they are living'. This is a version of 'reality' which includes the partial self-consciousness, the state which Stein describes as 'doing living', of the agents that make it up. On the other hand, 'composition' is the formal composition of the aesthetic object, which offers an account of the world which is always out of phase with the composition as it is lived. For Stein, the arts are ahead of life: they understand the formal possibilities within lived experience with a greater sense of possibility than the agents who live it.

War changes the relationship between the two kinds of composition:

And so there was the natural phenomena that was war, which had been, before war came, several generations behind the contemporary composition, because it became war and so completely needed to be contemporary became completely contemporary and so created the completed recognition of the contemporary composition. Every one but one may say every one became consciously became aware of the existence of the authenticity of the modern composition. This then the contemporary recognition, because of the authentic thing known as war having been forced to become contemporary made every one not only contemporary in act not only contemporary in thought but contemporary in self-consciousness made every one contemporary with the modern composition.[47]

War reveals to people the true condition of their actions; that condition is grasped in the 'authenticity' of the modern composition; thus the modernist aesthetic becomes the measure of their consciousness. 'Everyone but one may say everyone' becomes self-identical: everyone's place within the composition has become stable, and the composition itself has become the image of their being. The deconstructive movement shared between Stein's writing and everyone's living has ceased. Before the war, 'Everything is the same except composition and as the composition is different and always going to be different everything is not the same. Everything is not the same as the time when of the composition and the time in the composition is different. The composition is different, that is certain.' But in the war, there is a particular accord between psyche and history that will do away with this active living as difference: that accord identifies the self with something outside the self which is figured as 'the completed composition', at once the modernist artwork and martial culture.

'Doing living' ceases, life is hypostatised and tolerated, and the totalised form of the subject comes into being. Modernism and psychoanalysis have found their forms in martial culture. This is not just a momentary aberration, driven in the case of psychoanalysis by Freud's initial and perhaps surprising enthusiasm for the war. Freud's 1921 text, *Group Psychology and the Analysis of the Ego*, is governed by the same logic. The text is extremely important for one future of psychoanalysis. It formulates the central tenets of ego-psychology, offering a fully therapeutic vision of the function of psychoanalysis. In the section on 'The Church and the Army', Freud is still retrospectively intervening in the conduct of the war, and arguing that psychoanalysis might have saved the Central Powers:

> Prussian militarism, which was just as unpsychological as German science, may have had to suffer the consequences of this in the First World War. We know that the war neuroses which ravaged the German army have been recognised as being a protest of the individual against the part he was expected to play in the army; and according to the communication of Simmel (1918), the hard treatment of the men by their superiors may be considered as foremost among the motive forces of the disease. If the importance of the libido's claims on this score had been better appreciated, the

fantastic promises of the American President's Fourteen Points would probably not have been believed so easily, and the splendid instrument would not have broken in the hands of the German leaders.[48]

In the middle of a text that is both an expansion of psychoanalysis into new areas and a substantial re-formulation of the central tenets of ego-psychology, Freud is still arguing about how to hold an army together, about how to prolong a war over and against the protests of the individuals that it is killing.

The text is an intervention into a body of literature which is organised around the success of *The Psychology of the Crowd* by Gustave LeBon (1895). That literature explores the 'fact' that the behaviour of individuals in groups differs qualitatively from their normal behaviour. They become abnormally credulous, capable of acts of unusual violence and unusual heroism.[49] In *Group Psychology and the Analysis of the Ego*, Freud accepts these facts, but claims that psychoanalysis has some sort of conceptual priority over this area of social psychology:

> The contrast between individual psychology and social or group psychology,[50] which at first glance may seem to be full of significance, loses a great deal of its sharpness when it is examined more closely. It is true that individual psychology is concerned with the individual man and explores the paths by which he seeks to find satisfaction for his instinctual impulses; but only rarely and under certain exceptional conditions is individual psychology in a position to disregard the relations of this individual to others. In the individual's mental life someone else is invariably involved, as a model, as an object, as a helper, as an opponent; and so from the very first individual psychology, in this extended but entirely justifiable sense of the words, is at the same time social psychology as well.[51]

Psychoanalysis, then, is in a position to commandeer group-psychology, and provide its merely speculative endeavours with a properly scientific foundation. According to Freud, LeBon's work has fudged its analysis of the conditions of group behaviour by placing a magic word, 'suggestion' (and the related concepts of hypnosis and mental contagion), at the centre of its explanation of how groups are constituted. The individual, that is, behaves in an abnormal way because controlled from 'elsewhere'. Freud promises, by introducing the properly grounded notion of 'libido' (the inhibited action of the sexual instinct), to assimilate group behaviour to what we already know about the individual. This leads him in two directions: to including the tendency to form groups within the natural scope of Eros, the pleasure principle (binding the individual into larger organisms); and to stressing the role of the leader (which he disingenuously suggests that LeBon has largely ignored). For Freud, the group is held together as a new unity by the shared love of the individuals in the group for a leader or a leading idea. This libidinal tie gives rise to bonds of identification between the members of the crowd: they recognise that they stand in the same relation relative to the leader.

Mikkel Borch-Jacobsen places *Group Psychology and the Analysis of the Ego* at the centre of his analysis of Freudian politics.[52] He notes that Freud's 'advance' on LeBon's mass-psychology, based on the translation of the unstable and riddle-ridden terms of LeBon's work into what Freud sees as the properly scientific language of psychoanalysis, is problematic. Far from colonising and stabilising a new field, the mysteries of contagion, suggestion, and hypnosis begin to corrode the centres of psychoanalysis. The assertion of priority and authority rapidly becomes a rather desperate cover-up; a struggle over the origins and the autonomy of psychoanalysis itself. The uneasy differentiation of psychoanalysis from the magical suggestion theories of, for example, Bernheim, looks increasingly like a repudiation rather than an epistemic break, and thus threatens continually a disturbing return.

Borch-Jacobsen's argument is difficult to summarise, in that it takes the form of a careful and cumulative analysis of Freud's work. He suggests that Freud's interest in group psychology, and his concentration on the particular form of the organised group (the stable form of the institution with a single leader, the army and the crowd) functions to 'save' the notion of the 'subject' for psychoanalysis.[53] In the form of the (unanalysed) Master-subject, the God-commander-dictator, the originally complete, charismatic and narcissistic leader, Freud simply calls up the coherence of the Subject, against all evidence of its improbability. The structure of the group is a synchronic version of the culture narrative he produced in *Totem and Taboo*, where the properties of the individual are already contained in the mythical prehistoric Father-figure. This myth form, according to Borch-Jacobsen, 'states, decrees, institutes the Political (and the) Subject'.[54] That is, it carries with it an implied and necessary political model which is totalitarian. The only way to be a subject is to be entirely subjected to the Master-subject, the single leader. There is some evidence that Freud accepts this model literally; that is, it is given as the non-rigorous conditioning notion 'human nature', as well as being given within possibly heuristic analytical precepts. Freud seems to naturalise his model, for example in *Why War*, a text which claims that its rationale is to 'set out the problem of avoiding war as it appears to a psychoanalytic observer':[55]

> One instance of the innate and ineradicable inequality of men is their tendency to fall into the two classes of leaders and followers. The latter constitute the vast majority; they stand in need of an authority which will make decisions for them and to which they for the most part offer an unqualified submission.[56]

Borch-Jacobsen suggests that Freud rescues the category of the subject and the authority of psychoanalysis by instituting a 'naturalised' political model. I want to add that this saving of the subject happens in a context where psychoanalysis takes an institutionally politic relation to the traumatic revelations of war. The subject is rescued theoretically at the same moment as the war-neurotic individual is turned back into a soldier, and as psychoanalysis makes itself useful to the wartime State. Like the subject, psychoanalysis as an institution ensures its reproducible coherence through subjection to the ideal encoded in the totalitarian regimes of wartime nations. François Roustang has argued a parallel point through a reading of different materials, seeing the primal horde of *Totem and Taboo* as at least partly representing the institution, with Freud as its primal father, which is then in the position to 'think' its origins.[57]

Some theorists, beginning with Georges Bataille in 1933, have claimed that, in *Group Psychology*, Freud performed a remarkably prescient, even prophetic, analysis of the subsequent rise of totalitarianism in Germany. Borch-Jacobsen's analysis allows this prescience to be re-phrased. Freud prophesied the future only in so far as he was locked into its production; only to the extent that he subscribed in advance to a totalitarian political structure, that he wrote down, or dictated its myth.

> 'Me', 'Myself,' and 'I': all this (psychoanalysis, in short), was nothing but a great egoistic dream – that of 'Sigmund Freud,' but also 'ours,' that of the throng of parricidal listeners and readers. A subject will be born here, identifying itself with all positions, assassinating everything and playing all the roles. Without being born, then. This birth will have been merely mythical, fantasmatic, fictive, and doubtless nothing (no Father, no Narcissus, no Master) has preceded the situa-

tion of *Dichter* – that is, of actor, mime. Everything will have begun through the angle – the primordial angle – of an identification without model, an identification that is blind. And nothing, as a result, will have ever really begun.[58]

The necessity, the fatality of totalitarianism, and the myth of a completed subject which Freud couples to it, is called up directly in response to a fantasy of coherence that has no proper ground. Borch-Jacobsen uses this emptiness to propel him, in a later rewriting of the argument, 'beyond' politics, to ethics, an ethics grounded in groundlessness, in nothing, in what he calls 'death'.[59] Either there is the pointless, groundless, disastrous history that links the century across its two world wars, or there is nothing, pure aporia. Death, aporia, and 'ethics' as he reads them in and from Freud, are defined to coincide with and to confirm war and totalitarianism, however much they deconstructively undo them. Borch-Jacobsen approaches Barrès and Maurras when he imagines that the emptiness of the ideal is modelled on the unthinkable presentation of the death of the individual, and that an ethic can be designed out of this.

There is no historical passage out of this historical problem, in Borch-Jacobsen's account, and in that sense there is no counter-politics, unless it is a redemptive or a deconstructive one. There is nothing, for Borch-Jacobsen, apart from the personal, the political, and death. There is no way of knowing produced by psychoanalysis which does not lock our model of the human into the narrative of the twentieth century. The kind of substance that modernism has, and the kind of imagination necessary to conjure up that substance, have no place in this narrative. By paying attention, however, to the places which Freud calls private, to an aesthetic of underdetermination which links smoking and modernism, that imagination and that counter-politics can be articulated.

'I can heartily recommend the Gestapo to anyone'

To begin to construct this counter-politics, I want to look again at the 'Church and the Army' section of *Group Psychology*. The analysis of the libidinal structure of the army, where the psychology of the group functions to suppress the war-neurotic rationalities of the individual, is doubled by an argument about religion. It is clearly difficult to show what happens when the bonds that hold together the church break down, and when the love for Christ that produces a harmonious social identification as 'brothers in Christ' becomes disillusioned, for that would be to tell the story of modernity. In the two paragraphs he devotes to discussion of the Church, Freud does more or less this. And he tells the story of modernity by recounting the plot of a British popular novel, *When It Was Dark*, by Guy Thorne (a pseudonym for Cyril Edward Arthur Ranger Gull).[60] The novel gives, according to Freud, 'a clever and, as it seems to me, a convincing picture of [the dissolution of a religious group] and its consequences'.[61] He treats it, that is, as a reliable theoretical model, a plausible exposition of what would have happened in a situation which it is difficult to reproduce in the real world.

Freud takes the novel as transparent representation; he does not look at the novel as a material phenomenon; and *When It Was Dark* (subtitled *The Story of a Conspiracy*) did have rather an extraordinary material history. It was first published in 1903 by a modest publisher, Greening and Co., who gave it a sad second billing in their small advertisements to that season's favourite, Adair Fitzgerald's *The Love Thirst of Elaine*. *When It Was Dark* was barely reviewed on publication, and there is no evidence of any substantial early sales. But later in the year, the Bishop of London made it the subject of a sermon:

> I wonder whether any of you have read that remarkable work of fiction entitled *When It Was Dark*? It paints, in wonderful colours, what it seems to me the world would be if for six months, as in the story is supposed to be the case, owing to a gigantic fraud, the Resurrection might be supposed never to have occurred, and as you feel the darkness creeping over the world, you see how Woman in a moment loses the best friend she ever had, and crime and violence increase in every part of the world. When you see how darkness settles down upon the human spirit, regarding the Christian record as a fable, then you quit with something like adequate thanksgiving, and thank God it is light because of the awful darkness when it was dark.[62]

On the 1904 popular edition, these words finally became the book-jacket blurb that is their ambition and their adequate destiny. With this puff, it became a spectacular best-seller. Looking back over his life in a 1970 radio interview, Field-Marshal Montgomery noted that this book had been a major influence in his life, and in the lives of many others.

Freud summarises the plot usefully, giving slightly more detail than the Bishop:

The novel, which is supposed to relate to the present day, tells how a conspiracy of enemies of the person of Christ and of the Christian faith succeed in arranging for a sepulchre to be discovered in Jerusalem. In this sepulchre is an inscription, in which Joseph of Arimathaea confesses that for reasons of piety he secretly removed the body of Christ from its grave on the third day after its entombment and buried it in this spot. The resurrection of Christ and his divine nature are by this means disproved, and the result of this archaeological discovery is a convulsion in European civilisation and an extraordinary increase in all crimes and acts of violence, which only ceases when the forgers' plot has been revealed.[63]

The novel's plot demonstrates, within Freud's thesis, that the loosening of the libidinal bonds which took Christ as their focus allows previously controlled aggression to be acted upon. He educes it as evidence in support of his problematic claim that among members of a crowd, where rivalry might be expected, peaceful solidarity is preserved through a shared love for the 'leader', through unanimous placing of Christ in the position of ego-ideal.

However, in the accounts of Freud and of the Bishop, the need to preserve the theoretical or practical coherence of the church leads them to omit the central dynamic of the novel. This is an anti-Semitic novel. The plot to fool the world into momentary and disastrous disbelief is orchestrated by Constantin Schuabe, a millionaire Jewish genius, an antichrist with reptile eyes. He is introduced to the reader in the following passage:

The man was tall . . . and the heavy coat of fur he was wearing increased the impression of proportioned size, of massiveness, which was part of his personality. His hair was a very dark red, smooth and abundant. . . . His features were Semitic, but without a trace of that fullness, and sometimes coarseness, which often marks a Jew who has come to the middle period of life. The eyes, though, were cold, terribly *aware*, with something of the sinister and untroubled regard one sees in a reptile's eyes.

Most people, with the casual view, called him merely indomitable, but [. . .] now and again, two or three people would speak of him to each other without reserve, and on such occasions they generally agreed to this feeling of the sinister and malign.

Repeatedly referred to as a 'Judas', he has both arranged the forgery, by blackmailing the dissipate archaeologist, Llewellyn; and controlled its reception, through his majority shareholding in *The Daily Wire*, a thinly disguised *Times*.

> Once more commercial and political influences were at work, as they had been two thousand years before. The little group of Jewish millionaires who sat in [the office of the *Daily Wire*] had their prototypes in the time of Christ's Passion. Men of the modern world were once more enacting the awful drama of the Crucifixion.[64]

Freud has nothing to say about the anti-Semitism in the novel. He also simplifies the plot, and reduces the novel to an instantiation of his argument, by asserting that the violence and anarchy 'cease[ ] when the forgers' plot has been revealed'. When Basil Gortre, the humble curate whose faith has never wavered despite seemingly overwhelming evidence against it, reveals the source of the plot, violence is merely re-channelled, finding a sanctioned, and then a buried, outlet. First the deceived nation expresses its recovered harmony by lynching Llewellyn, the archaeologist. 'The nation was coming to take its revenge upon its betrayer. Mob law!'.[65] Then the novel's violence is expressed in representations of the defeated Schuabe.

> The beauty of Schuabe's face went out like an extinguished candle. His features grew markedly Semitic; he cringed and fawned, as his ancestors had cringed and fawned before fools in power hundreds of years back.[66]

The novel closes with a comic tableau, set several years after the rest of the plot. Two young society ladies are being shown round a lunatic asylum: the scene is presented as though this were a common practice, like going to the zoo. Schuabe – 'it' – is the prize exhibit.

> [. . .] 'Here, Mr Schuabe, some ladies have come to see you'.
> It got up with a foolish grin and began some ungainly capers.[67]

As the ladies leave, they discuss what they have seen:

> 'I liked the little man with his tongue hanging out the best', said one. 'Oh, Mabel, you've *no* sense of humour! That Schuabe creature was the funniest of *all*!'[68]

It appears here that the significant crowd, and the significant violence, the ones which the novel as a material and historical phenomenon is working to produce, in aligning the faith it propounds with this scapegoating reduction and representation of Schuabe, are not the negation of the 'organised' group, or its collapse into an anarchic release of previously bound aggression, but the means by which its restitution is imagined. Freud, Thorne, and the Bishop all claim to defend the idea or the practice of the church against a theoretical or an historical dissolution. What my reading of the novel proposes is that they produce its unity groundlessly and violently. Only modernist reading practices and the preservation of privacy can withstand that violence.

The myth of a second crucifixion is grounded not in its 'proof' or even in its insistence on the necessities of faith; neither the represented group, nor the group which the book performatively constructs in its readership, is held together by a 'shared ego ideal'. Rather, community is constructed through the enthusiastic insistence on the necessity of an act of violence directed against Jews. This is the sort of plot dynamic which René Girard has repeatedly analysed.[69] Girard makes the claim that, in the mode of representation of a persecutor or transgressor, we can read direct evidence of real violence in the past: the violence which is at the origin of the culture in which the representation circulates, and which lends it its guilty coherence. In Thorne's novel, an analysis of this kind would suggest, the coherence of the Christian culture that the story is aimed at, and within which it circulates, has been secured by an original founding violence, which is repeated in the legitimate violence directed against Schuabe; and that we can read the violence in the animus of Thorne's reductive depiction.

Reconsidering *When It Was Dark*, and Freud's predicament as a reader of the novel, struggling for theoretical authority, it is not clear that this morphogenetic account is the primary function of such myths of culture. Their performative function may be more significant. As Girard would argue, the founding murder revealed in the representation of the Jewish figure is in some sense real. Violence here is more than just represented: it has its proper existence outside the text, in the culture within which the novel circulates. But it is to be found in the future, rather than at the prehistoric origins of that culture. The unified and harmonious culture imagined to exist before and after the time 'when it was dark' is not so much already instituted, appearing disguised in the fiction in rationalisation of its guilty prehistory, as called up by the novel and charged with the scapegoating murder which will be the condition of its possibility.

Freud can only transmit the violent narrative about the future which is encoded in Thorne's novel and its reception. He cannot make it an object of analytical scrutiny, cannot read the performative twitchings of a gathering futurity; not, at any rate, from within psychoanalysis as institution and public discourse. Yet a sort of knowledge does appear in *Group Psychology and the Analysis of the Ego*. Immediately after his brief discussion of the novel, Freud adds a qualification. The peace which he has described as characterising relationships within the organised religious group may also be ensured by a violence directed outwards which supplements and overdetermines the internal bonds:

> even during the kingdom of Christ those people who do not belong to the kingdom of believers, who do not love him, and whom he does not love, stand outside this tie. Therefore a religion, even if it calls itself the religion of love, must be hard and unloving to those who do not belong to it [. . .] cruelty and intolerance towards those who do not belong to it are natural to every religion.[70]

This passage comes immediately after his brief account of Thorne's novel. The anti-Semitism which has no place within the terms in which he can read the novel finds its encrypted recognition here.[71] In a strange act of displacement, Freud seems to signal that this other sort of group violence may be directed at him.

> If another group tie takes the place of the religious one – and the socialistic tie seems to be succeeding in doing this – then there will be the same intolerance towards outsiders as in the age of the Wars or Religion; and if differences between scientific opinions could ever attain a similar significance for groups, the same result would again be repeated with this new motivation.[72]

Freud must be thinking here about psychoanalysis: he does not have a heated interest in other differences of scientific opinion. The harmony of interest between the nation and psychoanalysis in the maintenance of single coherent groups here turns against Freud; the approbation of group formation is momentarily imagined as working against psychoanalysis in the same way as it works against Jews. This significantly develops Roustang's argument in *Dire Mastery*. Roustang suggests that the psychoanalytic concept of the group (both as it externalises the psyche in social organisations and as it lives on as a structuring of the psyche) is formed in the image of the psychoanalytical institution. Here that group is briefly imagined as the object of a significant and bloody exclusion. Freud seems to be imagining that exclusion personally and institutionally, to be recognising, in a coded and displaced fashion, the message of *When It Was Dark*. Freud as an Austrian Jew and Freud as the author of psychoanalysis, in their historical contingency, are registered as potentially the scapegoat that would lend coherence to the totality, both of community and of the Subject. His fraught and 'private' critical position outside the totality is the source of his uneasy prophetic authority, his capacity to speak about an historical process into which the discipline he speaks from is intimately locked.

But this authority, this materially and historically contingent position, is private, coded, hidden. Freud speaks from outside psychoanalysis. Freud is trapped there, and the institutional and historical force of his ideas risks turning upon him: there is a danger of historical and theoretical autotomy. This threatened historical privacy provides the modality in which it may make sense to speak of psychoanalysis as a 'Jewish science'. Psychoanalysis expresses neither an essential nor a cultural Jewishness.[73] But its refusal to complete and close its construction of the psyche is partly motivated by the protection of the private; its construction of the psyche constantly refuses to become positivist, and that has something to do with the political pressures, including cultural anti-Semitism, which surround and inform the work of building relations between the ego and the world.

This modality is expressed rather neatly in an anecdote Ernest Jones relates about Freud in 1938, at the moment when Freud is contemplating the feared autotomy. After a series of increasingly pointed difficulties and worries, Freud and some of the members of his family were finally cleared to leave for Britain. After getting the *Unbedenklichkeitserklärung* (clearance as being no longer worth thinking about, harmless), he had to sign a statement that he'd been well treated, and had no reason to complain:

> When the Nazi Commissar brought it along Freud had of course no compunction in signing it, but he asked if he might be allowed to add a sentence, which was: 'I can heartily recommend the Gestapo to anyone'.[74]

This is all, in relation to its prophetic mode of 1921, that psychoanalysis can say to the rise of totalitarianism, 'heartily recommending' it, as a way of binding and controlling impulses that might otherwise result in anarchy or trauma, while reserving an ironic but unanalysed – a 'private' – distinction.[75] In one way, this is a conclusion to my argument. It claims that Freudian politics is contained within a sarcastic quietism; that it emerges as irony from within Freud's private and prophetic authority. Freud maintains here a difference between the private and the personal, between the psyche which grounds a discourse of psychoanalysis, and the historical body which accompanies that psyche; and that difference appears as an irony that evades the hold of history on his thought.

However, the story is probably apocryphal (despite appearing both in Jones's and Gay's biographies of Freud). And it depends upon a rather too brittle construction of relations between actions and history: the model of psychoanalysis constructed here, where its thought is trapped in a single position, where its therapeutic, theoretical, and institutional practices are perfectly concentric, needs to be refined. While I think that this model of psychoanalysis may be a necessary corrective to accounts which read the ideas of psychoanalysis as independent of their institutional history, psychoanalysis itself is not quite so coherent a discipline. The early 1920s was the time of *Beyond the Pleasure Principle* as well as of *Group Psychology*.

Consonant with this point, the model of reading constructed around *When It Was Dark*, where the reader is entirely controlled, hypnotised, subjected to the violent ambitions of the text, needs to be modified. While that model was constructed in an attempt to read the performative force of a particular phenomenon, an anti-Semitic best-seller, it leaves no space for divergent reading practices, no space for modernism. While both psychoanalysis and popular fiction may have been marked indelibly by the history and fantasy of totalitarianism, that history too is contingent. It had to be enacted and internalised, and thus it could be resisted by something more substantial than irony.

So while Freud's apocryphal recommendation of the Gestapo, his irony blackly isolated outside the currents of history, figures a kind of conclusion to my chapter, there is a little more to say. I will locate that 'more' within Freud's own private persistence. Freud's passion for smoking survived everything, including his better wisdom and his ambitious investment in a full self-analysis. He had to struggle to maintain his addiction: the shrunken scars, and the painful prosthesis from his first operations for cancer of the palate, together made it often physically difficult to keep on plugging in those clumsy stumps (he had at one stage to use a special tool to open his jaw wide enough to allow the introduction of a cigar). The present chapter will close with a reading of this edgy eloquent gesture; with a final sketch of the modernist constitution within modern history, in all of its disastrous and glamorous complexity.

'He was smoking when the Light of the World – the whole great world! – was flickering into darkness.'

Smoking has been celebrated recently as a mode of anti-totalitarian politics. Richard Klein's *Cigarettes are Sublime* makes extraordinary historical claims for the habit. He claims that 'There is nowhere in the world where people do not smoke if they are allowed to',[76] and suggests that this universal craving is an index of freedom. The argument expands. Noting that 'Napoleon, like Louis XIV and Hitler, was violently, personally disgusted by smoking', Klein derives a general principle:

> The relation between tyranny and the repression of the right to grow, sell, use, or smoke tobacco can be seen most clearly in the way movements of liberation, revolutions both political and cultural, have always placed those rights at the center of their political demands. The history of the struggle against tyrants has been frequently inseparable from that of struggle on behalf of the freedom to smoke.[77]

Even if it were true that movements of political and cultural revolution have in every instance placed the right to smoke 'at the centre of their political demands' – and, just for the record, as a kind of health warning: kids, it is *not* true – it does not follow that the act of smoking necessarily undoes or opposes tyranny. Klein's argument associates this force of freedom with two notions, which have been regularly related: the idea of literary textuality in its deconstructive moment, and the Freudian idea of the death drive.

> What [Freud] calls the 'death instinct,' which underlies the pleasure principle, organises the otherwise intermittent and wildly modulating discharges of the organism into repetitive, predictable patterns. By smoking a cigarette, ingesting a certain quantity of nicotine, the organism is hastening its death, is producing in itself more noxious effects than if it endured the discomfort of anxiety. But the death it is hastening is its own death; it substitutes its own path toward death for the process over which it otherwise has no control. Using cigarettes to master anxiety may be understood as preferring a certain

form of dying over an intolerable form of living. In that respect, it is a heroic activity, not nutritive or therapeutic at all. Under some circumstances, giving oneself more discomfort is preferable to passively enduring less, assuming a death of one's own choosing is more desirable than suffering a life over which one has no control. The only thing worse than war is to lose one's freedom.[78]

Klein aligns his definition of an ethic of resistance and freedom with 'death'. The mode of freedom which is entered by the smoker, in Klein's account, is the freedom of an aporetic textual unravelling of history around the solid kernel of singularity which is the death proper to the autonomous individual. I want to resist this movement towards death, the individual, ethically sponsoring death of Borch-Jacobsen and Klein.[79] While it aims to wrestle some special essential value away from the generalisations of history – producing something like irony – it thereby loses the little historical purchase which the smoker might have. It evacuates the historically positioned relative autonomy of the place of privacy. To see smoking as an heroic mode of owning your death within a history imagined as a fatal exteriority – as trauma – is to leave history excessively generalised.

If smoking does have some general form of relation to history, it is not in its instancing of heroic and ironic knowledge, to be analysed corrosively back into the big picture. Rather, it seems often just to allow people to cope. In this sense, it would be classed as what Michel de Certeau calls a 'tactic' rather than a 'strategy', having no critical relation to *structures* of power whatsoever, but embodying the capacity productively to survive power.[80] In the First World War, the most common way of resisting war neuroses was to smoke. Like psychoanalysis, this allowed individuals to carry on fighting when it was not in their best interests. Here is the reason why governments supplied cigarettes to troops, and why the US Army commandeered the entire production of Bull Durham tobacco: smoking, one psycho-pharmacological account suggests, offers a mastery of the moment, giving 'a feeling of decisive action when none is possible'.[81] But, unlike therapy, that feeling is not accompanied by the reconversion of the situated individual into a 'soldier', through the imposition of a healthy libidinal relation to the army. The mastery of the unmasterable situation is also a display of damage.

Smoking allows a person to cope with a murderous history without turning her into the subject of that history; the pain of not being able to influence her destiny is displayed by the smoker, at the same time as she survives the moment of pain. This damaged persistence appeals affectively out towards a possible private constituency, towards a world composed, not of subjects, but of underdetermined smokers.

This is why, I think, *When It Was Dark* hates the cigarette almost as much as it hates the figure of the Jew. Cigarettes are an oddly insistent textual presence in the novel, often being given a whole little paragraph to themselves. But nothing in the reading I have developed of the novel can tell us how to read their punctuating appearances. Initially, cigarette smoking seems to be just another of the fixed 'signs' that the novel manipulates. It is obvious something has gone wrong with Spence, the reporter charged with broadcasting the story of the forgery, as soon as we are shown his room: '[one] was immediately struck by [the moral as well as the material atmosphere] of the chambers, most unpleasantly so indeed. The air was stale with the pungent smell of Turkish tobacco'.[82] However, far from being a reliable indication of character, like Schuabe's features, or the heroine's hair, which is outrageously described as 'luxuriant and of a traditional "heroine" gold',[83] smoke is uncomfortably promiscuous. In the stress of the moment, everyone in the novel smokes cigarettes. Reverend Byars, 'a sure sign of disturbance with him, put down his pipe [. . .] and took a cigarette from a box on the table'.[84] Even the hero, Basil Gortre, whose faith is never for a moment rocked, at one point buys a packet of cheap cigarettes to calm his nerves. In this proliferation of cigarettes, some kind of recognition of an alienated relation to the *present* moment here and there overwhelms the novel's concentration on the future, and interrupts its performative production of a murderous unity.

When Spence, the reporter, first receives the news about the disastrous tomb, he lights a cigarette:

> As he did so he gave a sudden, sharp, unnatural chuckle. He was smoking when the Light of the World – the whole great world! – was flickering into darkness.[85]

This pause cuts through the inevitabilities of the fiction, opening up a brief unnatural moment of presence. How are we to read this pause? One kind of craving, the totalising religious faith identified with the procedures of narrative, which Gortre calls 'the craving for something to hold by which is outside [the self], and which cannot have grown out of the inner persuasions of men',[86] is momentarily replaced by a different one. The processes of reading through which the subject is locked into an historical process that binds aggressivities within the group, directing them at once together towards the coherence of Christ and closure, and outwards in anti-Semitic supplementation, gives way to a self-sufficient pause. Into this gap we can feel or project a desire that the novel and the world pause, in order to freeze and examine, in order to experience as damage, the social and ideological articulations which it has reflected or designed.

This other craving is the subject of a novel by the same author, published a year before: *The Cigarette Smoker*. There Thorne, writing as Cyril Gull, represents the threat that this pause may be sustained, that the desire to smoke might be able to persist. This novel displays the same fanaticism as *When It Was Dark*, the same plot structure, even. But here the enemy that the plot attacks is a second-order enemy, the cigarette and not the Jew. Cigarettes in the novel are a foreign habit, particularly French in this case, distinctly not English.[87] Addiction to smoking destroys the protagonist, the English painter Uther Kennedy. The novel draws upon a substantial literature on cigarette smoking, to which Gustave LeBon and Henry Ford are only two of the significant contributors, when it describes the mechanisms by which cigarettes seduce and destroy Kennedy. After offering a soothing decadent resolution to his anxieties, they take him over, until '[t]he very craving itself became its own safeguard for its existence'.[88] Then they kill: smoking cigarettes leads inevitably to monomania and then general mania, the brain shrinks and goes yellow, and then death is inevitable.

There is a strange side-effect to the process, though, in which modernism appears. Uther Kennedy's paintings change under the effects of cigarettes. From being decent but marketable English landscapes (the text even suspects that they are mediocre), they become nasty, abstract, economically pointless, 'French' paintings: the descriptions make them sound like immense *Gitanes* packets. They are, even to Kennedy's sceptical English friend, impressive:

> I shouldn't have thought you could have done it, or anyone else for the matter of that. Not that I think it's really worth doing, old fellow, you know. It's pretty, it's tricky, but is it art?[89]

With cigarettes comes a sort of painting which has 'that short lived modern notoriety', but not 'the sanity and discipline which alone can insure a public and permanent regard'.[90] Like the stories written by Blackwood's possessed humourist, which I discussed in Chapter 1, Kennedy's paintings are becoming modernist. Gull's novel offers an etiology of modernism as pathology, locked into a demonised vision of a private productivity. This elucidates the role of cigarettes in *When It Was Dark*, where the pause they offer, wildly contagious, indicates an oblique, but still historical, relation to the construction of history as totality. The cigarette, modernism, and pathology, indicate a private place of substantial pause. This is not the heroism of Klein's account, as it cannot be turned easily into a singular resistance to history. Modernism is not an accomplished revolution, in the form of the revolution of the word; rather it is an interruption of possibility, mirroring the brief and unsuccessful self-interruptions of Thorne's novel, and in the lives of smokers.

Anthony Easthope, commenting in a letter to the *Guardian* on Seamus Heaney's accession to the Nobel Laureateship, accused him of failing to be modernist:

> His poetry simply steps aside from Modernism, the great movement that transformed Western culture early this century [. . .]

Easthope, by suggesting that modernism was, has confused the kind of persistence that modernism can have. Where it does 'survive' in this triumphal mode, it does so, as Bruce Robbins, for example, has argued, as a form of distinction within a structure: as advertising, as the commodity, as 'style'.[91] Easthope suggests that the triumph of modernism would be a triumph of modernity, cleansing contingency right through to the addictions.

> A really modern culture should give up old fashioned things, however familiar and charming – horse-drawn cabs, smoking, the poetry of Seamus Heaney.[92]

Modernism, this book has argued, cannot be had in that way. It will always be accompanied by the fag-ends at least of its weak hopes, of its defeated relations with history. If we wish to invest modernism with the objectivity of an autonomous aesthetic, that wholeness and separateness will be like the autonomy that an addiction has, a 'craving' which becomes 'its own safeguard for its existence'.

Autonomy and freedom here are marked with refusal, retreat, failure, and historical relation. This is what is registered in Freud's unwillingness to allow psychoanalysis to encroach on the space of privacy, to become a tool in his struggle with the cigar. This is why, to return to the quotations with which I opened the chapter, Freud was unable to free himself of the addiction that was killing him slowly, or of the unpleasant interaction with Nazi Austria, without feeling that he had mutilated himself. In the image of autotomy, of a loss within the self which is not melancholy and which cannot be restored, there is an image of the disastrous importance of what lies *before* modernism. The damage comes from a surrounding and irresistible context; but it also signals a refusal to turn the individual into a subject of the history which will render him negligible. There may be no existing social arrangement – either in the historical past where modernism was, or in our own present – through which the private persistence in damage can be turned into a concrete social movement, but the affective possibility of constituency is urgently experienced here, its weight shared between the historical agents and the contemporary readers of modernism. In the figure of something lost through autotomy, and the gestures to which it gives rise – limping, smoking, haunting, adolescent sulking, Polish action, nervous scrutiny of our dogs – the embarrassing prospect of modernism opens before us.

Notes

Preface

1. Wyndham Lewis, *Blasting and Bombadiering* (London: John Calder, 1982), 256.
2. I have been challenged and supported in my attempts to think inside historical affect by the example and friendship of Pamela Thurschwell. The breadth of conversation and intimacy – with Pam herself, and with the dead, with writing, with adolescence, and with objects near and at a distance – which she has offered me over many years, has helped me to sense the sustaining constituency of this work. See Pam Thurschwell, *Literature,Technology, and Magical Thinking, 1880–1920* (Cambridge: Cambridge University Press, 2001), especially 12–36; 65–85. Chris Nealon has also provided a way of getting very close to writing, while remaining its friend, that has been inspiring for me. See Chris Nealon, *Foundlings: Lesbian and Gay Historical Emotion before Stonewall* (Durham NC: Duke University Press, 2001).
3. I return to Lewis regularly in my book for two reasons. First, his influence is difficult to discern in more recent writing: there is no clear 'Lewisian' strain in modern writing (in this he is different from Woolf, or Joyce, or Eliot, or even Lawrence or Stein). For this reason, the ways in which his writing is formed in relation to the pressures of its surrounding historical context are easier to see, easier to separate out from their 'literary' determinations, than for some other writers. Second – and this point is probably part of the reason for the neglect of his writing – his path through the twentieth century was considerably less happily chosen than those of some other writers. Under the pressures of a desire to experiment, and limited financial and psychical resources to support experiment, the choices he makes in the construction of his career often involve fantasised constituencies. His anti-Semitism, his fascism, his anti-liberalism, his anti-capitalism, his anti-communism, his anti-modernism, are all attempts to externalise these fantasised constituencies in the world, as markets for his writings and as confirmations of his social imaginary. I have written about Lewis in more detail in *A Career in Modernism: Wyndham Lewis, 1909–1931*, PhD thesis, Cambridge, 1995.
4. Wyndham Lewis, *Blasting and Bombadiering*, 256.
5. L. G. Chiozza Money, *Things That Matter: Papers on Subjects which are, or Ought to be, under Discussion* (London: Methuen, 1912).
6. This question has a longer history, of course. In his classic work, *Culture and Society: Coleridge to Orwell* (London: Hogarth, 1990), especially xiii–xx, Raymond Williams gives a history of the shifting meanings of the term 'industry', which he correlates with shifts in the ways in which the words 'culture', 'art', 'democracy', and 'class' are used after the industrial revolution.

7. Money, *Things That Matter*, 105.
8. Willa Cather, 'The Novel Démeublé', *Not under Forty* (1936; Lincoln NB: University of Nebraska Press, 1988), 43–51; Wyndham Lewis, *The Caliph's Design: Architects! Where is Your Vortex* (1919), ed. Paul Edwards (Santa Barbara CA: Black Sparrow Press, 1982), especially 19–49.
9. See Franco Moretti on *Ulysses*, in 'The Long Goodbye: *Ulysses* and the End of Liberal Capitalism', *Signs Taken For Wonders: Essays in the Sociology of Literary Form* (London: Verso, 1988); and Maud Ellmann on *The Waste Land* in 'Eliot's Abjection', in *Abjection, Melancholia, and Love: The Work of Julia Kristeva*, ed. Andrew Benjamin and John Fletcher (London: Routledge, 1990), 178–200.
10. Robert Musil, *The Man without Qualities*, trans. Sophie Wilkins and Burton Pike (London: Picador, 1995), 10–11.
11. Geoffrey Hawthorne cites Musil in *Plausible Worlds: Possibility and Understanding in History and the Social Sciences* (Cambridge: Cambridge University Press, 1991), his study of the role of counterfactuals in explanation in history and the social sciences. Hawthorne's discussion of how to talk about things which did not happen has been very useful to me, although his pragmatic conclusions, which depend upon the category of plausibility, are not appropriate for modernism.
12. Georg Lukács, 'The Ideology of Modernism', *The Meaning of Contemporary Realism* (London: Merlin, 1957), 17–46, rpt. in *Marxist Literary Criticism*, ed. Terry Eagleton and Drew Milne (London: Blackwell, 1995), 141–62.
13. Musil, 11.
14. See, notably, the multiplication of modernisms in Peter Nichols, *Modernisms: A Literary Guide* (Basingstoke: Macmillan Press – now Palgrave Macmillan, 1995), and the division of the term in Tyrus Miller, *Late Modernism: Politics: Fiction, and the Arts between the World Wars* (Berkeley CA: University of California Press, 1999). Both approaches depend upon the quiet assumption of a prior coherence of 'modernism' under which multiple versions can be ranged, or out of which fractions can be divided. For a radical gesture in the other direction, see Celeste Schenck, 'Charlotte Mew (1870–1928)', in *The Gender of Modernism: A Critical Anthology*, ed. Bonnie Kime Scott (Bloomington IN: Indiana University Press, 1990). Schenck refuses formal definition entirely in the name of a non-exclusive historical ideal: she makes the extremely rational claim that 'although a certain stylistic designation is lost if we open up "Modernism" to anything written between 1910 and 1940, we lose in an equal measure if we restrict this literary critical marker of periodization to experimental writing alone. We lose, in short, all the other modernisms against which a single strain of white, male, international "Modernism" has achieved such relief' (320, n. 1). See also Celeste Schenck, 'Exiled by Genre: Modernism, Canonicity, and the Politics of Exclusion', in *Women's Writing in Exile: Alien and Critical*, ed. Mary Lynn Broe and Angela Ingram (Chapel Hill NC: University of North Carolina Press, 1989).
15. Theorisation about literature in each of these contexts, for the reasons I have given, has some simple productivity, as it works within a historical fabric, in relation to established and shared distinctions. Literary theory becomes hysterical when it becomes engaged with modernist literature,

when it imagines itself as happening exorbitantly on the same ground as the work of modernism. In *The Future of Theory* (Oxford: Blackwell, 2002), Jean-Michel Rabaté has argued that this hystericisation of theory, visible in the regular sharing of ground between literary theorists and literary modernists, is also the condition of theory's future.

16. Michel Foucault, 'How Much Does It Cost for Reason to Tell the Truth?', interview with Gerard Raulet (1983), trans. Mia Foret and Marion Martius, *Foucault Live*, ed. Sylvère Lotringer (New York: Semiotext(e), 1989), 250.

17. T. S. Eliot, 'In Memoriam, Marie Lloyd', *Criterion* I.2 (January 1923), 192–5.

18. T. S. Eliot, 'The Function of Criticism', *Criterion* 2.5 (October 1923), 33.

19. For a detailed elaboration of one late and troubling moment in which modernist production is tied up with an imagined social arrangement, and in which discourses on modernism are developed to turn away from a recognition of this constituency, see Alex Houen, 'Ezra Pound: Anti-Semitism, Segregationism, and the "Arsenal of Live Thought"', *Terrorism and Modern Literature: From Joseph Conrad to Ciaran Carson* (Oxford: Oxford University Press, 2002). Houen details the relations between Pound and the anti-integrationist John Kasper, and between Pound's poetry and Kasper's arson attacks on integrationist schools in the South. Pound's writings in this moment, Houen argues, are deeply implicated in Kasper's action; but the discourses he produces *about* poetry, discourses that feed into the 'new criticism', exist to disavow this deep implication.

Introduction

1. Michel de Certeau, *The Practice of Everyday Life*, trans. Steven Rendall (Berkeley: University of California Press, 1984), 13–14. The interpolation is in the original.

2. Georg Lukács, *The Theory of the Novel* (London: Merlin Press, 1971), 23.

3. Constance Garnett translates the novel as *A Raw Youth* (London: Heinemann, 1916), but the Russian title, *Podrostok*, is both culturally and etymologically close to the English 'adolescent'. I have consulted Garnett's text, as this is the work – and the stylistic universe – that the British modernists would have known. However, I have chosen to quote from a recent translation, *The Adolescent*, trans. Richard Pevear and Larissa Volokhonsky (New York: Alfred Knopf, 2003), as the life and strangeness of Dostoevsky's novel, already visible in Garnett's work, are even more strongly conveyed there. On the character, and the strengths and weaknesses, of Garnett's translations, see A. N. Nikoliukin, 'Dostoevskii in Constance Garnett's Translation', in *Dostoevskii and Britain*, ed. W. J. Leatherbarrow (Oxford: Berg, 1995), 206–27.

4. One moment in the post-structuralist theorisation of relations between language and 'the literary' could be said to be compressed into the 'debate' between Lacan and Derrida over how to read Poe's 'The Purloined Letter'; over whether the letter – the signifier – always or never reaches its destination; over whether the relation between language and the subject is an absolutely closed or an absolutely opened one. That debate cannot even begin – Dostoevsky's fable suggests – until we have located the letter, until

we have caused the letter to come to rest, and thus turned the adolescent into a subject, somewhere outside the work of writing in history. See John P. Muller and William J. Richardson, eds, *The Purloined Poe* (Baltimore MD: Johns Hopkins University Press, 1987).

5. Dostoevsky, *The Adolescent*, 559.
6. *The Adolescent*, 563–4.
7. Fyodor Dostoevsky, *The Notebooks for* A Raw Youth, trans. Victor Terrass, ed. Edward Wasiolek (Chicago: University of Chicago Press, 1969), 203.
8. Versions of the phrase do appear, though. The narrator insists regularly that 'Of course, between me as I am now and me as I was then there is an infinite difference.' (59)
9. *The Adolescent*, 85.
10. *The Adolescent*, 39.
11. *The Adolescent*, 18.
12. *The Adolescent*, 5.
13. *The Adolescent*, 499.
14. *The Adolescent*, 10.
15. Richard Pevear, Introduction, *The Adolescent*, xxvi.
16. Mikhail Bakhtin, *Problems of Dostoevsky's Poetics*, trans., ed. Caryl Emerson (Minneapolis: University of Minnesota Press, 1984), 27.
17. *The Adolescent*, 47.
18. Jacques Copeau, 'Sur le *Dostoïevski* de Suarès', *Nouvelle Revue Française* 7 (1912), 229. My translation.
19. This is not intended as a survey of British responses to Dostoevsky. That work has been done very thoroughly by Helen Muchnic, in *Dostoevsky's English Reputation (1881–1936)*, Smith College Studies in Modern Languages 20.3–4 (Northampton: Smith College, 1939), and more recently by Peter Kaye, in *Dostoevsky and English Modernism: 1900–1930* (Cambridge: Cambridge University Press, 1999).
20. Virginia Woolf, 'More Dostoevsky' (1917), review of *The Eternal Husband and Other Stories*, *The Essays of Virginia Woolf*, ed. Andrew McNeillie, vol. 2 (London: Hogarth, 1994), 83.
21. Katherine Mansfield, 'Some Aspects of Dostoevsky', *Novels and Novelists*, ed. J. Middleton Murry (London: Constable, 1930), 111–14, 111.
22. See Claire Tomalin, *Katherine Mansfield: A Secret Life* (London: Viking, 1987).
23. André Gide, *Journal, 1889–1939* (Paris: Gallimard, 1951), entry for 26 January 1908.
24. See Mark Manganaro, 'Textual Play, Power, and Cultural Critique: An Orientation to Modernist Anthropology', *Modernist Anthropology: From Fieldwork to Text*, ed. Mark Manganaro (Princeton NJ: Princeton University Press, 1990), and Michael North, *Reading 1922: A Return to the Scene of the Modern* (New York: Oxford University Press, 1999), Chapter 1.
25. Valerie Eliot remembers him saying this, according to Peter Ackroyd, in *T. S. Eliot* (London: Penguin, 1993), 204.
26. One of the earlier British statements of this notion is in Maurice Baring's influential *Landmarks in Russian Literature* (London: Methuen, 1910). Baring notes a relation between crime and epilepsy, and argues that 'It is no doubt the presence of this disease and the frequency of the attacks, which were responsible for the want of balance in his nature and in his artistic

conceptions, just as his grinding poverty and the merciless conditions of his existence are responsible for the want of finish in his style. But Dostoevsky had the qualities of his defects' (162). These terms were picked up by psychologists, including Alfred Adler, who writes admiringly of Dostoevsky as an epileptic criminal, in 'Dostoevsky' (1918), *The Practice and Theory of Individual Psychology* (London: Kegan Paul, 1924), Chapter 23.

27. Woolf, 'The Russian Point of View', *The Essays of Virginia Woolf*, ed. Andrew McNeillie, vol. 4 (London: Hogarth, 1994), 182.

28. T. J. Clark, *Farewell to an Idea: Episodes from a History of Modernism* (New Haven CT: Yale University Press, 1999), 13.

29. Clark, *Farewell to an Idea*, 9.

30. Clark, *Farewell to an Idea*, 9.

31. Georg Lukács, *The Theory of the Novel*, 152–3.

32. Lukács, *The Theory of the Novel*, 20.

33. Lukács, *The Theory of the Novel*, 12.

34. Lukács, 'The Ideology of Modernism', 150.

35. Lukács, 'The Ideology of Modernism', 145.

36. Interestingly, in relation to *The Adolescent*, for Lukács the conditions of concrete possibility are 'inherited'; they depend upon given models of affiliation, which are not subject to contingencies.

37. Lukács, 'The Ideology of Modernism', 162.

38. Peter Bürger has suggested, in 'Naturalism, Aestheticism, and Modernist Subjectivity', *The Decline of Modernism*, trans. Nicholas Walker (Cambridge: Polity, 1992), that 'modernist subjectivity' registers an attempt to realise the dialectical synthesis of the separated appearances of naturalism and aestheticism. In naturalism, the social can be conceived of in its determining fullness, but without the presence of the individual. For aestheticism, the individual can register his presence fully, but only at the cost of withdrawal from social meanings. Together, the two modes of representation signal a single notion: the impossibility of formative intervention of the individual into the social. This is the legacy which modernism attempts to deal with, and the appearance which, I would suggest, Lukács misrecognises. This essay of Bürger's is, I believe, more productive than his classic anatomy of distinctions between 'modernism' and 'the avant-garde', *Theory of the Avant-Garde* (Manchester: Manchester University Press, 1984).

39. Mansfield, 'Some Aspects of Dostoevsky', 112.

40. John Middleton Murry, *Fyodor Dostoevsky: A Critical Study* (London: Martin Secker, 1916), v.

41. Murry, *Fyodor Dostoevsky*, 25. Dostoevsky arrives, in the literary communities of London, mediated by a range of Russian exiles, often political migrants. Sexologist Havelock Ellis, calling Dostoevsky 'the Saint of Sinners' and the 'Idealisation of Perversity', is confused that all of these Russians are not the same: 'Kropotkin, I should have thought, possessed the essential Russian temperament, the same impulse to saintliness, which should have made him sympathetic, even though he moved on another plane, to Dostoevsky', *Impressions and Comments: Third (and Final) Series, 1920–1923* (London: Constable, 1924), 197, 196. Kropotkin had written about Dostoevsky in *Russian Literature: Ideals and Realities* (1905, rev. edn; London: Duckworth, 1916). Apparently and understandably irritated by notions of

'the Russian soul', he notes that any spirit understood as characteristic of Russian literature should be ascribed to history – including the history of the specific persecutions of specific writers – rather than to 'race' or to the 'mystical soul' of Russia (iv–vi). In that context he distances himself from Dostoevsky, noting that he is a formally sloppy writer, and that 'whatever the hero says in the novel [...] you feel it is the author who speaks' (179–80). Kropotkin sees Dostoevsky's 'pleasure in describing the sufferings, moral and physical, of the downtrodden' as 'repulsive to a sound man' (180, 181).

42. Murry, *Fyodor Dostoevsky*, 25–6.
43. Murry, *Fyodor Dostoevsky*, 28.
44. Ten years later, D. H. Lawrence avowed a desire to read Dostoevsky again, in search of the abolition of fictional distance: 'I have been thinking lately the time has come to read Dostoevsky again: not as fiction, but as life. I am so weary of the English way of reading nothing but fiction in everything.' D. H. Lawrence to S. S. Koteliansky (11 January 1926), *The Quest for Rananim: D. H. Lawrence's Letters to S. S. Koteliansky*, ed. George J. Zytaruk (Montreal: McGill – Queen's University Press, 1970), 278.
45. Julia Kristeva defines the movement of abjection as an endless and impossible quest to cleanse the subject of all that is foreign to it, to turn abject things into objects, and thus to establish an identity which is proper to the ego. See *Powers of Horror: An Essay on Abjection* (New York: Columbia University Press, 1982), especially 1–89.
46. D. H. Lawrence to S. S. Koteliansky (15 December 1916), *The Quest for Rananim*, 102. Lawrence refers to *Pages from the Journal of an Author*, trans. Constance Garnett, intr. J. M. Murry (London: Heinemann, 1916). See Peter Kaye, *Dostoevsky and English Modernism*, Chapter 2, for a fuller account of Lawrence's intense reactions to Dostoevsky, and a reading of the heavy traces of Dostoevsky's influence on Lawrence's own writing.
47. D. H. Lawrence to J. M. Murry (28 August 1916), *The Letters of D. H. Lawrence*, vol. 2, *June 1913–October 1916*, ed. George J. Zyartuk and James T. Bolton *et al.* (Cambridge: Cambridge University Press, 1981), 646.
48. See George A. Panichas, 'F. M. Dostoevskii and D. H. Lawrence: Their Vision of Evil'; and Ralph E. Matlaw, 'Dostoevskii and Conrad's Political Novels', both in *Dostoevskii and Britain*, ed. W. J. Leatherbarrow (Oxford: Berg, 1995), 249–75; 229–48.
49. André Gide, 'Joseph Conrad', *Nouvelle Revue Française* 23 (1924): 659–62, 661. My translation.
50. André Gide, *Dostoïevski* (1923; Paris: Gallimard, 1981), 166.
51. The *NRF* was widely conflated with Gide, however little he had to do with its running. In 1921, he notes that 'the more I draw away from the *NRF*, the more people think that it is me who is in control'. Quoted in Martyn Cornick, *The Nouvelle Revue Française Under Jean Paulhan, 1925–1940* (Amsterdam: Rodolphi, 1995), 18. Dostoevsky was a regular subject in the journal, in essays by Jacques Rivière, Michel Arnauld, Emma Cabire, Léon Schestof, Jean Schlumberger, and Jacques Copeau, as well as by Gide.
52. Henri Massis, 'André Gide et Doistoïevsky', *La Revue universelle* 15 (1 November 1923; 15 November 1923): 329–41; 476–93, 329.
53. Massis, 477.

54. For a full and beautiful account of how a sexualised socius might be figured, of what social relations founded on a generalised narcissism, on the inhabiting of a world filled with non-exact replications of the self, might look like, see Leo Bersani, 'Sexuality and Sociality', *Critical Inquiry* 26 (Summer 2000). Bersani approaches these questions in relation to Gide in *Homos* (Cambridge MA: Harvard University Press, 1995), 113–29. For a further rehabilitation of narcissism within its psychoanalytical frame, as a mode of historical being – loving who you wish you were – which indicates a political idealisation, see Michael Warner, 'Homo-Narcissism: or, Heterosexuality', in *Engendering Men: The Question of the Male Feminist Critique*, ed. Joseph Boone and Michael Cadden (New York: Routledge, 1990). In a different vein, Denise Riley, in *The Words of Selves: Identification, Solidarity, Irony* (Stanford CA: Stanford University Press, 2000), has articulated a mode of linguistic solidarity which can be grasped within the ironies of narcissism. Finally, narcissists can look themselves in the face with pride.

55. Roger Martin du Gard, *Notes on André Gide*, trans. John Russell (London: André Deutsch, 1953), 35.

56. Du Gard, 36. He also admits that '[. . .] we mustn't forget that Gide has never had the patience to keep a completed manuscript in his drawer for very long' (38).

57. T. S. Eliot, 'Lettre d'Angleterre', trans G. d'Hangest, *Nouvelle Revue Française* 21 (1923), 621–2. My translation. In an earlier 'Lettre d'Angleterre: le style dans la prose Anglaise contemporaine', *Nouvelle Revue Française* 19 (1922), 751–6, he had denied that his friend Wyndham Lewis's writing was stylistically similar to Dostoevsky's.

58. Virginia Woolf, *The Letters of Virginia Woolf*, vol. 1, *The Flight of the Mind (1888–1912)* (London: Hogarth, 1977), 5. Woolf refers to *Crime and Punishment* here in the French translation.

59. I am grateful to Laura Marcus for drawing this allusion to my attention. See Jenny Uglow, *George Eliot* (London: Virago, 1987), 246–9, for a brief account of the event.

60. One of her earliest diagnoses of this problem refers, in a 1913 letter to Lytton Strachey, to *The Adolescent* (again, I presume, in French translation), which she finds 'more frantic than any, I think, twelve new characters on every page and the mind quite dazed by conversations'. The letter is cited in Peter Kaye, *Dostoevsky and English Modernism*, 68.

61. Virginia Woolf, 'A Minor Dostoevsky' (1917), review of *The Gambler and Other Stories*, *The Essays of Virginia Woolf*, vol. 2, 166.

62. Woolf here is reviewing *The Gambler*, which Dostoevsky wrote extremely quickly under extraordinary economic pressure, making himself ill in the process. The result, in the text as well as for the author, is pathology, a convulsive body; rather than rejecting this text as anomalous *because* of its circumstances of production, I would wish to note the continuity between the materiality which is evidenced here and, for example, the tropes which Mansfield and Murry use about Dostoevsky's work, which include an account of the revealed materiality of the book in their reactions to the text. These relations between the economics of authorship and the contents of fiction will be discussed more fully in Chapter 1.

63. Woolf, 'A Minor Dostoevsky', 166. In 'The Russian Point of View', 183, Woolf notes that characters in Russian fiction constantly call one another brother; such intimacy would destroy the English novel, which borrows its forms from a social order in which relations are clearly and unchangeably structured. She suggests that the whole plot of a Galsworthy novel is produced in reaction against the fact that two men have inadvertently, in a moment of weakness, hailed one another as 'brothers'.

64. I would like to register here my admiration for three of the works that have helped me to conceive this project, in which the cultural project and the deconstructive energies of reading are held in careful tension: Tim Armstrong, *Modernism, Technology, and the Body: A Cultural Study* (Cambridge: Cambridge University Press, 1998), Mark Seltzer, *Bodies and Machines* (New York: Routledge, 1992), and Maud Ellmann, *The Hunger Artists: Writing, Starving, and Imprisonment* (London: Virago, 1993).

65. The relations and social identities established between humans and animals have become the focus of a range of interesting recent work. For just one example, see Donna Haraway, *The Companion Species Manifesto: Dogs, People, and Significant Otherness* (Chicago: Prickly Paradigm Press, 2003).

1 Property: The Preoccupation of Modernism

1. Max Stirner, *The Ego and Its Own* (1844, trans. Stephen Byington, 1907), ed. David Leopold (Cambridge: Cambridge University Press, 1995), 35.

2. Now it is time that gods came walking out of lived-in Things . . .
   Time that they came and knocked down every wall
   inside my house. New page. Only the wind
   from such a turning could be strong enough
   to toss the air as a shovel tosses dirt:
   a fresh-turned field of breath.
   Rainer Maria Rilke, '[Now it is time that gods came walking out]' (1925), *The Selected Poetry of Rainer Maria Rilke*, ed., trans. Stephen Mitchell (1980; London: Picador, 1987), 276.

3. 'First Report of the Committee on Haunted Houses', *Proceedings of the Society for Psychical Research* I (1882), 115.

4. R. C. Morton, 'Record of a Haunted House', *Proceedings of the Society for Psychical Research* 8 (1892), 315.

5. Jean-Pierre Dupuy has explored the spectral logic of the free market, in terms of the language of crowd theory, in 'De l'Economie considérée comme théorie de la foule', *Stanford French Review* 7 (Summer 1983).

6. 'Report of the General Meeting', *Journal of the Society for Psychical Research* 16 (April 1884), 35.

7. *Journal of the Society for Psychical Research* 16 (May 1884), 52.

8. Lawrence Rainey, *Institutions of Modernism: Literary Elites and Public Culture* (New Haven CT: Yale University Press, 1998), 3. The modernist text in Rainey's account becomes the plausible object of a series of contractual exchanges between individuals operating within briefly stable quasi-institutional structures. This is refreshing at least: there is something undeniably right in his claim, talking of *The Waste Land*, that 'the best reading

of a work may, on some occasions, be one that does not read it at all' (106). But, in replacing the text as text with the text as object, Rainey is in danger, I think, of losing a sense of how strange and charged all this appeared to the individuals involved in the positing of the modernist object; strange, I would argue, to the point of upsetting the grounds on which a liberal individual can be imagined to stand. The strangeness returns in Rainey's book as an incommensurable allergy to H. D.'s writing, such that his descriptive accounts of institutions turns into hyper-suspicious close readings of what is wrong equally with H. D.'s writing and her social networks.

9. I follow Pierre Bourdieu's account of the role of disavowal as a relay between the general economy and restricted – relatively autonomous – fields such as the field of cultural production. For Bourdieu, a disavowal of an interest in money is never disinterested; nor, however, is it merely disingenuous. Rather, it is part of the logic through which the reward specific to cultural production is produced as a component of the (potentially) perfectly sincere faith specific to the field of art. I depart from Bourdieu where he argues that this process is *always* recontained by the general economy; that cultural capital is always, eventually, by definition reconverted into economic capital. Bourdieu implies that the field of cultural production is defined by its success, whereas, for modernism, it is necessary to recognise the extent to which the constant fracturing of the field of cultural production into sub-fields is hedged by disaster, by perversion, and by negligibility. See particularly 'The Field of Cultural Production, or: The Economic World Reversed', in *The Field of Cultural Production* (Cambridge: Polity, 1993), 29–63, and 'The Production of Belief: Contribution to an Economy of Symbolic Goods', in *The Field of Cultural Production*, 74–111.

10. Virginia Woolf, 'Mr Bennett and Mrs Brown' (1924), *A Woman's Essays*, ed. Rachel Bowlby (London: Penguin, 1992), 82.

11. Woolf, 'Mr Bennett and Mrs Brown', 80. Henry James's objection to Bennett is couched in similar terms: his work is 'a monument exactly not to an idea, a pursued and captured meaning, or in short *to* anything whatsoever, but just simply *of* the quarried and gathered material it happens to contain, the stones and bricks and rubble and cement and promiscuous constituents of every sort that have been heaped in it and thanks to which it quite massively piles itself up. Our perusal and our enjoyment are our watching of the growth of the pile and of the capacity, industry, energy with which the operation is directed.' ('The New Novel' (1914), *The Critical Muse: Selected Literary Criticism*, ed. Roger Gard (London: Penguin, 1987), 604).

12. Woolf, 'Mr Bennett and Mrs Brown', 77.

13. Woolf, 'Mr Bennett and Mrs Brown', 84.

14. Virginia Woolf, *To the Lighthouse* (1927), ed. Stella McNichol (London: Penguin, 1992), 137.

15. Woolf, *To the Lighthouse*, 151.

16. Woolf, *To the Lighthouse*, 151.

17. Closure in *To the Lighthouse* is presented as forced and limited: the sense of ending inherent in Lily's vision (pointedly only *hers*) co-ordinates 'extreme fatigue' (226) and relief (225) with aesthetic closure; held in imaginary – impossible – simultaneity with the arrival at the lighthouse. The text's

accordance with that co-ordination partakes consciously in the relief, the fatigue, and the sense of limitation.

18. I borrow this notion from Lyndsey Stonebridge, *The Destructive Element: British Psychoanalysis and Modernism* (Basingstoke: Macmillan Press – now Palgrave Macmillan, 1998). See especially Chapter 3 for a beautiful articulation of how the rhythmical movements 'beneath' Woolf's writing are seen to trope an extra-discursive force; but *in* figuring it they place it infirmly within the spaces of the historical and the discursive.

19. Woolf, *To the Lighthouse*, 214.

20. Quoted in Avner Offer, *Property and Politics* (Cambridge: Cambridge University Press, 1981), 294.

21. See, for example, Forest Capie and Geoffrey Wood, 'Money in the Economy, 1870–1939', in *The Economic History of Britain since 1700*, ed. Roderick Floud and D. N. McCloskey, vol. 2, *1860–1939*, second edition (Cambridge: Cambridge University Press, 1994).

22. Rae, *The Country Banker*, quoted in Offer, *Property and Politics*, 115.

23. José Harris, *Private Lives, Public Spirit: A Social History of Britain, 1870–1914* (Oxford: Oxford University Press, 1993), 97.

24. Woolf, *To the Lighthouse*, 189.

25. J. A. Hobson, *The Crisis of Liberalism: New Issues of Democracy* (London: P. S. King and Son, 1909), vi. Hobson published one piece, 'The Extension of Liberalism', in Hueffer's *English Review*, in November 1909.

26. Algernon Blackwood, 'The Empty House', *The Empty House and Other Ghost Stories* (London: Eveleigh Nash, 1906), 2.

27. Blackwood, 'The Empty House', 20, 25.

28. 'Mr Bennett and Mrs Brown', 70–1.

29. Blackwood, 'The Empty House', 14.

30. Sharon Marcus has outlined the sub-genre of the Victorian fiction of urban haunted properties in *Apartment Stories: City and Home in Nineteenth-Century Paris and London* (Berkeley CA: University of California Press, 1999), especially 116–27. She notes that these stories stage and overcome the sense that the urban crowd is already present in the private space of the urban domestic interior.

31. Algernon Blackwood, *John Silence: Physician Extraordinary* (London: Eveleigh Nash, 1908). The ghost is a woman 'of singularly atrocious life and character who finally suffered death by hanging' (69). She is 'large, dark-skinned, with white teeth and masculine features, and one eye – the left – so drooping as to appear almost closed' (21). 'She came to her end in 1798' (69).

32. Blackwood, *John Silence*, 7.

33. Blackwood, *John Silence*, 12, 25, 24, 29.

34. This is one of the moments in which modernism holds most tightly to decadence. If there is a clear distinction to be made, I would suggest that where the decadent writer disavows successfully the economic grounds for her position, imagining it perhaps in purely psychological or aesthetic terms, the position of 'modernist' is intensely materially self-conscious, hyper-aware of the economic disaster of decadence, of the fact that writing which will not sell threatens physical personhood not through a delicious internal process but through circuits which include the economic and the political.

35. Blackwood, *John Silence*, 59.
36. '[B]eing at heart a genuine philanthropist' (3), Silence does not charge his clients. But neither does he rid the very poor of their ghosts, reckoning rather oddly that they can make use of charitable agencies. His interest is solely with that 'very large class of ill-paid, self respecting workers, often followers of the arts' (3), to which Blackwood's target reader will also belong.
37. Algernon Blackwood, *Episodes Before Thirty* (London: Cassell, 1923), 222.
38. Blackwood, *Episodes Before Thirty*, 303.
39. Blackwood, *Episodes Before Thirty*, 224.
40. According to *The Book Monthly* 6.1 (October 1908), 12.
41. Walter Besant, *The Pen and the Book* (London: Thomas Burleigh, 1899), 30. See also, for example, Arnold Bennett, *Fame and Fiction* (London: Grant Richards, 1901).
42. See Peter Keating, *The Haunted Study: A Social History of the English Novel 1875–1914* (London: Fontana, 1991), 15.
43. Michael Anesko, *'Friction with the Market': Henry James and the Profession of Authorship* (New York: Oxford University Press, 1986), 34.
44. Besant, *The Pen and the Book*, vi.
45. On the 'courting' and 'management' of the 'mob' by the author, see Arnold Bennett, *How to Be an Author* (London: C. Arthur Pearson, 1903), 26. We might also cite the proliferation of institutions which gather around authorship at the end of the nineteenth century (Society of Authors (1883); London Booksellers' Society (1890), Associated Booksellers of Great Britain and Ireland (1895); Publishers Association (1896)) as part of an attempt to control the implications of this. See Keating, *The Haunted Study*.
46. 'Light and Leading, New Fact and Current Opinion Gathered from the Book World', *The Book Monthly* 6. 8 (May 1909), 651, quoting *The Observer*.
47. David Trotter, *The English Novel in History, 1895–1920* (London: Routledge, 1993), especially 62–79.
48. Ford Madox Hueffer, 'The Function of the Arts in the Republic', *The English Review* I (December 1908), 157.
49. Douglas Goldring, *South Lodge: Reminiscences of Violet Hunt, Ford Madox Ford and the English Review Circle* (London: Constable, 1943), 23. In contrast, Goldring notes that, during the planning in 1914 of the avant-garde journal *Blast*, '[Wyndham] Lewis insisted on regarding me (rather to my annoyance) as a kind of useful business man' (67).
50. Ezra Pound, 'Editorial on Solicitous Doubt'. First printed in the suppressed edition of October 1917 (suppressed by the US post office because of an 'obscene' story by Wyndham Lewis), then reprinted in *The Little Review* 4. 8 (December 1917), 54.
51. Hueffer, 'The Function of the Arts in the Republic', 160.
52. 'Algernon Charles Swinburne', *English Review* 2 (May 1909), 194.
53. 'George Meredith, OM', *English Review* 2 (June 1909), 409.
54. 'Two Poets', *English Review* 2 (June 1909), 627.
55. H. G. Wells, *Tono Bungay* (London: Macmillan, 1909). Perhaps it shouldn't be too surprising that the serialisation of Wells's novel was not completed, due, it seems, to Wells's discomfort with the financial operation of the journal.

56. Wells, *Tono Bungay*, 341. This of course is the image that Galsworthy, another contributor to the first issue of *The English Review*, made central to *The Forsyte Saga* in general and *Man of Property* (1906) in particular.

57. The other story James published in *The English Review* was 'The Velvet Glove' (March 1909), which charts the refusal of John Berridge to consecrate the work of the mediocre but socially fabulous Princess; a refusal to allow anything – social success, sexual desire, even the recognition of the fabulous refinement of the Princess – to cash in the value of his writing.

58. Leon Edel notes the relations between this story and James's purchase of Lamb House in Rye, in *Henry James*, vol. 4, *The Treacherous Years: 1895–1901* (New York: Avon Books, 1978), 317–28.

59. Henry James, 'The Third Person' (1900), *The Jolly Corner and Other Tales*, ed. Roger Gard (London: Penguin, 1990), 30.

60. It seems that James wasn't particularly impressed with the story; it was not included in the New York edition.

61. Henry James, 'The Jolly Corner', *The English Review* I (December 1908), rpt. in *The Jolly Corner and Other Tales*, 162.

62. James, 'The Jolly Corner', 162–3.

63. James, 'The Jolly Corner', 163–4.

64. James, 'The Jolly Corner', 166.

65. James, 'The Jolly Corner', 168.

66. James, 'The Jolly Corner', 167.

67. James, 'The Jolly Corner', 165.

68. Strangely, the billionaire ghost is sensed first in the servants' quarters: 'the rear of the house affected him as the very jungle of his prey. The place was there more subdivided; a large "extension" in particular, where small rooms for servants had been multiplied, abounded in nooks and corners, in closets and passages' (176).

69. Henry James, *Autobiography*, ed. Frederick W. Dupee (1956; Princeton NJ: Princeton University Press, 1983), 476.

70. Henry James, *Autobiography*, 476.

71. Michael Anesko *'Friction With the Market'*, 27.

72. James, 'The Jolly Corner', 175.

73. James, 'The Jolly Corner', 165.

74. Deborah Esch, 'A Jamesian About-Face: Notes on "The Jolly Corner"', *ELH* 50.3 (Fall 1983), 595.

75. Esch, 588.

76. Harry Roberts, 'The Art of Vagabondage', *The Tramp* I (June–July 1910), 387.

77. Goldring, *South Lodge*, 66.

78. Advert for Ozonair Ltd., *The Tramp* I (June–July 1910), xxiii.

79. *The Tramp* I (September 1910).

80. The stories are 'The Pole' (May 1909, 255–65), 'Some Innkeepers and Bestre' (June 1909, 471–84), and 'Les Saltimbanques' (August 1909, 76–87). For a discussion of these stories, and the stories he published in *The Tramp*, in this context, see Geoffrey Gilbert, *A Career in Modernism: Wyndham Lewis, 1909–1931* (PhD thesis, Cambridge, 1995), Chapter 3.

81. Wyndham Lewis to J. B. Pinker, nd, quoted in Paul O'Keefe, *Some Sort of*

Genius: A Life of Wyndham Lewis (London: Jonathan Cape, 2000), 96. I discuss the non-publication of *Mrs Dukes' Millions* in 'Intestinal Violence: Wyndham Lewis and the Critical Poetics of the Modernist Career', *Critical Quarterly* 36.3 (Autumn 1994).

82. Wyndham Lewis, 'Unlucky for Pringle', *The Tramp: An Open Air Magazine*, 2 (February 1911), rpt. in C. J. Fox and Robert T. Chapman, eds, *Unlucky for Pringle: Unpublished and Other Stories* (London: Vision, 1973). He published three other stories there: 'A Spanish Household' (June–July 1910); 'A Breton Innkeeper' (August 1910); 'Le Père Françoise (A Full Length Portrait of a Tramp)' (September 1910).
83. Lewis, 'Unlucky for Pringle', 23.
84. Lewis, 'Unlucky for Pringle', 28–29.
85. James, 'The Jolly Corner', 178.
86. Lewis, 'Unlucky for Pringle', 28, 30, 29, 29.
87. Lewis, 'Unlucky for Pringle', 25.
88. Lewis, 'Unlucky for Pringle', 24–5.
89. Lewis, 'Unlucky for Pringle', 32.
90. Lewis, 'Unlucky for Pringle', 36–7.

2 Boys: Manufacturing Inefficiency

1. Mina Loy, 'Giovanni Franchi', In *Rogue* 2.1 (October 1916), rpt. in *The Lost Lunar Baedeker*, ed. Roger L. Conover (Manchester: Carcanet, 1997), 29.
2. Françoise Dolto, *La Cause des adolescents* (Paris: Lafont, 1998), 13. Dolto, like most broadly psychoanalytic writers on adolescence, sees that variety of being as the name for the difficulty of becoming adult: becoming economically independent, psychically both autonomous and related to another – reproductive, broadly. As with all such accounts, investigation of the adolescent serves less to highlight the values earned through the difficult processes of maturing, than to make it seem increasingly unlikely that anyone should ever either be able to or want to become adult. In that sense I think that the adolescent, tied up in material historical process, the affective unrecognizable image of ourselves, may be *all* we know; and the ideals dear to analysis – of the reproducing adult and the infinitely potential child – may well be fetish objects made to paper over our refusal of that evidence.
3. Walter Benjamin, 'The Destructive Character', *One Way Street and Other Writings*, trans. Edmund Jephcott and Kingsley Shorter (London: Verso, 1979), 158.
4. Benjamin, 157.
5. Charles Altieri, 'Can We Be Historical Ever? Some hopes for a dialectical model of historical self-consciousness', in *The Uses of Literary History*, ed. Marshall Brown (Durham NC: Duke University Press, 1995).
6. Wyndham Lewis to Augustus John (Summer 1915), *The Letters of Wyndham Lewis*, ed. W. K. Rose (Norfolk CT: New Directions, 1963), 70–1.
7. Wyndham Lewis, 'History of the Largest Independent Society in England', *Blast* 2 (1915; facs. rpt, Santa Barbara CA: Black Sparrow Press, 1981), 80–1.
8. Wyndham Lewis to Augustus John, 70.

9. 'History of the Largest Independent Society', 81.
10. Ford Madox Hueffer, 'Literary Portraits – XLII: Mr Wyndham Lewis and "Blast"', *The Outlook* 34 (4 July 1914), 15.
11. Sigmund Freud, 'Family Romances', *Pelican Freud Library*, vol. 7, *On Sexuality* (Harmondsworth: Penguin, 1977), 221.
12. Wyndham Lewis, 'Our Vortex', *Blast* 1 (1914; facs. rpt, Santa Barbara CA: Black Sparrow, 1981), 147. Peter Nicholls has articulated the distinction between the anti-historicism of *Blast* and the 'presentism' of the superficially similar pronouncements of the Italian Futurists, in *Modernisms: A Literary Guide* (Basingstoke: Macmillan Press – now Palgrave Macmillan, 1995), 172–4.
13. 'Long Live the Vortex', *Blast* 1, 7.
14. Paul de Man, 'Literary History and Literary Modernity' (1969), in *Blindness and Insight: Essays in the Rhetoric of Contemporary Criticism* (1971; rev. edn, London: Methuen, 1983), 148.
15. De Man, 164. De Man typically explodes the predicate – here the mutual exclusivity of history and modernity – on which his argument had been based. For a critique of de Man's argument – for its faulty reading of Nietzsche's *Untimely Meditations* and for the clumsiness of its concept of history – see Astradur Eysteinsson, *The Concept of Modernism* (Ithaca NY: Cornell University Press, 1990), 54–9.
16. 'Manifesto', *Blast* 1, 30–42.
17. Wyndham Lewis, 'The New Egos', *Blast* 1, 141.
18. 'Manifesto', 30–1.
19. 'Long Live the Vortex', 7.
20. A more frequent name for this territory in *Blast* and in modernism generally is the 'primitive', which should be read as a formal gathering of the contradictions of the 'modern' (most especially when it claims to offer a resolution of these contradictions). See Julian Stallabrass, 'The Idea of the Primitive: British Art and Anthropology 1918–1930', *New Left Review* 183 (September–October 1990). I would want to widen the scope of this claim such that all a-historical objects of modernist projects would be tested against it. The promulgation in *The Egoist* of Stirnerian egoism appeals to the 'nature' of a pre-conceptual individual force, but it does this, I would argue, from within the field defined by militant suffrage, deriving the natural ego – and the state of nature which is its natural condition – from the critical violence of conscious historical struggle. For an account of the place of Stirnerian egoism in British modernism, see Jean-Michel Rabaté, *The Ghosts of Modernity* (Gainesville FL: University of Florida Press, 1996).
21. Karl Marx and Friedrich Engels, *The Communist Manifesto* (1848; trans. Samuel Moore, 1888; Harmondsworth, Middlesex: Penguin, 1967), 79.
22. 'Ja, der Fortschritt der Gesellschaft beruht überhaupt auf dieser Gegensätzlichkeit der beiden Generationen' ('Der Familienroman der Neurotiker', *Gessamelte Werke*, vol. 7, *Werke aus den Jahren 1906–1909* [London: Imago, 1941], 227); and 'Die Geschichte aller bißherigen Gesellschaft ist die Geschichte von klassenkämpfen' (*Manifest der Kommunistischen Partei* [London: Bildungsgesellschaft für Arbeiter, 1848; facs. rpt Bonn-Bad Godesberg, NG Reprint, 1970], 3).
23. Freud, 'Family Romances', 222–3.

24. George Dangerfield, *The Strange Death of Liberal England* (London: Constable, 1936).

25. For just one representative example, see Martin Pugh, *State and Society: British Political and Social History, 1870–1992* (London: Edward Arnold, 1994), 132–44.

26. See *The Adolescent Idea: Myths of Youth and the Ideal Imagination* (1981; London: Faber, 1982), especially 236–56; see also John Neubauer, *The Fin-de-Siècle Culture of Adolescence* (New Haven CT: Yale University Press, 1992).

27. Oddly, the novel which most explicitly aligns an opening of the spirit to possibility with adolescence is Henry James's *The Ambassadors*. Strether, basking in a fresh set of conditions, which he is absorbing from Parisian relations, finds himself young. This state of being (which is held in a consciousness and a prose gradually sure enough of itself to hold no judgement whatsoever) includes adolescence. 'Though they're young enough, my pair, I don't say they're, in the freshest way, their *own* absolutely prime adolescence; for that has nothing to do with it. The point is that they're mine.' (305–6). Strether sees the dangers here too: 'He saw himself [. . .] recommitted to Woolett as juvenile offenders are committed to reformatories' (314); the danger comes not from a 'discipline' that is exactly *of* Woolett, but from his own potential 'concession' to a set of norms there, such that he would be dissociated from – through judgement or knowledge – the adolescence that he is growing into in Paris.

28. I argue something like this in 'Intestinal Violence: Wyndham Lewis and the Critical Poetics of the Modernist Career', especially 111–19.

29. Wyndham Lewis, *Blasting and Bombadiering* (1937; rev. edn, 1967; London: John Calder, 1982), 253.

30. *Blasting and Bombadiering*, 50.

31. Solomon Eagle [J. C. Squire], 'Current Literature: Books in General', *The New Statesman* 3 (4 July 1914), 406.

32. *Blast* 1, 27.

33. See Michelle Perrot, 'Worker Youth: From the Workshop to the Factory', in Giovanni Levi and Jean-Claude Schmitt, eds, *A History of Young People*, vol. 2, *Stormy Evolution to Modern Times* (1994; trans. Carol Volk, Cambridge MA: Belknap Press, 1997), especially 68–71.

34. See Geoffrey Pearson, *Hooligans: A History of Respectable Fears* (London: Macmillan, 1983), 74–116. Pearson notes that the modes of British hooligan violence sensationally recorded in the late Victorian and Edwardian press were continually seen as new and as 'foreign', as a deflection from structural analysis of the relations between, for example, delinquency and unemployment.

35. In *The Emergence of Social Space: Rimbaud and the Paris Commune* (London: Macmillan, 1988), Kristin Ross reads the 'adolescent' poetry of Rimbaud in relation to the 'adolescent' history expressed by the Paris Commune of 1871.

36. A similar argument is put forward by a writer who becomes very important for the British avant-garde, Georges Sorel, in *The Illusions of Progress* (1908, trans. John and Charlotte Stanley, Los Angeles CA: University of California

Press, 1969). Neubauer relates Sorel's thought to adolescence in *The Fin-de-Siècle Culture of Adolescence*, 182–5.

37. G. Stanley Hall, *Adolescence: Its Psychology, and its Relations to Physiology, Anthropology, Sex, Crime, Religion, and Education*, 2 vols (New York: D. Appleton, 1904), I, xviii.
38. Hall, II, 94.
39. I can think of no more urgent mental exercise for modernist criticism than to take Hall's insistent concretion of these terms and reconcile them with T. S. Eliot's finessing of them.
40. Hall, I, 164–5.
41. Hall, I, 216.
42. For an attractive history of juvenile rebellion and resistance, see Steve Humphries, *Hooligans or Rebels? An Oral History of Working-Class Childhood and Youth, 1889–1939* (Oxford: Blackwell, 1981).
43. Hall, I, 310.
44. Hall, I, 157.
45. There is something of the same pattern in Baden-Powell's designs on boys and empire: the same energies which result in delinquent behaviours will be channeled into regenerative social creativities. See Michael Rosenthal, *The Character Factory: Baden-Powell and the Origins of the Boy Scout Movement* (New York: Pantheon, 1986). On other regenerative projects which tap into disarranged youthful energies, see Seth Koven, 'From Rough Lads to Hooligans: Boy Life, National Culture and Social Reform', in *Nationalisms and Sexualities*, ed. Andrew Parker, Doris Sommer, and Patricia Yaeger (New York: Routledge, 1992).
46. Hall, I, 166.
47. Cyril Burt, *The Young Delinquent* (London: University of London Press, 1925), 157–8. For a similar point, see Reginald Bray, *The Town Child* (London: T. Fisher Unwin, 1907).
48. The classic text is Benjamin's essay on shock in Baudelaire ('On Some Motifs in Baudelaire', *Illuminations: Essays and Reflections* [1955, trans. Harry Zohn, ed. Hannah Arendt, 1968; rev. edn, New York: Schocken, 1979]); the present chapter could be described as an attempt to articulate across another ground the relation between that essay and Benjamin's own delinquent meditation, 'The Destructive Character', *One Way Street and Other Writings*, trans. Edmund Jephcott and Kingsley Shorter (London: Verso, 1979).
49. Paul Thompson has noted that, as a result of marriage ages higher than ever before in British history, 'for the average Edwardian the gap between leaving school and full independence was twice as long as it is today', in *The Edwardians: The Remaking of British Society* (1975; rev. edn, London: Routledge, 1992), 51.
50. Michel Foucault, *Discipline and Punish: The Birth of the Prison* (1975; trans. Alan Sheridan, 1977; London: Penguin, 1991), 292. See also Foucault's *Les Anormaux: cours au College de France, 1974–1975* (Paris: Gallimard, 1999), which deals at greater length with relations between youth and monstrosity and between law and its convulsive officers (see particularly 217–303).
51. See Certeau, *The Practice of Everyday Life* (Berkeley CA: University of California Press, 1988), 45–9.

52. Arnold Freeman, *Boy Life and Labour: The Manufacture of Inefficiency*, preface by M. E. Sadler (London: P. S. King, 1914), 2.
53. See Reginald Bray, *Boy Labour and Apprenticeship* (London: Constable, 1911).
54. Freeman, *Boy Life and Labour*, 2–3.
55. Freeman, *Boy Life and Labour*, 3, 92.
56. Stanley Hall is similarly unable to provide any absolute material limits to the period of adolescence; what is outside boyhood is qualitatively rather than quantitatively beyond it. Gareth Stedman Jones notes that a separate and 'stunted race[ ]' was recorded as being produced and reproduced in this place of labour uncertainty. 'No town bred boys of the poorer classes [. . .] ever except in very rare instances attain the [standard] development of form [. . .] at the age of 15'. *Outcast London: A Study of the Relationship between Classes in Victorian Society* (Oxford: Clarendon Press, 1971), 129, quoting '23rd Annual Report of the Poor Law Board', Parliamentary Papers XXVII (1871), 207.
57. Freeman, *Boy Life and Labour*, 206.
58. Freeman, *Boy Life and Labour*, 158.
59. For most boys, of course, this will not be the case for many years to come, until the property criteria for franchise are reformed.
60. Freeman, *Boy Life and Labour*, 159.
61. Arnold Freeman, *How to Avoid a Revolution* (London: George Allen and Unwin, 1919).
62. *Blasting and Bombadiering*, 51–2.
63. *Blasting and Bombadiering*, 256.
64. See Victor Bailey, *Delinquency and Citizenship: Reclaiming the Young Offender, 1914–1948* (Oxford: Clarendon Press, 1987), 5–114.
65. Burt, *The Young Delinquent*, 17.
66. For a useful outline of this material, see James Bennett, *Oral History and Delinquency: The Rhetoric of Criminology* (Chicago: University of Chicago Press, 1981), especially 104–78.
67. William Healy, 'The Psychology of the Situation in Delinquency and Crime', in *The Child, the Clinic, and the Court* (New York: New Republic, 1927), 117. Healy's ideas are laid out in *The Individual Delinquent: A Text Book of Diagnosis and Prognosis for all Concerned in Understanding Offenders* (London: William Heinemann, 1915).
68. Freud, Foreword to August Aichhorn, *Wayward Youth* (1925, trans. London: Imago, 1951), ix.
69. Anna Freud, 'Adolescence' (1958), *The Writings of Anna Freud*, vol. 5, *Research at the Hampstead Child Therapy Clinic and Other Papers, 1956–1965* (New York: International Universities Press, 1969), 147.
70. Ben B. Lyndsey and Rube Borough, *Dangerous Life* (New York: Horace Liveright, 1925), 6–7. See also Judge Ben B. Lyndsey and Wainright Evans, *The Revolt of Modern Youth* (London: John Lane, 1928).
71. See Allison Morris and Henri Giller, *Understanding Juvenile Justice* (London: Croom Helm, 1987), 26.
72. Burt, *The Young Delinquent*, 21.
73. John Gillis, 'The Evolution of Juvenile Delinquency in England, 1890–1913', *Past and Present* 67 (May 1975).
74. Hall, I, 350.

75. Gillis, 97.
76. Jürgen Habermas, 'Moral Consciousness and Communicative Action', in *Moral Consciousness and Communicative Action* (1983; trans. Christina Lenhardt and Shierry Weber Nicholsen, 1990; Cambridge: Polity, 1995), 126.

3   Poles: The Centre of Europe

1. Virginia Woolf, 'Mr Bennett and Mrs Brown' (1924), *A Woman's Essays*, ed. Rachel Bowlby (London: Penguin, 1992).
2. Letter from Stanislaw Ignacy Witkiewicz to Bronislaw Malinowski (26 May 1921), *A Witkiewicz Reader*, ed. Daniel Gerould (Evanston IL: Northwestern University Press, 1993), 144.
3. Alfred Jarry, 'Conférence Prononcée à la Création d'Ubu Roi' (December 1896), *Ubu* (1931; Paris: Gallimard, 1984), 342. Popular literature, too, had marked central Europe as a particularly *unmarked* site. An anonymous reviewer notes that 'the imaginary principality in Eastern Europe, where the Englishman is a *persona grata*, and where the English constitution and language is more or less the adopted practice of the country, has become of late a common device of the novelist'. 'Rev. of *The Princess Sophia*, by E. F. Benson', *The Bookseller: A Newspaper of British and Foreign Literature* 510 (4 May 1900), 373.
4. 'The Critical Attitude: Little States and Great Nations', *English Review* II (May 1909), 355.
5. 'The Critical Attitude', 358.
6. 'The Critical Attitude', 359.
7. Henry W. Nevinson, 'Notes on the Balkans, with a Table', *English Review* I (December 1908), 186.
8. T. S. Eliot, '*Ulysses*, Order, and Myth', *Dial* 75.5 (November 1923), 482.
9. Eliot, '*Ulysses*, Order, and Myth', 483, 482.
10. Eliot, '*Ulysses*, Order, and Myth', 483.
11. Eliot's work in Lloyds bank involved consideration of the financial consequences of the Treaty of Versailles. See his letters to his mother (18 December 1919, and 6 January 1920), *The Letters of T. S. Eliot*, vol. 1, *1898–1922*, ed. Valerie Eliot (London: Faber, 1988), 351, 353. David Craig notes the importance of the Russian Revolution to *The Waste Land*, in 'The Defeatism of *The Waste Land*', *Critical Quarterly* 2.3 (Autumn 1960). My argument in this section is indebted to that of Stan Smith, in *The Origins of Modernism: Eliot, Pound, Yeats and the Rhetorics of Renewal* (New York: Harvester Wheatsheaf, 1994), especially Chapter 2, Chapter 7, to which I refer the reader for further details of Eliot's relation to Central European politics.
12. Bronislaw Malinowski, *Argonauts of the Western Pacific: An Account of Native Enterprise and Adventure in the Archipelagoes of Melanesian New Guinea* (London: Routledge, 1922; Prospect Heights: Waveland, 1984). This is a photographic reprint of the 1922 edition.
13. Malinowski, *Argonauts*, 9–10.
14. Malinowski, *Argonauts*, 518.

15. Bronislaw Malinowski, *A Diary in the Strict Sense of the Term* (1967; London: Athlone, 1989). There has been some controversy over the ethics of publishing the diary, summarised in Raymond Firth's introduction to the 1989 edition. Further details of this period have emerged with the publication of *The Story of a Marriage: The Letters of Bronislaw Malinowski and Elsie Masson*, vol. 1, *1916–20*, ed. Helena Wayne (London: Routledge, 1995).
16. Raymond Firth, Introduction, *A Diary*, xxvi.
17. Michael Levenson, *A Genealogy of Modernism* (Cambridge: Cambridge University Press, 1984), 218. On modernism's institutional role, see Chris Baldick, *The Social Mission of English Criticism 1848–1932* (Oxford: Clarendon Press, 1983); Louis Menand, *Discovering Modernism: T. S. Eliot and his Context* (Oxford: Oxford University Press, 1987), 97–132; Bruce Robbins, 'Modernism in History, Modernism in Power', *Modernism Reconsidered*, ed. Robert Kiely, assisted by John Hildebidle (Cambridge MA: Harvard University Press, 1983). On the professionalisation of the academy, see Harold Perkin, 'The Professionalisation of University Teaching', *The Structured Crowd: Essays in English Social History* (Sussex: The Harvester Press, 1981).
18. 'Textual Play, Power, and Cultural Critique: An Orientation to Modernist Anthropology', *Modernist Anthropology: From Fieldwork to Text*, ed. Mark Manganaro (Princeton NJ: Princeton University Press, 1990), 31.
19. This argument depends on a substantial body of work on anthropological writing as a cultural product. The central theoretical texts are: James Clifford, *The Predicament of Culture: Twentieth Century Ethnology, Literature, and Art* (Cambridge MA: Harvard University Press, 1988); *Writing Culture: The Politics and Poetics of Ethnology*, ed. James Clifford and George Marcus (Berkeley CA: University of California Press, 1986); Clifford Geertz, *Works and Lives: The Anthropologist as Author* (Stanford CA: Stanford University Press, 1988); Dan Sperber, *On Anthropological Knowledge* (Cambridge: Cambridge University Press, 1985); and Johannes Fabian, *Time and the Other: How Anthropology Makes its Object* (New York: Columbia University Press, 1983). George Stocking, in the collection he edited, *Functionalism Historicised: Essays in British Social Anthropology* (Madison WI: University of Wisconsin Press, 1984), and his *Victorian Anthropology* (New York: The Free Press, 1987), provides useful historical contexts for the theoretical claims. The relation between a new anthropological writing and literary modernism is discussed in Edward Ardener, 'Social Anthropology and the Decline of Modernism', in *Reason and Morality*, ed. Joanna Overing (London: Tavistock, 1985); James Clifford, 'On Ethnographic Self-Fashioning: Conrad and Malinowski', in *Reconstructing Individuality: Autonomy, Individuality and the Self in Western Thought*, ed. Heller, Sosna, and Wellbery (Stanford CA: Stanford University Press, 1986), and in the collection *Modernist Anthropology*, ed. Manganaro.
20. Malinowski, *Argonauts*, xv.
21. T. S. Eliot, 'In Memoriam, Marie Lloyd', *Criterion* I.2 (January 1923), 194.
22. Eliot, 'In Memoriam', 195. W. H. R. Rivers was not just a psychologist, whose work on shell-shock will be discussed in Chapter 5, but also an important ethnographer. See *Functionalism Historicised*; and *Malinowski, Rivers, Benedict and Others: Essays on Culture and Personality*, ed. George W. Stocking Jr. (Madison WI: University of Wisconsin Press, 1984).

Malinowski's functionalism drew on the genealogical methods developed by Rivers.

23. Eliot, 'In Memoriam', 195.
24. T. S. Eliot, 'The Function of Criticism', *Criterion* II.5 (October 1923), 31–2.
25. For a digest of the contents of *The Criterion*, see Agha Shahid Ali, *T. S. Eliot as Editor* (Ann Arbor MI: UMI Research Press, 1986).
26. Eliot, '*Ulysses*, Order, and Myth', 482. Malinowski writes at one point in his *Diary* that 'it occurred to me that the purpose in keeping a diary and trying to control one's life and thoughts must be to consolidate life, to integrate one's thinking, to avoid fragmenting themes' (175).
27. Eliot, 'The Function of Criticism', 33.
28. Sigmund Freud, 'Lecture 31: The Dissection of the Psychical Personality', *New Introductory Lectures on Psychoanalysis* (1933), *Pelican Freud Library*, vol. 2 (Harmondsworth: Penguin, 1981), 112.
29. Freud, 'Lecture 31', 105.
30. Freud's bitterness at Wilson's role in the Versailles treaty re-surfaces in *Group Psychology*, 124, and in the study of Wilson he co-wrote with W. C. Bullit.
31. Eliot, 'The Function of Criticism', 32.
32. See Robert Ackerman, *J. G. Frazer: His Life and Work* (Cambridge University Press, 1987). Frazer's sense that his work could serve 'serious tourists' as well as academic demands marks him as part of a culture innocent of professional anthropology. On modernism's relation to this anthropological paradigm, see particularly *Sir James Frazer and the Literary Imagination: Studies in Affinity and Influence*, ed. Robert Fraser (Basingstoke: Macmillan, 1990).
33. Andrew Lang, *The World's Desire* (1890; London: Longman's, 1929).
34. See Rider Haggard, 'Introduction', *King Solomon's Mines* (1885; rev. edn, London: Cassell, 1907), xi–xii.
35. Walter Besant, *The Pen and the Book*, 30. See also Derek Hudson, 'Reading', in *Edwardian England*, ed. Nowell-Smith.
36. *The Haunted Study*, 164. See also Joseph Bristow, *Empire Boys: Adventures in a Man's World* (London: Unwin Hyman, 1991); Wayne Koestenbaum, *Double Talk: The Erotics of Male Literary Collaboration* (New York: Routledge, 1989), Part 3; and Eve Kosofsky Sedgwick, *Between Men: English Literature and Male Homosexual Desire* (New York: Columbia University Press, 1985).
37. The relation between Frazer and Malinowski is complicated. See, for example, Marilyn Strathearn, 'Out of Context: The Persuasive Fictions of Anthropology', *Modernist Anthropology*, ed. Manganaro.
38. Malinowski, *Argonauts*, 18.
39. Malinowski, *Argonauts*, fig. 1, facing 16.
40. Malinowski, *Argonauts*, 9.
41. Malinowski, *Argonauts*, 25.
42. 'The Natives of Mailu', 650–2. This notion of the social owes much to the Durkheimian influence on British social anthropology. See George Stocking, 'Dr. Durkheim and Mr. Brown: Comparative Sociology at Cambridge in 1910', *Functionalism Historicised*, ed. Stocking.
43. Malinowski, *Argonauts*, 22.
44. Geertz, *Works and Lives*, 1–24.

45. One of the philosophical models of modernist 'immediate knowledge', Bergson's *Les Données immediates de la conscience*, translated as *Time and Free Will* (London: Swann Sonnenschein, 1911), negotiates intuitive knowledge of ontologically distinct realms through a relaxation of pragmatic designs on the objective world. In a cancelled version of the account of his 'beginning', Lewis links the experience of Brittany with Bergson. 'In Paris I began my education [. . .] I attended Bergson's lectures [. . .] *Les Données immediates de la conscience* produced a great effect in my just awakened mind. [. . .] My first stories and literary sketches were written in Brittany [. . .]'. 'Early Draft of Chapter XXI, "How One Begins"', *Rude Assignment*, 248.

46. There is still no full biography of Malinowski. Biographical information used in this chapter is taken from *Man and Culture: An Evaluation of the Work of Bronislaw Malinowski*, ed. Raymond Firth (London: Routledge, 1957); *Malinowski: Between Two Worlds*, ed. Ellen *et al.* (Cambridge: Cambridge University Press, 1988); Robert Thornton and Peter Skalnìk, Introduction, *The Early Writings of Bronislaw Malinowski*, ed. Thornton and Skalnìk (Cambridge: Cambridge University Press, 1993); and R. S. Ashley Montagu, 'Bronislaw Malinowski (1884–1942)', *Isis* 34 (Autumn 1942). On Malinowski's Polish intellectual background, see Jan Jerschina, 'Polish Culture of Modernism and Malinowski's Personality', *Malinowski: Between Two Worlds*; Andrzej K. Paluch, 'The Polish Background to Malinowski's Work', *Man*, ns 16 (1981); Ivan Strenski, 'Malinowski: Second Positivism, Second Romanticism', *Man* ns 17 (1982).

47. Bronislaw Malinowski, 'Observations on Friedrich Nietzsche's *The Birth of Tragedy*' (1904), *The Early Writings*.

48. Paul Carter, *Living in a New Country: History, Travelling and Language* (London: Faber and Faber, 1992), 105.

49. Malinowski, *Argonauts*, 21. George Stocking, in 'Fieldwork in British Anthropology', *Observers Observed: Essays in Ethnographic Fieldwork* (Madison WI: University of Wisconsin Press, 1983), notes that Seligman, Malinowski's mentor at the London School of Economics, had considered that Malinowski might do fieldwork in Poland (96). This would have been almost to repeat the literary ethnography of an earlier generation of Polish modernists, including the poet and playwright Wyspianski, who experimented with living as 'genuine peasants' in rural communities. See Jerschina, 'Polish Culture of Modernism', 140.

50. A critique of the idea (which also summarises some statements of Eliot, on poetry as 'sinking to the most primitive and forgotten, returning to the origin and bringing something back', *The Use of Poetry and the Use of Criticism* [1933; London: Faber, 1964], 119) that participation produces a valuable, 'authentic' knowledge, which can then be returned to the community as a particularly effective writing, is set out influentially in Michel de Certeau, 'Montaigne's "Of Cannibals": The Savage "I"', *Heterologies: Discourse of the Other* (Manchester: Manchester University Press, 1986). See also 'Ethno-Graphy: Speech, or the Space of the Other, Jean de Leery', *The Writing of History* (New York: Columbia University Press, 1988).

51. The Polish state was reconstituted by the Versailles treaty in 1919, whereupon it immediately became involved in the territorial wars which constituted the new Balkan crisis. Between 1918 and 1921, six wars were fought:

with the Ukraine, Germany, Silesia, Lithuania, Czechoslovakia, and the Soviet Union.
52. Norman Davies, *God's Playground: A History of Poland*, vol. 2, *1795 to the Present* (1981; Oxford: Clarendon Press, 1991), 11.
53. Malinowski, *Argonauts*, 9–10.
54. *Argonauts*, 7.
55. According to Strenski, and Edmund Leach in *Man and Culture*, the translation here is faulty, and 'Nigger', translating the coined Polish word 'nigrami', should be replaced by a relatively neutral word choice. In his letters to Elsie Masson, written in English, however, Malinowski repeatedly uses the words 'nigg' and 'nigger'. See *The Story of a Marriage*, x.
56. The *Diary* is written in Polish. Italicised passages in the translation are in other languages, predominantly English.
57. Malinowski, *Diary*, 69.
58. *Diary*, 4.
59. *Diary*, 17.
60. *Diary*, 7.
61. *Diary*, 16.
62. *Diary*, 26, 33, 51.
63. See, for example, *Diary*, 25, 211–12.
64. Pierre Bourdieu, 'The Disenchantment of the World', *Algeria 1960* (1963; trans. Cambridge: Cambridge University Press, 1979). See also *The Algerians* (1958; trans. Boston MA: Beacon Press, 1962). *Outline of a Theory of Practice* (1972; trans. Cambridge: Cambridge University Press, 1977), Bourdieu's classic general theory of social action, was also derived from this period of fieldwork.
65. Nicholas Thomas, in *Entangled Objects: Exchange, Material Culture, and Colonialism in the Pacific* (Cambridge MA: Harvard University Press, 1991), reinterprets exchange in the Pacific to include analysis of the negotiation of power relations within a larger historical and political context, including the history of colonialism and cultural contact. See particularly Chapters 3 and 4.
66. Malinowski, *Argonauts*, 330.
67. Malinowski, *Argonauts*, 465.
68. Bourdieu, *The Algerians*, 155–9.
69. Malinowski, *Diary*, 240.
70. *Diary*, 145.
71. Johannes Fabian, *Time and the Other: How Anthropology Makes its Object* (New York: Columbia University Press, 1983), 171, n. 28.
72. Malinowski, *Diary*, 157. An ethnographer visiting the Trobriand Islands years later was told that Malinowski had great skill in chasing off witches.
73. *Diary*, 105.
74. See Witkiewicz's fictional version of the relationship, in *The 622 Downfalls of Bungo* (1910–11), a section of which is reprinted in *A Witkiewicz Reader*, ed. Daniel Gerould (Evanston: Northwestern University Press, 1993), especially 64–6.
75. Malinowski, *Diary*, 246.
76. Malinowski, *Diary*, 156.

77. Malinowski, *Diary*, 54.
78. Malinowski, *Diary*, 103, 136, 204, 174, 105.
79. Witkiewicz's extraordinary novel, *Insatiability: A Novel in Two Parts* (1932; trans. London: Quartet, 1985), describes the effects of a drug, 'Murti Bing', which causes intellectuals to feel useful and comfortable, and which turns out to be an instrument of colonisation.
80. Letter from Stanislaw Ignacy Witkiewicz to Bronislaw Malinowski (26 May 1921), *A Witkiewicz Reader*, 144.
81. This turning inwards also expresses a melancholia which Malinowski shares with Eliot. Freud, in 'Mourning and Melancholia', a paper written just after 'Thoughts for the Times on War and Death', which registers the complicated disillusionment that attended Freud's initial wartime identification with Austria (and is briefly discussed in Chapter 5), argues that the melancholic, unable to resolve his or her attitude to the lost object, experiences that guilty relation as an ambivalent narcissism. *Pelican Freud Library*, vol. 11, *On Metapsychology: The Theory of Psychoanalysis* (Harmondsworth: Penguin, 1985), especially 266–8.
82. Malinowski, *Diary*, 289, 13.
83. Malinowski, *Argonauts*, 174–94.
84. *Argonauts*, 186, 170.
85. Malinowski to Elsie Masson (15 April 1918), *The Story of a Marriage*, I, 128.
86. *Argonauts*, 3–4.
87. *Argonauts*, 4.
88. For example, *Argonauts*, 55. On Malinowski's admiration for Frazer's narrative style, see Edmund Leach, 'The Epistemological Background to Malinowski's Empiricism', *Man and Culture*, ed. Firth (London: Routledge and Kegan Paul, 1957), 119.
89. Malinowski to Frazer (May 1921), quoted in Robert J. Thornton, ' "Imagine yourself set down . . .": Mach, Frazer, Conrad, Malinowski and the Role of Imagination in Ethnography', *Anthropology Today* I.5 (1985), 12.
90. Malinowski, *Argonauts*, 25.
91. Beatrice Webb (1903), quoted in Sydney Caine, *The History of the Foundation of the London School of Economics and Political Science* (London: G. Bell, 1963), 2.
92. See Beveridge, *The London School of Economics and Its Problems, 1919–1937* (London: George Allen and Unwin, 1960); José Harris, *William Beveridge: A Biography* (Oxford: Clarendon, 1977); Ralf Dahrendorf, *A History of the London School of Economics and Political Science, 1895–1995* (Oxford: Oxford University Press, 1995).
93. Malinowski, *Diary*, 298.
94. Carter, *Living in a New Country*, 1–2.
95. For the most complete English-language outline of the events of Witkiewicz's life, and their relation to Malinowski, see 'Chronology: Stanislaw Ignacy Witkiewicz and Bronislaw Malinowski', in *A Witkiewicz Reader*, 345–52.
96. Witkiewicz to his father (29 June 1914), *A Witkiewicz Reader*, 88–9.
97. There is considerable internal evidence in *A Primitive Arcadia: Being the Impressions of an Artist in Papua* (London: T. Fisher Unwin, 1926), Silas's account of his trip, that he had read *Argonauts of the Western Pacific*.

Malinowski's novelistic account of a generalised first investigation of the massim is repeated almost verbatim as Silas's experience.

98. Quoted in 'Ellis Silas, F.R.G.S., and his Papuan Paintings', *Sketch* 91 (January 1926), 38.

99. Huntley Carter, 'The Post-Savages', *New Age* 8.6 (8 December 1910), 140.

100. E. Wake Cook, 'Post-Savages', *New Age* 8.10 (5 January 1911), 238.

101. On modernism and primitivism, see particularly Robert Goldwater, *Primitivism in Modern Art* (Cambridge MA: Belknap Press, 1986); Gill Perry, 'Primitivism and the "Modern"', in *Primitivism, Cubism, Abstraction: the Early Twentieth Century*, by Harrison, Frascina, and Perry (New Haven CT: Yale University Press, 1993); *'Primitivism' in Twentieth Century Art: The Affinity of the Tribal and the Modern*, ed. William Rubin, 2 vols (New York: Museum of Modern Art, 1984); Julian Stallabrass, 'The Idea of the Primitive: British Art and Anthropology 1918–1930', *New Left Review* 183 (September–October 1990), which discusses Lewis's work briefly, and Marianna Torgovnick, *Gone Primitive: Savage Intellects, Modern Lives* (Chicago IL: University of Chicago Press, 1990), which includes a chapter on Malinowski.

102. Wyndham Lewis, 'Inferior Religions', *Complete Wild Body*, 315.

103. Martine Segalen, *Fifteen Generations of Bretons: Kinship and Society in Lower Brittany, 1720–1980* (Cambridge: Cambridge University Press, 1991), 146–7.

104. 'Inferior Religions', 315.

105. Wyndham Lewis, *Rude Assignment*, 250.

106. Wyndham Lewis, '[untitled]', in 'Beginnings', *Complete Wild Body*, 373–4.

107. Wyndham Lewis, 'The Death of the Ankou', *The Complete Wild Body*, 110.

108. 'The Death of the Ankou', 111.

109. 'The Death of the Ankou', 113, 115.

110. 'The Death of the Ankou', 115.

111. Keith Spence, *Brittany and the Bretons* (London: Gollancz, 1978), 171.

112. Wyndham Lewis, 'Fêng Shui and Contemporary Form', *Blast* I, 138.

113. Emile Souvestre, *Les Derniers Bretons* (Paris, 1836).

114. Spence, 172.

115. The traditions Lewis inhabits are invented. Fishing in Brittany had been big business only since the turn of the century, with the arrival of the canning factories. See Segalen, 21–4. See also Fred Orton and Griselda Pollock, 'Les Données Bretonnantes: la Prairie de Représentation', *Art History* 3.3 (September 1980), for a suggestive discussion of material relations between emergent modern art and the economic history of Brittany at the turn of the century.

116. Wyndham 'The "Pole"', *English Review* 2 (May 1909), *Complete Wild Body*, 211.

117. 'The "Pole"', 209.

118. Lewis's whimsy should perhaps here be placed in some context. Two million people left Malinowski's region, Galicia (with an average population over this period of less than 7 million), in the twenty-five years before the First World War. They left, simply, because Galicia was the poorest province in Europe. See Davies, 145–7.

119. 'The "Pole"', 210, 209 note 2.

120. 'The "Pole"', 211.

121. On Vollard and the art market in Paris before the war, see Michael Baxendall, *Patterns of Intention: On the Historical Explanation of Pictures* (1985; New Haven CT: Yale University Press, 1992), 50–8.
122. Robert Goldwater, *Paul Gauguin* (London: Thames and Hudson, 1985), 14. For Gauguin's entertaining and economically obsessed account of this period, see *The Intimate Journals of Paul Gauguin* (1923; trans. London: KPI, 1985).
123. This is, then, *not* an argument, like that so beautifully constructed by Lewis Hyde, which looks at art as apart from cultural function, a pure 'value' that adds something to the world. His description of the 'gift' of art is one that does not create nor respond to any uncomfortable debts. 'With two or three brief exceptions I do not [. . .] take up the negative side of gift exchange – gifts that leave an oppressive sense of obligation, gifts that manipulate or humiliate, gifts that establish and maintain hierarchies, and so forth and so on [. . .] I have hoped to write an economy of the creative spirit: to speak of the inner gift that we accept as the object of our labour, and the outer gift that has become a vehicle of culture. I am not concerned with gifts given in spite or fear, nor those gifts we accept out of servility or obligation; my concern is the gift we long for, the gift that, when it comes, speaks commandingly to the soul and irresistibly moves us.' *The Gift: Imagination and the Erotic Life of Property* (1979; New York: Random House, 1983), xvi–xvii.
124. 'The "Pole"', 210.
125. 'The "Pole"', 210–11.

4 Dogs: Small Domestic Forms

1. Septimus Clarke, 'Bulldogs in the South: Ten Years' Retrospect', *The Kennel* 2 (1910), 63.
2. Clarke, 63.
3. 'Great Dane', 'Some Breeding Hints', *The Kennel* 6 (1910), 243.
4. For a persuasive comparative account of some European discourses around degeneration, see Daniel Pick, *Faces of Degeneration: A European Disorder, c.1848–c.1918* (Cambridge: Cambridge University Press, 1989).
5. Kate Spencer, 'Is the Dandie degenerate?', *The Kennel* 11 (February 1911), 550. It is tempting here to find in the vision of an emulation of Irishness a non-arbitrary worry. As I'll go on to argue briefly, the relation between questions of form – debates about representation and abstraction – and geographies of Britain reserves a special place for Ireland.
6. Spencer, 550.
7. That is, between a quarter and a half of the subsistence wage for a human family, as defined by, for example, Mrs Pember Reeves, in *Round about a Pound a Week* (1913; London: Virago, 1979).
8. 'Vocomontis', 'The Dachshund in England and Germany', *The Kennel* 2 (1910), 89.
9. 'Vicomontis', 89.
10. Andrew Benjamin, *What is Abstraction?* (London: Academy, 1996), 10.
11. Charles Altieri, *Painterly Abstraction in Modernist American Poetry: The Contemporaneity of Modernism* (Cambridge: Cambridge University Press, 1989), 57–8.

12. See Charles Altieri, 'Can We Be Historical Ever? Some Hopes for a Dialectical Model of Historical Self-consciousness', in *The Uses of Literary History*, ed. Marshall Brown (Durham and London: Duke University Press, 1995).

13. See David Peters Corbett, *The Modernity of English Art, 1914–30* (Manchester: Manchester University Press, 1997) for a careful account of how this question might be answered by opening art history up to a radical cultural materialism.

14. Wyndham Lewis, 'A Review of Contemporary Art', *Blast* 2, 41.

15. Wyndham Lewis, 'The Melodrama of Modernity', *Blast* 1, 144.

16. Wyndham Lewis, 'Futurism, Magic, and Life', *Blast* 1, 135. Possibly the most self-parodying example of futurism is Carra's literalisation of Futurist theories of movement in the image of a sausage dog with multiplying, desperate, blurry little legs.

17. 'Bless England!', *Blast* 1, 22–4.

18. 'Manifesto', *Blast* 1, 34.

19. See, for example, the discussion of Flinders Petrie in Annie Coombes, *Reinventing Africa: Museums, Material Culture and Popular Imagination in Late Victorian and Edwardian England* (New Haven CT: Yale University Press, 1994), 57–9.

20. 'A machine is in a greater or a lesser degree, a living thing. It's [sic] lines and masses imply force and action, whereas those of a dwelling do not.' *Blast* II, 44. This distinction between ways in which the world is inhabited is also imagined as a kind of mimetic competition: 'When you watch an electric crane, swinging up with extraordinary grace and ease a huge weight, your instinct to admire this power is, subconsciously, a selfish one. It is a pity that there are not men so strong that they can lift a house up, and fling it across a river' (43). This might be the ground on which to think the distinction between the abstract and the representational – the distribution between modernism and late capitalism: a distinction between seeing the forms of the outside world as places to settle in and as a blocked model for one's own political-aesthetic willing of the world. This is called – as the piece develops – 'doing what nature does'.

21. 'Bless English Humour', *Blast* 1, 26.

22. Wyndham Lewis, *Tarr* (1918), ed. Paul O'Keefe (Santa Rosa CA: Black Sparrow, 1990), 204–5.

23. Lewis, *Tarr*, 58–9.

24. 'Plain Home-Builder: Where is Your Vorticist?' (1934), *Creatures of Habit and Creatures of Change: Essays on Art, Literature and Society*, ed. Paul Edwards (Santa Rosa CA: Black Sparrow Press, 1989), 248.

25. 'Manifesto', *Blast* 1, 39.

26. 'Manifesto', 39–40 (emphasis mine).

27. *Blasting and Bombadiering* (1937; rev. edn 1967, London: Calder, 1982), 100.

28. Willhelm Worringer, *Abstraction and Empathy: A Contribution to the Psychology of Style* (1908), trans. Michael Bullock (London: Routledge and Kegan Paul, 1953), 5.

29. Worringer, 15.

30. See William Vaughan, 'The Englishness of British Art', *The Oxford Art Journal* 13. 2 (1990), 11–23.

31. His differences from Worringer here lie in the translation from the affect of fear to the condition of separation; and in his disinterest in the aspects shared between abstraction and empathy in Worringer. This makes him more of a formalist than Worringer is and less of a psychologist, and that tendency is clearly completed in Lewis.

32. T. E. Hulme, 'Modern Art and Its Philosophy' (1914), *The Collected Writings of T. E. Hulme*, ed. Karen Csengeri (Oxford: Clarendon Press, 1994), 278.

33. Hulme, 'Modern Art and Its Philosophy', 278.

34. T. E. Hulme, 'Note on the Art of Political Conversion', *The Collected Writings*, 210–11.

35. Cited in José Harris, *Private Lives, Public Spirit: A Social History of Britain, 1870–1914* (Oxford: Oxford University Press, 1993), 256.

36. J. A. Hobson, 'The Inner Meaning of Protectionism' (1903), *Writings on Imperialism and Internationalism*, ed. Peter Cain (London: Routledge, 1992), 367.

37. 'Our Vortex', *Blast* I, 149.

38. 'The Purposes of Jokes', in *Jokes and Their Relation to the Unconscious* (1905), *Pelican Freud Library*, vol. 6 (London: Penguin, 1976), 141.

39. Lisa Tickner, *The Spectacle of Women: Imagery of the Suffrage Campaign, 1907–1914* (Chicago IL: University of Chicago Press, 1988), 52.

40. *Annual Report of the National Canine Defence League* (1910), 39.

41. Quoted in Helen Blackburn, *Women's Suffrage: A Record of the Women's Suffrage Movement in the British Isles* (London: Williams and Norgate, 1902), 85.

42. T. S. Eliot, *The Waste Land: A Facsimile and Transcript of the Original Drafts*, ed. Valerie Eliot (London: Faber, 1971), 144 (V, l. 359).

43. *The Waste Land*, 148.

44. T. S. Eliot to his mother (23 April 1919), *The Letters of T. S. Eliot*, vol. 1, *1898–1922*, ed. Valerie Eliot (London: Faber, 1988), 287.

45. This is the affect which Eliot beautifully captures in the prose poem 'Hysteria' (1917), *Collected Poems 1909–1962* (London: Faber, 1974), 34.

46. Michael Levenson, 'Does *The Waste Land* Have a Politics?', *Modernism/Modernity* 6.3 (1999), 1, 5.

47. Douglas Mao, *Solid Objects: Modernism and the Test of Production* (Princeton NJ: Princeton University Press, 1998).

48. *Annual Report of the National Canine Defence League* (1910), 2.

49. *Annual Report of the National Canine Defence League* (1910), 27.

50. *The Kennel* I (December 1910), 386.

51. James Turner, *Reckoning with the Beast: Animals, Pain, and Humanity in the Victorian Mind* (Baltimore MA: Johns Hopkins, 1980), 27.

52. Judith R. Walkowitz, *Prostitution and Victorian Society: Women, Class, and the State* (Cambridge: Cambridge University Press, 1986), 73.

53. See Nancy Boyd, *Josephine Butler, Octavia Hill, Florence Nightingale: Three Victorian Women Who Changed Their World* (London: Macmillan, 1982), 40–9.

54. Walkowitz, *Prostitution and Victorian Society*, 86.

55. Susan Kingsley Kent, *Sex and Suffrage in Britain, 1860–1914* (London: Routledge, 1990), 86.

56. See Eve Sedgwick, *Between Men: English Literature and Male Homosocial Desire* (New York: Columbia University Press, 1985); Gayle Rubin, 'The Traffic in

Women: Notes Towards a Political Economy of Sex', in *Towards an Anthropology of Women*, ed. Rayma Reiter (New York: Monthly Review Press, 1975).

57. Walkowitz, *Prostitution*, 78.
58. See Sheila Jeffreys, *The Spinster and Her Enemies: Feminism and Sexuality 1880–1930* (London: Pandora, 1985), Chapter 2.
59. This is the trajectory of Wayne Koestenbaum's reading – which draws on Sedgwick's advances – of Eliot's work, in *Double Talk: The Erotics of Male Literary Collaboration* (New York: Routledge, 1989), 112–39.
60. Quoted in Walkowitz, *Prostitution*, 130.
61. *The Lancet* (1891), I, 342.
62. *The Lancet* (1911), I, 1282.
63. David Sime, MD, *Rabies: Its Place Among Germ-Diseases, and its Origin in the Animal Kingdom* (Cambridge: Cambridge University Press, 1903), 39.
64. *Report of the National Canine Defence League* (1906), 49–50.
65. *Report of the National Canine Defence League* (1887), 2.
66. See Kingsley Kent, *Sex and Suffrage*, 48.
67. J. Sidney Turner, 'The Scientific Case for Vivisection', *The Kennel* 1 (April 1910), 13.
68. Turner, 14.
69. David A. Warrell, 'Rabies in Man', in *Rabies: The Facts*, ed. Colin Kaplan (London: Oxford University Press, 1977), 37.
70. *Report of the National Canine Defence League* (1887), 3.
71. *Report of the National Canine Defence League* (1896), 1369.
72. *Report of the National Canine Defence League* (1899), 14.
73. There is an interesting glimpse of the generalisation of the notion that rabies is an effect of repression, in a letter from one of the sexologist Krafft-Ebing's correspondents, a Belgian, who suggests that the pathologies which are attributed to homosexuality, rather than being inherent in his 'Urning' identity, are a result of its repression: 'we are considered sick for a completely valid reason, that we really become sick and that one then confuses cause and effect. . . . We certainly become sick, as animals are stricken by rabies if they are prevented from engaging in the sexual act which is adequate to their nature.' *Psychopathia sexualis*, 5th edition (1890), 129–30, quoted in Harry Oosterhuis, 'Richard von Krafft-Ebing's "Step-Children of Nature": Psychiatry and the Making of Homosexual Identity', *Sexualities in History: A Reader*, ed. Kim M. Phillips and Barry Reay (New York: Routledge, 2002), 281.
74. I'm speaking here of furious rabies, which is by far the more common form the disease takes in man. The rarer condition, 'dumb' or 'paralytic' rabies, is just as fatal, but less theatrical.
75. Warrell, 'Rabies in Man', 37.
76. D. A. Haig, 'Rabies in Animals', in *Rabies: The Facts*, 57.
77. Warrell, 'Rabies in Man', 39.
78. Haig, 'Rabies in Animals', 57.
79. Sime, *Rabies*, 39.
80. Sime, *Rabies*, 42–3.
81. Warrell, 'Rabies in Man', 35.
82. Sime, *Rabies*, 240.

83. Warrell, 'Rabies in Man', 38.
84. Warrell, 'Rabies in Man', 38.
85. Warrell, 'Rabies in Man', 39.
86. Warrell, 'Rabies in Man', 36.
87. Warrell, 'Rabies in Man', 41.
88. *Report of the National Canine Defence League* (1898–99), 2.
89. The animal liberation movement has tended to meet the same limits as other historical instantiations of enlightenment thought. See Charles Dickens, for example, commenting on the excitement surrounding touring groups of 'savages', and on the 'whimpering over him with maudlin admiration, and the affecting to regret him, and the drawing of any comparison of advantage between the blemishes of civilisation and the tenor of his swinish life.' Dogs clinch it for Dickens: 'For evidence of the quality of his moral nature, pass himself for a moment and refer to his "faithful dog." Has he ever improved a dog, or attached a dog, since his nobility first ran wild in woods, and was brought down (at a very long shot) by POPE? Or does the animal that is the friend of man always degenerate in his low society?' *Household Words* (11 June 1853), rpt. in *Selected Journalism, 1850–70* (London: Penguin, 1997), 561.
90. *Report of the National Canine Defence League* (1912), 21.
91. *Report of the National Canine Defence League* (1906), 151.
92. *Report of the National Canine Defence League* (1914), 15.
93. Christabel Pankhurst, *Unshackled: The Story of How We Won the Vote* (London: Hutchinson, 1959), 49. The title was added to the text on its posthumous publication.
94. 'Leaflet 379' (London: National Canine Defence League, nd [1915?]), np.
95. Quoted in Peter Ballard, *A Dog is for Life* (London: National Canine Defence League, 1990), 23.
96. Richard Aldington, *Death of a Hero* (London: Chatto and Windus, 1929), 26, 27.
97. *Report of the National Canine Defence League* (1903), 9.
98. *Report of the National Canine Defence League* (1916), 13.
99. 'Leaflet 361' (London: Canine Defence League, nd [1914]), np.
100. *Report of the National Canine Defence League* (1916), 19.
101. To give just one example: '"Robina," a young greyhound, rescued by a Wigan Police Constable, who found its owner, a collier, slowly cutting its throat with a pocket knife. The dog, moaning piteously and bleeding profusely, was taken to a veterinary surgeon, who successfully treated it, and it is now a lady's much loved companion and pet'. *Annual Report of the National Canine Defence League* (1908), 41.
102. 'Leaflet 354', (London: Canine Defence League, nd [1913]), np.
103. *Captain Loxley's Little Dog*, by the author of *Where's Master* (London: Hodder and Stoughton, 1915), 50. *Where's Master*, by Caesar the King's Dog (London: Hodder and Stoughton, 1911), an elegy for the death of Edward VII, which was one of the best-selling books of that year, displays much of the same intense and strange eroticism.
104. Virginia Woolf, *The Diary of Virginia Woolf*, vol. 4, *1931–35*, ed. Anne Olivier Bell (1982; London: Penguin, 1983), 178.

5   Smoke: Craving History

1. Edmund Gosse, 'War and Literature', *Inter Arma: Being Essays Written in Time of War* (London: Heinemann, 1916), 38.
2. Guy Thorne, *When It Was Dark: The Story of a Conspiracy* (1903; popular edition, London: Greening and Co., 1904).
3. Freud to Ernest Jones, cited in Ernest Jones, *The Life and Work of Sigmund Freud* (1961), ed., abr. Lionel Trilling and Steven Marcus (Harmondsworth, Middlesex: Penguin, 1993), 423–4.
4. For an account of Freud's interest in thought transference, see Pamela Thurschwell, *Literature, Technology and Magical Thinking, 1880–1920* (Cambridge: Cambridge University Press, 2001), Chapter 5: 'Freud, Ferenczi, and Psychoanalysis's Telepathic Transferences'.
5. Eli Zaretsky, *Capitalism, the Family, and Personal Life* (NY: Harper & Row, 1976).
6. Noted in Jones, 438.
7. Sigmund Freud to Martha Freud (9 April 1930), in Michael Molnar, ed. *The Diary of Sigmund Freud, 1929–1939: A Record of the Final Decade* (New York: Scribner, 1992), 64.
8. Sigmund Freud to Sandor Ferenczi (7 May 1930), in Molnar, 69.
9. Sigmund Freud to Minna Bernays (20 May 1938), in Molnar, 227.
10. Cathy Caruth, *Unclaimed Experience: Trauma, Narrative, and History* (Baltimore MD: Johns Hopkins University Press, 1996), 21.
11. Caruth, *Unclaimed Experience*, 18.
12. Caruth, *Unclaimed Experience*, 72.
13. Sigmund Freud, 'Thoughts for the Time on War and Death' (1915), trans. E. C. Mayne, 1925, rev. edn 1957, *Pelican Freud Library*, vol. 12, *Civilisation, Society and Religion* (Harmondsworth, Middlesex: Penguin, 1985), 75.
14. S[andor] Ferenczi, Karl Abraham, Ernst Simmel, and Ernest Jones, *Psychoanalysis and the War Neuroses* (London, 1921), 1.
15. For an outline of this material, see Martin Stone, 'Shellshock and the Psychologists', *Institutions and Society* (London and New York: Tavistock, 1985), vol. 2 of *The Anatomy of Madness: Essays in the History of Psychiatry*, ed. W. F. Bynum, Roy Porter, and Michael Shepherd, 3 vols (1985–88). For a nuanced account of some of the difficulties of psychoanalysis's advance in this context, see Ruth Leys, 'Traumatic Cures: Shellshock, Janet, and the Question of Memory', *Critical Inquiry* 20.4 (Summer 1994).
16. 'The brilliant initial success of the treatment with strong electric currents afterwards proved not to be lasting' (Jones, 23). See also K. R. Eissler, *Freud as Expert Witness: The Discussion of War-Neuroses between Freud and Wagner-Jauregg* (New York, 1986), which notes that Wagner-Jauregg makes the claim that psychoanalysis originates in Janet rather than Freud.
17. See Eric J. Leed, *No Man's Land: Combat and Identity in World War I* (Cambridge: Cambridge University Press, 1979).
18. Sigmund Freud, *Group Psychology and the Analysis of the Ego*, 1921, trans. James Strachey, 1922, rev. edn 1955, *Pelican Freud Library*, vol. 12, *Civilisation, Society and Religion* (Harmondsworth, Middlesex: Penguin, 1985), 126.
19. Ferenczi *et al.*, *Psychoanalysis and the War Neuroses*.
20. *Psychoanalysis and the War Neuroses*, 24.

21. Freud, 'Thoughts', 61.
22. Freud, 'Thoughts', 67.
23. Freud, 'Thoughts', 89.
24. Henri Bergson, *Creative Evolution* (1907; trans. London: Macmillan, 1911), 285.
25. Henri Bergson, *La Signification de la guerre* (Paris: Bloud et Gay, [1915]). Translations are mine. The pamphlet is constructed from two speeches Bergson gave, at the end of 1914 and the beginning of 1915, to the annual public meeting of l'Académie des Sciences Morales et Politiques, and two short papers: 'La Force qui s'use et celle qui ne s'use pas', which develops a point made in the speeches; and 'Hommage au roi Albert et au peuple belge' which is reprinted from an article requested by *The Daily Telegraph*.
26. Émile Durkheim, the sociologist, was another major French intellectual who found that his prestigious ideas could serve propaganda purposes. See *'L'Allemagne au-dessus de tout': La mentalité allemande et la guerre* (Paris: Librairie Armand Colin, 1915), and, with E. Denis, *Qui a voulu la guerre: Les origines de la guerre d'après les documents diplomatiques* (Paris: Armand Colin, 1915).
27. Bergson, *La Signification*, 7.
28. Bergson, *La Signification*, 7, and see also 12, 18, etc.
29. Bergson, *La Signification*, 19.
30. Bergson, *La Signification*, 8.
31. Bergson, *Creative Evolution*, 3
32. Quoted in René Puaux, *Marshal Foch: His Life, His Work, His Faith*, trans. E. Allen (London: Hodder & Stoughton, 1918), 79.
33. Freud too had for a moment a sense of other possibilities within disillusionment, responding to the 1917 revolution with the comment: 'How much one would have entered into this tremendous change if our first consideration were not the matter of peace'; and then noting that: 'I believe that if the submarines do not dominate the situation by September there will be in Germany an awakening from illusions that will lead to frightful consequences' (Jones, 439). Here, though, the 'illusion' is exactly the illusion of an invincible national ego, which had earlier served to disillusion Freud of the possibility of international harmony.
34. Freud 'Thoughts', 64.
35. Freud 'Thoughts', 78–9.
36. When Ferenczi suggests that Freud is like Goethe, Freud enjoys the comparison, but rejects the status as national hero on the ground of 'my attitude toward tobacco which Goethe simply loathed, whereas for my part it is the only excuse I know for Columbus's misdeed.' Freud to Ferenczi (1915), quoted in Jones, 433–4.
37. Freud, 'Thoughts', 79.
38. Freud, 'Thoughts', 79–80.
39. See for example Samuel Hynes, *A War Imagined: The First World War and English Culture* (London: The Bodley Head, 1990); for an account of British writers' enthusiastic involvement in the propaganda campaigns, see Peter Buitenhuis, *The Great War of Words: Literature and Propaganda, 1914–18 and After* (1987, London: Batsford, 1989).

40. Henry James, 'France', *The Book of France*, ed. Winifred Stephens (London: Macmillan, 1915), 7–8.

41. P. J. Flood, in *France 1914–1918: Public Opinion and the War Effort* (Basingstoke: Macmillan Press – now Palgrave Macmillan, 1990), defines the new national subjection: 'It is the nation which unites, and politics which divides. Partisans of all political persuasions were invited to submerge their differences in the higher interests of the nation. Thus stood condemned as "anti-patriotic" the idea of politics and political activity during the war. Thus also did *Union-Sacrée* become synonymous with "sacrifice" ' (22).

42. This harmony was of course occasionally interrupted in its material forms. There were strikes in Paris in 1917, discussed in Jean-Jacques Becker, *The Great War and the French People* (1983; trans. Leamington Spa: Berg, 1985), 205–10, and in Frank Field, *Three French Writers and the Great War: Studies in the Rise of Communism and Fascism* (Cambridge: Cambridge University Press, 1975), 24; and mutinies in most armies at some point in the war. See John Keegan, *The Face of Battle: A Study of Agincourt, Waterloo and the Somme* (London: Pimlico, 1992), 270–2. Becker's study contests the descriptive value of the notion of the *union sacrée*, providing material rather than ideological explanations for the continued consent of populations to the war.

43. Maurice Barrès, *The Undying Spirit of France* (New Haven CT: Yale University Press, 1917), 19. Becker reports that, 'Much later [. . .] Jean Guéhenno called him the "national undertaker," applying to Barrès, as to other journalists of his ilk, the advertising slogan of American undertakers: "You die, we do the rest" ' (162).

44. This is one strain in the argument of Paul Fussell, in *The Great War and Modern Memory* (London: Oxford University Press, 1979).

45. Edmund Gosse, 'War and Literature', *Inter Arma: Being Essays Written in Time of War* (London: Heinemann, 1916), 38, 35.

46. Margaret Anderson, 'The War', *The Little Review* 4.2 (June 1917), 13. I discuss this moment in more detail in 'Shell-Shock, Anti-Semitism, and the Agency of the Avant-Garde', in *Wyndham Lewis and the Art of Modern War*, ed. David Peters Corbett (Cambridge: Cambridge University Press, 1998), 86–92.

47. Gertrude Stein, 'Composition as Explanation' (1926), *Look at Me Now and Here I Am: Writings and Lectures 1909–45*, ed. Patricia Mayerowitz (Harmondsworth, Middlesex: Penguin, 1971), 28.

48. Freud, *Group Psychology*, 124.

49. The stress of most of LeBon's writing is conservative. He sees group behaviours as socially dangerous: the originary instances of the crowd are the Paris Commune of 1871 and Algerian resistance to colonial rule during the same moment. However, during the war – in *Enseignements psychologiques de la guerre européene* (Paris: Ernest Flammarion, 1916), for example – he pragmatically shifted this focus, suggesting that the mechanisms through which the crowd functions can be controlled in order to build successful armies. His theories had substantial impact on the technologies of military control: for details, see Robert A. Nye, *The Origins of Crowd Psychology: Gustave LeBon and the Crisis of Mass Democracy in the Third Republic* (London: Sage, 1975), particularly chapter 6.

50. 'Group psychology' is a slightly unfortunate translation of both Freud's 'Massenpsychologie' meaning both mass-psychology and crowd-psychology and LeBon's *La Psychologie des Foules*, meaning 'crowd psychology'. Strachey's translation dissolves some of the ordinary-language political charge of each, while rhetorically assimilating the notion to the therapeutic situation.

51. Freud, *Group Psychology*, 95.

52. See for example 'The Primal Band', in *The Freudian Subject* (1982) trans. Catherine Porter (Basingstoke: Macmillan, 1988).

53. 'Save', both in the sense of saving phenomena with a new model, and in the more desperate sense of, well, just saving appearances. Borch-Jacobsen notes usefully that the 'subject' is not a particularly Freudian notion, but one that is native to a Lacanian world in which the philosophical and the psychological can be made to coincide, which is a world in which history has been reduced to 'composition'. Being as a subject 'should not be understood in the sense of an "egoist" or "subjectivist" determination of being, but rather in the sense that the whole of being is henceforth to be conceived on the initially Cartesian model of the autofoundation or auto-positioning of a subject presenting itself to itself as consciousness, in representation or in the will, in labor or in desire, in the State or in the work of art.' 'The Freudian Subject', in *The Emotional Tie: Psychoanalysis, Mimesis, and Affect* (1991), trans. Douglas Brick, Xavier Callahan, Angela Brewer, and Richard Miller (Stanford CA: Stanford University Press, 1992), 17.

54. Borch-Jacobsen, 'The Primal Band', 237.

55. Sigmund Freud, 'Why War', (1932), *Pelican Freud Library*, vol. 12, *Civilisation, Society and Religion* (Harmondsworth, Middlesex: Penguin, 1985), 349.

56. Freud, 'Why War', 359.

57. François Roustang, *Dire Mastery: Discipleship from Freud to Lacan*, (1976), trans. Ned Lukacher (Baltimore MD and London: Johns Hopkins, 1982).

58. Borch-Jacobsen, 'The Primal Band', 239.

59. Borch-Jacobsen, 'The Freudian Subject', *The Emotional Tie*.

60. Guy Thorne, *When It Was Dark: The Story of a Conspiracy* (1903; popular edition, London: Greening and Co., 1904).

61. Freud, *Group Psychology*, 127.

62. Quoted in Claud Cockburn, *Bestseller: The Books that Everyone Read* (London: Sidgwick & Jackson, 1972), 19–20.

63. Freud, *Group Psychology*, 127–8.

64. Thorne, *When It Was Dark*, 223.

65. Thorne, *When It Was Dark*, 408.

66. Thorne, *When It Was Dark*, 347.

67. Thorne, *When It Was Dark*, 158.

68. Thorne, *When It Was Dark*, 158.

69. See, for example, 'Generative Scapegoating', in *Violent Origins*, ed. Robert G. Hammerton-Kelly (Stanford CA: Stanford University Press, 1987); *The Scapegoat* (1982), trans. Yvonne Freccero (Baltimore MD: Johns Hopkins University Press, 1986).

70. Freud, *Group Psychology*, 128.

71. The same sort of unassimilated evidence can be found in the earlier text, 'Thoughts for the Time on War and Death'. Speaking about the oceanic and disarticulated state of 'civilisation' which precedes disillusionment, Freud qualifies his earlier remarks, noting that: 'Observation showed, to be sure, that embedded in these civilised states there were remnants of certain other peoples, which were universally unpopular and had therefore been only reluctantly, and even so not fully, admitted to participation in the common work of civilisation, for which they had shown themselves suitable enough' (63). This flash of constituency is a significant modification of the earlier claim, that only unaccountably paralysed individuals were blocked from full enjoyment of the pre-war world. But again, this datum is never integrated; it remains an aside to the alternately enthusiastic and resigned work of the essay, which aligns its expression with the 'reality' of wartime nationalisms.

72. Freud, *Group Psychology*, 128.

73. There are elements of psychoanalysis which draw upon aspects of Jewish culture, and the ascription from outside of essential Jewishness to psycho-analytical ideas has been a constant accompaniment to the development of the institution.

74. Jones, 241.

75. See Slavoj Zizek, *For They Know Not What They Do: Enjoyment as a Political Factor* (London: Verso, 1991).

76. Richard Klein, *Cigarettes are Sublime* (Durham NC: Duke University Press, 1993), 12.

77. Klein, 12. Klein does give some speculative rationalisation of the relations between tyrants and smokers: 'the reasons may have to do with these tyrants' moralizing tendency and their allergic reaction to individual acts of expressive freedom' (12).

78. Klein, 143.

79. One visceral reason, perhaps, for resisting this alignment of freedom and death is that the unconscious conflation has been a constant trope in the tactics of the tobacco corporations. Philip Morris, for example, sponsored the publication and distribution of the Bill of Rights. See Hans Haake's artwork 'Helmsboro Country', and the discussion of it in Hans Haake and Pierre Bourdieu, *Free Exchange* (Cambridge: Polity, 1995), 8–10.

80. Michel de Certeau, *The Practice of Everyday Life*, 29–42.

81. Kieran O'Connor, 'Individual Differences and Motor Systems in Smoker Motivation', in *Smoking and Human Behaviour*, ed. Ney and Gale (Chichester: Wiley, 1989), 157.

82. Thorne, *When It Was Dark*, 100.

83. Thorne, *When It Was Dark*, 9.

84. Thorne, *When It Was Dark*, 11.

85. Thorne, *When It Was Dark*, 67.

86. Thorne, *When It Was Dark*, 50.

87. The ascription of the origin of the cigarette habit to a demonised elsewhere, to somewhere outside the healthily constituted nation or person, is a con-stant one. In Britain, which was the fastest of all nations in its conversion from other forms of tobacco consumption to cigarette smoking, cigarettes were seen as either French or 'Eastern' (often Turkish). In the United States,

which 'resisted' conversion to the cigarette habit for longer than Britain, they were seen as broadly and perversely European. See Ans Nicolaides-Bouman, *International Smoking Statistics* (London: Wolfson Institute, 1993), for an historical account of the details of the differential patterns of global tobacco consumption. For an excellent narrative overview of global conversion to the cigarette, see Jordan Goodman, *Tobacco in History: The Cultures of Dependence* (London: Routledge, 1993), particularly chapter 5.

88. Cyril Edward Arthur Ranger Gull, *The Cigarette Smoker* (London: Greening, 1902), 62–3.
89. Gull, *The Cigarette Smoker*, 138.
90. Gull, *The Cigarette Smoker*, 137–8.
91. Bruce Robbins, 'Modernism in History, Modernism in Power', in *Modernism Reconsidered*, ed. Robert Kiely (Cambridge MA: Harvard University Press, 1983).
92. Anthony Easthope, Letter, *The Guardian* (7 October 1995), 28.

Bibliography

Ackerman, Robert. *J.G. Frazer: His Life and Work*. Cambridge: Cambridge University Press, 1987.

Ackroyd, Peter. *T. S. Eliot*. London: Penguin, 1993.

Adler, Alfred. *The Practice and Theory of Individual Psychology*. London: Kegan Paul, 1924.

Advert for Ozonair Ltd. *The Tramp* I (June–July 1910): xxiii.

Aichhorn, August. *Wayward Youth*. 1925. Trans. London: Imago, 1951.

Aldington, Richard. *Death of a Hero*. London: Chatto and Windus, 1929.

'Algernon Charles Swinburne'. *English Review* 2 (May 1909): 194.

Ali, Agha Shahid. *T. S. Eliot as Editor*. Ann Arbor MI: UMI Research Press, 1986.

Altieri, Charles. 'Can We Be Historical Ever? Some Hopes for a Dialectical Model of Historical Self-consciousness'. *The Uses of Literary History*. Ed. Marshall Brown. Durham NC and London: Duke University Press, 1995. 219–32.

——. *Painterly Abstraction in Modernist American Poetry: The Contemporaneity of Modernism*. Cambridge: Cambridge University Press, 1989.

Anderson, Margaret. 'The War'. *The Little Review* 4.2 (June 1917): 13.

Anesko, Michael. *'Friction with the Market': Henry James and the Profession of Authorship*. New York: Oxford University Press, 1986.

Ardener, Edward. 'Social Anthropology and the Decline of Modernism'. *Reason and Morality*. Ed. Joanna Overing. London: Tavistock, 1985. 47–70.

Armstrong, Tim. *Modernism, Technology, and the Body: A Cultural Study*. Cambridge: Cambridge University Press, 1998.

Ayers, David. *Wyndham Lewis and Western Man*. Basingstoke: Macmillan, 1992.

Bailey, Victor. *Delinquency and Citizenship: Reclaiming the Young Offender, 1914–1948*. Oxford: Clarendon Press, 1987.

Bakhtin, Mikhail. *Problems of Dostoevsky's Poetics*. Trans., ed. Caryl Emerson. Minneapolis: University of Minnesota Press, 1984.

Baldick, Chris. *The Social Mission of English Criticism 1848–1932*. Oxford: Clarendon Press, 1983.

Ballard, Peter. *A Dog is for Life*. London: National Canine Defence League, 1990.

Baring, Maurice. *Landmarks in Russian Literature*. London: Methuen, 1910.

Barrès, Maurice. *The Undying Spirit of France*. Trans. Margaret W. B. Corwin. New Haven CT: Yale University Press, 1917.

Baxendall, Michael. *Patterns of Intention: On the Historical Explanation of Pictures*. 1985. New Haven CT: Yale University Press, 1992.

Becker, Jean-Jacques. *The Great War and the French People*. 1983. Trans. Arnold Pomerans. Leamington Spa: Berg, 1985.

Benjamin, Andrew. *What is Abstraction?* London: Academy, 1996.

Benjamin, Walter. 'The Destructive Character'. *One Way Street and Other Writings*. Trans. Edmund Jephcott and Kingsley Shorter. London: Verso, 1979. 157–9.

——. 'On Some Motifs in Baudelaire'. *Illuminations: Essays and Reflections*. 1955. Trans. Harry Zohn. Ed. Hannah Arendt. 1968. Rev. edn New York: Schocken, 1979. 155–200.

Bennett, Arnold. *Fame and Fiction*. London: Grant Richards, 1901.

——. *How to Be an Author*. London: C. Arthur Pearson, 1903.

Bennett, James. *Oral History and Delinquency: The Rhetoric of Criminology*. Chicago: University of Chicago Press, 1981.

Bergson, Henri. *Time and Free Will: An Essay on the Immediate Data of Consciousness*. 1899. Trans. F. L. Pogson. London: Swann Sonnenshein, 1910.

——. *Laughter: An Essay on the Meaning of the Comic*. [1900]. Trans. Cloudesley Brereton and Fred Rothwell. London: Macmillan, 1911.

——. *La Signification de la guerre*. Paris: Bloud et Gay, n.d. [1915].

——. *An Introduction to Metaphysics*. [1903]. Trans. T.E. Hulme. London: Macmillan, 1913.

——. *Matter and Memory*. 1896. Trans. Nancy Margaret Paul and W. Scott Palmer. 1910. New York: Zone Books, 1991.

——. *Creative Evolution*. 1907. Trans. Arthur Mitchell. London: Macmillan, 1911.

Bersani, Leo. 'Sexuality and Sociality'. *Critical Inquiry* 26 (Summer 2000): 641–56.

Besant, Walter. *The Pen and the Book*. London: Thomas Burleigh, 1899.

Beveridge, William. *The London School of Economics and Its Problems, 1919–1937*. London: George Allen and Unwin, 1960.

Blackburn, Helen. *Women's Suffrage: A Record of the Women's Suffrage Movement in the British Isles with Biographical Sketches of Miss Becker*. London: Williams and Norgate, 1902.

Blackwood, Algernon. *The Empty House and Other Ghost Stories*. London: Eveleigh Nash, 1906.

——. *Episodes Before Thirty*. London: Cassell, 1923.

——. *John Silence: Physician Extraordinary*. London: Eveleigh Nash, 1908.

Borch-Jacobsen, Mikkel. *The Freudian Subject*. 1982. Trans. Catherine Porter. Basingstoke: Macmillan, 1988.

——. *The Emotional Tie: Psychoanalysis, Mimesis, and Affect*. 1991. Trans. Douglas Brick, Xavier Callahan, Angela Brewer, and Richard Miller. Stanford CA: Stanford University Press, 1992.

Bourdieu, Pierre. *The Algerians*. 1958. Rev. edn 1961. Trans. Alan C. M. Ross. Boston MA: Beacon Press, 1962.

——. 'The Disenchantment of the World'. *Algeria 1960*. 1963. Trans. Richard Nice. Cambridge: Cambridge University Press, 1979. 1–94.

——. *Outline of a Theory of Practice*. 1972. Rev. edn Trans. Richard Nice. Cambridge: Cambridge University Press, 1977.

——. *Distinction: A Social Critique of the Judgment of Taste*. 1979. Trans. Richard Nice. 1984. London: Routledge, 1992.

——. *The Logic of Practice*. 1980. Trans. Richard Nice. 1990. Cambridge: Polity Press, 1992.

——. *The Field of Cultural Production: Essays on Art and Literature*. Ed. Randal Johnson. Trans. Richard Nice, R. Swyer, Claud DuVerlie, Priscilla Parkhurst Ferguson, Juliette Parnell, Charles Newman. Cambridge: Polity Press, 1993. Collects articles first published between 1968 and 1987.

——, and Hans Haake. *Free Exchange*. Cambridge: Polity, 1995.

——, and Jean-Claude Passeron. *Reproduction in Education, Society, and Culture*. 1970. Trans. Richard Nice. 1977. Rev. edn London: Sage, 1990.

Boyd, Nancy. *Josephine Butler, Octavia Hill, Florence Nightingale: Three Victorian Women Who Changed Their World*. London: Macmillan, 1982.

Bray, Reginald. *Boy Labour and Apprenticeship*. London: Constable, 1911.

——. *The Town Child*. London: T. Fisher Unwin, 1907.

Bristow, Joseph. *Empire Boys: Adventures in a Man's World*. London: Unwin Hyman, 1991.

Buitenhuis, Peter. *The Great War of Words: Literature and Propaganda, 1914–18 and After*. 1987. London: Batsford, 1989.

Bürger, Peter. *Theory of the Avant-Garde*. 1974. Trans. Michael Shaw. Manchester: Manchester University Press, 1984.

——. *The Decline of Modernism*. Trans. Nicholas Walker. Cambridge: Polity, 1992.

Burt, Cyril. *The Young Delinquent*. London: University of London Press, 1925.

Caesar the King's Dog. Where's Master? London: Hodder & Stoughton, 1911.

Capie, Forest and Geoffrey Wood. 'Money in the Economy, 1870–1939'. *The Economic History of Britain since 1700*. Ed. Roderick Floud and D. N. McCloskey. Vol. 2. *1860–1939*. Second edition. Cambridge: Cambridge University Press, 1994. 217–46.

Captain Loxley's Little Dog. By the author of *Where's Master?* London: Hodder and Stoughton, 1915.

Caine, Sydney. *The History of the Foundation of the London School of Economics and Political Science*. London: G. Bell, 1963.

Carter, Huntley. 'The Post-Savages'. *New Age* 8.6 (8 December 1910): 140.

Carter, Paul. *Living in a New Country: History, Travelling and Language*. London: Faber, 1992.

Caruth, Cathy. *Unclaimed Experience: Trauma, Narrative, and History*. Baltimore MD: Johns Hopkins University Press, 1996.

Cather, Willa. *Not Under Forty*. 1936. Lincoln NB: University of Nebraska Press, 1988.

Certeau, Michel de. *Heterologies: Discourse of the Other*. Manchester: Manchester University Press, 1986.

——. *The Practice of Everyday Life*. Berkeley CA: University of California Press, 1988.

——. *The Writing of History*. New York: Columbia University Press, 1988.

Clark, T. J. *Farewell to an Idea: Episodes from a History of Modernism*. New Haven CT: Yale University Press, 1999.

Clarke, Septimus. 'Bulldogs in the South: Ten Years' Retrospect'. *The Kennel* 2 (1910): 63.

Clifford, James. 'On Ethnographic Self-Fashioning: Conrad and Malinowski'. *Reconstructing Individuality: Autonomy, Individuality and the Self in Western Thought*. Ed. Heller, Sosna, and Wellbery. Stanford CA: Stanford University Press, 1986. 140–62.

——. *The Predicament of Culture: Twentieth Century Ethnology, Literature, and Art*. Cambridge: Harvard University Press, 1988.

——, and George Marcus, eds. *Writing Culture: The Politics and Poetics of Ethnology*. Berkeley CA: University of California Press, 1986.

Cockburn, Claud. *Bestseller: The Books that Everyone Read*. London: Sidgwick & Jackson, 1972.

Cook, E. Wake. 'Post-Savages'. *New Age* 8.10 (5 Jan 1911): 238.

Coombes, Annie. *Reinventing Africa: Museums, Material Culture and Popular Imagination in Late Victorian and Edwardian England*. New Haven CT: Yale University Press, 1994.

Copeau, Jacques. 'Sur le *Dostoïevski* de Suarès'. *Nouvelle Revue Française* 7 (1912): 226–41.

Corbett, David Peters. *The Modernity of English Art, 1914–30*. Manchester: Manchester University Press, 1997.

Cornick, Martyn. *The Nouvelle Revue Française under Jean Paulhan, 1925–1940*. Amsterdam: Rodolphi, 1995.

Craig, David. 'The Defeatism of *The Waste Land*'. *Critical Quarterly* 2.3 (Autumn 1960): 241–52.

Dangerfield, George. *The Strange Death of Liberal England*. London: Constable, 1936.

Davies, Norman. *God's Playground: A History of Poland*. Vol 2. *1795 to the Present*. 1981. Oxford: Clarendon Press, 1991.

Dickens, Charles. *Selected Journalism, 1850–70*. Ed. David Pascoe. London: Penguin, 1997.

Dolto, Françoise. *La Cause des adolescents*. Paris: Lafont, 1998.

Dostoevsky, Fyodor. *Notebooks for* A Raw Youth. Ed Edward Wasiolek. Trans. Victor Terras. Chicago: University of Chicago Press, 1969.

——. *A Raw Youth*. Trans. Constance Garnett. London: Heinemann, 1916.

——. *The Adolescent*. Trans. Richard Pevear and Larissa Volokhonsky. New York: Alfred Knopf, 2003.

Dupuy, Jean-Pierre. 'De l'Economie considérée comme théorie de la foule'. *Stanford French Review* 7 (Summer 1983): 245–63.

Durkheim, Emile. 'L'Allemagne au-dessus de tout': La mentalité allemande et la guerre*. Paris: Librairie Armand Colin, 1915.

Durkheim, Emile, and E. Denis. *Qui a voulu la guerre: Les origines de la guerre d'après les documents diplomatiques*. Paris: Librairie Armand Colin, 1915.

Eagle, Solomon. [J. C. Squire]. 'Current Literature: Books in General'. *The New Statesman* 3 (4 July 1914): 406.

Easthope, Anthony. Letter. *The Guardian* (7 Oct 1995): 28.

Edel, Leon. *Henry James*. Vol. 4. *The Treacherous Years: 1895–1901*. New York: Avon Books, 1978.

Eissler, K. R. *Freud as Expert Witness: The Discussion of War-Neuroses between Freud and Wagner-Jauregg*. New York, 1986.

Eliot, T[homas] S[tearns]. *Collected Poems 1909–1962*. London: Faber, 1974.

——. 'The Function of Criticism'. *Criterion* 2.5 (October 1923): 31–42.

——. 'In Memoriam, Marie Lloyd'. *Criterion* I.2 (Jan. 1923): 192–5.

——. *'The Letters of T. S. Eliot*. Vol 1. *1898–1922*. Ed. Valerie Eliot. London: Faber, 1988.

——. Ulysses, Order, and Myth'. *Dial* 75.5 (Nov. 1923): 480–83.

——. *The Use of Poetry and the Use of Criticism*. 1933. London: Faber, 1964.

——. *The Waste Land: A Facsimile and Transcript of the Original Drafts*. 1922. Ed. Valerie Eliot. London: Faber, 1971.

——. 'Lettre d'Angleterre', trans G. d'Hangest, *Nouvelle Revue Française* 21 (1923): 619–25.

Ellen, Roy, Ernest Gellner, Grazyna Kubica, and Janusz Mucha, eds. *Malinowski: Between Two Worlds*. Cambridge: Cambridge University Press, 1988.

Ellis, Havelock. *Impressions and Comments: Third (and Final) Series, 1920–1923.* London: Constable, 1924.

'Ellis Silas, F.R.G.S., and his Papuan Paintings'. *The Sketch* 91 (January 1926): 38–43.

Ellmann, Maud. 'Eliot's Abjection'. In *Abjection, Melancholia, and Love: The Work of Julia Kristeva.* Ed. Andrew Benjamin and John Fletcher. London: Routledge, 1990. 178–200.

——. *The Hunger Artists: Writing, Starving, and Imprisonment.* London: Virago, 1995.

Esch, Deborah. 'A Jamesian About-Face: Notes on "The Jolly Corner"'. *ELH* 50.3 (Fall 1983): 587–605.

Eysteinsson, Astradur. *The Concept of Modernism.* Ithaca NY: Cornell University Press, 1990.

Fabian, Johannes. *Time and the Other: How Anthropology Makes its Object.* New York: Columbia University Press, 1983.

Ferenczi, S[andor], Karl Abraham, Ernst Simmel, and Ernest Jones. *Psychoanalysis and the War Neuroses.* London, 1921.

Field, Frank. *Three French Writers and the Great War: Studies in the Rise of Communism and Fascism.* Cambridge: Cambridge University Press, 1975.

'First Report of the Committee on Haunted Houses'. *Proceedings of the Society for Psychical Research* I (1882): 101–15.

Firth, Raymond, ed. *Man and Culture: An Evaluation of the Work of Bronislaw Malinowski.* London: Routledge, 1957.

Flood, P. J. *France 1914–1918: Public Opinion and the War Effort.* Basingstoke: Macmillan, 1990.

Foucault, Michel. *Les Anormaux: cours au College de France, 1974–1975.* Paris: Gallimard, 1999.

——. *Discipline and Punish: The Birth of the Prison.* 1975. Trans. Alan Sheridan. 1977. London: Penguin, 1991.

——. 'How Much Does It Cost For Reason to Tell the Truth?'. Interview with Gerard Raulet. 1983. Trans. Mia Foret and Marion Martius. *Foucault Live.* Ed. Sylvère Lotringer. New York: Semiotext(e), 1989. 233–56.

Fraser, Robert, ed. *Sir James Frazer and the Literary Imagination: Studies in Affinity and Influence.* Basingstoke: Macmillan, 1990.

Freeman, Arnold. *Boy Life and Labour: The Manufacture of Inefficiency.* London: P. S. King, 1914.

——. *How to Avoid a Revolution.* London: George Allen & Unwin, 1919.

Freud, Anna. 'Adolescence'. *The Writings of Anna Freud.* Vol. 5. *Research at the Hampstead Child Therapy Clinic and Other Papers, 1956–1965.* New York: International Universities Press, 1969. 137–66.

Freud, Sigmund. *Five Lectures on Psycho-Analysis.* 1910. Trans. James Strachey. 1957. *Two Short Accounts of Psycho-Analysis.* Harmondsworth, Middlesex: Penguin, 1984. 31–87. First English translation 1910.

——. *Totem and Taboo.* 1913. Trans. James Strachey. 1950. Rev. ed. 1953. *Pelican Freud Library.* Vol. 13. *The Origins of Religion.* Harmondsworth: Penguin, 1985. 45–224. First English translation 1918.

——. 'Family Romances'. *Pelican Freud Library.* Vol. 7. *On Sexuality.* Harmondsworth: Penguin, 1977.

Bibliography 207

——. 'Der Familienroman der Neurotiker'. *Gessamelte Werke*. Vol. 7. *Werke aus den Jahren 1906–1909*. London: Imago, 1941.

——. 'Thoughts for the Time on War and Death'. 1915. Trans. E. C. Mayne. 1925. Rev. edn 1957. *Pelican Freud Library*. Vol. 12. *Civilisation, Society and Religion*. Harmondsworth, Middlesex: Penguin, 1985. 58–89. First English translation 1918.

——. 'Mourning and Melancholia'. 1917. Trans. Joan Riviere. 1925. Rev. ed. 1957. *Pelican Freud Library*. Vol. 11. *On Metapsychology: The Theory of Psychoanalysis*. Harmondsworth, Middlesex: Penguin, 1985. 247–68. Written May 1915.

——. *Group Psychology and the Analysis of the Ego*. 1921. Trans. James Strachey. 1922. Rev. edn 1955. *Pelican Freud Library*. Vol. 12. *Civilisation, Society and Religion*. Harmondsworth, Middlesex: Penguin, 1985. 93–178. Translation of *Massenpsychologie und Ich-Analyse*. Leipzig: Internationaler Psychoanalytischer Verlag, 1921.

——. *New Introductory Lectures on Psychoanalysis*. 1933. Trans. James Strachey. 1964. *Pelican Freud Library*. Vol. 2. Harmondsworth, Middlesex: Penguin, 1981. First English translation 1933.

——. *Jokes and Their Relation to the Unconscious*. (1905). *Pelican Freud Library*. Vol. 6. London: Penguin, 1976.

Fussell, Paul. *The Great War and Modern Memory*. 1975. London: Oxford University Press, 1979.

Gard, Roger Martin du. *Notes on André Gide*. Trans. John Russell. London: André Deutsch, 1953.

Gauguin, Paul. *The Intimate Journals of Paul Gauguin*. 1923. London: KPI, 1985.

Geertz, Clifford. *Works and Lives: The Anthropologist as Author*. Stanford CA: Stanford University Press, 1988.

Gide, André. *Journal, 1889–1939*. Paris: Gallimard, 1951.

——. *Dostoïevski*. 1923. Paris: Gallimard, 1981.

Gilbert, Geoffrey. *A Career in Modernism: Wyndham Lewis, 1909–1931*. PhD thesis. Cambridge, 1995.

——. 'Intestinal Violence: Wyndham Lewis and the Critical Poetics of the Modernist Career'. *Critical Quarterly* 36.3 (Autumn 1994): 86–125.

——. 'Shell-Shock, Anti-Semitism, and the Agency of the Avant-Garde'. *Wyndham Lewis and the Art of Modern War*. Ed. David Peters Corbett. Cambridge: Cambridge University Press, 1998. 78–98.

Gillis, John. 'The Evolution of Juvenile Delinquency in England, 1890–1913'. *Past and Present* 67 (May 1975): 99–103.

Girard, René. 'Generative Scapegoating'. *Violent Origins*. Ed. Robert G. Hammerton-Kelly. Stanford CA: Stanford University Press, 1987. 73–105.

——. *The Scapegoat*. 1982. Trans. Yvonne Freccero. Baltimore MD: Johns Hopkins University Press, 1986.

'George Meredith, OM'. *English Review* 2 (June 1909): 409.

Goldring, Douglas. *South Lodge: Reminiscences of Violet Hunt, Ford Madox Ford and the English Review Circle*. London: Constable, 1943.

Goldwater, Robert. *Paul Gauguin*. London: Thames and Hudson, 1985.

——. *Primitivism in Modern Art*. Cambridge MA: Belknap Press, 1986.

Goodman, Jordan. *Tobacco in History: The Cultures of Dependence*. London: Routledge, 1993.

Gosse, Edmund. *Inter Arma: Being Essays Written in Time of War*. London: Heinemann, 1916.

'Great Dane' [pseud]. 'Some Breeding Hints'. *The Kennel* 6 (1910): 243.

Gull, Cyril Edward Arthur Ranger. *The Cigarette Smoker*. London: Greening, 1902.

Habermas, Jürgen. 'Moral Consciousness and Communicative Action'. *Moral Consciousness and Communicative Action*. 1983. Trans. Christina Lenhardt and Shierry Weber Nicholsen. 1990. Cambridge: Polity, 1995. 116–94.

Haggard, Rider, *King Solomon's Mines*. 1885. Rev. edn. London: Cassell, 1907.

——, and Andrew Lang. *The World's Desire*. 1890. London: Longman's, 1929.

Hall, G. Stanley. *Adolescence: Its Psychology, and its Relations to Physiology, Anthropology, Sex, Crime, Religion, and Education*. 2 vols. New York: D. Appleton, 1904.

Haraway, Donna. *The Companion Species Manifesto: Dogs, People, and Significant Otherness*. Chicago: Prickly Paradigm Press, 2003.

Harris, José. *Private Lives, Public Spirit: A Social History of Britain, 1870–1914*. Oxford: Oxford University Press, 1993.

——. *William Beveridge: A Biography*. Oxford: Clarendon, 1977.

Harrison, Charles, Francis Frascina, and Gill Perry. *Primitivism, Cubism, Abstraction: The Early Twentieth Century*. New Haven CT: Yale University Press, 1993.

Hawthorne, Geoffrey. *Plausible Worlds: Possibility and Understanding in History and the Social Sciences*. Cambridge: Cambridge University Press, 1991.

Healy, William. *The Child, the Clinic, and the Court*. New York: New Republic, 1927.

——. *The Individual Delinquent: A Text Book of Diagnosis and Prognosis for All Concerned in Understanding Offenders*. London: William Heinemann, 1915.

Hobson, J. A. *The Crisis of Liberalism: New Issues of Democracy*. London: P.S. King and Son, 1909.

——. 'The Extension of Liberalism'. *The English Review* 2 (November 1909).

——. 'The Inner Meaning of Protectionism'. 1903. *Writings on Imperialism and Internationalism*. Ed. Peter Cain. London: Routledge, 1992.

Houen, Alex. *Terrorism and Modern Literature: From Joseph Conrad to Ciaran Carson*. Oxford: Oxford University Press, 2002.

Hudson, Derek. 'Reading'. *Edwardian England 1901–1914*. Ed. Simon Nowell-Smith. London: Oxford University Press, 1964. 303–26.

Hueffer, Ford Madox. 'The Critical Attitude: Little States and Great Nations'. *English Review* 2 (May 1909): 355–9.

——. 'The Function of the Arts in the Republic'. *The English Review* I (December 1908): 175–6.

——. 'Literary Portraits – XLII: Mr Wyndham Lewis and "Blast"'. *The Outlook* 34 (4 July 1914): 15–16.

Hulme, T. E. *The Collected Writings of T. E. Hulme*. Ed. Karen Csengeri. Oxford: Clarendon Press, 1994.

Humphries, Steve. *Hooligans or Rebels?: An Oral History of Working-Class Childhood and Youth, 1889–1939*. Oxford: Blackwell, 1981.

Hurley, Frank. *Pearls and Savages: Adventures in the Air, on Land and Sea in New Guinea*. New York: G.P. Putnam's Sons, 1924.

——. *Argonauts of the South: Being a Narrative of Voyagings in Polar Seas and Adventures in the Antarctic with Sir Douglas Mawson and Sir Ernest Shackleton*. New York: G.P. Putnam's Sons, 1925.

Hyde, Lewis. *The Gift: Imagination and the Erotic Life of Property*. 1979. New York: Random House, 1983.

Hynes, Samuel. *A War Imagined: The First World War and English Culture*. London: The Bodley Head, 1990.

James, Henry. *The Ambassadors*. 1903. Ed. Harry Levin. Harmondsworth, Middlesex: Penguin, 1986.

——. *Autobiography*. Ed. Frederick W. Dupee. 1956. Princeton NJ: Princeton University Press, 1983.

——. 'France'. *The Book of France*. Ed. Winifred Stephens. London: Macmillan, 1915.

——. 'The Jolly Corner'. *The English Review* I (December 1908). Rpt. in *The Jolly Corner and Other Tales*. Ed. Roger Gard. London: Penguin, 1987. 161–93.

——. 'The New Novel'. 1914. *The Critical Muse: Selected Literary Criticism*. Ed. Roger Gard. London: Penguin, 1987.

——. 'The Third Person'. 1900. *The Jolly Corner and Other Tales*. Ed. Roger Gard. London: Penguin, 1990. 15–45.

——. 'The Velvet Glove'. *The English Review* 2 (March 1909). Rpt in *The Jolly Corner and Other Tales*. Ed. Roger Gard. London: Penguin, 1987. 194–220.

Jarry, Alfred. 'Conférence Prononcée à la Création d'Ubu Roi'. Dec. 1896. *Ubu*. 1931. Paris: Gallimard, 1984.

Jeffreys, Sheila. *The Spinster and Her Enemies: Feminism and Sexuality 1880–1930*. London: Pandora, 1985.

Jerschina, Jan. 'Polish Culture of Modernism and Malinowski's Personality'. In *Malinowski: Between Two Worlds*. Ed. Roy Ellen, Ernest Gellner, Grazyna Kubica, and Janusz Mucha. Cambridge: Cambridge University Press, 1988. 128–48.

Jones, Gareth Stedman. *Outcast London: A Study of the Relationship between Classes in Victorian Society*. Oxford: Clarendon Press, 1971.

Jones, Ernest. *The Life and Work of Sigmund Freud*. Ed., abr. Lionel Trilling and Steven Marcus. 1961. Harmondsworth, Middlesex: Penguin, 1993.

Kaplan, Colin, ed. *Rabies: The Facts*. London: Oxford University Press, 1977.

Kaye, Peter. *Dostoevsky and English Modernism: 1900–1930*. Cambridge: Cambridge University Press, 1999.

Keating, Peter. *The Haunted Study: A Social History of the English Novel 1875–1914*. London: Fontana, 1991.

Keegan, John. *The Face of Battle: A Study of Agincourt, Waterloo and the Somme*. 1976. London: Pimlico, 1992.

Kent, Susan Kingsley. *Sex and Suffrage in Britain, 1860–1914*. 1987. London: Routledge, 1990.

Klein, Richard. *Cigarettes are Sublime*. Durham NC: Duke University Press, 1993.

Koestenbaum, Wayne. *Double Talk: The Erotics of Male Literary Collaboration*. New York: Routledge, 1989.

Koven, Seth. 'From Rough Lads to Hooligans: Boy Life, National Culture and Social Reform'. *Nationalisms and Sexualities*. Ed. Andrew Parker, Doris Sommer, and Patricia Yaeger. New York: Routledge, 1992. 365–91.

Kristeva, Julia. *Powers of Horror: An Essay on Abjection*. 1980. Trans. Leon. S. Roudiez. New York: Columbia University Press, 1982.

Kropotkin, Peter. *Russian Literature: Ideals and Realities*. 1905. Rev. edn. London: Duckworth, 1916.

Lawrence, D. H. *The Letters of D. H. Lawrence*. Vol. 2. *June 1913–October 1916*. Ed. George J. Zyartuk and James T. Bolton. Cambridge: Cambridge University Press, 1981.

Leach, Edmund. 'The Epistemological Background to Malinowski's Empiricism'. *Man and Culture*. Ed. Raymond Firth. London: Routledge and Kegan Paul, 1957.

Leatherbarrow, W. J., ed. *Dostoevskii and Britain*. Oxford: Berg, 1995.

LeBon, Gustave. *La Civilisation des Arabes*. Paris: Mesnil, 1884.

——. *The Crowd: A Study of the Popular Mind*. 1895. Translation anonymous. 1896. Harmondsworth, Middlesex: Penguin, 1977.

——. *The Psychology of Peoples: Its Influence on their Evolution*. n.d. Translation anonymous. London: T. Fisher Unwin, 1899.

——. *The Psychology of Revolution*. n.d. Trans. Bernard Miall. London: T. Fisher Unwin, 1913.

——. *Enseignements psychologiques de la guerre européene*. Paris: Ernest Flammarion, 1916.

——. *Hier et demain: pensées brèves*. Paris: Ernest Flammarion, 1918.

Leed, Eric J. *No Man's Land: Combat and Identity in World War I*. Cambridge: Cambridge University Press, 1979.

Levenson, Michael. 'Does *The Waste Land* Have a Politics?', *Modernism /Modernity* 6.3 (1999): 1–13.

——. *A Genealogy of Modernism: A Study of English Literary Doctrine 1908–1922*. Cambridge: Cambridge University Press, 1984.

Lewis, Wyndham. 'The "Pole" '. *The English Review* 2 (May 1909): 255–65. Rpt. in *The Complete Wild Body*. Ed. Bernard Lafourcade. Santa Barbara CA: Black Sparrow Press, 1982. 209–20.

——. *Blasting and Bombadiering*. 1937. Rev. edn. 1967. London: John Calder, 1982.

——. 'Some Innkeepers and Bestre'. *The English Review* 2 (June 1909): 471–84. Rpt. in *The Complete Wild Body*. Ed. Bernard Lafourcade. Santa Barbara CA: Black Sparrow Press, 1982. 221–36.

——. 'Les Saltimbanques'. *The English Review* 3 (August 1909): 76–87. Rpt. in *The Complete Wild Body*. Ed. Bernard Lafourcade. Santa Barbara CA: Black Sparrow Press, 1982. 237–50.

——. 'A Spanish Household'. *The Tramp: An Open Air Magazine* I (June-July 1910): 356–60. Rpt. in *The Complete Wild Body*. Ed. Bernard Lafourcade. Santa Barbara CA: Black Sparrow Press, 1982. 259–68.

——. 'A Breton Innkeeper'. *The Tramp: An Open Air Magazine* I (August 1910): 411–14. Rpt. in *The Complete Wild Body*. Ed. Bernard Lafourcade. Santa Barbara CA: Black Sparrow Press, 1982. 269–76.

——. 'Le Père François (A Full-length Portrait of a Tramp)'. *The Tramp: An Open Air Magazine* I (September 1910): 517–21. Rpt. in *The Complete Wild Body*. Ed. Bernard Lafourcade. Santa Barbara CA: Black Sparrow Press, 1982. 277–86.

——. *Rude Assignment: A Narrative of My Career Up to Date*. London: Hutchinson, 1950. Ed. Toby Foshay. Santa Barbara CA: Black Sparrow, 1984. Foshay changes the subtitle to *An Intellectual Autobiography*.

——. 'Unlucky for Pringle'. *The Tramp: An Open Air Magazine* 2 (February 1911): 404–14. Rpt. in *Unlucky for Pringle: Unpublished and Other Stories*. Ed. C. J. Fox and Robert T. Chapman. London: Vision, 1973. 23–38.

——. *The Caliph's Design: Architects! Where is Your Vortex*. 1919. Ed. Paul Edwards. Santa Barbara CA: Black Sparrow Press, 1982.

——. 'Plain Home-Builder: Where is Your Vorticist?'. 1934. *Creatures of Habit and Creatures of Change: Essays on Art, Literature and Society*. Ed. Paul Edwards. Santa Rosa CA: Black Sparrow Press, 1989.

——, ed. *Blast* 1 (1914). Facs. rpt. Santa Barbara CA: Black Sparrow Press, 1981.

——, ed. *Blast* 2 (1915). Facs. rpt. Santa Barbara CA: Black Sparrow Press, 1981.

Leys, Ruth. 'Mead's Voices: Imitation as Foundation, or, The Struggle against Mimesis'. *Critical Inquiry* 19.2 (Winter 1993): 277–307.

——. 'Traumatic Cures: Shellshock, Janet, and the Question of Memory'. *Critical Inquiry* 20.4 (Summer 1994): 623–62.

'Light and Leading, New Fact and Current Opinion Gathered from the Book World'. *The Book Monthly* 6.8 (May 1909): 651.

Loy, Mina. 'Giovanni Franchi'. *Rogue* 2.1 (October 1916). Rpt. *The Lost Lunar Baedeker*. Ed. Roger L. Conover. Manchester: Carcanet, 1997. 29.

Lukács, Georg. *The Theory of the Novel*. 1920. Trans Anna Bostock. London: Merlin Press, 1971.

——. 'The Ideology of Modernism'. *The Meaning of Contemporary Realism*. London: Merlin, 1957. 17–46. Rpt. in *Marxist Literary Criticism*, ed. Terry Eagleton and Drew Milne. Oxford: Blackwell, 1995. 141–62.

Lyndsey, Ben B. and Rube Borough. *Dangerous Life*. New York: Horace Liveright, 1925.

——, and Wainright Evans. *The Revolt of Modern Youth*. London: John Lane, 1928.

Malinowski, Bronislaw. *Argonauts of the Western Pacific: An Account of Native Enterprise and Adventure in the Archipelagoes of Melanesian New Guinea*. London: Routledge, 1922. Prospect Heights: Waveland, 1984.

——. *A Diary in the Strict Sense of the Term*. 1967. London: Athlone, 1989.

——. *The Early Writings of Bronislaw Malinowski*. Ed. Robert Thornton and Peter Skalnìk. Cambridge: Cambridge University Press, 1993.

——. 'The Natives of Mailu: Preliminary Results of the Robert Mond Research Work in British New Guinea'. 1915. Rpt. in *Malinowski among the Magi*. Ed. Michael Young. London and New York: Routledge, 1988. 77–331.

——. *The Story of a Marriage: The Letters of Bronislaw Malinowski and Elsie Masson*. Vol 1. *1916–20*. Ed. Helena Wayne. London: Routledge, 1995.

Man, Paul de. 'Literary History and Literary Modernity'. 1969. *Blindness and Insight: Essays in the Rhetoric of Contemporary Criticism*. 1971. Rev. edn. London: Methuen, 1983.

Manganaro, Mark. 'Textual Play, Power, and Cultural Critique: An Orientation to Modernist Anthropology'. *Modernist Anthropology: From Fieldwork to Text*. Ed. Mark Manganaro. Princeton NJ: Princeton University Press, 1990. 3–47.

——, ed. *Modernist Anthropology: From Fieldwork to Text*. Princeton NJ: Princeton University Press, 1990.

Mao, Douglas. *Solid Objects: Modernism and the Test of Production*. Princeton NJ: Princeton University Press, 1998.

Mansfield, Katherine. *Novels and Novelists*. Ed. J. Middleton Murry. London: Constable, 1930.

Marcus, Sharon. *Apartment Stories: City and Home in Nineteenth-Century Paris and London*. Berkeley CA: University of California Press, 1999.

Marx, Karl and Friedrich Engels. *The Communist Manifesto*. 1848. Trans. Samuel Moore, 1888. Harmondsworth, Middlesex: Penguin, 1967.

——. *Manifest der Kommunistischen Partei*. London: Bildungsgesellschaft für Arbeiter, 1848. Facs. rpt. Bonn-Bad Godesberg, NG Reprint, 1970.

Massis, Henri. 'André Gide et Doistoïevsky'. *La Revue Universelle* 15 (1 November 1923; 15 November 1923): 329–41; 476–93.

Matlaw, Ralph E. 'Dostoevskii and Conrad's Political Novels'. In *Dostoevskii and Britain*. Ed. W. J. Leatherbarrow. Oxford: Berg, 1995. 229–48.

Menand, Louis. *Discovering Modernism: T.S. Eliot and his Context*. Oxford: Oxford University Press, 1987.

Michaels, Walter Benn. *The Gold Standard and the Logic of Naturalism: American Literature at the Turn of the Century*. Berkeley: University of California Press, 1987.

——. *Our America: Nativism, Modernism, and Pluralism*. Durham NC: Duke University Press, 1995.

Miller, Tyrus. *Late Modernism: Politics, Fiction, and the Arts between the World Wars*. Berkeley CA: University of California Press, 1999.

Molnar, Michael, ed. *The Diary of Sigmund Freud, 1929–1939: A Record of the Final Decade*. New York: Scribner, 1992.

Money, Leo George Chiozza. *Things That Matter: Papers on Subjects Which Are, or Ought to be, Under Discussion*. London: Methuen, 1912.

Montagu, M. F. Ashley. 'Bronislaw Malinowski (1884–1942)'. *Isis* 34 (Autumn 1942): 146–50.

Moretti, Franco. *Signs Taken For Wonders: Essays in the Sociology of Literary Form*. Trans. Susan Fischer, David Forgacs, and David Miller. 1982. Rev. edn. London: Verso, 1988.

Morris, Allison and Henri Giller. *Understanding Juvenile Justice*. London: Croom Helm, 1987.

Morton, R. C. 'Records of a Haunted House'. *Proceedings of the Society for Psychical Research* 8 (1892): 311–32.

Muchnic, Helen. *Dostoevsky's English Reputation (1881–1936)*. Northampton: Smith College, 1939.

Murry, John Middleton. *Fyodor Dostoevsky: A Critical Study*. London: Martin Secker, 1916.

Musil, Robert. *The Man without Qualities*. Trans. Sophie Wilkins and Burton Pike. London: Picador, 1995.

Muller, John P., and William J. Richardson, eds. *The Purloined Poe: Lacan, Derrida, and Psychoanalytic Reading*. Baltimore MD: Johns Hopkins University Press, 1987.

Nealon, Chris. *Foundlings: Lesbian and Gay Historical Emotion before Stonewall*. Durham NC: Duke University Press, 2001.

Neubauer, John. *The Fin-de-Siècle Culture of Adolescence*. New Haven CT: Yale University Press, 1992.

Nevinson, Henry W. 'Notes on the Balkans, with a Table'. *English Review* I (December 1908): 182–7.

Nicolaides-Bouman, Ans. *International Smoking Statistics*. London: Wolfson Institute, 1993.

Nicholls, Peter. *Modernisms: A Literary Guide*. Basingstoke: Macmillan, 1995.

Nikoliukin, A. N. 'Dostoevskii in Constance Garnett's Translation'. In *Dostoevskii and Britain*. Ed. W. J. Leatherbarrow. Oxford: Berg, 1995. 206–27.

North, Michael. *The Dialect of Modernism: Race, Language, and Twentieth-Century Literature*. New York: Oxford University Press, 1994.

——. *Reading 1922: A Return to the Scene of the Modern*. New York: Oxford University Press, 1999.

Nye, Robert A. *The Origins of Crowd Psychology: Gustave LeBon and the Crisis of Mass Democracy in the Third Republic*. London: Sage Publications, 1975.

O'Connor, Kieran. 'Individual Differences and Motor Systems in Smoker Motivation'. *Smoking and Human Behaviour*. Ed. Ney and Gale. Chichester: Wiley, 1989.

Offer, Avner. *Property and Politics*. Cambridge: Cambridge University Press, 1981.

O'Keefe, Paul. *Some Sort of Genius: A Life of Wyndham Lewis*. London: Jonathan Cape, 2000.

Oosterhuis, Harry. 'Richard von Krafft-Ebing's "Step-Children of Nature": Psychiatry and the Making of Homosexual Identity'. In *Sexualities in History: A Reader*. Ed. Kim. M. Phillips and Barry Reay. New York: Routledge, 2002. 271–92.

Orton, Fred, and Griselda Pollock. 'Les Données Bretonnantes: la Prairie de Représentation'. *Art History* 3.3 (September 1980): 314–44. The text of this article is in English.

Paluch, Andrzej K. 'The Polish Background to Malinowski's Work'. *Man* ns 16 (1981): 276–85.

Panichas, George A. 'F. M. Dostoevskii and D. H. Lawrence: Their Vision of Evil'. In *Dostoevskii and Britain*. Ed. W. J. Leatherbarrow. Oxford: Berg, 1995. 249–75.

Pankhurst, Christabel. *Unshackled: The Story of How We Won the Vote*. London: Hutchinson, 1959.

Pearson, Geoffrey. *Hooligans: A History of Respectable Fears*. London: Macmillan, 1983.

Perkin, Harold. *The Structured Crowd: Essays in English Social History*. Sussex: The Harvester Press, 1981.

Pevear, Richard. Introduction. *The Adolescent*. By Fyodor Dostoevsky. New York: Alfred Knopf, 2003.

Perrot, Michelle. 'Worker Youth: From the Workshop to the Factory'. *A History of Young People*. Vol. 2. *Stormy Evolution to Modern Times*. Ed. Giovanni Levi and Jean-Claude Schmitt. 1994. Trans. Carol Volk. Cambridge MA: Belknap Press, 1997. 66–116.

Pick, Daniel. *Faces of Degeneration: A European Disorder, c.1848–c.1918*. Cambridge: Cambridge University Press, 1989.

Pound, Ezra. 'Editorial on Solicitous Doubt'. *The Little Review* 4.8 (December 1917): 53–5.

——. 'Our Contemporaries', *Blast* 2 (1915): 21.

Puaux, René. *Marshal Foch: His Life, His Work, His Faith*. Trans. E. Allen. London: Hodder & Stoughton, 1918.

Pugh, Martin. *State and Society: British Political and Social History, 1870–1992*. London: Edward Arnold, 1994.

——. *Women's Suffrage in Britain, 1867–1928*. London: The Historical Association, 1988.

Rabaté, Jean-Michel. *The Ghosts of Modernity*. Gainseville FL: University of Florida Press, 1996.

——. *The Future of Theory*. Oxford: Blackwell, 2002.

Rainey, Lawrence. *Institutions of Modernism: Literary Elites and Public Culture*. New Haven CT: Yale University Press, 1998.

R. C. Morton, 'Record of a Haunted House'. *Proceedings of the Society for Psychical Research* 8 (1892): 311–32.

Reeves, Mrs Pember. *Round about a Pound a Week*. 1913. London: Virago, 1979.

'Report of the General Meeting', *Journal for the Society for Psychical Research* 16 (April 1884): 35.

Reiter, Rayma, ed. *Towards an Anthropology of Women*. New York: Monthly Review Press, 1975.

Review of *The Princess Sophia*, by E. F. Benson. *The Bookseller: A Newspaper of British and Foreign Literature* 510 (4 May 1900): 373.

Riley, Denise. *The Words of Selves: Identification, Solidarity, Irony*. Stanford CA: Stanford University Press, 2000.

Rilke, Rainer Maria. '[Now it is time that gods came walking out]' (1925). *The Selected Poetry of Rainer Maria Rilke*. Ed., trans. Stephen Mitchell. 1980. London: Picador, 1987.

Robbins, Bruce. 'Modernism in History, Modernism in Power'. *Modernism Reconsidered*. Ed. Robert Kiely. Cambridge MA: Harvard University Press, 1983. 229–45.

——, ed. (for the Social Text Collective). *The Phantom Public Sphere*. Minneapolis MN: University of Minnesota Press, 1993.

Roberts, Harry. 'The Art of Vagabondage'. *The Tramp* I (June–July 1910).

Rose, W. K. *The Letters of Wyndham Lewis*. Norfolk CT: New Directions, 1963.

Rosenthal, Michael. *The Character Factory: Baden-Powell and the Origins of the Boy Scout Movement*. New York: Pantheon, 1986.

Ross, Kristin. *The Emergence of Social Space: Rimbaud and the Paris Commune*. London: Macmillan, 1988.

——. *Fast Cars, Clean Bodies: Decolonization and the Reordering of French Culture*. Cambridge MA: MIT, 1995.

Roustang, François. *Dire Mastery: Discipleship from Freud to Lacan*. 1976. Trans. Ned Lukacher. Baltimore MD and London: Johns Hopkins, 1982.

Rubin, William, ed. *'Primitivism' in Twentieth Century Art: The Affinity of the Tribal and the Modern*. 2 vols. New York: Museum of Modern Art, 1984.

Schenck, Celeste. 'Charlotte Mew (1870–1928)'. In *The Gender of Modernism: A Critical Anthology*. Ed. Bonnie Kime Scott. Bloomington IN: Indiana University Press, 1990. 316–20.

——. 'Exiled by Genre: Modernism, Canonicity, and the Politics of Exclusion'. In *Women's Writing in Exile: Alien and Critical*. Ed. Mary Lynn Broe and Angela Ingram. Chapel Hill NC: University of North Carolina Press, 1989.

Scott, Bonnie, ed. *The Gender of Modernism: A Critical Anthology*. Bloomington IN: Indiana University Press, 1990.

Sedgwick, Eve Kosofsky. *Between Men: English Literature and Male Homosexual Desire*. New York: Columbia University Press, 1985.

Segalen, Martine. *Fifteen Generations of Bretons: Kinship and Society in Lower Brittany, 1720–1980*. Cambridge: Cambridge University Press, 1991.

Seltzer, Mark. *Bodies and Machines*. New York: Routledge, 1992.

Silas, Ellis. *A Primitive Arcadia: Being the Impressions of an Artist in Papua*. London: T. Fisher Unwin, 1926.

Sime, David, MD. *Rabies: Its Place Among Germ-Diseases, and its Origin in the Animal Kingdom*. Cambridge: Cambridge University Press, 1903.

Sorel, Georges. *The Illusions of Progress*. 1908. Trans. John and Charlotte Stanley. Los Angeles CA: University of California Press, 1969.

Smith, Stan. *The Origins of Modernism: Eliot, Pound, Yeats and the Rhetorics of Renewal*. New York: Harvester Wheatsheaf, 1994.

Souvestre, Emile. *Les Derniers Bretons*. Paris, 1836.

Spacks, Patricia Meyer. *The Adolescent Idea: Myths of Youth and the Ideal Imagination*. 1981. London: Faber, 1982.

Spence, Keith. *Brittany and the Bretons*. London: Gollancz, 1978.

Sperber, Dan. *On Anthropological Knowledge*. Cambridge: Cambridge University Press, 1985.

Spencer, Kate. 'Is the Dandie Degenerate?'. *The Kennel* 11 (February 1911): 550.

Stallabrass, Julian. 'The Idea of the Primitive: British Art and Anthropology 1918–1930'. *New Left Review* 183 (September-October 1990): 95–115.

Stein, Gertrude. 'Composition as Explanation'. 1926. *Look at Me Now and Here I Am: Writings and Lectures 1909–45*. Ed. Patricia Mayerowitz. Harmondsworth, Middlesex: Penguin, 1971.

Stirner, Max. *The Ego and Its Own*. 1844. Trans. Stephen Byington. 1907. Ed. David Leopold. Cambridge: Cambridge University Press, 1995.

Stocking, George. *Victorian Anthropology*. New York: The Free Press, 1987.

——, ed. *Functionalism Historicised: Essays in British Social Anthropology*. Madison WI: University of Wisconsin Press, 1984.

——, ed. *Malinowski, Rivers, Benedict and Others: Essays on Culture and Personality*. Madison WI: University of Wisconsin Press, 1984.

——, ed. *Observers Observed: Essays in Ethnographic Fieldwork*. Madison WI: University of Wisconsin Press, 1983.

Stone, Martin. 'Shellshock and the Psychologists'. In *The Anatomy of Madness: Essays in the History of Psychiatry*. Vol. 2. *Institutions and Society*. Ed. W. F. Bynum, Roy Porter, and Michael Shepherd. London and New York: Tavistock, 1985. 242–71.

Stonebridge, Lyndsey. *The Destructive Element: British Psychoanalysis and Modernism*. Basingstoke: Macmillan, 1998.

Strathearn, Marilyn. 'Out of Context: The Persuasive Fictions of Anthropology'. *Modernist Anthropology: From Fieldwork to Text*. Ed. Mark Manganaro. Princeton NJ: Princeton University Press, 1990. 80–130.

Strenski, Ivan. 'Malinowski: Second Positivism, Second Romanticism'. *Man* ns 17 (1982): 266–71.

Tickner, Lisa. *The Spectacle of Women: Imagery of the Suffrage Campaign, 1907–1914*. Chicago IL: University of Chicago Press, 1988.

Thomas, Nicholas. *Entangled Objects: Exchange, Material Culture, and Colonialism in the Pacific*. Cambridge MA: Harvard University Press, 1991.

Thompson, Paul. *The Edwardians: The Remaking of British Society*. 1975. Rev. edn. London: Routledge, 1992.

Thorne, Guy. *When It Was Dark: The Story of a Conspiracy*. 1903. London: Greening and Co., 1904.

Thornton, R. J. ' "Imagine Yourself Set Down. . . .": Mach, Frazer, Conrad, Malinowski and the Role of the Imagination in Ethnography'. *Anthropology Today* 1.5 (1985): 7–14.

Thornton, Robert, and Peter Skalnìk. Introduction. *The Early Writings of Bronislaw Malinowski*. Ed. Robert Thornton and Peter Skalnìk. Cambridge: Cambridge University Press, 1993.

Thurschwell, Pamela. *Literature, Technology and Magical Thinking, 1880–1920*. Cambridge: Cambridge University Press, 2001.

Tomalin, Claire. *Katherine Mansfield: A Secret Life*. London: Viking, 1987.

Torgovnic, Marianna. *Gone Primitive: Savage Intellects, Modern Lives*. Chicago IL: University of Chicago Press, 1990.

Trotter, David. *The English Novel in History, 1895–1920*. London: Routledge, 1993.

Turner, James. *Reckoning with the Beast: Animals, Pain, and Humanity in the Victorian Mind*. Baltimore MD: Johns Hopkins, 1980.

Turner, J. Sidney. 'The Scientific Case for Vivisection'. *The Kennel* 1 (April 1910): 13.

'Two Poets'. *English Review* 2 (June 1909): 627.

Uglow, Jenny. *George Eliot*. London: Virago, 1987.

Vaughan, William. 'The Englishness of British Art'. *The Oxford Art Journal* 13. 2 (1990): 11–23.

'Vocomontis'. 'The Dachshund in England and Germany'. *The Kennel* 2 (1910): 89.

Walkowitz, Judith R. *Prostitution and Victorian Society: Women, Class, and the State*. Cambridge: Cambridge University Press, 1986.

Warner, Michael. 'Homo-Narcissism: or, Heterosexuality'. In *Engendering Men: The Question of the Male Feminist Critique*. Ed. Joseph Boone and Michael Cadden. New York: Routledge, 1990. 190–206.

Wells, H. G. *Tono Bungay*. London: Macmillan, 1909.

Williams, Raymond. *Culture and Society: Coleridge to Orwell*. 1958. London: Hogarth, 1990.

Witkiewicz, Stanislslaw Ignacy. *Insatiability: A Novel in Two Parts*. 1932. Trans. London: Quartet, 1985.

——. *A Witkiewicz Reader*. Ed. Daniel Gerould. Evanston IL: Northwestern University Press, 1993.

Woolf, Virginia. 'A Minor Dostoevsky'. 1917. Review of *The Gambler and Other Stories*. *The Essays of Virginia Woolf*. Ed. Andrew McNeillie. Vol. 2. London: Hogarth, 1994.

——. 'More Dostoevsky'. 1917. Review of *The Eternal Husband and Other Stories*. *The Essays of Virginia Woolf*. Ed. Andrew McNeillie. Vol. 2. London: Hogarth, 1994.

——. 'The Russian Point of View'. *The Essays of Virginia Woolf*. Ed. Andrew McNeillie. Vol. 4. London: Hogarth, 1994.

——. 'Mr Bennett and Mrs Brown'. 1924. *A Woman's Essays*. Ed. Rachel Bowlby. London: Penguin, 1992.

——. *The Diary of Virginia Woolf*. Vol 4. *1931–35*. Ed. Anne Olivier Bell. 1982. London: Penguin, 1983.

——. *To the Lighthouse*. 1927. Ed. Stella McNichol. London: Penguin, 1992.

——. *The Letters of Virginia Woolf*. Vol. 1. *The Flight of the Mind (1888–1912)*. London: Hogarth, 1977.

Worringer, Willhelm. *Abstraction and Empathy: A Contribution to the Psychology of Style*. 1908. Trans. Michael Bullock. London: Routledge and Kegan Paul, 1953.

Zaretsky, Eli. *Capitalism, the Family, and Personal Life*. New York: Harper and Row, 1976.

Zizek, Slavoj. *For They Know Not What They Do: Enjoyment as a Political Factor*. London: Verso, 1991.

Zytaruk, George J., ed. *The Quest for Rananim: D. H. Lawrence's Letters to S. S. Koteliansky*. Montreal: McGill – Queen's University Press, 1970.

Index

Abraham, Karl, 140–1, 147
Ackerman, Robert, 186n.32
Ackroyd, Peter, 170n.25
Acton, William, 122
Adler, Alfred, 170–1n.26
Aichhorn, August, 70
Aldington, Richard, 131–2
Altieri, Charles, 52, 106–7, 111, 192n.12
Anderson, Margaret, 147, *see also The Little Review*
Anesko, Michael, 36, 41
Ardener, Edward, 185n.19
Armstrong, Tim, 174n.64
Arnauld, Michel, 172n.51
Asquith, Herbert Henry, 67, 68, 117

Baden-Powell, Robert, 182n.45
Bailey, Victor, 183n.64
Bakhtin, Mikhail, 6, 19
Baldick, Chris, 185n.17
Baring, Maurice, 170–1n.26
Barrès, Maurice, 141, 147, 153, 198n.43
Baxendall, Michael, 191n.121
Becker, Jean-Jacques, 198n.42, 198n.43
Bell, Clive, 29, 113
Benjamin, Andrew, 106, 113
Benjamin, Walter, 51, 182n.45
Bennett, Arnold, 27, 46, 175n.11, 177n.45
Bergson, Henri, viii, 24, 82, 142–4, 147, 187n.45, 197n.25
Creative Evolution, 142–4
La Signification de la guerre, 143–4
Bersani, Leo, 173n.54
Besant, Walter, 33, 81
Blackwood, Algernon, 30–3, 37, 38, 43, 49–50, 164, 177n.36
The Empty House, 30–1, 37, 38
John Silence: Physician Extraordinary, 31–2, 33

Blast, 21, 53–5, 56, 58, 59, 60, 64, 67, 68, 72, 97, 107, 108, 109, 110, 111, 112, 116, 117, 147, 177n.49, 180n.12, 180n.20
Borch-Jacobson, Mikkel, 151–3, 162, 199n.53
Bourdieu, Pierre, 54, 85, 86, 98, 175n.9, 188n.64, 200n.79
Bray, Reginald, 65, 183n.53
Boy Labour and Apprenticeship, 65
Buitenhuis, Peter, 197n.39
Bürger, Peter, 171n.38
Burt, Cyril, 63–4, 69, 72
Young Delinquent, The, 69
Butler, Josephine, 122, 123–4

Caesar the King's Dog
Where's Master, 102, 195n.103
Captain Loxley's Little Dog, 133
Carter, Huntley, 94
Carter, Paul, 82, 83, 92–3
Caruth, Cathy, 137–8
Cather, Willa, x
de Certeau, Michel, 1, 65, 162, 182n.51, 187n.50
Chamberlain, Joseph, 115, 117, 129
Chesterton, G. K., x, xiii
Churchill, Winston, 30, 31
Clark, T. J., 10–11, 14
Conrad, Joseph, 16, 19, 34, 74, 84, 87, 88, 89
Coombes, Annie, 192n.19
Copeau, Jacques, 8, 15–16, 172n.51
Corbett, David Peters, 192n.13
Cornick, Martyn, 172n.51
Craig, David, 184n.11
The Criterion, xv, 79

Dangerfield, George, 57–8, 59
Despard, Charlotte, 120–1
Dickens, Charles, 195n.89
Dolto, Françoise, 51, 179n.2